C0066 43494

D0756594

Glasgow libraries

This book is d.. .u,

renew...

Bri...een jotting down stories as far

Th...

2...member but decided that 2013

...r that she finished a full-length

her debut novel, *It Started at Sunset Cottage*, was shortlisted for the Contemporary Romantic Novel of the Year and RNA Joan Hessayon New Writers Award.

Bella's stories are about friendship, love and coping with what life throws at you. She likes to find the humour in the darker moments of life and weaves these into her stories. Bella believes that writing your own story really is the best fun ever, closely followed by talking, eating chocolate, drinking fizz and planning holidays.

She lives in the Midlands, UK with her lovely husband and wonderful daughter, who thankfully, both accept her as she is (with mad morning hair and a penchant for skipping).

The Promise of Summer

BELLA OSBORNE

avon.

Published by AVON
A division of HarperCollins*Publishers* Ltd
1 London Bridge Street
London SE1 9GF

www.harpercollins.co.uk

HarperCollins*Publishers*
1st Floor, Watermarque Building, Ringsend Road
Dublin 4, Ireland

A Paperback Original 2021
1
First published in Great Britain by HarperCollins*Publishers* 2021

Copyright © Bella Osborne 2021

Bella Osborne asserts the moral right to be identified as the author of this work.

A catalogue copy of this book is available from the British Library.

ISBN: 978-0-00-846490-5

This novel is entirely a work of fiction. The names, characters and incidents portrayed in it are the work of the author's imagination. Any resemblance to actual persons, living or dead, events or localities is entirely coincidental.

Typeset in Minion Pro by Palimpsest Book Production Limited, Falkirk, Stirlingshire
Printed and Bound in the UK using 100% Renewable Electricity at
CPI Group (UK) Ltd

All rights reserved. No part of this text may be reproduced, transmitted, downloaded, decompiled, reverse engineered, or stored in or introduced into any information storage and retrieval system, in any form or by any means, whether electronic or mechanical, without the express written permission of the publishers.

MIX
Paper from
responsible sources
FSC
www.fsc.org **FSC C007454**

This book is produced from independently certified FSC™ paper to ensure responsible forest management.
For more information visit: www.harpercollins.co.uk/green

Chapter One

'What a knob,' said Ruby, looking at her mobile phone. She couldn't quite believe it.

'Another dick pic?' asked Kim, arranging flowers into a bouquet.

'Not this time. It's my ex. The one with the homemade knuckle tattoos. They wouldn't have been so bad if he could have at least spelled them properly. Anyway him. He's selling my bloody microwave on eBay. The one he stole from me.'

'That's despicable!' Kim sounded outraged on her behalf. 'Is this the same one who peed in your kettle?'

Ruby shook her head. She'd tried very hard to forget about that incident but just the thought of it brought the smell of boiling urine to her nostrils. 'No, this loser was between the kettle pisser and the one who wanted to video us having sex for *training purposes*.' It was fair to say she'd not had much luck on the dating front for some time or, in fact, ever.

Ruby had a woefully bad track record when it came to men. She had tried to remain optimistic but, over the years, experience had taught her that however much effort she made it was still, most likely, going to end badly. Perhaps she had some cosmic ability to attract men of a particularly low calibre. Bald chancers on Tinder aside, she had had her fair share of good-looking men, but they were frequently the worst. All the pretty ones she had dated had cheated on her – every single one.

The shop entry bell chimed, and Ruby shoved the phone in her back pocket and went to serve, leaving Kim in the back room with a large sheet of cellophane and an armful of antirrhinums.

Bloom with a View was a little flower shop tucked out of the way down a side street, a stone's throw from Sheffield's railway station. So, despite its name, the view wasn't great unless trains and stressed commuters was your thing. On entering you were met by an explosion of colour and scent all year round, although summer was Ruby's favourite, when the shop was full of sweet-smelling stocks and vibrant roses.

A suited man came in.

'Hi, Adrian,' said Ruby. 'How are you?' Adrian was a regular customer. He called in every Friday on his way home from work to get flowers for his wife and he'd been doing it since before Ruby had started working at the tiny florist's three years ago.

'Fine, thanks. No Kim today?' he asked, leaning to one side to look through the archway to the back room.

'Hi, Adrian,' called Kim. 'I'm wrestling with a hand-tied bouquet. You all right?'

'Good thanks. Busy week. I'm looking forward to a glass of wine and putting my feet up.' He directed his answer at the beaded curtain separating the main part of the shop from the back room where they kept most of the stock in a walk-in cooler and the orders were made up.

'I bet Justine is too. We've got some lovely yellow roses in. I know they're her favourite,' called back Kim.

'Perfect,' said Adrian.

'On it,' said Ruby and she began making up a bunch. She knew the price Adrian liked to pay so they always made the spray up to that amount, although both Ruby and Kim usually added in a couple of extra sprigs of whatever was in season because he was a loyal customer and also a genuinely lovely person.

'Ey, up,' said Kim, coming through the archway with a flourish like a game show host.

'What are you up to this weekend, Kim?' asked Adrian, getting out his wallet.

'I'm working here as usual. No other plans. What about you?'

'Off to the Crucible tomorrow night.'

'How lovely. I haven't been to the theatre since I used to go with Vince but I'm not sure why because he never liked it. He only came for the ice cream in the interval. I adore plays. There's something vibrant about it – the excitement of a live performance. It's like you're part of the show somehow.' Kim looked wistful as she spoke.

'Couldn't agree more. I've been hooked since a school trip to see *West Side Story*. It's more personal than TV. There's something special about being allowed to experience it up close,' said Adrian.

Ruby wasn't sure what they were going on about. 'Nah, you can't beat curling up on the sofa in your PJs with pizza and Netflix. If it's rubbish you can just pick something else.'

Adrian and Kim both looked mildly horrified at her suggestion. She shrugged and passed Adrian the flowers and he tapped his debit card on the machine.

'Thanks,' said Adrian, 'see you next week.'

'Enjoy the play,' said Kim.

The door chimed and Adrian was gone. Kim stood staring at the door.

'Earth to Kim. You all right?'

Kim sighed. 'Yes. It's been seven years and I still miss Vince. I don't suppose that ever goes away.'

Ruby had heard many stories about Kim's husband. Their marriage sounded ideal. Maybe not the perfect relationship she read about in her favourite romantic novels but certainly a sound partnership built on love and trust. They had set up the florist's together, and from Kim's accounts enjoyed each other's company. This had all been cut abruptly short when Vince had suffered a heart attack leaving Kim on her own at forty-two. So even if you found someone you wanted to spend the rest of your life with, there were no guarantees.

Ruby would be happy with what Kim and Vince had had but what she truly wanted was the full-scale fairy tale. She wanted to meet a man who would sweep her off her feet and ideally look like Chris Hemsworth or better still actually be Chris Hemsworth, although she knew looks weren't her number-one priority. She liked a laugh so a fun person was essential. Maybe Peter Kay but with Chris Hemsworth's body – that would work. Most importantly she needed somebody who would stick around, not do a runner at the first sign of trouble or a bouncing cleavage. She needed a man who was a match for her quick tongue and would accept her as she was. Although that was looking less and less likely. She was heading for thirty-five and everyone she'd dated had a major personality flaw. However much she liked the idea of a long-term relationship, her wishes didn't come true so she was temporarily off men and focusing on something else that would bring her guaranteed joy.

Kim was still gazing at the closed door. Ruby didn't like to see her looking sad, so she tried to jolly her out of it.

'You need to get on Tinder or that over-fifties app. I could set up a profile for you. You'd find someone for sure.'

'No, thank you, and anyway I'm not fifty *yet*,' said Kim, folding her arms across her ample chest. 'I've seen the wasters you've been matched with. They're not exactly the pick of the bunch. No offence.'

'None taken. I mean look at this lot.' Ruby pulled out her phone and brought up the latest dating app she was subscribed to for a couple more days. She scrolled to the first picture: a bald man asleep in a deckchair. 'Forty my arse – he's seventy if he's a day.' She scrolled to the next one. 'Picture of his dog. Delete.'

'Why? He likes dogs. That's a good thing. I was thinking about getting a puppy.'

'I could see you with a Labrador.'

'I'm fed up coming home to an empty house. A man with a dog might be nice.' Kim pointed at Ruby's phone. 'For you I mean.'

'But there's no photo of him, which most likely means he's either so ugly he'd curdle milk, or he's worried I'll recognise him on *Crimewatch*.'

'He looks all right,' said Kim, pointing at the next one who popped up. 'At least he's got hair.'

'But most of it appears to be nasal,' said Ruby, zooming in.

'Don't be so picky. It says he's a wine enthusiast,' added Kim.

'Nope,' said Ruby swiping the screen. 'Wine enthusiast means he's a drunk.'

'How can you tell?' asked Kim, trying to have another look before the picture was swiped away.

'You need to learn to translate. Dating app speak is a whole other language. It's a bit like when an estate agent says a property is compact and bijou but actually what they mean is it's so small that when you wipe your bum you'll bang your head on the cooker.'

Kim gave her an odd look. 'That's one weird layout you've got.'

'I don't mean my place. It was just an example.' Ruby scrolled to another profile. 'Look, let me explain. For example, *Has a love of classic cars* probably means his old banger failed its MOT. *No ties* – homeless. *Enjoys the outside* – recently released from prison. And *Animal lover* – has a police record for something unspeakable.'

Kim recoiled. 'It was a lot easier in my day when everyone went to clubs. You'd check someone out one week, snog them the next and if he took you for chips when the club closed you'd arrange to meet him in daylight.'

'Ah, the good old days,' said Ruby, turning the door sign to closed.

'Watch it, cheeky. I knew my Vince was the one when he gave me his sausage.'

'Eurgh. Too much information,' said Ruby.

'Battered sausage . . .' clarified Kim.

'Now there's kinky,' said Ruby. Kim gave her a playful swipe as she passed.

They busied themselves with tidying up the stock, refreshing water and binning the stems past their best. Ruby sorted out the back room while Kim began checking what orders had to go out over the weekend.

Each time Ruby bent down her hair flopped into her face. She swept it into an impromptu bun and stuck a pencil in it. 'My hair needs a cut,' she said. It would have to go to the bottom of a very long list.

'I like it long. It's such a beautiful colour. Mine's mud brown with grey highlights.'

Ruby had grown to like her red hair. 'You could always dye yours a similar colour to mine.'

'Knowing my luck, it'd come out orange and I'd look like an angry traffic cone. Oh, I meant to say earlier, will you be okay on your own next Friday morning?' asked Kim. 'My cousin is going to pop round to mine and give me a cut and colour on the cheap. I've got to get my roots done.' Kim tilted her head in Ruby's direction as evidence. 'I'll be the full Father Christmas by autumn at this rate,' she added with a chuckle.

'Ah, I've booked next Friday off as holiday. I put it on the calendar.' Ruby went a bit stiff. She hadn't prepared an excuse for what she was up to as she hadn't expected she'd have to explain. She'd been planning to pass it off as a long weekend.

'Okay. Not to worry. I can rearrange it. I mean I'll look like Worzel Gummidge's scruffy older sister but that's okay, I've got no one to impress.'

Ruby felt instantly bad. 'I'm really sorry but it's a thing I can't change.'

Kim tilted her head. 'A thing? Does the thing have a name?'

Ruby didn't want to lie to Kim. She was her friend, as well as her boss, but she could hardly tell her the truth either. Ruby busied herself with cashing up. 'No . . . it's an appointment.' It was the first thing that popped into her head. She could feel Kim's eyes were scrutinising her and she concentrated on counting out the notes.

'Ruby, is everything okay?' Kim's voice was full of concern.

Now she'd gone and worried her. Lying was a minefield. 'Everything's fine. It's just a routine appointment.' She glanced at Kim and instantly felt guilty.

Kim gave Ruby's arm a squeeze. 'You're sure?'

'Totally,' said Ruby. Although totally sure was absolutely the last thing she was.

Chapter Two

It was the next Friday morning and Ruby had changed her outfit four times, but she wasn't sure why. What she wore for her trip to London really didn't matter although it somehow did to her. She'd eventually gone for her favourite vintage dress in a classic pattern. She felt good in it, it was comfortable and she had a long journey ahead of her. She had a bottle of water, some gum and a novel for the journey – she was all set. She rarely ventured out of Sheffield, let alone all the way to London so she was a bit nervous. But this was something she was serious about and if the best she could afford was in London then that was where she had to go.

When she walked into the station there were a lot of cross-looking people milling about. She glanced at the board and saw that two trains to Manchester Piccadilly were cancelled. She started to panic. She'd not considered there being a problem with the train although she had left plenty of time, mainly because she was hoping to buy a hot chocolate and have a browse through the magazines. She hastily scanned the board. There was a train to London leaving from platform two in five minutes and she felt an urgency to get this earlier one. She spun around looking for signs and when she spotted platform two on the other side of the crowd her pulse quickened.

'Excuse me! Train to catch. Whoops. Sorry. Thank you.' She made her way through the grumbling commuters and raced for the platform. When she got there a train was pulling in and her heart was pounding to the beat of Beyoncé's 'Single Ladies'. That song felt like an anthem for her life and she chuckled to herself, which elicited a frown from a nearby man. There was someone in a railway uniform further down the platform and she almost jogged up to them. 'Is this the train to London?' she asked. They just nodded their reply. 'Thank goodness.' She puffed out a breath. That had been close.

She could see it was quite busy so she made her way to the last carriage and sat in the first free seat. It was an earlier train than she'd planned to get but after the panic of the cancellations she was just glad to be on one. She now had a ridiculous amount of contingency time but that might be handy if she couldn't find where she was going at the other end. The London underground with all its zones and multiple lines in fancy colours looked like you needed to be a member of Mensa to negotiate it.

She popped her water on the table in front of her, got out her book and tried to relax. She had no sooner started to read when the carriage door slid open, someone entered and stopped right next to her.

'Excuse me,' he said. He had one of those sensual voices you were drawn to.

'Yeah,' replied Ruby looking up. He was tall, smartly dressed with neat dark hair and remarkable blue eyes. She put on her best smile. 'Can I help you?' she asked.

'That's my seat,' he said. The voice was still delicious but his manner was belligerent.

'Look, there's seats right there.' She pointed at the spare pair of seats across the aisle.

The man's eyes followed her finger. 'But those are pointing the wrong way. I like to sit facing the direction of travel.'

Ruby had a quick look down the carriage, but she couldn't see any free seats facing the same way as she was.

'I'm sure those seats are fine or maybe you could check if there are others facing the direction of travel in another carriage.' She was settled now and this was a window seat, unlike the ones across the aisle.

'But this is the *quiet* carriage. I always travel in the quiet carriage because I like to work in peace.'

He might have had cheekbones to die for but he was getting irritating now. Why did handsome men think they could boss women around? 'Sorry, but it's only a seat and I got here first. So . . .' She gave a jaunty shrug and went back to her book hoping that would give him the message that the conversation was over.

The man cleared his throat. 'I've pre-booked this seat. Carriage A. Seat seventeen.' He placed what looked like a train ticket on the table in front of Ruby and when she pulled her nose out of her book, he pointed from the ticket to a small digital display above her, which was flashing Reserved from Sheffield. *Bugger,* she thought. She'd not been on a train in years and hadn't even known you could book seats.

'I am really sorry. I didn't realise,' she said with a grimace and she picked up her water and moved across the aisle, giving him a series of apologetic expressions as she went.

'Thank you,' he said, taking the vacated seat.

Ruby had no sooner settled herself down again than the carriage door opened and another man came in. This one was dressed in a leather jacket and jeans. He nodded at the empty seat next to hers. 'Is that seat free?' He gave her a hopeful smile.

'Sure,' she said, and got up to let him in.

She retook her seat and reread the same sentence of her book for the third time. The man next to her got something out of his pocket and started fiddling with it. Her Tinder date experiences told her not to look directly at something like that – there were some things you couldn't unsee. She glanced furtively across. He was handling a small black velvet box. It looked like a ring box and it now had her full attention. He caught her looking and beamed at her.

'Excuse me,' he said. 'I'm not a weirdo or anything but you look like a nice sensible woman. Could I ask your opinion on something?'

Ruby closed her book. She'd never been called a sensible anything in her life before. 'Fire away,' she said, giving him the once-over. He was casual but clean with a faint aroma of aftershave, no homemade knuckle tattoos and a friendly smile – it was a promising start.

'I'm going to propose to my girlfriend and this is the ring. What do you think?' He flicked open the small box and the ring inside took Ruby's breath away. It was a simple platinum band with the biggest sparkly diamond she had ever seen, with two yellow stones on either side.

'Wow, it's beautiful.'

'Thank you. I'm ridiculously nervous – I'm shaking like a leaf. These are yellow diamonds because yellow is her favourite colour.' He pointed at the smaller stones. 'I've been planning this for weeks and now it's here I'm a mess.' He ran a hand through his hair. 'I'm meeting her in London and taking her on the London Eye. When we get to the top I'm going to ask her to marry me.'

Ruby's heart gave a flutter. Why weren't the guys on the apps like this one? 'I think that's perfect . . . um . . . sorry, what was your name?'

'No, that's my fault – my head's in a spin. I'm Lewis.' He put the ring away and offered her a hand to shake.

'Hi, Lewis; I'm Ruby.' In her head she added, *And do you happen to have a brother you could introduce me to who is as caring as you are and as sane and normal as you appear to be?*

The next few minutes flew by as Lewis waxed lyrical about his girlfriend. It was only interrupted by the occasional tut from the man who had kicked her out of her seat earlier. Although she was eternally grateful to him because Lewis was a great distraction from what lay ahead of her in London.

Lewis was a true romantic. It was like a hero from one of her favourite books had been brought to life. He was funny, interesting and clearly besotted with his soon-to-be fiancée. He got out his phone and showed her a photograph of a pretty woman leaning against a palm tree. A picture clearly taken on holiday as she was wearing a bikini and holding a cocktail but it was the way she was laughing into the lens that caught Ruby's attention. She wanted to swap places with the woman in the photo.

'Sorry, I'm boring you,' said Lewis, putting his phone in his pocket.

'No, not at all. It's great to see someone so happy. I hope everything goes well today.'

'Thank you. You're a lovely person,' said Lewis and the compliment caught Ruby off-guard.

Lewis seemed to jump and pulled his phone from his pocket. 'Sorry I'd better take this.' It must have been on silent as she hadn't heard it ring but then they were in the quiet carriage. Perhaps she should have put hers on vibrate too.

'Yes, that's right . . . Four o'clock . . . What do you mean there's a problem?' His voice was starting to get louder. The man from across the aisle tutted and pointed at the quiet carriage sticker on the window.

'Sorry, I'd better take this outside,' said Lewis.

'Outside? Don't go leaping off the train,' said Ruby, and then wanted to curl into a ball for being lame. Lovely Lewis gave her terrible attempt at wit a smile as she got out of her seat and let him escape.

She sat back down again and sighed deeply. Lewis was proof that romance wasn't dead and that maybe she shouldn't give up on the fairy tale just yet. A few questions about her planned trip to London whirled around her mind. Was she doing the wrong thing?

The carriage door opened and the ticket inspector came in. Ruby gasped. In her rush to catch a train buying a ticket had completely slipped her mind. Ruby could hear Lewis arguing with someone on the phone and he was sounding fraught. She tried to listen in but the door automatically slid closed.

'Tickets please,' said the inspector.

'I'm really sorry,' said Ruby. 'You see I don't often take the train . . . actually can't remember the last time . . . anyway it was busy and . . .' The inspector was looking bored. She flashed an apologetic smile. 'I need a ticket please.'

'You're not meant to travel without one,' he said.

'I was cutting it fine to catch the train because of all the cancellations so I didn't have time. Sorry,' she said.

He tutted. 'Single?' he asked in a gruff voice.

What about her was screaming lonely singleton? 'How did you know?'

The ticket inspector's eyebrows pulled together. 'Single or *return* ticket to . . .'

'Ah, right, yes. I see. Return, not single – ha. Well I am single but . . .' She gave a dry laugh. 'London please.'

She paid with her card and sheepishly took her ticket. She saw the man in seat seventeen, across the aisle, was grinning broadly at her error and it irked her. 'Is something funny?' she asked him.

He turned in her direction. 'It wasn't funny that you were travelling without a ticket and most likely had no intention of purchasing one unless you were caught out.'

Ruby bristled. Thankfully the inspector was at the other end of the carriage. 'That's not true. Trains were being cancelled so I jumped on one quickly and anyway I bought a ticket, didn't I?' That should shut up the smartarse.

'The only cancelled trains were going in the opposite direction to Manchester. You had no excuse not to purchase a ticket.'

Before she had time to come up with a riposte, Lewis came into the carriage looking highly stressed. 'My phone battery has just died on me. And there's some issue with the booking I've made so the proposal is in jeopardy. Have you got a charger?'

'No, but here, use my phone.' Ruby unlocked the screen and handed it to him.

'Thank you so much. You're a life-saver.' Lewis took the phone and left the carriage.

The man across the aisle was shaking his head. Ruby ignored him. She got out her book and huffily turned to the right page and reread the same sentence for a fourth time which annoyed her even further. After a couple of minutes her irritation levels eased as she got back into her novel. Oddly the hero in her story now looked a lot like Lewis in her mind's eye.

The train began slowing for the next station and lots of people started standing up and sorting out jackets and bags. Ruby was now thoroughly engrossed in her book and was only vaguely aware of people leaving the train.

'Excuse me,' said someone and she had to drag herself away from a dramatic scene to see who was speaking to her. It was the irritating man from seat seventeen leaning across the aisle.

Ruby pointedly stuck her finger on the page where she had read to, so she didn't end up rereading anything again, and gave him a look that she hoped conveyed her annoyance at being interrupted. As people were leaving the train she had to wait a few moments before the aisle was free and she could see him.

'Yes?' she said.

'He's still got your phone,' said the man.

'Lewis? Yeah, I know,' said Ruby. 'I gave it to him to use. His battery is dead.'

Seat seventeen pursed his lips. 'Only he's on the platform.' He pointed out of the window and Ruby's eyes followed.

She was aware of an insistent beeping noise as she stared at the sight of Lewis, still talking animatedly on her mobile phone but standing with his back to the train.

'What the f . . .' Ruby bolted from her seat but was halted by the closed sliding door, which took ages to open even though she was pressing the button. In the vestibule, between carriages, she hit the exit button on the door to the platform repeatedly but nothing happened. She banged on the glass.

Lewis turned around and the look on his face went from troubled to shocked as the train started to move off.

'Noooo!' shouted Ruby. Lewis began running along at the pace of the train holding out Ruby's phone to her as if somehow trying to return it but as the train picked up speed he slowed to a walk and disappeared from view. 'Noooo!'

'Is everything all right?' asked seat seventeen, stepping into the vestibule to join her.

'Obviously not,' she snapped. She spun around, trying to think what to do. Next to seat seventeen's head was a red lever and a sign saying *Emergency Stop*. In blind panic, Ruby lurched for it but was intercepted.

'You can't do that,' he said blocking her.

'But I need to stop the train.' She reached around the other side and was blocked again.

'But it's only for emergencies.'

'This is a bloody emergency. He's got my phone!' She dodged him and made another lunge for the emergency switch but missed.

'Wrong sort of emergency. If you pull it you'll get a hefty fine. And a lot of angry passengers after you.'

'I don't care.'

'Even if you stop the train, they can't exactly turn around and go back. I think maybe we should retake our seats.' He stayed firmly in front of the switch. Her shoulders sagged as she realised he was right. It was a simple mistake not an emergency. Lewis was such a lovely romantic person who had become engrossed in sorting out his special proposal and simply forgotten he had her phone. Poor thing was probably beside himself. Seat seventeen was watching her closely with those pretty blue eyes. If he wasn't such an arse he would be highly attractive.

'Shall we?' he suggested, ushering her back into the carriage.

'I'll have to get off at the next station and get a train back to . . . back to . . . Where the hell was that?' She waved her arm about – it was something she did when she felt anxious.

'Derby,' said seat seventeen. 'But why?' He was looking at her quizzically.

'Because I need my phone back.'

'But it's been stolen.'

'No, it hasn't,' said Ruby, with a splutter.

'Yes, it has.' Seat seventeen looked confused at her response.

'Lewis wasn't planning on getting off there. He's going to London. He had to get off because of all of those people and he didn't get back on in time. It was an accident.'

'No, it wasn't.'

Ruby sighed. This bloke was exasperating.

Ruby gathered up her things and, in her haste, dropped her book on the floor and out fell her bookmark. 'Bugger.' She'd be rereading whole chunks of it now. She scrabbled about under the seat and her hand touched something velvety. Her fingers closed around it and she pulled it from under the seat. It was the ring box. She flicked it open and Lewis's engagement ring sparkled back at her.

Chapter Three

Ruby snapped the box shut. This was a complete and utter disaster. Lewis was about to propose but she had the ring.

'Is that the engagement ring?' asked seat seventeen.

'Someone was earwigging.' She gave him a pointed look but his expression didn't change. 'Yeah. It's the ring. See.' She held it out for inspection. He took it and studied it closely.

'It certainly looks real.'

'Of course it's real. And I need to get off at this stop,' she said, as the train announced its next calling point. She held her hand out for the ring. 'Can I have it back, please?'

Seat seventeen's brow furrowed – he seemed deep in thought. 'I think I should keep hold of this,' he said.

'Why? I found it.' She was indignant.

He stared at her and his intensity made her feel all funny. 'It's not finders, keepers.'

'I know that. I'm going to return it and save the day. And get my phone back.' She waved her empty palm for him to hand it back.

'I don't think you're trustworthy,' he said.

'What?' she snapped.

Someone coughed and they both turned. A lady pointed at the quiet carriage sticker.

'My apologies,' said seat seventeen, popping the ring box in the pocket of a battered leather laptop bag and exiting the carriage.

'Hey! You can't just take that,' said Ruby, hastily throwing her things into her bag and following him only to have the stupid sliding door almost take her nose off as it shut on her again. She stabbed a finger at the button, it opened and she marched into the vestibule to join him.

'You have no right to call me untrustworthy without even knowing me,' she said.

'I know you don't pay for train travel. That is an offence and *that* makes you untrustworthy.'

'That was a simple mistake because I was rushing. I'm completely honest. I want to return the ring so Lewis can propose to his very lucky girlfriend.' A picture of the smiling woman in the photograph swam into her mind. 'Anyway, he has my phone.'

'I would suggest your phone is worth a lot less than the ring.' He raised one eyebrow.

'For goodness' sake. Stop being pompous and give me the ring.' She held out her hand, her patience all but expired.

'No,' he said and he turned to face the door.

He was infuriating. 'Why should I trust *you* with the ring?'

This got his full attention. He turned slowly to face her, which she found slightly unnerving but she tipped her chin up and held his gaze. 'We've not been properly introduced. I'm Curtis Walker.' He held out his hand.

Ruby eyed it suspiciously before giving it a brief shake. 'Ruby Edwards.'

Curtis reached into the side pocket of his laptop bag and for a moment she thought he was going to hand her the ring. Instead he pulled out a business card. 'My card,' he said.

Ruby read the details. 'What's a technical consultant?'

'It can be quite varied. From digital strategy to large-scale technical change.' Ruby had no idea what he'd just said. He continued. 'But generally, that means I gather extensive amounts of data to determine the organisation's data management and security needs, as well as potential scalability.'

'Ri-ight,' said Ruby. 'It sounds . . . interesting. But that hardly makes you more qualified to return the ring than me. It was me Lewis made friends with, not you. Hand it over.'

Curtis sighed. 'I will return to Derby and hand it in to the lost property office. Okay?'

'No!' Her vehement response made them both jump. 'He needs it today. He's proposing this afternoon. Just give it here.' She tried to wrestle his laptop bag off him.

'Stop!' he said forcefully, which had the desired effect. 'Let's take it one step at a time.' He checked his watch. 'I have ample time to return to Derby, catch the later train and still be in London on time. Do you?'

'Yep. I've left loads of time for my thing.' Ruby felt quite smug.

'Do you really want to waste your time chaperoning me?' he asked.

'Fine by me,' said Ruby. She wasn't going to let this guy fob her off. This was the most exciting thing to happen to her since someone pissed in her kettle.

Curtis sighed. 'Fine. Then we work together.'

An announcement told them they were pulling into

Long Eaton. They got off the train and watched it depart. It was a quiet little station with only a couple of people milling about.

'Tickets,' said Curtis.

'Got mine.' Ruby held hers up and gave him a cheesy grin.

'We'll need additional tickets for the trip back to Derby.'

Ruby huffed a bit but followed him to the small ticket office where they both purchased return tickets to Derby. Curtis checked the departures board and marched off towards the bridge and the other platform. Ruby followed.

'I've an idea,' said Curtis. His face had changed from its resting bored accountant look to enthusiastic human.

'Hmm,' replied Ruby.

'What's your mobile number? I'll ring it, speak to the man with your phone and resolve all this.'

'Genius.' She was impressed. 'It's zero seven eight three . . . um four no hang on two then four. Actually, I'm not sure. I changed the number to get rid of this guy who . . . Anyway there's definitely a four in it.' He gave her a pained look. 'Stop it.' She put her index fingers on her temples and tried to conjure up the number. 'Right, it's definitely zero seven eight three . . . bugger.'

'Sorry, I don't think I have a number for bugger. At least I don't think I do,' he said. He gave a flicker of a smile. 'Do you really not know your own telephone number?'

'Who knows their own number anyway?' Ruby waved her hands about.

'Most people,' said Curtis.

'No, they don't. Normal people get the other person's number and then give it a quick call. They don't remember all those digits.'

'A friend's phone number then? Perhaps we can call

them and ask them for your number.' Curtis returned his eyes to his phone screen, his thumbs poised.

Ruby bit her lip. She had no idea of anyone's number. 'They're all in my phone.'

'Parents?'

'She . . .' Her pause made him look up. 'She died.' The statement took the wind out of her sails. Every time she had to tell someone it took her by surprise. The renewed shock that her mother was actually gone was like a physical slap.

Curtis put his phone away. His expression softening. 'I see. And this happened recently, did it?'

'Eight months ago.' She felt the familiar lurch of her gut at the thought of her mum dying. Grief was her constant companion. A sneaky little bugger who she sometimes thought had disappeared but popped up unexpectedly.

'And, you were close?' he asked, whilst guiding her to sit on a nearby bench.

'Very.' It had always been just Ruby and her mum. As a single mother, she'd played the role of both parents and, to Ruby's mind, had done an exceptional job. She was biased, of course, and it hadn't been easy financially but she'd always felt they could face anything together. Although, it seemed, death had other ideas.

'My mother died before her time too,' said Curtis, and something passed between them – a shared sense of understanding. 'I am very sorry for your loss,' he added.

'Thank you. You too.'

There was an awkward silence thankfully broken by the sound of the approaching train.

* * *

The trip back to Derby was quiet and uneventful. They were sitting across the aisle from each other because Curtis had to face the direction of travel. She felt a bit exposed having told Curtis about her mum's death. But it had just tumbled out. Her friends had been hugely supportive at the time and Kim had been a life-saver, but the world had slowly moved on. People had stopped asking her how she was. Maybe they didn't want to hear that she was sad every day, but that was the truth. But today was the start of her looking to the future. About her taking control and she was sure it was for the best.

Derby station was announced and they both got up ready. Curtis had his finger poised over the exit button as if to reassure other passengers that he was prepared for the responsibility bestowed on him as the person nearest the door.

Ruby craned her neck to look out of the window in all directions to see if she could catch a glimpse of Lewis. They left the train and Ruby darted about, not knowing where to look first, until a cough halted her.

'I suggest we try lost property,' said Curtis and he headed off towards the exit.

The person at the counter said nothing had been handed in at all that day – they were back to square one.

'But he could be anywhere,' said Ruby, twirling her arms about and making Curtis take a step away from her. 'The platform where he got off. The coffee shop. Another train.'

This made Curtis stop walking. 'Those are all possibilities. He could also have got on the next train. We could be chasing each other in circles. Perhaps we should have continued to London and waited for him there?'

'Don't say that now we've done this.' She threw up her arms in despair.

'Okay. Let's at least search this station and make certain he isn't here. You cover that side; I'll do this. Meet back here in ten minutes.'

'Okay.' Ruby dashed off and began shouting Lewis's name. She got some odd looks but she didn't care. She was used to odd looks – her vintage outfits frequently prompted them. Her initial energy soon waned as there was no sign of Lewis anywhere. She decided to pop to the loo. When she came out Curtis was nearby.

'Was he in there?' asked Curtis, twitching an eyebrow.

'I was being thorough,' she said. 'What's the plan now?'

'I need to get the next train to London. I suggest we discuss options on the way, assuming we can find seats together.'

'If not, we can come up with a plan at the other end.' Ruby was quite into the adventure. It felt a bit like the books she used to read as a child. They were only missing a couple of other people and a dog.

'Actually, we can't. I'll be cutting it fine to make my meeting. So, I'll have to head straight off.'

'Hang on, I've got an appointment too. You can't just dash off and take the ring. Lewis needs it.'

'But I have a meeting.'

'My appointment might be more important than your meeting.' This was a pivotal point in Ruby's life. It didn't get much more important than that. Ruby folded her arms across her chest and stared him down.

'I somehow doubt it. I am presenting the final analysis and recommendations for a multimillion-pound technical infrastructure replacement for a large financial institution.' He nodded emphatically as if to say, 'Beat that'.

Ruby raised one eyebrow. 'I'm getting a baby.'

Chapter Four

Kim concentrated hard on the excited bride-to-be explaining her vision for the perfect wedding while her young daughter viciously pulled the petals off a peony.

'The theme for the flowers is natural woodland with accents of indigo and magenta,' explained the woman.

'When you say indigo, are you thinking blue like an iris or purple like those tulips over there?' She pointed behind her customer. 'Ooh,' said Kim, spotting what the small child was doing. 'I don't think eating those petals is a good idea.'

The mother spun around. 'Are they poisonous?'

'No, but I shouldn't think they'll do her much good.'

'Oh, that's fine. I believe in freedom of expression.' She smiled at Kim, making her unsure how to respond. It appeared that 'freedom of expression' translated to *doing whatever the heck she liked.*

'Do you think she'd prefer a biscuit?'

The child dropped the petals and ran to Kim at the mention of the word 'biscuit', which was a reaction Kim could relate to. Recently, thanks to the menopause, biscuits were making up her main food group. Kim retrieved the biscuit barrel from the back room and offered the open tin to the little girl. She promptly snatched the tin from Kim and began sifting through the contents while her mother watched on with pride.

'Anyway . . .' began Kim, making a mental note to buy more. 'What sort of colour are you picturing when you say indigo?'

'Well, *indigo*,' said the woman, scrunching up her features as if Kim had asked the most stupid question ever in the history of stupid questions.

Kim wobbled her head to buy her some time to phrase her reply. As she got older she found she had to give herself a moment to avoid blurting out what she was thinking, which wasn't always very customer-friendly. 'Indigo is open to interpretation, so I want to be sure to get it right. Let me show you the sort of thing I mean.'

Kim gathered some samples of flowers she had in: cornflower, forget-me-nots and irises, as well as showing her some example bouquet photos from her binder.

The bride-to-be ummed and ahhed her way through them all before finally shaking her head. 'No, none of those are indigo.'

'Right. We can look at dyed flowers – that way you can get a near perfect colour match.'

'Near perfect?' She didn't appear convinced.

An hour later and Kim was wondering if it might be her who was losing the plot – she was pretty sure one of them was.

'Let's recap the bridesmaids,' said Kim. 'Eight trailing bouquets that each need to end just above the hem of their respective dress and are therefore bespoke to each bridesmaid. Although none of them should be on a par with or greater than the size of your bouquet. Four flower girls each with baskets of real petals in shades of *indigo* and magenta with alternating flowers of those colours entwined around the handle.' The bride-to-be nodded along while her daughter drew on the carpet with the last of Kim's custard creams. 'And finally, two doggy-maids with flower collars, one in indigo and one in magenta. Is that everything?'

'Confetti. I want you to make confetti from tiny, weeny chopped-up real petals in shades of—'

'Indigo and magenta?'

'Yes,' said the woman clapping her hands together.

Save me, thought Kim. And to think she'd missed a cut and colour for this. Where was Ruby when she needed her?

Curtis had been very quiet for the rest of the journey, so much for planning out their next steps – her baby announcement seemed to have killed conversation.

'When you say you're getting a baby, I'm assuming not an actual baby?' he asked with a puckered brow.

'Not an *actual* baby. No . . . but—'

Curtis brightened. 'That's good then.' He opened his laptop and she went back to her novel although her mind was somewhere else.

He was quick to get to his feet a moment before the announcement came that they were arriving into St Pancras station.

'Shall we spread out and search the station?' asked Ruby, following his lead and packing her things away.

'I've no time for that I'm afraid. But you feel free to check.' They filed off the train.

'What about getting the ring to Lewis at the London Eye before four o'clock? That's when he said he was proposing.'

'I think it would be best to hand it in to lost property.'

'No!' She said it louder than she'd intended, making a few passers-by give her a wider berth. 'No. This is the most romantic thing I've ever heard of. And trust me I've read all the best romance novels. We absolutely have to get the ring to Lewis on time. Don't he and his girlfriend deserve their happy ever after?'

Curtis appeared confused by the question. 'I believe there will be endless opportunities for Lewis to suggest marriage to this woman. It doesn't have to be at four o'clock today.'

'Yes, it does. We don't want to be the people who wreck his plans. We want to help. Don't we?' She knew she was pleading but she wanted this to work out for Lewis. He'd seemed so nice and genuine. And if it had been her, she'd hope someone else would put themselves out to save the day.

Curtis checked his watch. He pulled in a deep breath. 'Where and what time are you getting . . . the um . . . baby? More importantly, what time will you be finished?'

She did some rough calculations. 'Done by three-ish and it's in Newham.' She almost sounded like she knew where she was going.

'Newham is a huge area. Can you be more specific? What's the nearest Tube station?'

Ruby pulled the printed-off email from her bag and quickly scanned it. 'West Ham.'

Curtis stared at his watch. 'Nearest Tube for the London Eye is Waterloo. It's tight but West Ham and Waterloo are both on the Jubilee line, which makes it doable.'

Ruby didn't want to be, but she was impressed by his underground knowledge. 'Hang on,' said Ruby realising something. 'You're not coming with me for my . . . my . . . appointment.'

'Are you prepared to go our separate ways and meet me at the London Eye?'

'No way.'

'Then I'm afraid you are going to have to come to my meeting and I am coming to your . . . appointment.' His expression conveyed that he could barely believe what he was suggesting.

'Fine,' she said, and for no apparent reason she held out her hand for him to shake, which he cautiously did.

'Right. Follow me.'

She followed Curtis across St Pancras station. A sign flashed up to say which lines were closed due to essential maintenance. She was secretly pleased that she was with someone who knew where they were going. He instructed her on how to use her contactless debit card to get through the ticket barrier – it had been an extremely long time since she'd been on the Tube.

A couple of escalators conveyed them to the depths of the underground. Curtis suddenly broke into a run. 'Quick.'

She didn't have time to question him. He was already leaping onto a train. Ruby followed close behind as a now familiar beeping noise surrounded her. The doors closed with the speed of a guillotine but she was inside. However, when she went to move, she realised she was pinned to the door. It had managed to shut with her on the inside and her bag on the outside. She began frantically tugging on the bag handles but it wouldn't budge. She started to panic. If she lost her bag her appointment would be off. She'd already lost a phone today; she couldn't lose anything else. She tugged harder.

Curtis appeared at her side, gripped the door firmly and forced it back open and, just like that, her bag was freed.

'Thank heavens for that,' she said. Curtis looked at his black-stained hands with dismay. 'And thank *you*,' she added.

'You're welcome,' said Curtis pulling some hand gel and a pack of tissues from his bag. They moved further along the carriage where others were sitting but there was enough space for them to stand.

'How many stops?' asked Ruby, peering at the very long map on the wall.

'Hold on tight,' said Curtis and on cue the train took off, making Ruby lurch forward. She managed to grab the support post, but her weight continued travelling and the momentum swung her right around the pole. She lost her balance and couldn't stop herself from falling. She landed with a bump.

She wasn't sure who was more surprised: her or the poor woman whose lap she landed on. Ruby burst into hysterical laughter. The woman's face was stony. Ruby used the pole to pull herself to her feet. 'I am so sorry,' she said through the giggles. 'Are you okay?' The woman nodded but it was clear she didn't want to discuss the matter and neither did she find it remotely amusing.

Two stops later Ruby was still chuckling. It was the funniest thing she'd done in ages. Every time the woman glanced up Ruby mouthed another apology. As the train pulled into a station the poor woman made good her escape. Ruby apologised again and took her seat.

'Don't sit down – there's only two more stops,' said Curtis.

'Did you do that without looking at the map?'

It appeared his underground knowledge extended far beyond the Jubilee line. Ruby was soon entertaining herself by testing Curtis.

'Liverpool Street to Mayfair,' she said.

'Mayfair isn't a Tube station. Are you just citing places off the Monopoly board?'

She was but she wasn't going to admit it. 'How about Liverpool Street to Wimbledon?'

'Central line to Notting Hill Gate then District line,' he replied. She loved how he pronounced all the words properly. His voice had a deep timbre and she thought how fabulous he'd be at narrating audio books.

'Okay, what about Paddington to Covent Garden?'

'Bakerloo to Piccadilly Circus, then Piccadilly line to Covent Garden.' He puckered up his features. 'I think we've established I have a good working knowledge of the Tube map.'

'I'd love to go to Covent Garden,' she said. It was one of those places that always seemed to be on people's lists when they went to London and she wanted to see for herself what all the fuss was about.

'What's stopping you?' asked Curtis.

'I don't often come to London.' She'd been three times: once with school to see the crown jewels, once with her mum to see the Christmas lights, and the last time was on a hen weekend that ended very messily when they got kicked out of their B and B after too much tequila.

'Really?' he asked. Was he being sarcastic? She wasn't sure.

'Covent Garden's not somewhere you go on your own though, is it?'

'There's no reason why you couldn't go alone. It's well lit and there are usually quite a few people. It's relatively safe for a woman on her own.'

He'd kind of missed the point.

The carriage flooded with light as they came into Bank

Tube station. It was busy and she had to walk like a race walker to keep up with Curtis. He had long legs and an enviable stride. He did keep checking over his shoulder, every so often, which reassured her that he wasn't trying to give her the slip. They seemed to walk a long way before popping out at another platform.

'For crying out loud. How much further?' asked Ruby, feeling a stitch in her side and a throbbing in her feet.

'DLR,' said Curtis.

'PMT,' said Ruby. They both looked equally confused.

'DLR is Docklands Light Railway.'

'Ahh. There was a sign at St Pancras saying there was essential maintenance being carried out on DLR and the something and city line.'

'Neither of those relate to the section we need,' he said.

'I thought DLR was some text speak I wasn't up on.' Curtis gave her an odd look. 'You know, like NVM.'

Curtis appeared interested. 'Do you mean Node Version Manager?' he asked.

'No. Never mind.'

A train pulled in and Curtis ushered Ruby into the front carriage. There weren't as many people on this one and they sat down at the front. It wasn't until the train pulled away that Ruby let out a squeak of alarm. 'There's no driver.' She was sitting at the very front of the train with a large glass screen in front of her and it was bombing along with no visible person driving it.

'Relax. It's a driverless train.'

'Oh, right.' She loosened her grip on the seat.

Once her heart rate had returned to normal, she quite liked the view at the front, especially when it went above ground and then back under again. They arrived at Canary Wharf and Curtis set off on another march. Ruby felt like her head was spinning as they walked through what appeared to be a shopping centre. They passed a sandwich shop and her stomach growled.

'Can we grab something to eat?' she asked.

'There will be coffee and food at the meeting.'

'But I'm guessing that doesn't include me.'

'It should be fine,' said Curtis.

'Are you sure I can have some?' Free food was even better. 'I thought I'd be waiting outside. Like a puppy.' She made her hands into paws and whimpered like a lost dog.

Curtis slowed his pace and furrowed his brow. 'I don't think that's necessary. If you attend as my assistant that shouldn't be an issue.'

'Promotion already. I'll be after a pay rise soon,' said Ruby with a grin and Curtis eyed her suspiciously. 'I'm joking.'

He nodded but didn't seem convinced.

They were soon above ground and it was good to feel sunlight on her skin. She whipped out her Audrey Hepburn-style sunglasses and tried to take in her surroundings. Lots of people were hurrying past. Most of the latest fashions were literally passing her by although many were teamed with trainers, which made for an odd combination. Though her throbbing toes told her the trainers were a good idea.

They crossed a bridge in front of a glass building so tall that Ruby couldn't see the top of it, even if she tilted her head right back, which she had to stop doing for fear of toppling over. Inside it was all very swish, modern and airy and full of busy-looking people. Curtis walked up to a circular reception desk while Ruby tried to work out how the queuing system would work or if it was just a free-for-all.

'Curtis Walker to see Cordelia Stuart-Bruce.'

Ruby stepped forward. 'And his assistant, Ruby Edwards, to see Cordelia, Stuart and Bruce.' The smartly dressed receptionist smiled before tapping away on her keyboard.

'Cordelia's assistant will be with you shortly,' said the receptionist, handing them each a visitor's badge on a blue lanyard. 'Fire escape instructions are on the reverse, please have a read. Please help yourself to refreshments while you wait.' She indicated a plush seating area with lavish half-moon sofas and a large bowl of individually wrapped biscuits.

Curtis took a seat and Ruby took a handful of biscuits. 'If I'd known there was free stuff I'd have brought a bigger bag. Drink? Coffee?' she asked, pulling a paper cup from a dispenser.

'I'll wait until the meeting thanks.'

'Or there's mint tea or camomile or hot chocolate or—'

'Really. I'm fine.' He seemed to be getting irritated. Ruby shrugged and helped herself to a hot chocolate.

After a few minutes someone approached. 'Hi, Curtis, good to see you again,' said a trendy-looking young man thrusting out a hand for Curtis to shake.

'Hi, I'm Curtis's assistant, Ruby Edwards.' She was quite getting into her role now. She swapped her biscuits to her other hand so she could shake his. 'Bruce or Stuart?'

Curtis did a slow blink. The man tilted his head appearing unsure how to react. 'I'm Jonty, Cordelia Stuart-Bruce's assistant.'

'Ohhhh,' said Ruby as the penny dropped. 'Double-barrelled name. Wicked,' she added, biting into a biscuit that promptly exploded into crumbs.

Chapter Five

The meeting was on the sixteenth floor and the super-fast lift made Ruby's stomach tumble. They walked out across luxurious carpet to a large glass meeting room where Jonty left them to set up. Ruby rushed to the floor-to-ceiling windows to take in the view.

'Wow. Look, it's the O2 arena and the Thames. You can see for miles and miles.' She stared out at the sight of London laid before her like a pop-up book coming to life.

'Ruby, would you like to take a seat?' suggested Curtis.

'In a minute.' She was scanning the scene to work out what buildings she could identify from her sketchy knowledge of London. 'Can you see the tower from here?' she asked without pulling her eyes away.

'No. Completely the wrong direction.'

'Shame.' She watched a boat moving up the river quite slowly. It was a long way down.

'Ruby, as we're cutting it finer than I would like please can you write out a few flip charts for me?' asked Curtis, moving the flip chart board nearer to her.

'Hmm.' She was distracted, wondering who was on the boat and where they were going. Was today just another day in London for them or was it like her day, with the potential to change their life forever?

'Ruby, please.' Curtis was sounding exasperated.

At his words Ruby snapped out of her daydream and spun around. Not expecting the flip chart stand to be so close, she clattered into it sending it crashing to the floor.

'Whoops, sorry,' she said wincing. She was often inept when she was uneasy. And a meeting in a London office was definitely starting to make her feel that way. She had no place here and now she was anxious that she was going to mess things up. The best she could do was front it out.

Curtis smoothly lifted up the stand and set it upright. 'I suggest you sit here and do something quietly.' He pointed to a chair at his end of an extra long white table.

'What, like colouring in?'

'That would be perfect.' Curtis looked relieved.

Ruby grinned. 'I was joking. I'm not a child, Curtis. I can be trusted.' The twitch of his eyebrow said he disagreed. 'What? Do you think I'm going to mess this up for you?'

'Not on purpose, no,' he said, popping out a piece of plastic from the middle of the table and connecting his laptop to a cable that magically appeared.

'I promise I will be on my best behaviour. Now what can I do to help?'

'Maybe take some notes,' said Curtis, handing her a notepad and a posh-looking black pen with a fun white splosh on the end.

'I could do that.' She was excited at the opportunity to do something useful and fulfil her new role even though it was just for today. 'What shall I write down?' she asked, taking her seat and straightening her back.

'Just my actions.'

Ruby frowned. Did he think she was an idiot? 'What? Curtis is standing up. Curtis is waving his fist at me. Don't take the p—'

'No. Anything where I need to do something,' he clarified.

Now she felt stupid. 'Oh, right. That kind of action. You should have said. I can definitely do that.'

Jonty returned with a posse of well-groomed people at the same time as a woman appeared with a trolley. She watched as plate after plate of delicious-looking food was unloaded – and she'd thought the biscuits were a highlight.

Jonty sidled up to Ruby and handed her a small plate. 'The mini eclairs go really fast so grab a couple while you can,' he whispered.

In her haste Ruby quickly pushed back her wheelie chair and heard someone squeal. She turned to see she'd run over a man's toes. 'Whoops, sorry. I'm Ruby.'

'Bob,' he said, before limping away.

Ruby took a steadying breath. She was way out of her comfort zone and in her experience she occasionally acted a bit ditsy and panicky when she was in uncharted waters. She needed to keep that little quirk of hers under control for the next couple of hours. She checked the coast was clear before she reversed some more and followed Jonty. 'I've been to weddings with less food than this,' said Ruby and she wasn't lying.

Jonty chuckled and moved along the buffet. 'How come you're working for the infamous lone wolf?' He tipped his head.

'What, Curtis?' Jonty nodded and fixed her with interested eyes. 'You've heard the phrase – it's not what you know it's who you know?'

'Ahh,' said Jonty, with a sage nod. 'Well done. He's the best in the business.'

'Yeah, I know,' said Ruby. 'So am I.' She bit into a samosa. The filling was a bit hotter than she was expecting and she spent the next few minutes listening to Jonty while nodding wisely and waiting for her mouth to cool down. At least she hadn't embarrassed herself again.

After some light chat they all took their seats and Ruby felt a frisson of excitement. She could tell it was an important meeting and she felt like she was on *The Apprentice*.

An elegant woman took the seat at the opposite end of the table to Curtis. 'I can see we have a few new recruits.' She smiled warmly at Ruby. 'Shall we do a quick round of introductions? I'm Cordelia Stuart-Bruce, Head of Information Technology Development.' She nodded to the man to her left and he reeled off a very long job title. It was like a competition; as it moved to the next person the job titles got longer and longer.

When they reached Curtis, he tapped his laptop and the wall behind him lit up and emblazoned on it was Curtis Walker, Technical Consultant. Ruby spontaneously clapped and then, realising nobody else was, picked up her pen and pretended to write something down. 'I'm Curtis Walker and this is my assistant, Ruby Edwards.' Ruby gave a wave and then instantly wished she hadn't. It was met mostly by puckered brows with the exceptions of Jonty and Cordelia who smiled.

The meeting that followed could have been conducted in Swahili for the amount of sense it made to Ruby. Every sentence was littered with technical jargon. She doodled a dragon during the excruciatingly dull bit. A couple of times Curtis pointed at her, which she took as an indication she should be taking notes. Each time he pointed she hastily wrote something down, which prompted a brief nod from him and that made her feel like she was doing okay.

'I agree with everything you've suggested with the exception of the timelines,' said Cordelia.

'If you implement any quicker you lose your contingency window and will be loading on unnecessary risk as per slide fourteen,' said Curtis.

'Surely you could mitigate that risk?'

'Not really. I don't want to compromise the testing and this slide shows our maximum capacity.' Curtis tapped his laptop and a previous slide appeared.

Ruby looked at the slide. 'Is that based on people working nine to five?' she asked.

Curtis spun in her direction as if he'd momentarily forgotten she was there. 'Yes,' replied Curtis. He turned back to Cordelia. 'My recommendation—'

'Five days a week?' continued Ruby.

'Yes.' Curtis's tone was clipped.

'I've a suggestion,' said Ruby. Curtis slowly turned back to look at her as if in disbelief.

'Go ahead,' encouraged Cordelia.

'In my um . . . previous job, if we were up against a deadline we worked around the clock. Maybe get in some extra workers. Could you get some more of those um . . .' Ruby pointed at the slide where it said headcount.

'Testers,' offered Jonty.

'Yeah, testers and have them work a night shift? Wouldn't that shorten the testing phase?'

Curtis opened and closed his mouth but didn't make a sound.

'Excellent suggestion,' said Cordelia. Jonty gave her a little thumbs up just visible above the table. Ruby felt a glow from the inside out. She'd helped.

'Whilst that is an option, it brings with it its own level of risk. Additional testers would need training. I think the testing phase would then need overseeing,' said Curtis, finally finding his voice again.

'Fine,' said Cordelia. 'You can take offices on site here for the duration. Jonty, can you liaise with Ruby so they have everything they require?'

'Certainly,' said Jonty.

'I'm sorry. I need to dash to another meeting,' said Cordelia getting to her feet and swiftly heading for the door. 'Thank you, Curtis . . . and Ruby,' she added as she exited the room, followed quickly by a few others.

Jonty came over. 'What's your direct line, Ruby?' He was poised with a pen.

'Ahh funny story,' said Ruby.

'Which we don't have time for,' said Curtis, packing up his laptop at speed.

Jonty accompanied them back to the airy entrance, relieved them of their badges and lanyards and they said their goodbyes. As they walked away Ruby leaned into Curtis. 'How did I do?' she asked.

'Unmitigated disaster,' he replied.

Ruby was niggled by his grim view. 'Hey, I solved your problem back there.'

Curtis stopped walking and swivelled on his heel. 'No, you *caused* me a problem.'

'How?' Ruby threw up her arms.

'With my assistance they now need to recruit additional top-level testers, get them inducted, briefed and in place and up to speed on a bespoke system in a very short timescale. On top of that I am expected to decamp to London for the duration of testing supposedly with my new assistant.'

'You can tell them I got headhunted and left for an offer I couldn't refuse.' She gave him a cheeky grin.

Curtis looked as if he was going to add something but then thought better of it, shook his head and strode off in the direction of the DLR station. Next stop – baby central.

On the train Ruby passed Curtis back his notepad and fancy pen. He glanced at what she'd written.

'What's this?' he asked pointing to the first point.

Ruby tilted her head to see what she'd written. "'Bald man next to Bob said could you do something about data mining."'

'Helpful,' said Curtis, with a straight face.

'Thank you,' said Ruby.

'And this?'

"'Lady in floral print top, possibly Stella McCartney . . .'"

'Her name is Daksha not Stella.'

Ruby let that go and continued reading word for word. "'She just said future something or other. I don't know exactly because I wasn't listening but you pointed to me so now I'm writing this.'"

'Excellent. And the dinosaur?' he said, tapping the picture.

She grinned. 'That's a dragon. Sorry, I zoned out for a bit.'

'For a bit?' Curtis put the pad away. 'You said you were drawing on experience in your day job for the twenty-four-hour working suggestion.'

'Yep.'

'What is it that you do?' he asked.

'I'm a florist,' said Ruby proudly and Curtis dropped his head into his hands.

* * *

Kim was rubbing her temple and wondering if she could break her no alcohol mid-week rule when the door chime sounded and in walked Adrian doing a bad job of trying to hide something behind his back.

'Blimey I know it's been a long day but don't tell me it's half five already,' she quipped.

'No. Day off. I just popped in to um . . .' He looked around as if searching for the answer. 'To say thanks for last week's flowers.'

'Okay.' Kim sensed there was something amiss as Adrian looked uncomfortable and this was the first time in about three years that she'd seen him outside of their usual end-of-day window. 'I'm glad she liked them. Is everything okay?'

Adrian took a breath. 'Yep. Fine . . . It's fine. I just thought you seemed a bit low last week and I feared I may have contributed to that in some way, so I was checking you were all right.' He gave a shaky smile.

'That's kind of you, Adrian. I'm okay, really. Did you enjoy the theatre?'

'Yes, very much.'

There was an awkward pause where they looked at each other and waited for the other to speak. Kim was about to say something when Adrian jolted into life and thrust something green at her and almost up her left nostril.

'And I brought you this,' he said. 'It's a tomato plant.'

Kim leaned back until it was in focus. 'Oh, thank you. That's kind. Who's the gardener? You or Justine?'

'Me. I'm not a gardener as such. I potter about in the greenhouse and mow the lawn.'

'Can I interest you in a cuppa or do you need to dash off?' asked Kim.

'That'd be lovely. I had a bit of surplus holiday, so took

the day off. But now I've run out of things to do.' He scratched his ear and looked about as if seeking inspiration.

With that the door swung open, causing the bell to clang rather than its usual chime, making both Kim and Adrian jump. Kim placed the plant on the counter.

'Did we leave Bunnykins in here?' It was the bride-to-be looking rather fraught as she scanned the floor.

'I don't think so,' said Kim. She'd had plenty of biscuit crumbs to tidy up so she was fairly sure she would have noticed. 'I'm assuming Bunnykins is a cuddly toy?' These days they gave kids such odd names it wouldn't have surprised her if it had been a sibling.

'Of course it is.' The woman came fully into the shop, towing the red-faced child. Adrian stepped out of their way. 'She won't be able to sleep without him. It's a complete disaster. We've only been in here and the coffee shop.'

Kim began having a root around the corner where the child had spent some of her time destroying her stock.

'Ooh, now I like that,' said the woman, running a finger along a frond of Adrian's tomato plant. 'Very rustic.'

'I grew it,' said Adrian proudly.

'What, locally?'

'In my greenhouse. From seed. No pesticides. No growth enhancers.' Adrian pulled his shoulders back.

Kim noticed a flash of grubby pink amongst the lilies. She grabbed hold of the soaked mass and pulled it free. 'Bunnykins, I presume.' She held up the soggy, dripping toy.

'Oh, my word. How did that happen?' The bride-to-be was aiming her question at Kim.

'I think your daughter might have been using her freedom of expression,' said Kim, trying to hand over the soaked toy.

'What?' said the woman. 'Oh, yes.' She pasted on a fake

smile. 'Ah, ha, ha, ha.' Her laughter matched her smile perfectly. The woman gingerly took the rabbit by the tip of his ear.

Kim returned to the counter. 'Was there anything else?'

'Yes,' said the woman, picking up the tomato plant. 'I also want lots of these as table centres.' Kim looked at Adrian's shocked face and tried hard not to laugh.

Chapter Six

Curtis and Ruby had left West Ham Tube behind them and turned into a narrow street with garages on one side and what looked like the back of a row of terraced houses on the other. Ruby studied the address on the piece of paper again. This couldn't be right, could it? She inched down the road, looking for numbers or anything to confirm that this hopefully wasn't the right place. She stopped outside a property with an orange front door. A plastic two and a stuck-on number six confirmed her worst thoughts.

'I don't like to intrude,' said Curtis. 'However, I fear we may have taken a wrong turn.' As a breeze scattered litter at their feet, Curtis blinked at the row of grubby little houses with their fallen wheelie bins, abandoned like forgotten soldiers.

'No. I think it's the right place,' she said, her voice almost a whisper.

'I'm sorry. I have to ask. This baby.' He made inverted commas with his fingers. 'Is it something illegal?' He looked about him. 'Well, obviously it is.' He answered his own question. 'Ruby, could I suggest you have a rethink before you commit a serious offence. I mean—'

'It's legal,' said Ruby, finally pulling her eyes away from the peeling paint of number twenty-six. 'And it is a real baby . . . well, it will be.'

Ruby paced up and down. A myriad of thoughts vied for attention. All the arguments she'd been sure she'd silenced were banging their own drums and drowning out any rational thought.

Now she considered it, she'd made a lot of assumptions. She'd been focused on family health and cost but had failed to ask certain things that now seemed fundamental.

'Is there a problem?' asked Curtis, checking his watch.

'Yeah . . . No . . . Yes . . .'

'I'm going to take a stab and say if you can't decide between yes and no then there is a problem.'

'Arghhhh!' The sound came from somewhere in the pit of her stomach. It was a good way to release a bit of the tension.

He stepped back. 'Do you want to discuss it?'

'No.' She shook her head. 'Yeah. Maybe. I don't know.' He stepped forward as she spun around and they were suddenly very close together. 'I want a baby.'

His eyebrows shot up and stayed glued in position. 'As we've only just met, I'm going to say thank you for the offer but . . .'

'Not with you.' She waved his embarrassed babbling away. 'With the guy who lives here.' She stabbed a finger towards the house.

'I see. You have an appointment with . . .' Curtis scratched his head. 'Your boyfriend, partner, an experimental biologist?'

She shook her head. 'Some guy off the internet.'

Curtis opened and closed his mouth a few times. 'No, you're going to have to explain that a bit more.'

47

'I've come here to see a sperm donor.'

Curtis jolted. 'That I was not expecting,' he said.

She flopped onto a nearby wall. Curtis brushed the top of the low wall and sat down gingerly next to her.

'I'm almost thirty-five. Do you know what they call women who have a baby after thirty-five?'

'A mother,' said Curtis hesitantly.

'Well, yes, obviously. But they call them geriatric mothers. *Geriatric* at thirty-bloody-five. It happened to a friend of mine. That's the medical world saying you're officially past it. And that's what's missing in my life. Another person to love.' She took a breath, her mind swimming with memories of her mother. She had so much love she wanted to share. 'I want a child. I want to be a mum before it really is too late.'

'Is that all?'

'No. I had this list of stuff I was going to achieve by the time I was forty and I've done none of it.'

'Have you got a copy of the list?' he asked.

'What?'

'The list you made. What's on it?' He looked at her expectantly.

'There wasn't an *actual* list.'

'How were you expecting to achieve it? For a goal to be achievable you should—' She intensified her glare. 'Okay. Clearly not important. Please continue.'

'I guess there was just one big thing on the list. I thought I'd be married with children by now.'

'Technically that's two or possibly more things if it's . . .' He seemed to sense her stare. 'But I get your drift. What I'm not understanding is why someone who believes so blindly, or should I say fervently, in the existence of romance would then look to conceive a child in this manner.'

'Because at some point you get fed up of waiting for your happy ever after and realise if *you* don't make it happen nobody else will. This is me taking control of my dreams.'

'And you believe the path to your happy ever after lies here?' He indicated the house and they both turned to study the litter, marauding weeds and broken path that led to the shabby front door.

Ruby's chin hit her chest. 'I don't know any more. I thought I did. I really did. But then the guy on the train . . .'

'Stole your phone,' suggested Curtis as an end to her sentence.

'No. He borrowed it. It was so romantic – how he talked about his girlfriend. Everything he's planned for the proposal. It's going to be magical and I want that. I want someone to love me that much that they make my dreams come true. Someone I could raise a family with.'

'I see,' said Curtis. 'It's more of a package deal you're after rather than merely sperm.' He was frowning hard as if he was concentrating and it made Ruby smile despite everything.

'Yes, Curtis. I'm after the package deal.' She didn't like to admit the sad little love story her imagination had conjured up, that the man at number twenty-six just might be her true love. He would open the door, there would be an instant spark and they'd look back on this as the funny story that brought them together. That was looking less and less likely by the second. She sighed. 'Why is love so complicated?'

'Love interests me,' said Curtis. 'I understand that it is a mix of emotions but if you *become* sad, are *made* angry and *feel* happy then why do you *fall* in love? You don't fall into any other emotional state.'

'Huh,' said Ruby, giving it some thought. 'I guess because with love you are totally out of control.'

Curtis seemed to shiver, his expression stern. 'I feared that might be the case.'

'So, what do I do?' asked Ruby. 'Do I keep searching for something I might never find? Or do I take control and go down the clinical route?'

'If it's love you're seeking then I'm thinking that perhaps you need to date someone for a while rather than rush into . . .' He glanced across the road. 'Well, this.'

Ruby couldn't stop the huge sigh. 'But that is what I've been doing for years and years. I've dated hund—' His wide eyes made her adjust her sentence. 'I've dated lots of men and none of them have been *the one.*'

'The one who . . .' He gestured for her to continue.

'Just the one.'

'No, I'm sorry. I have no idea what you mean.' He tilted his head towards her. 'Please enlighten me.'

All the romantic heroes she'd read about tumbled into her mind. 'That one person who makes you feel alive. Who does all the romantic stuff because they love you and not because they think it'll get them a quick shag. Someone who makes your heart flip—'

'That's not technically possible.'

'Okay. Makes your heart beat faster or miss a beat.'

'Like arrhythmia?' He looked genuinely confused and it brought another unexpected smile to her face.

'No, not like arrhythmia. Like love.'

'Ahhh,' said Curtis, nodding firmly. 'We appear to be back at the same impasse – love.'

He was right. It did all come back to love. Love in all its guises. Feeling it, sharing it, finding it – love was fundamental. 'Do you love someone, Curtis?'

'No. I'm not well versed in that arena.'

'No. Nor am I,' said Ruby. 'Which is why I came to the conclusion that this was my best option to become a mother.' She took a deep breath and stood up. 'Right, let's stick with the plan.' She walked across the road and Curtis followed her.

Twenty minutes after the woman had left the shop, Kim and Adrian were still laughing about her wanting tomato plants at her wedding reception. Kim had made up Adrian's usual Friday bouquet with a beautiful selection of mixed roses. They were now sitting in the back room chatting over a cup of tea. Kim glanced at her phone. She'd been hoping to hear from Ruby. She had tried not to go full-on mother hen around her but she was more than a little concerned about this appointment she'd said she had.

She'd known Ruby a few years and in all that time she had always been very open about her personal life. They had grown close and it was out of character for Ruby to keep the details of something like this to herself, and it worried Kim.

'Am I keeping you from your work?' asked Adrian.

'No, I'm sorry. I was hoping Ruby was going to message me. That's all. I'm enjoying having the company if I'm honest. Don't get me wrong, I think the world of Ruby and we get on well. But it's nice to chat to someone my age who doesn't start looking up iPads when I say I need a tablet or think I mean the internet when I say I'm thinking about going on safari.'

'I know what you mean,' said Adrian. Kim instantly wondered if he meant his wife and something in her expression must have given her away. 'Oh, I didn't mean

Justine,' he added quickly. 'I mean people at work mainly. Lots of youngsters coming in now. Not many of the old guard left. People around me keep taking early retirement or redundancy.'

'Have you thought about doing the same?'

'For a nanosecond. And then I decided against it. I'm not sure what I'd do with all that time to myself.'

'Gardening?' She tipped her head in the direction of the tomato plant.

'That can only fill so many hours.'

'Holidays? Or maybe you could start a new hobby.'

Adrian sipped his tea. 'There was a time when Justine took up pottery.' He smiled at the memory. 'She was atrocious. More clay on her than on the wheel. It's all still in the garage.'

'There you are then. That's something you could take up together. You could be throwing pots or whatever it is potters do. Not like at a Greek wedding you understand.'

Adrian smiled. 'I'm not that creative. How about you? Any retirement plans?'

'I wish,' said Kim. 'I can't afford to retire. Vince said this place was our pension – no work means no money. And if I'm honest I wouldn't want to stop working. I don't do much outside of the shop. Between you and me, my day off is the worst day of the week. I'm afraid I've never really adjusted to life on my own.'

'Have you thought about a companion?' Adrian was watching her closely.

'Like a dog? I have actually. It would be nice to have someone to talk to. Them not answering back could be a bonus. And goodness knows I need to lose some weight so walking it would be good exercise.'

'Um, right. Yes, a dog might be the answer then. I know

someone who works at the rescue centre. We could go and have a look on your day off if you wanted to.'

'You know what, Adrian? I might just take you up on that.'

Curtis waited on the pavement while Ruby knocked on the door. A middle-aged man answered it. She looked him up and down. He was, at least in part, as he had described in his emails, with dark hair, dark eyes and he appeared generally well kempt. However, he was somewhat older and shorter than she was expecting and he certainly hadn't set her heart a flutter – so much for her fanciful meet-cute. She was now very thankful this baby wasn't going to be made the traditional way.

'Neil?' she asked.

'Ruby?'

'Yeah. I'm sorry I'm late. I got delayed and . . .' She turned to look at Curtis at the other end of the path. 'It's a long story.'

'Come in.' Neil stood back and held the door open. Ruby looked inside. It was neater than the outside, which was an improvement. What had she been expecting? She knew this was no London fertility clinic.

Curtis stepped forward. 'I hate to hurry you along, but we have an appointment with a giant Ferris wheel that is fast approaching. The appointment time . . . not the actual wheel.'

Neil looked unsettled. 'Is he with you?'

'Err, yeah. I guess.'

'Good afternoon,' said Curtis, striding forward and attempting to shake Neil's hand. Neil stepped back as he looked Curtis over.

'Are you the police?' He clutched the front door tighter.

'No. But why does the thought that I might be alarm you?' asked Curtis, narrowing his eyes.

'No reason. Not doing anything wrong.' He turned his attention back to Ruby. 'Do you have the cash?'

She produced an envelope from her bag and held it in front of her. She bit her lip. This was it. If she handed over the money then this was happening. She was having a baby.

'Excuse me,' said Curtis. 'I'm sorry to interrupt but could I have a word?' He took Ruby gently by the arm and steered her back down the wonky path to the pavement. She shoved the money back in her bag. Curtis fixed her with a sombre gaze. 'I understand that you may have been considering this for some time; however, it appears to be a very ill-thought-through plan of action. May I suggest you consider all your options.'

'Consider my options?' Ruby laughed. 'That's what I've been doing my whole adult life and my options are all a bunch of wasters or worse still wasters disguised as decent people. Either way I waste my time and money on men who always leave me in the end. This is my only option for a child before my ovaries retire. I've been planning it for ages. I've researched fertility and IVF clinics. They were too expensive as it turns out. But I looked up lots of other donor possibilities. I've been taking vitamin supplements for weeks. And I'm a regular in the John Lewis pushchair department. I'm ready to have a baby.' She took a breath. 'A donor means I get the baby but without the baggage of a man who is inevitably going to let me down. And worse still let a child down. This way there are no expectations. It's a business transaction. And I have sifted through loads of potential donors to find Neil.'

'And he is the best you could find?'

They turned and both studied Neil who was half hiding behind the door. Ruby pulled the now somewhat dog-eared email from her bag and handed it to Curtis. He speed-read it.

'I see. He claims to be incredibly fertile although his evidence is inconclusive. The four children he claims are his may not be unless there is DNA proof and even if they are his they were likely conceived some time ago. Sperm motility decreases with age.'

Neil shouted from the door. 'Look, I need to be at the new Spider-Man movie in an hour. I've got tickets. If you wanted to um . . . do this take-away, I've got some little pots so I could be getting on with that.'

'Two more minutes, sir,' said Curtis, leading Ruby a little further away. 'This is a very big decision. I just want to check that you're sure.'

'Grrr!' Ruby made the noise with gusto and Curtis jolted. 'Of course I'm not sure. I'm confused. The last thing my mum said to me was . . .' Ruby stopped talking.

'Continue,' said Curtis, giving her a nod of encouragement.

Ruby took a deep breath. 'She said I was what made her life a happy one. And then she said, "Be happy, Ruby."' Ruby ran her hands through her long hair and tugged when she got to the ends. 'I don't know what to do any more.'

'I don't think her telling you to be happy was an instruction to get pregnant.'

'My mum searched her whole life for a good man and she didn't find one. But because of me she was happy. It was like she realised at the end that maybe romance wasn't the answer to happiness. Don't you see?' At that moment a young mother strolled past pushing a buggy and she caught a glimpse of a snoozing toddler. Her heart ached at the sight.

Curtis's voice pulled her back to the discussion. 'Whilst I do not subscribe to the notion of romance, per se, I do believe there is such a thing as a good genetic match. So, if you were looking to balance your genetic failings—'

'Hey,' said Ruby. 'How to kick a girl when she's down.'

'I meant your height.'

'Oh, right okay. Carry on.' She was bang on average height but that didn't stop her feeling short most of the time. Besides Curtis was right – she had been looking for someone taller to balance things out for any offspring.

'He's lied about his height. There's no way he's six feet tall. Five ten, tops.'

Ruby pouted. 'How tall are you?'

'Six feet and a half. By that I mean six feet and a half inch. Not six and a half feet. It's a difficult measurement to convey. Six feet, one inch would be easier to communicate.'

'Then say six foot one.'

'But that would be incorrect . . . and a lie.'

A cough from behind the shabby front door drew their attention back to the decision that was required.

Ruby was beyond confused. All the doubts she'd had about doing this were fighting bare knuckle with her desire to be a mother. She studied Curtis's face. He seemed sensible. The sort of person who made good choices. 'What should I do?' she asked.

'Only you can make that decision,' said Curtis.

Chapter Seven

Friday afternoon was dragging. Kim ate another Hobnob and instantly regretted it. It felt like every biscuit she'd ever eaten was now stored as a fat cell on her bum. Ruby, on the other hand, seemed to eat as many biscuits as she liked and didn't put on an ounce. Kim wondered if there was some strange sort of osmosis at work, where Ruby ate the biscuits and they went on Kim's hips. She'd given up weighing herself; she didn't need the scales to tell her she was getting fatter, her jeans screamed that at her each morning and the mark they left across her middle reminded her every evening.

She popped her head into the flower shop's tiny washroom and surveyed the state of her hair. She really did need to get it done. The grey was no longer strolling through; it was rampaging. It was mainly on one side, which would soon give her an air of Cruella de Vil unless she took some action. The dark circles under her eyes added to the sorry picture. She was getting older and she didn't like it. Almost immediately her mother's voice popped into her head: 'It beats the alternative.' That was what she always used to say. She knew she was lucky to be alive and healthy. Even so it was hard to look in the mirror and see a tired older person staring back.

She returned to her work bench in the back room and set about the order she'd deliver on her way home. A bouquet and balloons for the arrival of twins. A boy and a girl. Even now, after all this time, she still felt it. That hollow pang of loss – if, of course, it was possible to lose something you never actually had. She'd so wanted to have children but all her attempts had come to nothing.

Just as she tried to tie the ribbon to keep the flowers together, the shop bell chimed.

'Hang on,' she called.

A face peered through the beaded curtain making her jump. 'Hiya,' said Gloria the postwoman. 'Need to sign for this one.' She put the envelope on the countertop. 'That's pretty,' she said, nodding at the bouquet Kim was grappling with.

'Thanks. Can you just hold that there?'

'Sure.' Gloria did as instructed and Kim tied off the knot. 'Twins huh? Nightmare. My Jade has three nippers now. She spends most days tearing her hair out.'

'I'm sure she wouldn't be without them,' said Kim.

'No, she would. She often says she wishes she'd never had them. And she's got a new fella so I'm expecting grandchild number four to be announced soon. Signature,' said Gloria, thrusting the electronic box at Kim.

'It's funny how those who really want children don't get them and then those who maybe don't . . . do.' She was thinking out loud as she signed something that barely resembled her signature.

'That's because these days they let anyone do it, don't they,' said Gloria, appearing serious.

'I guess they do,' agreed Kim, although she was fairly sure that was how it had always been.

'Have a good day,' added Gloria, already on her way out.

'Thanks.' Kim picked up the envelope. The sight of the handwriting made her freeze. The letter was from Vince.

Ruby was standing on Neil's doorstep chewing her lips, but stopped when she tasted blood. This was it. This moment could change her life. But once she'd done it there was no going back.

A woman walked by, weighed down by two large bags of shopping. 'All right, Neil?' she asked but her eyes were dancing over Ruby.

'Um, good thanks,' said Neil, scratching his head. Once the woman had passed he stepped out of the house. 'Look, we either do this now or the deal is off. And there aren't that many like me with a four-point-three rating.' He fixed her with a cold gaze.

'Right. Okay.' She took a deep breath. 'Let's do this.'

She followed Neil inside and right before he shut the door, she glanced over her shoulder at Curtis who was watching her intently. The door closed and she was alone in the hallway with Neil.

'You've got the cash?' asked Neil eyeing her handbag.

'Yeah. Sorry. Here you go.' She handed it over and he began counting it, which she found slightly offensive. Who would short-change someone over something like this? 'It's all there,' she added.

Neil didn't look up. 'Best results if you lie on your back afterwards with your legs in the air for fifteen minutes.'

Ruby nodded but she was struggling to speak. Her mouth was dry but her palms were sweaty.

'It's okay,' said Neil. 'I've done this loads of times before.'

'Good,' managed Ruby. Although her overactive imagination was filling up with babies and they all looked like Neil and wore the same cardigan.

'Top of the stairs is the bathroom. Bedroom next to the bathroom is mine. I'll be in there . . . getting the merchandise.'

Merchandise? She'd heard it called lots of things in her time but never that. 'Okay. And where will I be?'

'Bedroom next door. In there is the baster and a glass of water.'

'What's the water for?' Her mind was racing.

He gave her an odd look. 'In case you're thirsty.'

'Right. Good. Okay.'

She followed Neil upstairs and when he peeled off to his bedroom she carried on.

'I'll be a few minutes,' he said and he closed the door.

Ruby's pulse started to quicken. She was fairly sure stress wasn't a good thing for conception. She pushed open the door of the spare room. Inside it was all quite ordinary. Magnolia walls with no pictures. Net curtains hung at the window on a slightly drooping cord. There was a single bed with a plain cream throw on it. A pile of mismatched cushions in an assortment of colours littered the headboard end. On the bedside table was a turkey baster and a glass of water – just as Neil had explained.

Ruby sat on the bed. She closed her eyes and tried to calm herself down. This was what she wanted. This was exactly what she'd planned. Well, maybe not exactly . . . but it was, at least, very definitely Plan B. This was the least complicated way of having a baby. And that was what she had to focus on. Getting pregnant was what mattered – not exactly how or where she went about it.

Men were unreliable. Certainly the men she attracted

were. At least if she started off on her own as a single mother she knew what she was letting herself in for. No broken promises and no broken families. No weekends alternated between warring parents. No guilt-riddled child worrying about letting one of them down. No fights for maintenance.

The formal IVF approach was far too expensive and there was no proof that the results would be any better than the turkey baster.

No, this was definitely the best option. Her mother had been on her own and she had managed just fine as a single parent. Sure, Ruby had missed out on a few things growing up, but she hadn't missed out on love and that was the most important thing a parent could give their child. She thought about her mum. Maybe Curtis was right about her mother's words not being an instruction to get pregnant but he wasn't there. She could picture her mother lying in the hospice bed. A shadow of her former self but still beautiful and still smiling. She'd taken Ruby's hand and held it tightly. She must have sensed she was fading. Her words were clear in her mind but Ruby feared a day when she wouldn't be able to recall the sound of her mother's voice. 'Ruby, you were a beautiful baby, an adventurous child, a perfectly monstrous teenager and now you are an amazing woman. My life has been full of ups and downs but all my happy memories are of you. I love you, Ruby, you made me happy.' She'd taken a shaky breath. 'Be happy, Ruby.' Then she'd squeezed her hand and closed her eyes for the last time.

Ruby wiped away a stray tear. She looked at the turkey baster. It looked clean but then you couldn't be too sure. She popped her antibacterial hand gel out of her bag, squirted some on her hands and gave the baster the once-over. She popped it back on the side. Then she had a thought: wasn't there alcohol in hand gel? Would that kill the sperm? She figured as long as none had gone up the tube it would be okay. She picked it up and peered up the pointy end. She couldn't see any.

There was a tap on the door. She jumped and almost poked herself in the eye with the baster.

'Come in,' she said, cautiously. The irony of her words not lost on her.

Neil's hairy hand snaked around the door. He was holding a small plastic pot. Eurgh. She suddenly wasn't very keen on plan B. She'd need a shower after this. In fact, she'd probably need scrubbing down with a Brillo pad.

Neil coughed. 'Are you going to take this then?'

'Oh sorry,' said Ruby, getting to her feet. She reached for the pot with the tips of her fingers. She averted her eyes. Think about the baby, she told herself. The other half of your child is swimming in there. With just a quick squeeze she could be making her very own baby. It would all be over in minutes. 'Thanks.'

Neil's hand gave the thumbs up sign. 'I'll put the kettle on. Tea or coffee?'

'Um, no I'm all right thanks.' She was having a baby with someone who didn't even know that she didn't drink tea or coffee. This was beyond weird.

She returned to the bed slowly, holding the pot like an unexploded bomb, and placed it carefully on the cabinet next to the baster.

She'd watched quite a few videos online about how to complete the procedure. It had been more than a bit alarming how many videos there were. Then again it had reassured her that she could do it on her own and if all these other women were doing it then why not her?

Ruby picked up the turkey baster and squeezed the air out of the bulbous rubber end. Whilst trying not to look directly in the pot she manoeuvred the end into place and released her grip. Whoosh! The contents shot up the baster at lightning speed and promptly disappeared into the rubber bulb.

'Bugger,' said Ruby. That wasn't supposed to happen. She'd have to give it a seriously big squeeze to shoot it all out again.

Holding the baster in her right hand she now realised she'd omitted a key part of the process. She was still fully dressed. She popped the baster on the side, took off her shoes and managed to writhe her way out of her pants.

Ruby arranged some cushions on the bed, hopped on and got herself into a suitable position, trying not to think about how many other bare bums had been on this bed before hers. She reached for the turkey baster. This was it. There was no going back now.

Chapter Eight

Ruby was poised with the turkey baster. She closed her eyes and hoped for the best. A sudden banging from downstairs made her halt what she was doing. She listened hard. She heard Neil muttering as he went to answer the door. All sorts of scenarios flashed through Ruby's mind. Was it a police raid? Or the bailiffs? Or—

The voice was muffled but the low melodic timbre was recognisable all the same. It was Curtis. She heard feet on the stairs and a tap on the bedroom door.

'Ruby? It's Curtis. We need to talk,' he said through the door.

'I'm a bit busy right now.' Although pointless, she waved the baster at the door as evidence.

'I know but I've been thinking.'

'And?' Ruby tried to hurry him along.

'When the child is old enough to ask about their parentage, what will you tell them?'

It was like electricity jolting through her. What a question. She pictured a child. Worryingly it looked creepily like Neil. The child was looking up at her waiting for an answer. She glanced around the room. Was this a story she'd want to share?

'Ruby?'

'I don't know. All right? I don't know what I'd tell them. But at least they'd be here to tell.'

'There's no guarantee of that. I've been doing some research . . .' She didn't want to think what his internet search history must look like. 'And it's likely you only have a ten to fifteen per cent chance of success. And whilst that is in line with conception via sexual intercourse this is obviously a one-off unlike having sex which can be repeated ad infinitum, increasing your chances. I say ad infinitum but that's assuming a brief recovery period and that you're—'

'Okay.' He clearly didn't know the men Ruby did. 'I get the picture. Rather too vividly, thank you.'

'So?'

She pictured Curtis on the other side of the door awaiting her response. 'But then men are involved. I don't need a man.' Ruby returned her concentration to the job, literally, in hand.

'No. I'm sure you don't. But maybe your child does. However feckless, however unreliable, surely any father is better than none? I know my life would be very different without mine.'

It took the wind out of her sails. Deep down she knew this wasn't the ideal solution even though she'd tried to convince herself that it was. But what he was saying did ring true. Despite her mum being amazing she still felt she had missed out on something by not having a dad around. Curtis was messing with her head.

'And what if something happened to you? As a single parent if you were to die without making someone a guardian, your child would be taken into the care of social services. Also . . .' he continued. 'Stress can have a negative impact on conception. I'm sensing you might be stressed at the moment.'

'You think?'

'Yes.'

She shook her head at the door. Her heart was pounding. She was beyond stressed.

'Ruby!' His voice was impatient.

A flash of temper made her grip the turkey baster and its contents squirted across the room.

'Bugger!'

'You okay?'

She surveyed the scene. Yuck. That was it. Her decision made for her. In that moment she wasn't sure if what she was feeling was pure relief or devastation. But there was little point mithering over it now – there was plenty of time for that.

Ruby grabbed a few tissues and sorted the worst of it out. Her stomach heaved a couple of times but she managed the job. She quickly got dressed and opened the door. Curtis looked her up and down. 'Well? Have you been artificially inseminated?'

'No. And has anyone ever told you that you really have a way with words?'

'No, they haven't,' said Curtis, his face deadpan.

'Funny that.' She took a moment to compose herself. She'd deal with the emotional fallout later but for now she had to concentrate on what was time-critical. Come on. We've got a Ferris wheel to catch.'

West Ham Tube station had been relatively quiet when they'd arrived almost an hour ago but now it was swarming with people. Ruby stuck close to Curtis. He was able to cut through the crowds effectively. She figured being tall enough to see where you were going rather than the armpit of the person in front was a distinct advantage.

'Jubilee line is closed due to a passenger incident,' said Curtis, his lips pulling tight.

'Passenger incident? What . . . someone else has got their bag stuck?'

'No, I'm afraid it means someone has committed suicide on the line.'

Ruby was shocked. 'That's awful. Poor soul.'

'Indeed.'

'West Ham to Waterloo without the Jubilee line,' said Ruby enjoying picking up her game from earlier. 'Go.'

'I'm afraid that should be DLR to Bank and then Waterloo and City line but that's got essential works too.'

Ruby looked at her watch – quarter past three. 'Bugger! What do we do? Taxi?'

They strode back outside to see a mammoth snake of a queue at the taxi rank and not a single cab in sight.

'Bus?' she suggested.

Curtis looked alarmed. 'I have no idea about the bus timetable.'

'Come on, it can't be that hard. If I can get from Firth Park to Sharrow by bus I'm sure I can figure this out.'

A few minutes at the bus stop told them it wasn't quite that easy. The bus timetable was harder to crack than the Enigma code. It became quickly apparent that there was no direct bus. Half an hour later they were sitting on their second bus, stuck in traffic watching the minutes tick by as four o'clock loomed closer.

'Are you aware that you're biting your lip?' asked Curtis.

'Huh?' She rubbed her lips together. Having geared herself up for the turkey baster and the hope that she'd be heading home with a precious cargo on board, she was now feeling out of sorts. Everything had changed very quickly and she wasn't entirely convinced she'd done the right thing. In fact, she hadn't really made a decision either way at all. It had been taken out of her hands, so to speak.

'I suggest when we get to the wheel that we go directly to the ticket office and ask. I'm assuming Lewis would have some sort of specific reservation.'

'I guess.'

'Is everything all right?' asked Curtis.

Ruby absently scratched her eyebrow. 'I don't know.' It was an honest answer.

'Is it the failed artificial insemination that has upset you?' he asked and every head on the bus swivelled in their direction.

'Shhh! Bloody hell, Curtis. If you must know, I'm not sure I did the right thing. What if that was my one and only chance to have a baby?'

'Statistically that's not likely. Unless you're planning on never having sex.'

The head swivelling continued. 'For crying out loud. Will you please keep your voice down?'

'Sorry.' He lowered his voice to a stage whisper. 'You would have far more chance of increasing the odds of a successful fertilisation by regular sex. That could be with one or more partners—'

'Curtis!' All newspapers had been abandoned, headphones had been removed and all the other passengers were unashamedly staring directly at them. Ruby hit the request stop button. 'I'm getting off here.'

Curtis peered out of the window. 'I don't know where we are. This is a very bad idea.'

'I don't care!' Her voice was rising.

The bus pulled into the next stop.

'Ruby. Please can we just stay on the bus. I promise not to mention . . .' She turned and glared at him. 'Anything.' He mimed locking his lips and throwing away the key. Despite everything it made her smile.

'Are you getting off or what?' asked the surly driver.

Curtis tipped his head at Ruby. She let out a sigh. 'No. We're staying on,' said Ruby.

'Thank you,' replied Curtis, nodding at Ruby.

'Bloody tourists,' said the driver, closing the doors and pulling back into the traffic. Ruby reluctantly retook her seat.

Her mind unhelpfully played back the day like a comedy film reel. The plan she'd been working on for weeks had been scuppered. What had she done? She'd been tracking her cycle, popping folic acid and saving up the money. It was cash she could ill afford to throw away and yet that was exactly what she had done. She could have cleared her credit card instead. Now it was wasted. And worst of all she'd allowed a complete stranger to influence probably the biggest decision of her life.

She checked her watch. They were cutting it fine to make it to the London Eye for four o'clock. Curtis saw her looking.

'I'm afraid we're going to be late with the ring,' he said.

'You think?'

'Yes, I do,' said Curtis. 'I'm sensing I may have said something to upset you. In which case I am truly sorry.'

'It's not just what you said very loudly here on the bus. It's what you said at the . . . at Neil's house. But it's really me I'm upset with. I shouldn't have allowed you to influence my decision.' They sat in silence for the rest of the trip.

When it finally pulled up at their stop, they were both waiting for the doors to open. Ruby was off the bus first.

'Which way?' she asked, almost toppling over as she spun around on the spot.

Curtis studied his phone. 'This way,' he said, striding off.

They passed a little market and some restaurants with tables outside. Delicious wafts assaulted Ruby, making her realise she was still hungry despite her free lunch. But she was on a mission. She refocused her mind on Lewis. Excited butterflies fluttered inside her. She hoped they would be able to save the day. She so wanted *something* to go right today. She knew it wasn't about her but it was exciting to think they could play a part by returning the ring in time. She glanced at her watch; they were almost out of time. Curtis turned left and they were suddenly walking alongside the River Thames. The summer sun made it sparkle and look quite pretty. She could see the London Eye up ahead. It was far bigger than she'd imagined. Now she was close to it, it was huge.

She desperately wanted to return the ring in time. Somehow it felt like her own happy ending was dependent on Lewis and his girlfriend getting theirs. Ruby broke into a run and Curtis followed. They reached the base of the wheel where a massive queue wound around it. Ruby pictured Lewis in her mind. His leather jacket was quite distinctive but there were hordes of people.

'Now what?' asked Ruby, catching her breath. She really needed to do more exercise.

'Ticket office,' said Curtis, marching into a nearby building.

They joined a short queue. Ruby was sure she could hear actual seconds ticking by in her head.

'Next,' said a smiley woman and they both charged forward.

'We believe a proposal is about to happen and—' started Curtis.

'But he dropped the ring and I found it,' butted in Ruby.

'Do you have a name?' asked the woman.

'Lewis,' said Ruby proudly.

'Last name?'

'I'm afraid not,' said Curtis.

'Did they book a pod?' asked the woman.

'Dunno,' said Ruby. 'He was proposing at four o'clock. I guess that's what time he had tickets for.'

'Let me have a look.' The woman smiled but it was one of those smiles that said they were wasting her time and she was humouring them. More seconds thudded past. 'I'm sorry. No private pods booked this afternoon. There's one this evening for a corporate event but that's all.'

Ruby felt her shoulders sag. This wasn't the result she wanted.

'Could I leave my card in case Lewis gets in touch?' Curtis passed his card under the glass.

'Okay. Can I help you with anything else?' she asked.

'No,' said Ruby, managing to convey her glumness in the single word. It was four o'clock. They had failed their mission. Her big day out in London was a big waste of time.

'Come on.' Curtis steered her away. 'He might still be in the queue or they might already be on the wheel in which case we can intercept them when they come off. He doesn't have to have the ring to propose.'

'You're a bloody genius.' Ruby was instantly heartened.

'I scored 159 on an IQ test so technically I'm not a genius as you need 160 to . . .' Ruby wasn't listening. She

71

was back on her mission to find Lewis. They rushed outside and towards the vast queue. Curtis started scanning the crowd. Ruby had a better idea.

'LEW-IS!' she yelled at the top of her voice. Most of the people turned in her direction. She tried again just to catch any stragglers. 'LEW-IS!'

Hundreds of faces stared at them but none of them were Lewis. An attendant in a red uniform stepped forward. 'Can I help you?'

'We're looking for someone called Lewis,' said Curtis.

'Call me Sherlock Holmes but I gathered that.' The attendant grinned at them and they both stared back with humourless expressions.

'He's proposing to his girlfriend here this afternoon.' Ruby checked her watch. 'At like now o'clock. But he lost the ring and we found it.'

'Right. Not sure there's anything we can do.' The attendant shrugged his shoulders.

'Thank you. We'll wait,' said Curtis, guiding Ruby away from the queue and over to a grassy area. Ruby plonked herself down and the familiar feeling of gloom rested on her again.

Curtis took off his jacket. 'Up,' he instructed.

Ruby did as she was told and he laid his jacket down for her to sit on. 'Thanks.'

'You're most welcome.' He sat down beside her and they waited.

Ruby fixed her gaze on the pods that slowly came level with the ground. More attendants ushered the people out. None of them were Lewis. 'We could be here for hours,' she said with a huff.

'Thirty minutes,' said Curtis. 'The wheel takes thirty minutes to complete one full rotation. If he's not in the queue and he's not come off within half an hour then we've missed him.'

'Oh, okay. That's not too bad.' She watched closely as another pod glided in. The wheel was moving all the time and the people had to hop off. She studied the attendants as they helped an elderly lady off and there behind her was someone she thought she recognised. 'Lewis.'

Ruby jumped to her feet and started to run but then realised she didn't have the ring. She spun around. 'Curtis. Ring!'

Chapter Nine

Ruby was filled with excitement. Curtis jumped to his feet and looked over the top of her head towards the wheel.

'Where's Lewis?' he asked.

'In the jacket and jeans. Bring the ring!' She was going to save the day.

'It's not Lewis.'

'What?'

Ruby turned back for a second look. Someone in jeans and a jacket, a similar colour to Lewis's, was walking towards them but Curtis was right – it wasn't Lewis. She watched the man walk past them. Ruby's stomach plummeted. She'd thought for a moment that everything was going to be okay. Neither of them said anything; they simply returned to their positions sitting on Curtis's suit jacket and continued the vigil.

Over the next thirty minutes Curtis checked his phone and tapped out a few messages but Ruby's eyes didn't leave the base of the wheel. She studied everyone coming out of each pod. The couples grabbed her attention the most. She told herself it was because she was looking for Lewis. The young couple who were laughing as they stepped out of the pod, clutching their sides as they shared a joke. The pair who looked like they were in a new relationship, all coy looks and indecision as to where to go next. The older couple holding hands and chatting, completely at ease in each other's company. Why was that so hard for some people to attain?

Ruby wondered what it was like to see London from up there and then thought about the glass office earlier. She'd had a bird's eye view of London without it costing her a penny. And a very nice free lunch too. Maybe her day wasn't a total disaster. Then thoughts of her lost phone, the money she'd given to Neil and the turkey baster swam into her brain and reminded her that it was exactly that – a total disaster. She'd had a firm plan when she'd left home that morning and thanks to Lewis and Curtis the whole day had been derailed – and perhaps even the rest of her life. She let out a deep sigh, which caught Curtis's attention.

He checked his watch. 'It's four forty-five,' he said. 'Perhaps he's rearranged.'

Ruby flopped back onto the grass. The sun was warm. It was quite a nice spot. 'What do we do now?'

'I'm not sure about what *we* do. But *I* need to get back to St Pancras. And I'm assuming you have a train to catch too?'

'I guess so,' said Ruby.

'It's okay. The ticket you purchased is an open one. Which means you can get any train back.'

'But I don't want to give up on Lewis.'

'I think you've done far more than most people would have done if faced with the same situation.'

She knew he was right but something inside her compelled her to keep trying. 'Let's have another look at the ring.' She held out her hand.

Curtis scanned the area. 'You are aware that London has a very high crime rate? Although statistically West Yorkshire has the highest rate of crime in England.'

'And?'

'And brandishing an expensive piece of jewellery in the open is both foolhardy and irresponsible.'

'Is that a no?' She fixed him with a hard stare.

He looked contrite. 'I didn't say that exactly.' Curtis opened the side pocket of his laptop bag and handed her the ring box. She moved her body so she was facing Curtis and the box was shielded from prying eyes. She opened it carefully. Even though she'd seen it before the ring still took her breath away. The central diamond glinted magically in the sun. She tilted the box to read the wording inside the lid. 'East's Fine Jewellers since 1875. County Arcade, Leeds. Do you think they keep a record of what they sell?'

Curtis was watching her intently and there was a delay before he spoke. 'It's possible. We could give them a call.'

'Great idea.'

Curtis pulled out his phone, searched for the number of the jewellers and dialled. When someone answered he put the call on speakerphone so Ruby could listen.

'Good afternoon, Easts,' said a friendly but efficient female voice.

'Good afternoon, I hope you can help me. I've found an item of jewellery and I'm trying to return it to the owner. The box and therefore its contents purport to have been purchased at your shop. I was wondering if you kept records of customer purchases and might be able to help us return the item?' Ruby listened, rapt by what he said. Well, not so much by *what* he said, more the deep rhythmic sound of his voice.

'We do keep records,' said the woman. 'However, due to data protection we wouldn't be able to share any details with you I'm afraid.'

Ruby pouted. Curtis held up a finger. 'I completely understand but if you were to contact the purchaser and pass on our details they could get in touch with us and be reunited with their item.' Ruby gave him a double thumbs up.

'If you'd like to bring the item in, we could certainly take a look.'

'We're currently in London,' said Curtis. 'Can we send a photograph?'

'Sorry, we'd need to see the piece to be sure.'

'I understand,' said Curtis as Ruby slumped back on the grass. 'Thank you for your help.' He ended the call.

'She was barely any help at all,' said Ruby. 'Now what do we do?'

'How about we get a drink?'

'What about the train home?' she asked from her horizontal position.

'Let's aim for the two minutes past seven,' he suggested. Trust him to know the train timetable off by heart.

'Okay.' There was nobody waiting for her at home, with the possible exception of her neighbour's cat. Curtis helped her to her feet and picked up his jacket. 'There was a sandwich bar near the bus stop,' she suggested.

He smiled at her. 'I've got a better idea.'

Kim's hot flushes were worse this afternoon, probably because the shop caught the afternoon sun. She wasn't sure if it was a change in the weather or the thought of the letter that was bringing them on. It wasn't a busy day in the florist's but Kim managed to find tasks to procrastinate over and avoid the inevitable. She'd brought her accounts up to date and she'd done a spot of googling about different dog breeds. She was really warming to the idea of getting a dog. In fact, after all the cute puppy videos she'd been watching online recently it was pretty much a done deal. She'd even scoped out where she would put the dog's bed and water bowl when it was with her in the shop.

Despite all this the envelope kept taunting her every time she went into the back room, so she shoved it under some paperwork and went to serve customers. But it didn't help because she knew it was there waiting for her. As it neared closing time, Kim marched into the back room and lifted up the papers to reveal the letter just as the door chimed. She dropped the pile.

'Hang on, I'll be there in a minute,' she called.

'It's okay. I'm after Ruby,' came the voice.

Kim hurriedly replaced the paperwork and stepped into the shop. It was Dean. He was probably a similar age to Ruby and his height, weight, and looks were all average. Apart from the most soulful dark eyes Kim had ever seen. Dean was what she'd term a sporadic regular. Sometimes they'd see him a couple of times a week for months and then he'd disappear for a while, like he had for the last couple of months.

'Hello, stranger, what brings you back?'

'I need something expensive and I was hoping Ruby would craft me one of her special messages.'

Some people knew exactly what to put on a note to accompany flowers, others kept it simple, and then there were the ones who hadn't got a clue at all. Dean fell into the latter camp.

Whilst Ruby was an excellent florist, she wasn't exactly known for her poetic prose. However, one day when all words had escaped Dean, she had penned something to go with his flowers and apparently it had hit the spot with the recipient. Since then she'd been his go-to person.

'I'm sorry, Dean. Ruby's not in today. Maybe I can help?' Kim was keen not to lose a sale. The words 'something expensive' were still ringing in her ears.

Dean's shoulders sagged. 'It needs to say something. You know?'

Nope, Kim didn't know. She really wasn't sure what he was on about. 'Absolutely. Shall we choose the stems first and then come up with the perfect note?'

Dean looked glum. 'Okay.'

Kim went through to the cooler to pick out some of her best and most expensive blooms. When she'd finished, she had a stunning bouquet. It was like summer in her arms. 'Smell those,' she said, proffering the armful.

Dean sniffed. 'Yeah, they're all right. But what about the note? Ruby always knows what to put.'

Ruby and Kim had a theory about Dean – when the shop was quiet one of their favourite things to do was to speculate about the lives of customers. Given Dean's inter-mittent flower-purchasing habits, they reckoned he had intense but brief relationships until he got dumped, which made him a little more needy next time. Whatever his story, it meant when he visited the shop it was usually a lucrative few weeks for Kim – something she was very grateful for.

'Are we saying something specific with these?' asked Kim, wrapping the bouquet in cellophane. Dean was scrunching up his features. 'Sorry? Thank you? I love you?' she offered.

Dean's head shot up. 'It's only flowers ya know. But I want her to feel they've come from the heart.'

'Then let's say that,' said Kim. 'These come from the heart.'

Dean pouted whilst Kim put the finishing touches to the expensive creation. 'Ruby wouldn't put it like that though,' he said at last.

Kim winced. She didn't want to lose this sale. How would Ruby phrase it? 'Got it. From my heart to yours,' she said, feeling like she should do a ta-dah at the end.

Dean's lips twisted. 'Yeah, all right. That'll have to do.'

Phew, she thought as she rang it through the till.

Kim made herself a cup of tea whilst wishing she was the sort of person who kept a bottle of gin at work. She pulled out the ominous letter from under the pile of papers and scowled at it. Her name was emblazoned on the front. Her heart began to race at the sight of the handwriting. The way the letter K had a sweeping curl to it was the giveaway; surely nobody else had writing like that. The thought of who had written it loomed large in her mind. The husband everyone thought was dead.

Vince had been in her thoughts all afternoon. He'd mainly been stomping around her head giving her a head-ache. Images of him were wallpapering her mind. Him laughing, snoozing on the sofa, raising a glass of fizz, expertly flipping burgers on the barbecue and finally him lying motionless in a hospital bed. The last picture was impossible to shift, like gum on your shoe.

She took her scissors and slit the envelope open. Out fell a neatly typed letter. She took a deep steadying breath and skim-read it. Her mouth was dry despite the tea. How could this be happening? Her pulse quickened with every word she read. She closed her eyes and focused on her breathing. Heat swept over her. She flapped her top to cool herself down. After a sip of tea she tried to reread it, properly this time.

Kim reached the end, snatched up the letter, scrunched it into a tight ball and hurled it into the wastepaper bin. That might work for now, but she knew she could no longer ignore the truth, however much she wished she could.

Chapter Ten

They took a leisurely stroll alongside the Thames and Curtis pointed out a few sights. Ruby was impressed with the Royal Festival Hall and, once they had crossed over Waterloo Bridge to the other side of the river, even more wowed by Somerset House. They chatted amiably, although she was more of a talker than he was. She was dazzled by the Savoy Hotel, tucked down a side street, which she definitely would have missed if Curtis hadn't pointed it out. They turned a few corners and she found herself in an open cobbled courtyard.

Curtis stopped walking. Ruby looked about her. It was familiar.

'Curtis,' she said, giving him a friendly nudge. 'Covent Garden?'

'You said you wanted to visit.' Ruby put on her sunglasses and tried to take everything in: the pub on the corner like it was straight out of an old gangster film, the cobbled street and all the little shops. Tourists were taking selfies with a bright red telephone box and beyond that an old building had centre stage.

'That's the market building,' explained Curtis, following her gaze. 'There's been a market here for over three hundred and fifty years, but this building was built almost two hundred years ago.'

There was so much to see. 'Ooh, pretty shoes,' she said, spotting Kurt Geiger's.

'Right. If you have a look in there, I'll be back in ten minutes,' said Curtis. 'Then we can have a drink and something to eat?'

'Okay.'

He turned and walked off.

Ruby checked out all the latest designs and even tried a couple on from the sale section. She couldn't afford them but it was fun to pretend. When she emerged, Curtis was waiting nearby but appeared to have found a friend. A man in a suit was standing next to him with an uncannily similar gait and facial expression to Curtis.

'No purchases?' asked Curtis. Ruby shook her head and the man next to him pretended to be shocked.

'Hi,' said Ruby, waving to the man.

'He doesn't speak. He's a mime artist,' explained Curtis, pulling a five-pound note from his pocket and handing it to the street performer who did an elaborate bow.

'Cool,' said Ruby but Curtis was already walking away. They passed a few more performers before they reached a café with a large dark red awning and tables outside.

A waiter quickly appeared and offered them a menu. 'It's a little early for dinner . . . unless . . .' Curtis looked at Ruby.

'We do need to eat but . . .' She leaned forward and lowered her voice. 'How expensive is it?' She had a feeling it would be pricey and she had already blown five hundred quid today.

'It's reasonable for London and the food is good quality.'

'Then I'm in,' said Ruby, taking the proffered menu. The long list of food made her mouth water.

'Anything to drink?' asked the waiter.

'Ruby, would you like to join me in a bottle of wine?' asked Curtis.

'Sure.' She could definitely do with a drink and the setting was so perfect she felt all it needed was a nice glass of something chilled.

'Red, white or rosé?' he asked.

'White please,' said Ruby.

'A bottle of the Marlborough Sauvignon Blanc, please,' said Curtis.

'Certainly, sir.' And the waiter retreated.

Ruby ordered the ravioli as it was one of the cheapest things on the menu and they sipped wine while they waited. She tried to take everything in, all the people around her chatting and laughing like they did this every day. Maybe they did. The comings and goings of people across the cobbles – different shapes, sizes and outfits. Summer was in full swing and it felt like they'd all come to Covent Garden. The whole atmosphere had her hooked.

'Are you okay?' asked Curtis, leaning back in the bistro chair and looking relaxed for the first time that day.

'Yes and no.'

Curtis's mouth lifted at one side. 'You're not one for a straight answer, are you?'

'Well, this is lovely. I mean *really* lovely.' She made a sweeping gesture with her wine glass and then put it down so she didn't spill any. At those prices it would have brought her close to tears. 'But the rest of the day hasn't been great, you know? My plan got derailed.' She gave him a pointed look. 'And I kind of feel that I've let Lewis down,' said

Ruby, sipping her wine and then putting it down again so she didn't glug it too fast.

'I'm supposing he would have realised that he'd lost the ring long before now. In which case he's either improvised with something else, gone ahead without it or postponed the proposal. Either way it will be a nice surprise when we are finally able to return it to him.'

'I guess.'

'Would you like to discuss the artificial—'

'Can you not keep saying that? Please,' said Ruby.

Curtis nodded. He looked about the surrounding tables before eventually speaking. 'Would sperm donor be better?'

'I'm not sure it would but okay, fine.' She wasn't entirely convinced but it was a marginal improvement.

'Good,' said Curtis, seeming pleased. 'What would you like to discuss about the sperm donor?'

His factual approach wasn't conducive to a relaxed natter. It felt a bit like being interviewed. But at the same time it made it easier to give an honest answer. 'I'm mad at myself because in two minutes flat I let you talk me out of a decision I had spent a long time planning.'

'Does that not mean it was merely a bad decision?'

'No.' She heard the irritation in her own voice. 'I don't have many options for a baby. I'm almost thirty-five. I'm single. And even when I'm not single, I have a habit of choosing highly unsuitable men. This was a logical next step. I'm young enough to cope on my own as a single parent. It avoids any of the hassle that comes with a relationship and I wouldn't have to answer to anyone else. I could have done the whole pregnancy and birth my way. Grrr!' She made a growling noise and Curtis recoiled. 'I'm furious with myself. It was a good decision. I've done the wrong bloody thing as usual. I've let someone else change my mind. And now I'm not pregnant, never likely to be and I've chucked away five hundred quid for nothing.'

'Ah,' said Curtis, holding up a finger. 'I can help there.' He rummaged in his laptop bag and pulled out the envelope of money she'd given Neil.

Ruby felt her eyes pop wide. 'You nicked the cash?'

'No. I pointed out that the Human Fertilisation and Embryology Authority might be interested in his business and he reluctantly returned the money.' Ruby ran a thumb over the notes. This was a turn-up. 'I'm afraid he took fifty pounds out. For his . . . services.'

'Thank you.' She waved the envelope at him. 'This makes me feel a bit better.' She took a large swig of wine. She might even buy another bottle now her finances suddenly looked a bit healthier.

'Good. I wanted to do that, make you feel better. I did a small amount of investigation after you went inside and there are a number of far more reliable suppliers of sperm on the internet. Although they do seem to charge more in the region of a thousand pounds.'

'Yeah. I found those ones too. That was why Neil seemed like a bargain. But I did do lots of research and he was the best I could afford. The ones who send you stuff through the post looked seriously dodgy. I mean it could be anything in the little pot, right?'

'I think the phrase *you get what you pay for* probably applies here.'

Ruby put the money away and the waiter arrived with their food. The smell of the dishes was divine. 'Maybe I'll save up while I do a bit more research.' It was starting to feel like not all was lost; even if she wasn't pregnant today, she still had options.

'I think that's very wise. Have you completely ruled out sexual . . .' Ruby's hard stare seemed to have halted him. He rolled his lips together. 'Ruled out a more traditional approach?' he amended, cutting into his fishcake.

'Look, Curtis. I don't mean to be rude. But you need to trust me when I say that there are no decent men out there who are interested in me. And believe me I have done my research on this one too.'

'Fifteen per cent of people find their partners at work.'

Ruby giggled. 'I do love Kim but not like that, I'm afraid.'

Curtis frowned. 'I take it Kim is female.'

'She is.'

'Who else do you work with?' he asked.

'Nobody. It's just the two of us.'

'Ah.' Curtis took a sip of his wine. His cheek twitched and he took a slow intake of breath. 'Perhaps I could be of assistance?'

'Really? How?' She was intrigued and a little amused.

'You did a good job at convincing Jonty and the others at the meeting that you were my assistant. And you certainly seemed to win Jonty over very quickly. Whilst I don't particularly need a full-time assistant, I often find I spend a lot of time on admin work that could be completed by someone else. I also had some feedback that I should do more schmoozing, something I feel you would understand far better than me. As my admin clerk you would have access to a number of companies and therefore employees. Thereby increasing your pool of possible mates.'

Ruby burst out laughing. 'You make me sound like a chimp on a nature programme.' Curtis's expression was deadpan, making her moderate her amusement. 'Thank you, Curtis. That is a most generous offer. Which I promise you I will give full consideration to.' Was it her imagination or was she starting to talk like him now?

Kim cashed up the till, sorted out the flowers, prepped for the next day and readied herself to lock up. They had a wedding tomorrow so they'd need to be in early even though a lot of the work was already done. She hoped Ruby had remembered; she'd message her later to remind her. Kim picked up the twins' bouquet she was going to deliver on her way home and paused by the door. The bins hadn't been emptied. She let out a slow breath. However much she wanted to forget that the letter existed, she simply couldn't. She put down the bouquet and stomped through to the back room, grabbed the balled-up paper out of the bin and shoved it deep into her pocket. She locked up the shop and left.

The delivery was in Fulwood, which was on her way home. She parked the car and knocked on the door. As she waited, she could hear the screams of the babies. A flustered young woman opened the door and her troubled expression instantly dissolved at the sight of the balloons and the bouquet.

'The Taylor family?' asked Kim with a smile.

'Wow they're beautiful, thank you.'

'You're welcome. And congratulations!' said Kim, turning to leave. These were the moments of her job that she loved. She looked over the top of her car at the big old church on the other side of the street. She caught a fleeting glance of someone she recognised – Adrian. She remembered the offer he'd made to go with her to the dog rescue. She needed cheering up, and going to look at strays was definitely one way to do it. She crossed the road and walked around to the churchyard entrance. Adrian was sitting on a bench in the churchyard. She strode towards him but then slowed her pace. Maybe approaching him was being insensitive, realising where he was. He most likely wanted to be alone with his thoughts. Now was not the time – her rescue pup could wait. Kim turned on the gravel and began walking back to her car.

'Kim?'

She turned at the sound of Adrian's voice. 'I'm sorry. I didn't mean to disturb you,' she said as she walked back towards him. 'I was making a delivery across the road and . . .' Adrian was coming around the other side of the bench to meet her, but she carried on. 'I was heading back to my car and I looked across at the church. I quite like old churches and . . .' She might as well sit down now he'd spoken to her. He was clearly happy to chat. 'I spotted you and thought I'd just pop over.' She plonked herself down on the bench. Adrian hovered at the other end for a moment, making her look up at him. His eyes travelled from her to a nearby grave and hers followed.

The grave was neat and well-tended with a white stone headstone and a beautiful and very familiar bouquet of mixed roses. Kim's gaze travelled from the flowers up the headstone and the name – Justine Booth.

Ruby and Curtis caught a later train and found seats facing the direction of travel in the quiet carriage. Ruby was still buzzing from Covent Garden and a bit more than her fair share of a bottle of wine. Curtis had insisted on paying for everything because he said it was a business expense as, technically, they'd both been to a business meeting.

'This job you're offering me,' began Ruby, buoyed by the alcohol, 'is it paid?'

'Yes, if you're going to do administrative tasks.' Ruby twisted in her seat. Now she was interested. 'If it was purely you using my contacts to find a mate . . .' He stopped himself. 'A suitable partner, then I don't think there would be any associated remuneration.'

'No worky, no money. That's fair. But I'm not useless, honest. I know the action list I did today probably wasn't that useful.' Curtis's eyebrows twitched in agreement with her. 'And the cartoon dragon may have been a mistake. But I can do stuff. I worked in an office years ago. And at the florist's I do loads; as well as making up arrangements I answer the phone, serve customers, do the banking and I cover for Kim when she's not there. It's all proof I can be trusted. I could get Kim to write me a reference.' She was suddenly very keen to do this, especially if it was going to generate a bit more cash.

'Can you fit it around your full-time job?'

'Yeah, some days are quieter than others and I can work evenings and on my days off.'

Curtis pondered her statement. 'It could be on a trial basis, just for this project and purely until you found a donor, sorry, mate – partner.'

'Perfect, and it means we can work together to get the ring back to Lewis too. I could do some investigating. Maybe set up a conference call.' She was showing off now. She'd only ever done a conference call once before but he didn't need to know that.

'Hmm. Perhaps you could screen some of my calls and, if I give you access to my diary, set up some meetings.'

'Yes, I can do that. No problem.'

'And in return I could introduce you to suitable men.'

'Like a pimp?' She was teasing him.

'No. Not like that at all. For example, you could liaise with Jonty. I've known him for a number of years. He's reliable, trustworthy and seems popular in the office. He doesn't wear a wedding ring so it's likely he's single.'

'Are you setting me up, Mr Walker?' Ruby gave him a mock-shocked look.

'I thought that's exactly what we were doing?' Curtis seemed confused.

'I'm kidding. It's cool. One thing, do you trust me to do a good job?'

'I trust you to do your best and I'll remain undecided until I see a result.'

'Fair enough.' She held out her hand and he shook it. 'And you'll need to come up with someone better than Jonty – I'm pretty sure he's gay.'

Curtis's phone vibrated on the table and he left the carriage to take the call, leaving Ruby to contemplate what she was getting herself into. She'd spent the whole day with a stranger and when it came to strange Curtis fitted the brief completely. However, as the day had gone on, she'd kind of got used to him. He talked funny and he seemed confused by her most of the time but there was an innocence about him that made her feel safe in his company. He'd got her across London in one piece and taken her to Covent Garden, which she'd loved. She knew she wasn't a great judge of character but Curtis was very different to anyone else she'd ever met. For one thing he wasn't trying to impress her. He didn't put on a front and she liked his 'what you see is what you get' approach.

His idea of introducing her to men he knew wasn't conventional but she'd tried pretty much all the other options – clubs, bars, blind dates, speed dating, a multitude of apps and none of those had worked. If she thought about her friends, a lot of them had met people at work so maybe there was something in the statistics Curtis had spouted. And in her romance novels the heroine often found love when she least expected it, so you never knew. It was a crazy idea but perhaps it was worth having one last try to find love. If it failed, she always had the donor plan to fall back on.

Her evening in Covent Garden was catching up with her and now she needed a wee. She followed the signs, past Curtis who was scowling hard while listening on his phone. The toilet was a sort of round cubicle and seemed very space-age; when she pressed a button the door glided open. She went in, pressed another button and watched it slide shut – all very Dr Who.

She wiped the seat and sat down. Oh, the relief. She was mid-flow when the door majestically slid open, revealing her sitting on the loo in all her glory. She was horrified. But she was too far away to reach the close button. To stand up now would have dire consequences. In the doorway two men were having a conversation, oblivious to her situation. Most likely one of them had leaned on the button. Just behind them she could see Curtis speaking on his mobile. Could this get any worse? Curtis stepped forward, and without looking directly at her, he pressed the close door button. He turned his back and she watched the door slide across.

Ruby let out a huge sigh of relief. She quickly finished, washed her hands and left the cubicle. Curtis was still guarding it. She whispered a 'thank you', being sure not to make eye contact.

She hurried back to her seat and got her book out, so she had something to hide behind. The carriage door opened and Curtis entered and retook his seat. He'd seen her on the loo. She could feel the colour seeping into her cheeks.

'Thanks for closing the door. What a nightmare! I didn't know I had to press multiple buttons . . .' The look on his face made her stop babbling. 'You okay?' she asked.

'No.'

'Want to elaborate?'

'That was the police.'

'Bloody hell, what's wrong?'

'A truck left the road and smashed into the side of my house. Until it's been deemed safe, I cannot return. I'm homeless.' In that moment he looked utterly lost and alone.

'I'm so sorry. You poor thing.' She shook her fuzzy head. 'That's a real bummer.'

'Indeed, it is a . . . bummer.' He checked his watch. 'It'll be twenty past ten when we pull in. I'll need to make some calls to local hotels if I want a room at such short notice.'

'No way. You must stay at mine tonight.'

'What?' He looked alarmed at the prospect. 'No, thank you. That is kind but I'll go to a hotel.'

'At this time of night? I won't hear of it. You can sleep in my bed . . .' Curtis's eyebrows almost reached his hairline. 'And I'll sleep on the sofa.' His eyebrows returned to their normal position. He opened his mouth to speak. 'No. I'm not discussing it,' she said, patting his arm. 'After taking me to Covent Garden, shutting the loo door and giving me a new job it's the least I can do.'

Chapter Eleven

Kim stared at the headstone as the breeze tickled the roses. 'Justine's dead?'

Adrian came to sit on the bench next to Kim. When he spoke, he spoke to the headstone. 'She died two years ago.'

'But you buy her flowers every Friday.' Kim knew it sounded daft but it was all she could think to say; the shock was ricocheting around her mind.

He hung his head. 'I'm sorry, Kim. So many times I've tried to tell you the truth. The day I came in to tell you that she'd died and ask if you'd do the flowers for the funeral, you were so chuffed that you'd got some yellow roses in, and we talked about Justine as if she was still here and . . . this is going to sound strange but it was nice to be able to talk about her. Everyone around me was either devastated by her death or so awkward they avoided the subject.'

'It's okay,' said Kim at last.

'But it's not,' said Adrian. 'I feel awful that I've deceived you. The longer it went on, somehow the harder it was to explain. Hayley was devastated at losing her mum. It was such a shock.'

'Do you mind me asking what happened?'

'Heart attack.' Somehow Kim knew that was what he was going to say. 'Justine went off to work as normal and I got a phone call from her boss when I was having my lunch. The lift had been busy, she was late for a meeting and she'd run up three flights of stairs. She walked into the meeting room and collapsed and that was it. The post-mortem said it was a genetic condition.'

'Same as Vince,' she said in a low voice. Her lips were dry and she felt a little nauseous. It wasn't Adrian's revelation; it was the thought of having to share her own that was making her feel queasy. Now Adrian had shared his secret she could no longer keep hers hidden.

'And there you were, facing your grief at losing Vince whereas I was pretending—'

'No,' said Kim, interrupting abruptly. 'Let me stop you there. If it's confession time I've got something I need to share.' She felt a sheen of sweat come over her in a wave and this time it definitely wasn't a hot flush. She pulled the balled-up letter from her pocket and handed it to Adrian.

'What's this?'

'A letter, read it.' She couldn't watch him. She returned her gaze to Justine's headstone. Justine – who she asked after every week. The woman who she had pictured in her mind many times. The lucky wife who had a husband who brought her flowers every week, without fail. Justine who according to the headstone was a 'much-loved wife to Adrian and mother to Hayley, taken too soon'.

'It's from Vince?' asked Adrian. Kim nodded and swallowed hard. 'Your Vince? He's alive?'

'Sadly, yes,' said Kim. 'Despite how much I'd like to murder him.' She hoped that didn't sound insensitive.

'But . . . I don't understand,' said Adrian.

Kim had nothing to lose. She faced him. 'Do you fancy fish and chips and a bottle of wine?' she asked. Adrian deserved a proper explanation and she could definitely do with the company.

'Why not?' said Adrian, handing back the crumpled letter.

There had been further protests from Curtis but Ruby had waved them all away. She wanted to help. A truck through the front of your house was a bit of a shock and she knew she wouldn't want to spend the night alone in a hotel room if it had happened to her.

'We'll need to get a taxi as I can't drive after the wine,' she explained as they walked out of the station. 'Bugger it. I'll need to get a cab back in the morning to pick my car up from the station too.' The wine wasn't feeling like quite such a good idea now.

'Or I could drive. I only had one glass and that was over three hours ago. I have comprehensive insurance that covers me to drive another vehicle with the driver's permission.'

'Cool,' said Ruby, handing him a stuffed pineapple with her car keys jangling from its crown. Ruby paid her parking ticket and led the way to her bright yellow Kia. It was a happy colour and also easy to spot in a car park, although with only a handful of vehicles left it wasn't hard to locate. Curtis squeezed in behind the steering wheel and adjusted the seat until he was almost sitting in the back.

'Can you provide directions?' he asked, adjusting the rear-view mirror.

'So we don't argue over the best route I'll let the sat nav do it.' Ruby hit home on the screen and it sprang into life. 'No wheel-spinning or doughnuts, got it?'

Curtis frowned. 'You're joking, aren't you?'

'You might be a demon behind the wheel for all I know,' she said.

He laughed. 'You're right. I might be.'

He started the engine and 'Super Trouper' blared out. Ruby hastily killed the stereo. Curtis was grinning at her. 'What? I like ABBA, okay?'

'Yes. I like them too.'

'Really?' She wasn't sure if he was joking.

'Yes. It reminds me of being a child.'

'Me too. My mum played ABBA all the time.' She switched it back on but lowered the volume.

It felt a bit odd having someone else drive her car but it wasn't far and Curtis was a sedate driver. When the sat nav announced they were arriving at their destination, he indicated and pulled over outside a closed store. He stared out of the window. 'Greggs?'

'Ah, no. I'm a bit further up.'

'But home on your satellite navigation system is set to Greggs?' he queried.

'Sometimes I stop here on my way home. I really like their sausage rolls . . . anyway. Bit further up, before that road on the right.'

Curtis was quiet as he followed her up the stairs to the door of her flat. She wanted a chance to check it was presentable because she'd left in a bit of a hurry.

'Hang on a sec,' said Ruby, putting the key in the lock.

'Okay.' Curtis looked around the hallway.

'You can read the fire safety certificate if you like?' She pointed to a corkboard before slipping into the flat. She hit the light switch.

An outfit she'd tried on was strewn across the sofa and another one was on her bed. She quickly bundled them up and shoved them in her wardrobe. She grabbed the mouthguard she wore at night to stop her grinding her teeth and popped it in her pocket. She straightened the cushions on the small sofa as she passed. It was fine.

'Come in,' she said, opening the door. Curtis pulled his attention away from the fire safety certificate, which he appeared to actually be reading.

'Thank you.' He stepped cautiously inside.

'I'll do a quick guided tour. This is the living room cum dining room cum kitchen,' she said, splaying out her arms. She opened the door next to her. 'This is the bathroom. Well, it's a wet room really.' Curtis peered into the tiny space. 'Spare bedroom.' She opened the door to a small empty room and the one she had been hoping to decorate as a nursery. She nudged the paint tester pots to one side. 'And this is my bedroom.' She took a step to the right of the kitchen units and pointed through the open door.

'Right. Thanks again, Ruby. This is very kind of you.'

She filled up the kettle. 'My pleasure. Do you want a drink of anything? I say anything but I've only got hot chocolate, orange juice and some energy drinks. I don't drink tea or coffee.'

'Water will be fine, thank you.' Curtis looked around and then took a seat on the sofa. 'You own a cat,' he said, tipping his head at the cat flap and nearby food bowls.

'No. He's not mine.'

'You *stole* a cat?'

'No, he belongs to the flat next door but he comes and goes as he pleases.' She pondered their relationship for a moment. 'Basically, he likes to eat here, sleep with me and then he clears off. Pretty much like most men I know.'

Curtis was giving her a very odd look. 'I see.'

'It's a sort of time-share arrangement.' She handed him a glass of water. 'The flap was there when I moved in and

I wasn't about to buy a new door. I tried locking it but he just spent all night rattling it, so it was easier to let him in. It's not great coming home to an empty place after Mum . . .'

An awkward silence dominated the small room. Ruby couldn't say any more for fear of choking on her words as an unexpected surge of emotion squeezed her throat.

'I'm interested in the list you talked about. The one that wasn't written down and yet you expected to have achieved everything on it before you were forty.'

She gave him a look. He sounded like he was being sarcastic but his expression told her otherwise. 'It's just a phrase. Something people say. But there were a few things I kind of thought I would have done and I haven't.'

'I wasn't criticising. I mean I don't have a list at all. Real or figurative. So, you're doing better than me.' They exchanged weak smiles. 'I mean I have detailed financial projections for the next five years but that's not the same thing.'

'Buying this flat was on my list,' she said, feeling rather proud. It was thanks to her mother's life insurance that she'd been able to afford it, but she'd put the money to good use and she was proud of herself for not spending it all on holidays, clothes and Greggs sausage rolls.

'It's not a rental?' He looked beyond surprised.

'No, it's all mine. Every brick,' she said proudly. 'We can't all live in a mansion with butlers.' She handed him his glass of water.

'Are you implying that I do?'

'You clearly think this is below you.' She was hurt and a bit cross. She was very proud of her little flat. 'I'm mortgage-free.' She crossed her arms and raised her chin as if in challenge.

'I am very sorry if I have said something to offend you. Not my intention. It's purely that I look at property for its resale value. What you have done with the interior is . . . lovely. Very you.' He patted a bright orange cushion.

Ruby was a little mollified. She joined him on the sofa, tucking her feet underneath her and leaning back.

Curtis was watching her. He put down his glass of water and shuffled into what appeared to be a slightly more relaxed, although still quite stiff, seated position.

Ruby leaned to her right and checked her wall calendar. 'Bum.'

'Problem?'

'We've got a big wedding tomorrow so we're starting at six thirty.' Ruby liked the overtime but she didn't enjoy getting up early.

'I need to check in at the police station in the morning. I wonder if you'd be kind enough to take me into work with you?' he asked.

'Sure.' Curtis sat gingerly on the edge of the sofa and clutched his old laptop bag. 'You can put your stuff in the bedroom if you'd like.'

'I should take the sofa,' he said.

'Don't be daft, you're far too tall. It's one night. I'll be fine.' She led the way and switched on the light. He followed her in and his gaze was pulled to the teddy bear that sat on a chair in the corner. She followed his stare.

When she'd changed outfits earlier, she'd also changed underwear and her teddy now appeared to be wearing her purple lace bra as earmuffs. 'Bugger!' She grabbed the bra and stuffed it in the dirty clothes bin. She turned around and grinned at Curtis. 'I'll get some clean sheets for you.'

'No, really. It's fine,' he said, although a pulse in his jaw said otherwise as he put his bag on the floor. 'I don't want to put you to any trouble.'

'Here, have a clean sheet and we'll flip the duvet.' She pulled open the drawer under the bed and took out sheets and her winter duvet – that would do for her. 'Sleep tight. Mind the bed bugs don't bite.' Curtis's eyes widened. She took one of the pillows from the bed and exited the room, not bothering to hide her grin.

Kim and Adrian were sitting in her small back garden having eaten fish and chips out of the wrappers and were on their second bottle of wine. Kim had unburdened herself of the secret she'd been keeping for seven long years and it felt amazing.

'I can't believe Vince is alive,' said Adrian for about the fifth time.

'Disappeared without a trace until I registered his car as stolen and then he got in touch pretty quick. Apparently he couldn't say anything to my face because he didn't want to hurt me. But it was okay to tell me over the phone that he'd moved to Mablethorpe with his acupuncturist. Funny really because I'd love to stick pins in him.'

'But instead of telling people what actually happened you said Vince had died?'

'Family and close friends know the truth. I've never actually told anyone that he died. I haven't blatantly lied about it. I just didn't correct their assumptions.' Kim was beginning to feel awful. It turned out the relief of sharing the secret with someone was quite short-lived. She flopped back in her seat. 'I felt such an idiot. He had this massive heart attack and was rushed to hospital.' She saw Adrian swallow hard. 'I'm sorry.'

He waved her words away. 'It's fine. But it's very similar to Justine.'

'I know. But Vince survived. And I went to see him every day in hospital. Then one day, after I'd visited, a book I'd ordered for him was delivered and there were a few minutes of visiting left. So I charged over to the hospital with it. When I walked onto his ward there was another woman at his bedside holding his hand.'

'Crikey.'

'And you know, I still didn't twig. I introduced myself and rattled on about the book before the shocked looks on their faces registered. They both started talking over each other, a string of different excuses, and I finally cottoned on and well . . . I lost it a bit and walked out. I closed the shop for a few days. When Vince was discharged, he didn't come home. And when someone asked me, I burst into tears and they assumed he'd died.' She scratched her eyebrow. 'I know it was wrong of me but it was easier that way. I felt bad because I didn't want the sympathy but I also didn't want to have to explain that I'd been living a lie. I'd lost my perfect husband.'

'Does Ruby know the truth?'

Kim shook her head. 'I found I liked to talk about all the good times rather than focusing on how it ended. So, like all the others I finished the story with "and he had a heart attack" and let her assume he'd died.' Kim held her head in her hands. 'I'm a bad person.'

Adrian leaned forward. 'No, you're not.'

Kim lifted a hand to look at him. 'It's only really Ruby I feel bad about. Other folk were probably only going to gossip anyway. When I gave Ruby a job, I figured she'd not stick around too long. Telling her what I told everyone else seemed fine then. But now . . .'

'You're quite close, you two, aren't you?'

'We are. Apart from the shop we have nowt in common but somehow we find enough to talk about for hours on end. We're an odd couple.'

'Whoever said we all have to be a perfect match?'

Something about the way he was looking at her made something fizz in her stomach. *Probably just indigestion*, she thought.

Ruby stirred and adjusted her mouthguard. The sofa wasn't as comfy to sleep on as it was to sit on and watch TV. She was vaguely aware of a distant scratching sound. Then silence. She drifted back to sleep.

'Argh!' A half scream from the bedroom had her instantly awake and dashing across the room before her legs had been informed.

Ruby switched on the light and smiled, forgetting she had her blue mouthguard in. Curtis screamed again. 'Whoops, thorry,' she said, before popping out the guard.

'Um, can you help?' Curtis's voice was muffled by the large cat lying over his head with the tail across his face, making him look like he was wearing a furry helmet.

'There you are, Seymour,' said Ruby, lifting the Siamese cat into her arms.

Curtis spat out a mouthful of cat fur and proceeded to try to wipe his tongue with his hand.

'I told you I shared a cat.'

'So I see,' said Curtis as he and Seymour exchanged glares. Curtis blinked. 'Is it me or has he got—'

'Cross eyes. Yep.'

'And he's called See-More. Someone has a sense of humour.'

'It's quite common in Siamese cats apparently. Night,' said Ruby, turning to leave.

'Actually, it's almost four thirty. We both need to have showers and breakfast and allow circa fifteen minutes to drive to the florist's and find a parking space, so we should probably be getting up soon anyway.'

The long explanation and the thought that she wasn't getting any more sleep made her yawn. 'I guess.'

'Let me know when I can use the bathroom.'

Ruby nodded and left the room, feeling like she needed more sleep.

A shower woke her up a little bit and she busied herself with trying to be a good hostess and making breakfast for two. She even laid the little table and found a teabag at the back of the cupboard. It must have been there a while but she was fairly sure that tea didn't go off.

'Toast okay?' she called.

'Great, thanks,' came the reply from inside the bathroom.

'You want anything on it?' She began searching her cupboards for something she could put on toast and wished she'd done that before offering.

The bathroom door opened and Curtis stepped furtively out. He clutched the small towel around his waist. Ruby suppressed a snigger at him trying to hide his modesty. She hadn't thought about what Curtis's body might look like – why would she? But now she knew. And apart from being rather on the paler side of white, it was lean, trim and lightly toned.

'Marmite would be nice,' he said.

'Eurgh. That stuff is the devil's bottom.'

'Really? Where do you do your research?' he asked.

'It's a fact.' She stuck her head back in the cupboard. 'I've got something called Christmas marmalade. I'm not sure what that means.' She studied the label. 'I think it's just an excuse to add alcohol.'

'Butter will be fine.'

'Low-fat spread okay?'

'Lovely,' he said although she wasn't sure he meant it. He scurried into the bedroom, the flash of the white towel like a rabbit's tail as it runs away from danger.

After breakfast, Ruby finished drying her hair and returned to the kitchen, where she'd left Curtis washing up.

He was holding up the tea caddy and looking like he'd just discovered it was a portal to hell.

'What's wrong?' she asked.

His expression was stony. 'Drugs?' His voice had that air of parental disappointment.

'What?' She grabbed her car keys.

'I don't know what else to call it.' Curtis tilted the tea caddy up for Ruby to see inside. 'Actually, I think I can be more specific and say cannabis. I believe the colloquial term is marijuana. Or pot, weed, ganja, dope, hashish, skunk, leaf—'

'Blimey if there's a quiz round on that you'd ace it.' He was still holding the tea caddy at arm's length. 'It's not mine,' she said. Curtis's expression registered his disbelief. 'It's Seymour's.'

'I know there are times when I fail to notice I'm being ridiculed but this isn't one of them.' Curtis put the lid back on the caddy and returned it to the countertop with a thud. He picked up his bag and strode towards the door.

'Wait!' Ruby picked up something from the floor and returned to the tea caddy. She spooned some of the contents into what she was holding. 'Seymour,' she called and the cat eyed her suspiciously. She crouched down and waved what she was holding and the cat trotted over. When he got within a foot of Ruby, he leaped forward, snatched the toy and proceeded to go a bit crazy. Curtis was frowning hard. 'It's catnip,' she explained. 'I buy it in bulk off eBay to put in his favourite toy.'

'Catnip?' Curtis looked mortified. 'I am really very so—'

'No need,' said Ruby, waving his apology away. She turned around so he wouldn't see her suppressing a smile. 'Come on or we'll be late.'

Chapter Twelve

Kim yawned so hard her jaw clicked. She'd had a good evening with Adrian. They had a lot in common – not least lying about their spouses. He was a gentle soul with a self-deprecating sense of humour and a shy smile. She'd really enjoyed his company and if he hadn't waxed lyrical about Justine for most of the evening there was a possibility she would be developing feelings for him that went beyond a platonic friendship. The way Adrian talked was lovely to witness but it also cemented in Kim's mind just how much he was still in love with his wife.

Adrian had got a taxi home at midnight and she'd slept soundly until her alarm. But she had drunk quite a bit. Years ago, a bacon butty would have set her straight, but these days alcohol wiped her out. Kim had decided that after her confessional with Adrian, Ruby needed to be next. She cared a lot about what Ruby thought of her and needed to put things straight. On the journey to the flower shop she'd gone over and over the conversation in her mind. She very much hoped Ruby would understand.

She'd collected the fresh stock from the wholesaler en route. Opening the cooler door, she was greeted by the usual waft of flowers, which made her senses ping – she never grew tired of it. For some people it was the smell of freshly baked bread or coffee but for Kim it was flowers. She put down the crates of fresh blooms and went in search of the kettle – she'd not had nearly enough tea yet to get her started for the day.

The door chimed and Ruby walked in, closely followed by a smartly dressed man – one Kim hadn't seen before and would have definitely remembered because of his classic good looks.

'I'm saying there's a reason it's called a three-point turn,' he said to Ruby.

'And all I'm saying is, that's just a guideline.' Ruby turned to Kim. 'Morning.'

'Hello,' said Kim, unable to take her eyes off Ruby's companion.

'Kim, this is Curtis Walker. We met on the train yesterday,' explained Ruby.

'Hello, Kim, I'm very pleased to meet you,' said Curtis, offering her his hand.

'Oh. Yes, likewise,' she said, shaking his hand whilst desperately trying to catch Ruby's eye. 'Can I get you a tea or coffee?'

'Um. I don't want to put you to any trouble.' Curtis seemed to be taking his cue from Ruby. Had he stayed the night at her place?

'It's fine,' said Ruby. 'She's got all sorts of tea in case people get upset. You know, funerals and anniversaries. There's even some of that camomile stuff they had in London. And Earl Grey.'

'An Earl Grey would be lovely. No milk. Thank you.'

'Coming right up,' said Kim, shooing Ruby through the beads into the back room. She hit the switch on the kettle and lowered her voice. 'Train? London? Gorgeous man who smells of your strawberry shower gel? Spill,' said Kim, all thoughts of her Vince confession completely superseded.

'It's not what you think,' said Ruby, hanging up her jacket and pulling out the order for that day's wedding.

'Nope. You'll have to do better than that.' Kim put her hand on the order sheet to get Ruby's full attention.

Ruby shrugged. 'I sat in his seat on the train. I got chatting to a really hot guy—'

'Curtis.' Kim pointed towards the shop. Had she forgotten his name already? He certainly was hot and nothing like Ruby's usual type, which could only be a good thing.

'No, Lewis.'

'I'm not following,' said Kim, making drinks for herself and Curtis.

'It's a very long story.' Ruby ran herself a glass of water and disappeared through the beads. Kim's curiosity was piqued.

'Here you go, Curtis,' said Kim, returning to the shop and handing him his tea. 'Do you work in London?' She pulled out the stool and sat down opposite him while Ruby started sorting out the flowers from the cooler.

'Mainly from home but the majority of my clients are London-based, requiring me to travel down regularly.'

'And what is it that you do?'

'Kiiiim,' Ruby's tone was imploring. 'Stop interrogating him.'

'What? I'm making polite conversation.'

'You're prying.'

'It's fine,' said Curtis, handing Kim his business card. Now she was seriously impressed.

'Don't you need to check in at the police station?' Ruby

asked Curtis. Kim's automatic response would have been to check his ankle for a tag but surely that couldn't be the case with this smartly dressed individual?

'There's no rush,' he replied. He turned to Kim to explain. 'There was an accident at my home while I was in London. A truck came off the road and apparently has damaged the property.'

'Apparently?' said Kim, feigning innocence. 'Have you not been home then?' She could almost hear Ruby rolling her eyes. Kim sipped her tea.

'Ruby was kind enough to let me sleep in her bed last night.'

Kim almost spat out her tea.

'I was on the sofa,' said Ruby. 'Shall I finish the bride's bouquet?' she asked clearly trying to change the subject.

'Fine by me.' She turned her attention back to Curtis who was taking in his surroundings. 'Are you local?' she asked.

'Born in Sheffield. I now live near Nether Padley.'

'And you live alone?'

'Am I finishing these flowers on my own today?' asked Ruby, sounding a little huffy.

'Of course not,' said Kim. 'I'm just having a chat with Curtis whilst I drink my tea and then I'll be right with you.'

'I should probably make a move,' said Curtis, putting down his mug. 'It was lovely to meet you, Kim.'

'Likewise,' she said. 'Now you know where we are, you can pop in any time. I'll do you a good discount.'

'That's very kind. And thank you for the tea.' He rose to his feet and leaned over where Ruby was binding the bouquet's handle.

'I'll be in touch,' he said.

'Yep. Okay. Great. Bye,' said Ruby without looking up.

Curtis gave Kim a brief nod and left. As the door shut, Ruby's shoulders slumped. 'Thank heavens for that. I thought he'd never leave.'

'But now he has I need to know *all* the details.'

'There aren't any and we have work to do.' Ruby stabbed a finger at the flowers.

'Spoilsport,' said Kim, sticking her tongue out. But she wasn't that easily deterred.

They worked flat out for two hours and Ruby managed to keep Kim's questions at bay. It turned out she had a lot to share about Adrian and the revelation that his wife in fact died two years ago.

'It's a bit weird though isn't it, lying about that?' asked Ruby.

Kim pulled her chin in. 'Well, sometimes things are too hard to face.'

'Still. It feels a bit odd that we've been asking after her and all the while she was dead.' Ruby shivered. 'It's creeping me out. Are you sure he's not got her in his spare room or something? Like that film.'

'*Psycho*? And no, I've seen her grave. He takes her flowers every Friday. What I witnessed was a man who loved his wife very much and wasn't ready to let her go.'

'I guess that's quite sweet,' conceded Ruby. 'Mum didn't want me to feel I had to keep visiting a grave – that's why we scattered her ashes at Cleethorpes.' Ruby knew her mum didn't like the thought of her daughter standing in a miserable graveyard every birthday and Christmas. Instead she'd told her to remember all the good times they'd had, like their days out at the beach. Those days had been the best. Sand between her toes, paddling in the sea, building sandcastles and being wrapped in a big towel and hugged until she was dry. She missed her mum's hugs.

'Adrian suggested I get a dog. You're not allergic or anything?'

Ruby reluctantly left her memories and focused back on Kim. 'No, but it won't be living with me.'

'But it would be in here every day. I couldn't leave it at home on its own. I'm thinking about a rescue.' Kim looked pleased at the prospect.

'Fine by me. Just don't come back with a yappy one nobody else wants.'

'At least it won't steal my microwave,' quipped Kim.

'True. But it could do a lot worse than piss in your kettle.'

The chatter dwindled as they became engrossed in their work; fast fingers cutting stems and binding them together.

They were checking off the order when the door opened and in walked Curtis. Kim's face lit up but Ruby wanted to scream. What was he doing now?

'Curtis, how lovely to see you again!' said Kim wiping her hands on her apron.

'Yes, sorry,' he said. 'I realised we didn't agree next steps with the engagement ring? It's still safe in my bag.' He held up the weathered bag as if presenting evidence.

Kim's mouth dropped open and Ruby was tempted to push it shut. She turned to Curtis. 'I suppose one of us needs to trust the other one with it until we visit the jeweller's in Leeds.'

Ruby saw Kim looking zoned out and mouthing 'engagement ring' and 'Leeds' to herself but she chose to ignore her.

'Are you free Monday? It's my day off. We could go then?' suggested Ruby.

'I have some calls in the morning. But I'm free after twelve thirty if you wanted to take a trip over in the afternoon.'

'That's fine, Curtis.'

'And I wondered if we could have a chat about your new job?'

'Hey?' said Kim, suddenly perking up.

Curtis's phone rang. 'I'm sorry I need to take this,' he said, stepping outside.

Kim swivelled on her heel and fixed Ruby with a stare. 'New job?'

'Ah. Again, it's not what you think.' Ruby was starting to realise that yesterday was going to take a whole lot of explaining.

'How about you try?' said Kim, placing her hands on her hips in mock challenge.

'I need to get this order out. But I promise it's nothing to worry about and I'll explain later.'

Kim and Ruby ferried the boxes of flowers to the van. Curtis was marching up and down outside the shop.

'He's quite tasty,' said Kim.

'Tasty? What is he, a chicken nugget?'

'I'm just saying. He looks nice and he seems nice. So maybe he is . . . nice.'

'No. Just, no,' said Ruby, shutting the van door with a final bang.

Curtis ended his call but stared at his phone. 'Everything all right?' Kim called over.

Curtis looked up. 'No, Harry . . . my father has been taken ill.'

'Nothing serious, I hope?' said Ruby as Curtis joined them at the van.

'I'm not sure. I'd best get a taxi over there.'

'Where does your father live?' asked Kim.

'In a nursing home near Meersbrook Park.'

'Ruby's about to deliver to Woodford Hall, which is on the way. She'll give you a lift. Won't you, Ruby?' Kim gave her a nudge.

'Of course. Hop in,' she said, brandishing the van keys.

Curtis seemed to take a moment before opening the passenger door and getting in.

They didn't speak on the journey. Ruby wasn't sure what to say. She had had 'the phone call' a few times from the hospice where her mother spent her final days. You never knew if it really was the last time you'd get that phone call. She understood the need to get there as quickly as possible. She remembered wishing that teleporting had been invented because the fear of missing her mother's final moments had been overwhelming. It was like experiencing that same sensation all over again now. 'We'll go straight there. I'll deliver the flowers after I've dropped you off,' she suggested.

'That would be very inefficient to drive past the hotel. A few minutes won't make any difference.'

'If you're sure.' Ruby put her foot down and Curtis clutched the passenger seat.

She pulled into Woodford Hall, jumped out and opened up the rear van doors. The sky was grey and getting darker by the second. It didn't bode well for the poor bride who had most likely pinned her hopes on wall-to-wall sunshine. Curtis appeared next to her. 'What shall I bring?'

She nodded at the two crates of table centres. 'Either of those.' He picked one up and followed her into the grand Victorian building. It was one of Ruby's favourite wedding venues around the city and would definitely be on her shortlist if she ever got married.

Ruby was greeted warmly at the reception desk and directed through to where the wedding reception would be. The wedding co-ordinator joined them and after a couple more trips to the van all the floral arrangements were safely handed over. The bride made a brief appearance and sobbed over her bouquet – always a good sign.

They were soon on their way to Meersbrook. Curtis gave directions and Ruby dropped him off outside. He thanked her and left the van. She could have just driven off. She'd fulfilled her obligation; he'd been delivered to the nursing home. But there was something that struck her about Curtis – how alone he seemed. He was likely one of those people who preferred things like that. But even so the thought of leaving him didn't sit well with her.

Ruby found a place to park the van and walked back towards the nursing home. She perched on the wall outside, wondering exactly what she was doing there. A young man in a carer's uniform came out, lit up a cigarette and took a long drag.

'You can sit down if you like,' said Ruby, indicating the space on the wall next to her.

'A fellow exiled smoker?' he asked.

'The daughter of one.'

He nodded his understanding and sat down. 'Thanks.' They looked out through the row of trees to the park. 'Are you visiting?' he asked.

'No, I dropped a friend off. His dad's not well. I thought I should wait.'

With that the heavens opened. Rain bounced high off the pavement. 'Come on,' said the carer, stubbing out his cigarette and ushering her into the building, past a reception desk and through to the TV lounge.

'You might as well have a coffee while you wait,' he said.

'It's okay.'

'Tea then?' He waited expectantly by the door.

'Sorry. I don't drink tea or coffee.'

He gave her the look she'd seen many times – one of British bewilderment. She knew she was an embarrassment to her fellow countrymen but what could she do? She didn't like the taste – never had done.

'Orange squash?'

He was trying hard to please and she didn't have the heart to keep rejecting his offers. 'That'd be lovely. Thanks.'

He disappeared and she realised she was standing almost in the centre of the large room and all eyes were on her.

'Dot, wake up. I think your Barbara's here,' said a tiny lady in a large chair. The woman next to her, presumably Dot, came to with a start.

Ruby shook her head. 'Sorry. I'm not Barbara,' she said.

The woman put her glasses on. 'You're not.' She turned to Dot. 'It's not Barbara.'

'What are you saying, Kitty?' asked Dot, fiddling with her hearing aid.

'She's not Barbara. She's ...' Kitty stared straight at Ruby.

'Oh. I'm Ruby but I'm—' Dot's hearing aid screeched into life.

'She's Ruby,' explained Kitty to Dot.

'I know she is,' said Dot.

'Here's your squash,' said the carer, coming back into the room.

'Thank you. Please could you let my friend know that I'm waiting in here? Doesn't matter how long it takes but I don't want him having to get a taxi.'

'Sure. Resident's name?'

Ruby had a think. 'Mr Walker.'

The carer scrunched up his features in thought. 'Nah, don't think we've got a Mr Walker.'

'I'm waiting for Curtis Walker. I assumed . . .'

'Curtis.' His expression was unreadable. 'He'll be seeing Harry. I'll let him know.' Did she imagine it or did he just give her the once-over? He addressed the residents. 'Before you ask – the kettle's on. And I don't want to short-circuit your pacemakers but there's chocolate digestives today,' he added with a wink.

'Have a seat, Ruby, and tell us what you've been up to,' said Dot, moving the newspaper from the chair next to hers.

Ruby looked around. Most of the people were either asleep or reading; nobody was watching the telly. She had no idea how long she was going to have to wait. 'Sure.'

'How's that fella of yours?' asked Kitty.

Ruby was quite warming to the duo and decided to play along. 'Which one? The one who peed in my kettle or the one who stole my microwave?'

Kitty and Dot both hooted with laughter. This was fun. 'Didn't you go out with . . .' Dot was clicking her fingers as if trying to recall a name.

'Lenny?' suggested Kitty. Dot shook her head. 'Terry? Bert? George?'

'No!' said Dot, quite sharply. 'Gordon,' she said, clapping her hands in apparent pleasure that she'd remembered the name she was after. They both stared at Ruby.

'Nope. Never been out with a Gordon. I went out with a Greg once. He liked plaiting my hair with his huge sausage-like fingers.' The pair laughed again. There was a scraping sound. Ruby turned to see a lady dragging another chair over. 'Here, let me get that.' Ruby moved the chair and the surreal conversation continued.

She wasn't sure how but she ended up telling them the engagement ring story and those who were awake were enthralled.

'And then we went to Covent Garden and had a meal and wine.' The images of Covent Garden popped into her mind, making her feel wistful.

'But you found him, this Lewis?' asked Dot, leaning so far forward she was one sneeze away from toppling out of her seat.

'Nope,' said Ruby and the room seemed to give a collective sigh. 'But we're going to Leeds on Monday to see if the jeweller can help us.'

'Good idea,' said Kitty.

'Here you go, ladies and gents. Teas all round,' said the carer, wheeling in a trolley. 'Curtis said he'd be down in about ten minutes. And to thank you for waiting.'

'Cool,' said Ruby, taking a proffered biscuit. She turned back to her new friends. 'So tell me about Harry.'

Chapter Thirteen

Ruby was pretty sure she knew the moment Curtis had entered the room. Call it a sixth sense or intuition – but whatever it was it made her spin around. She was helping Dot to do the twist as Chubby Checker blared out from the television.

Curtis was standing in the doorway and cleared his throat. 'Are you ready to go?'

'Here he is. Come and join us,' called Kitty, grabbing her walking frame and heading towards him, although she'd been dancing for the last ten minutes quite happily without it.

'Ruby.' His tone contained a strong plea for help.

'Leave him be, ladies,' said Ruby, changing the channel back to BBC. There was a collective groan from the room.

'Spoilsport!' shouted someone.

'Next time, I'll bring some speakers and we'll have a proper rave,' said Ruby.

'Don't we need drugs for that?' whispered Kitty.

'We've got plenty. We're popping them all the time,' said Dot, with a giggle.

'It's been fun but I've gotta go. You all take care.' Ruby blew kisses to everyone and a round of applause broke out. She walked from the room, leaving Curtis frozen to the spot looking as if he was trying to work out what he'd witnessed.

'What were you doing in there?' he asked as he followed her out of the building.

She paused and smiled. He did seem genuinely confused. 'It's called having fun, Curtis. You should try it sometime. Anyway, how was your dad?'

Curtis swallowed hard. 'Not good. It's a chest infection. But the doctor doesn't want to move him to hospital. He's prescribed some antibiotics, which should help but they take a few days to have an effect . . .'

Ruby gave his arm a squeeze and he stared at her hand resting there. 'Anything I can do?'

'I can't impose any more.' He looked up and down the deserted street. 'I'll get a taxi.'

'Curtis, come on. I've waited half an hour for you. At least let me give you a lift somewhere.'

'Thank you,' he said with a slow smile. 'A lift home would be great.'

They walked in silence to the van. The rain had disappeared and the sun was fighting to escape from behind a cloud. She hardly knew him and yet it hurt her to see him look so sad. She couldn't help but study him across the bonnet before they got in. 'I know it looks bleak right now, but people frequently recover from chest infections. Let's hope for the best.'

'He has familial hypertrophic cardiomyopathy. Any additional pressure on his heart could be fatal.'

'Right. Familial? I'm guessing that means it's hereditary?'

'Yes.'

'I'm so sorry, Curtis.' All sorts of feelings pogoed around inside her. How awful to be dealt something like that. To watch someone suffer from something that was potentially coming for you next.

His eyebrows pulled tightly together. 'No, it's fine,' he said, shaking his head. 'There's no reason why I would have it.' And with that he got in the van. Ruby paused for a moment. Curtis really was an oddball.

Ruby got in the driver's seat and they set off. She decided to fill the silence.

'Your dad sounds like a bit of a hero.'

Curtis turned slightly. 'Have you been gossiping?'

'I'm shocked you'd even say that. I was merely showing an interest and those lovely ladies were happy to have a chat and share what they knew. That's all.'

'That's gossiping.'

'We'll have to agree to disagree.' Ruby felt this might be a bit of a theme. 'They said your dad was a policeman who rescued children and kittens.' Curtis gave her a sideways look. 'Okay, I might have added the kittens. Are they right?'

'He is a retired police inspector and he and his wife used to be foster parents, which isn't quite as dramatic as rescuing children.'

'Ah,' said Ruby as a piece of the puzzle slid into place. 'And were you one of those children?'

'I was,' said Curtis. 'Do you mind if we don't talk anymore?'

'Of course, that's fine,' said Ruby. The stack of questions she wanted to ask would have to wait.

Ruby was pleased she'd driven Curtis home because if she was shocked by the sight of his house then he must have been devastated. There was police tape all around it and the scene was exactly as the police had explained. What they'd failed to mention was that the truck was still wedged in the house. They got out of the van and stood aghast.

Ruby drew in a breath so hard she made herself cough. 'You all right?' he asked.

If she had covered one eye and viewed each half of the house separately it was like the before and after of the apocalypse. One side of the house was resplendent in ornate red brick with pretty divided windows and a neat garden full of colour. The other had a truck sticking out of the side of it. It had been carrying bricks, some of which remained on board, but most of the load had been shot across the grass. Rubble was strewn around the garden like there'd been an explosion and the window frame was hanging precariously. There was a truck-sized gap in the fence, revealing great troughs ploughed across the lawn where it had careered off the road, uprooting and demolishing plants, pots and pretty much everything in its path.

'Look at the state of it.' Unexpected emotion made her swallow hard. She instinctively linked her arm through his and hugged it tight to her. 'Oh, Curtis. This is awful.'

'It is rather inconvenient.'

'Inconvenient? Your beautiful home has been trashed.' She was heartbroken on his behalf. 'I'm so sorry.'

'None if this is your doing. In fact, you may well have saved my life. Had I not been with you in London I would have been at home here, sitting in the living room.'

'Bloody hell, Curtis. That's frightening.'

He pushed out his bottom lip and stared at the house. 'It's going to take a while to fix but that's what you have insurance for.'

She could hardly believe his unemotional response. 'Was the driver okay?'

'Surprisingly, yes. The police said he climbed out through the windscreen into my living room. They had to force the back door to let him out.'

'It's going to be a mess inside too,' she said, thinking out loud.

'I expect it is. My cleaner won't be pleased.'

'You're right. That's going to take more than a squirt of Mr Muscle.'

Curtis walked a little closer and she followed him. From this distance she could see through the window and it didn't look good.

'Bloody hell,' said Ruby, unsure what else to say. Ruby nodded at the 'How's my driving?' sticker on the back of the truck. 'Should I give them a call?'

'I think it's a little late for constructive feedback,' said Curtis, puffing out a breath like a plumber assessing a leak.

A recovery lorry was parked nearby and a man hopped out of the driver's side and came over. 'You Mr Walker?' he asked.

'I am,' said Curtis, whilst Ruby edged closer to the house for a better look at the damage.

'I was meant to be meeting the fire officer here twenty minutes ago only he's late. I can't tow that out until the building is shored up.'

'Of course. Let me make a few phone calls.'

Ruby looked about. They were on the edge of a village. There was a farm opposite and swathes of green fields surrounded them. It was like the places she had visited as a child. Her mother had always been one for trips out on the bus. And she loved looking around villages like this one, followed by a long walk and a picnic.

Curtis ended a call and came over. 'Have you got someone you can stay with?' she asked.

'No, but I'll check into a hotel. Honestly, I'll be fine.'

'There must be someone?' She didn't like the idea of him not having somewhere to crash. Off the top of her head she could come up with at least five people who she was sure would take her in if she were in the same situation.

Curtis smiled indulgently. 'I'm not big on friends. Are you?'

'Hell, yeah.' She was about to rattle off some names but when she thought about it, all her closest friends now had children and her best friend had moved away because of her husband's work so now they only spoke on the phone. Her friends were thinner on the ground than she liked to admit. Perhaps she'd let things drift because she was a little envious of them living the dream. Best she didn't analyse it too much. 'Life kind of gets in the way sometimes. I've got Kim.'

'Your employer?'

'She's more than that. Anyway, we were talking about *your* friends and family,' she said, keen not to dwell.

'Harry is my only family.'

'Look I still don't have a phone but you can call the florist's or pop in any time. This is a lot to deal with on your own. But hey, if you hire me, I could help with this too.' She gestured to the house.

'Thank you. That's kind.' His expression changed. 'Are you serious about doing some paid admin work for me?'

'If you mean, do I still want to be your part-time personal executive assistant? Then yes I do.' She was quite looking forward to it if she was being honest. She wanted to prove to him that she was more than capable of doing the job. She also felt a little responsible for the additional testing needed on the Cordelia Stuart-Bruce project. And there was also the promise of potentially meeting a decent man.

'I don't think you can be both personal and executive. And in an industry that loves a three-letter acronym do you really want to be a P-E-A?'

'I've been called worse things,' mused Ruby.

Curtis rummaged in his laptop bag and pulled out a small white box. 'Here, it's a new phone. I bought it in Covent Garden. You'll need one if you're going to be my PEA.'

Ruby was shocked but tried to hide it. She scrunched up her nose. 'I don't want to be referred to as your pee. Let's go with executive assistant. But I can't accept a phone like that; they cost hundreds.' She crossed her arms to stop her hand rushing out and grabbing it. She'd wanted one of the new iPhones for ages. Her mother's voice was in her head: 'There's no such thing as a free lunch.' And this was like the grown-up version of accepting sweets from strangers. Only was Curtis really a stranger? After the twenty-four hours they'd spent together she was already starting to get the measure of him.

'You can easily transfer over your old details to this one. You need to try to contact Lewis on the old one before you switch it all over. If Kim has your mobile number, get her to call your phone and see who answers.'

'Genius! I will but I don't think I can take the phone – I can't afford to pay you back for it.'

He thrust the phone at her. 'It comes with the job. A perk if you will.' He held it steady in front of her. It would be rude to say no again. She took it from him and resisted the urge to open it up then and there; she'd save that treat for later.

'Mr Walker. Fire officer is here.' The recovery driver was pointing to a uniformed man getting out of a nearby car.

'I need to get on,' he said.

'Thanks for this, Curtis.' She waved the phone box at him. 'I'll be off too then.' A thought struck her. 'Can I use this for everything, not just work?'

'Of course.'

'Cool,' she said, walking away. 'Thank you.'

'Although a word of advice,' he called and she turned to listen. 'If you're looking up sperm donors only go for the legitimate ones this time.'

The recovery driver's eyes almost popped out of his head.

Back at the florist's there was a queue of customers so Ruby got stuck in to serving. She loved her job. The smell in the little shop was the best. She'd always loved the scent of flowers – they had a calming effect on her and made her feel happy. And most of the time the customers were lovely. They'd usually come to Bloom with a View to do a nice thing – either buying plants or flowers for themselves or for someone else. She liked listening to people and choosing the right mix for them. That moment when they saw it come together and their face lit up was what gave Ruby the most job satisfaction.

Early afternoon there was a brief lull in customers and Kim was clearing down the bench in the back room, which tended to get strewn with cut stems and leaves. 'Can I borrow your mobile phone?' asked Ruby. 'I need to call my number and see if Lewis, the guy who borrowed it, answers.' She'd managed to bring Kim up to speed in between customers.

'Sure.' Kim handed it over.

They both paused while Ruby rang her number and waited. She heard her own voice begin. 'It went straight to voicemail. I'll try again later,' she said, jotting down her old number. A customer came in and they went back to work.

Before she knew it, Kim was handing her a can of Coke. 'Right, sit down and fill me in on the details of Curtis. He seems really ni—'

'Hang on,' said Ruby, holding up her palm. 'Before you go choosing hats, this is purely a business arrangement.'

'I thought there was an engagement ring?' Kim leaned forward and cupped her tea, her eyes fixed on Ruby.

'Yeah, there's that too. Seriously, I don't want you getting any ideas about matchmaking. He's *so* not my type.'

'Because he's nice? Dresses smartly? Has manners?'

Ruby stuck her tongue out. 'He's . . .' How could she describe him without sounding unkind? Her shoulders slumped. 'I don't know. He's a bit uptight and quite . . . unemotional. A bit robotic. He's all logic and no soul.'

'Like Mr Spock?'

'Is that *Star Wars*?' asked Ruby, taking a swig from her can.

'Heathen. He was in *Star Trek*.'

'I knew it was some sci-fi movie.'

'Movie,' muttered Kim. 'The Americans have a lot to answer for.'

'He is nice but it's buried way underneath all the stiff bits,' said Ruby and Kim grinned at the euphemism. 'Behave!'

'Seriously though,' said Kim, putting her mug to one side. 'What is it that you really want?'

Kim was watching her closely, so she pondered before answering. If the perfect partner didn't exist she didn't want to waste time looking for them. She knew for sure that she wanted to be a mother, which was definitely still her priority. But after yesterday something felt different – that maybe she should give love another shot and Curtis's madcap idea of finding her someone through his work contacts might be worth a try. 'I thought it was the fairy tale but I think I'm running out of time for that. Maybe I just need someone with promise.'

Chapter Fourteen

Ruby had gone home to set up her new phone. Kim was packing up for the day when the door chimed and she realised that while she'd turned the sign over to Closed, she'd forgotten to flick the catch on the door. *Damn,* she thought. It was inconvenient, but she couldn't go turning customers away.

'Be with you in a second,' she called.

'No rush,' replied Adrian.

Kim stuck her head through the beaded drapes. 'Two visits in two days. Tongues will start to wag. Won't be a minute.' Although she was pleased to see him. Their heart-to-heart over fish and chips had highlighted what she missed about having someone special in her life. Once her work surface was clean and ready for the next day, she joined Adrian in the shop. 'Right, what can I do for you?'

Adrian appeared a little coy. 'I hope you don't mind but I gave my friend a call. The one who works at the animal shelter. I didn't want you getting your hopes up if all they had were goats and chickens.' He waved his hands as if trying to hurry himself up. 'Anyway, they have a variety of dogs and she's working late tonight – if you wanted to have a bit of a private viewing, I can drive you over. Or you can drive. Or whatever.' Adrian swallowed hard.

Kim did want to investigate the possibility of a dog. But she wasn't very prepared. 'Adrian, that's really kind of you. But I don't have anything in – like dog food or a bed.'

'Oh, sorry. I should have explained. They have a process you have to go through. Even if you see one you like today they have to inspect your home to check it's suitable. The shelter has dogs coming in all the time – there's no pressure.'

Kim couldn't stand the look of disappointment on his face. He'd clearly gone out of his way and she was super keen to find a dog. 'If there's no pressure to bring one home today then looking can't do any harm.' She glanced at the clock. 'Shall we go now then?'

'Terrific!' Adrian jangled his car keys.

It was only a twenty-minute journey and Kim and Adrian chatted on the way. She found it was easy to talk to Adrian. Now she was on her way to the shelter she was starting to think about what sort of dog she would like – *something small and well trained would fit the bill perfectly*, she thought.

They pulled into a gravel car park and were met by a distant choir of barking and when they got out of the car, a border collie herded them over to a porta cabin.

'Hello, Adrian,' said a rosy-faced woman as she came down the steps. 'I'm Margaret,' she added, thrusting a hand at Kim.

'Kim,' she said as Margaret gave her arm a thorough workout.

'You don't mind if I rope you in for a spot of walkies, do you? Only, one of our volunteers has twisted her ankle. This way.' Margaret didn't wait for a reply; she was already striding off towards a series of farm buildings with the collie at her heels.

The barking grew louder as they made their way through a series of mesh doors, which were bolted firmly behind them. 'QUI-ET!' shouted Margaret and the sound rung in Kim's ears for a few moments afterwards. The barking dwindled. 'We'll do a full questionnaire and home check if you find a match today but just a couple of questions first, so we know we're not wasting our time. Okay?' Margaret fixed her with a steely gaze.

'Er, yes. Of course.' Kim felt like she was on a game show and the star prize was resting on her next few answers.

'Do you have a garden or nearby open space for exercise?'

'Yes, a garden,' said Kim.

'Any other pets or children?'

'No.'

'How many hours a day will the dog be left alone?' Margaret's stare intensified.

'None because I was planning on taking them to work with me.'

'Right answer,' said Margaret. 'Now then, what sort of dog are you after? And please don't say something small and well trained.' Margaret laughed hard.

Master plan thwarted. 'Oh, um. Not too big. Calm. Nice nature.'

Margaret nodded. 'Let's see who we have that fits the bill.'

Margaret rattled off a series of do's, don'ts and warnings as they walked along the kennels. They were greeted with barks and wagging tails from a variety of dogs in all shapes, sizes and colours. The kennels had indoor and outdoor sections with beds and toys but it nevertheless felt a bit like doggy prison, seeing them jump up at the mesh. There were two she rather liked: Jo-Jo the little Yorkshire terrier who walked on three legs due to an old injury and Sam, an eight-year-old chocolate Labrador with diabetes. Margaret had gone to fetch leads and harnesses so they could take them both out for a stroll. Kim and Adrian waited by the last kennel.

'Thanks for bringing me,' said Kim.

'That's okay. And thanks for last night . . . Goodness sorry, that sounded like I was thanking you for sex. I wish I hadn't said that. Sorry.' He stared off into the distance.

'Don't worry,' said Kim, trying hard not to smile at his awkwardness.

'Not that I wouldn't thank you . . . I'm not suggesting that we . . . I think I should stop talking now.'

'I enjoyed it too,' said Kim, checking out the kennels. It was easier than looking at each other. She was aware of a high-pitched whine coming from around the corner and she went to investigate. 'Adrian, come and see this one.'

In a kennel around the corner Kim found a splodgy blur of a dog who was racing around so fast it was hard to focus on him.

She crouched down and tried to get a better look. 'Hello,' she said gently. 'What's your name?'

'Boomerang!' bellowed Margaret from the indoor side of the kennels, giving Kim quite a start.

Adrian chuckled beside her. 'I think Margaret's ventriloquist routine needs some work,' he quipped as he joined Kim in crouching at the mesh.

'Hello, Boomerang,' said Kim to the blurry dog careering around his pen at breakneck speed. An arm, presumably Margaret's, appeared on the inside of the kennel and threw a bone across the concrete. The dog dived on it and began chewing. Kim now had a better view of the tan and white creature. 'Well, aren't you a sweetie?'

'I think he's a spaniel,' said Adrian. 'Hello, fella,' he said putting his fingers through the wire. But Boomerang was engrossed in demolishing his bone.

'Careful, he might bite them off,' said Kim – she'd heeded all of Margaret's warnings.

'He won't bite,' said Margaret, appearing with the Yorkshire terrier and the Labrador at her heels. 'But I think you can see the issue we have with him.'

Watching him now he looked like the perfectly well-behaved dog she was looking for.

'How do you mean?' She'd got Kim interested.

'He was from a raid on a puppy farm. He's lived most of his life in kennels vying for attention. We've tried rehoming but he keeps coming back.'

'Hence the name?' said Adrian standing up.

'Exactly.'

'Oh, that's awful.' Kim looked at Boomerang and he looked directly at her with big sad eyes, his tongue lolling out as he panted. Kim thought her heart would break. 'Poor soul. Can we take him for a walk?'

Margaret shook her head. 'He won't walk. We've got an animal psychologist coming out to him again this week but I fear he's a lost cause.'

Adrian pressed his lips into a flat line. 'Um, what does the future hold for him then?' he asked.

'Not a lot I can do with a dog I can't rehome. I will try to find another shelter who will take him long-term but if not . . .'

She didn't need to finish the sentence.

'That's awful,' said Kim. Poor Boomerang was either

going to be put down or, if he was lucky, spend the rest of his life in doggy prison.

'Let's take these two for a walk, shall we?' Margaret handed Kim and Adrian a lead each but Kim already knew neither of these was the dog she wanted to take home.

Ruby spent a while playing with her iPhone. She'd been puzzling over when Curtis had bought it and worked out it must have been when she'd been mooching around the fancy shoe shop. She wrote down her new number and tried very hard to memorise it. She tried calling her old phone. Same thing again – straight to voicemail. She thought about Lewis. He was lovely and she wondered what had happened with his proposal. A thought struck her and she began trawling social media in the hope of finding him. When 'Lewis engagement' returned nothing useful she resigned herself to having to find him the hard way.

She logged into her email and fired off a message to all her close friends saying she'd lost her phone and could she have their mobile numbers. She set up a new file to keep the replies in so she always had a backup – Curtis would be proud.

Ruby added Curtis's number to her new phone and sent him a text message – **Hey Curtis. Here's my new phone number. You can test me on it on Monday. CU then. Ruby x**

She always signed off with a kiss. She stared at it for a moment and then she deleted it. He was her boss now after all – well sort of. She didn't want him to think she was being inappropriate.

Her phone pinged and she leaped on it but then was embarrassed at her own desperation. It was Curtis – **What is your email address? I will send over contact** information and suggested actions following yesterday's meeting. Regards, Curtis.

It was very formal but then she'd expect nothing less. She sent back her email address in reply and then wished that all those years ago she'd chosen something more sensible than roonicorn @ her email provider but it had done her proud, why change it now?

Curtis replied – **Thank you, Curtis.**

There was a short delay and her phone pinged again – **And thank you for your hospitality, Curtis.**

She replied – **Any time** ☺

Ruby took a few selfies, played about with the filters until eventually the fun was over and she was bored and feeling alone again. This was how she felt most evenings. She put the phone down and looked around. She liked her little flat. The first couple of months it had kept her busy with painting and decorating and now it was finished it looked clean and modern. It wasn't as nice as the terraced house she'd shared with her mum but it had been too hard to live there without her, like she was squatting in her mother's life. So she'd made the decision to move.

Ruby lolled her head back on the sofa and her mother's photograph came into her peripheral vision. She missed her mum. She missed her so much. It was like a gnawing ache inside her. Ruby had always been popular and had a lot of friends but none, she now realised, that she was particularly close to. And the reason for that was her mum. She had been both parents as well as her best friend. Something that had been brilliant but now she was gone it was a double whammy of heartache. Ruby had never been this lonely in her life.

Chapter Fifteen

Kim sipped her tea. She had enjoyed walking the dogs and they had both been well behaved. The Yorkshire terrier lay down at one point and Margaret said she always did that in the hope someone would carry her the rest of the way – Kim sympathised. She'd left her details with Margaret and said she needed to have a think about the dogs, which was true. It was all she could think about despite now being in Adrian's very large and well-appointed kitchen. She had a picture of Boomerang in her head and it wouldn't go away. Even his name made her sad. Poor soul.

'. . . and I thought that's funny, and took a photo.' Adrian held his phone in front of Kim's face and she realised she'd completely zoned out.

Kim tried to focus on the picture of a squirrel hanging upside down from a bird feeder. 'Oh, that is funny.'

'Come on, what's the matter? It's Boomerang, isn't it?'

'Spot on. I keep seeing those eyes and the thought that he might live the rest of his life in a shelter is haunting me.'

'Then why not have him?'

She'd been mulling over this exact question all the way

home. 'Margaret said he wasn't up for rehoming. And anyway, what do I know about dogs? He probably needs some dog whisperer if he's to live a normal life.'

Adrian did a slow rise and fall of his eyebrows, something she'd noticed he did sometimes before speaking. 'Before we had Hayley, just before she was born, I had a bit of a meltdown.'

'Really?' Adrian didn't strike her as the meltdown kind of guy.

'Yep. I was worried I'd be a useless dad. My parents were quite distant and I was worried I was going to be the same. But Justine said something that helped. She said, "We will both monumentally stuff this up because that's what parents do but our baby will be loved and that's all a child really needs." And she was right.'

Kim found she was smiling. 'Basically you're saying I will be a crap dog owner but if my heart is in the right place then it's okay?'

'Precisely. You might be Boomerang's last chance.'

'Oh heavens. Don't say that.' The pressure was instant.

Adrian held up his hands. 'Sorry. Look I'll pledge to help however I can. Come to dog training classes with you. Take him for a . . . run because he doesn't do walks. Maybe introduce him to the theatre. We'll find a solution.' The way Adrian looked at her made something flip inside her.

'I would love him. I'm sure of that. I feel like I've got a connection with him already. Does that sound daft?'

Adrian briefly scanned her face. 'No, not at all.' He blinked. 'I loved Hayley from the moment I saw her. And she was hairless and screaming at the time and covered in this disgusting goo.' He pulled an exaggerated yuk face.

'That's a baby though. This is a dog.'

'Love is love,' he said and returned to his coffee.

137

'I wanted to have children.' As soon as she'd said it, she wished she could rewind and suck the words back in.

'And Vince?' His voice was gentle, making her feel it was safe to share and he already knew her biggest secret.

'He seemed keen. We tried everything. Lots of rounds of IVF but it wasn't meant to be.'

'I'm sorry,' said Adrian.

'It's okay. I mean it wasn't at the time. I was a mess. I felt like I'd failed – as a woman and as a wife. It was rubbish. And then we considered adoption. We did the course, the many *many* interviews and form filling and we waited. Eventually they matched us with a little girl. We were waiting for a date for the match to be made official when Vince had his heart attack.' Her voice cracked. Kim hadn't expected to get emotional. She took a moment to compose herself. 'And, you know the rest. He buggered off to Mablethorpe with the acupuncturist and with them they took my dreams of motherhood.'

'Oh, Kim, I'm sorry.' Adrian rested his hand on hers and she was grateful for the contact. 'Couldn't you have gone ahead on your own?'

'I was a mess. I could barely feed and dress myself let alone a toddler.' She wiped away a stray tear. 'I suppose some things aren't meant to be.'

'And maybe some things are,' said Adrian. Their eyes rested on their now clasped hands.

A rap of knuckles on the kitchen window made them both spring apart. A young woman was glaring at them.

'Hayley,' said Adrian, getting to his feet. He went through to the utility room to let her in. Hayley kept her glare firmly trained on Kim.

* * *

On Monday morning Ruby woke early and was feeling quite excited about the day ahead. Curtis had messaged her to say he was staying at Woodford Hall until his house was safe to move back into. She'd meet him there this afternoon before they headed off to Leeds. Today was the first day in her new job. Ruby dressed in the most conservative clothes she had and those she felt were befitting an executive assistant and happily set to work on her day off.

She logged into her emails and was a bit surprised by how many there were from Curtis. It looked like she'd be earning her money. He'd even sent a spreadsheet for tracking her progress. She had a quick scan of each email and prioritised them. Top of the list was Jonty. She practised what she was going to say with Seymour but he merely looked at her and did the sort of yowl only Siamese cats can do. Although with his wonky eyes Ruby was never a hundred per cent certain where he was looking. When she was happy with her spiel, she dialled Jonty's number.

'Good morning, Jonty. It's Ruby Edwards. Curtis's—' She didn't get as far as her title before Jonty was speaking.

'Hey, Ruby. Happy Monday to you. How was your weekend?'

She hadn't been expecting the social chit-chat but she was pleased by it. 'Crazy Friday. A truck crashed into Curtis's house!'

She loved the gasp that came. 'No way?'

'It's a total war zone. He's had to move into a hotel.'

'That's awful. Will it impact our project plans?'

She'd not been expecting that either. 'No, absolutely not.' She crossed her fingers as she spoke. 'I wanted to firm up dates for the testing recruitment and for when Curtis is on site with you.' She checked the dates she'd scribbled down from Curtis's email.

'No problem, but first of all I was talking to a colleague and he thinks he's worked with you before.' Her bullshit radar went into overdrive. 'Did you work at Goldman Sachs?'

'No. I must have a double.'

'Where did you work before this?' he asked.

Shit! She could already see her reputation plummeting. She said the first thing that popped into her head. 'It's confidential.'

'Really? Do you mean you worked for celebrities?'

'I couldn't possibly say.' She was warming to her deception.

'Are you that PA who had an affair with—'

'No! Bloody hell, Jonty.' The real Ruby was back.

'Sorry.' She could tell even from the one word how disappointed he was.

'Anyway, I need to book accommodation for when Curtis is on site. I think he's already explained to Cordelia that there's no need for me to be there. I've been looking at hotels in the area and they all seem very similar and business-focused. Are there any you'd recommend?'

'There are a couple we use regularly. They all have good Wi-Fi, gym, swimming pool and room service. I'll email over the details.'

'Okay.' Now she was wishing she was going too. 'Shall we look at dates then?' She straightened her back and poised her pen. She was serious about this – and she'd prove it.

The morning whizzed by and she was pleased with what she'd achieved. She made a list to show Curtis and left for his hotel. He'd told her to get the lift to the second floor and follow signs for the Harris Suite. She felt a bit odd just walking into the hotel and heading up to one of the rooms. At least she was familiar with some of the hotel staff from bringing flowers to events there, but what she needed was a badge or even better a badge and a lanyard, to make her look official and not like a sex worker on a client call.

When she found the room there was a lit-up sign and a doorbell. She'd not seen a doorbell for a hotel room before. This was super fancy. She rang it and waited.

Curtis opened the door.

'Hiya, Curtis, this is a bit swish and—' Curtis immediately indicated that she needed to be quiet because he was on the phone. 'Right. Got it,' she said in a whisper and for no apparent reason gave him a double thumbs up. She decided to have a snoop around. It wasn't like it was his home or anything, so she figured it was allowed. When he'd said it was a room he'd been way off. The bit Curtis had let her into had a dining room table and four chairs, a large black desk where Curtis was now seated – and that was just for starters. Further in was a large sofa, which sat opposite the biggest TV she'd seen outside of Currys. A door was ajar, so she stuck her head through into a huge bedroom. A giant bed held centre stage and an ornate chandelier dangled above it. 'Bloody hell,' she said under her breath.

She wandered into the bedroom to be presented with a series of double doors. The first was a wardrobe. The second opened into the largest bathroom she'd ever stepped foot in. Wall-to-wall marble, with a hydro bath, a massive shower and two sinks. Who needed two sinks? She wasn't sure about the mirrored wall – that might be a bit of a shock if she'd pruned herself in the bath for a few hours, which was exactly what she'd do if she was staying there. She missed having a bath – her little flat only had a shower. She ran her fingertips along the cool marble surround.

'Here you are,' said Curtis, startling her. 'Sorry, my meeting overran. You all right?'

'This room. It's amazing. It's bigger than my flat.'

'You like it? There wasn't a lot of choice at such short notice and I didn't fancy the hostel-style hotel on the ring road.' He scrunched up his nose and she did the same although she clearly wasn't as fussy as him. She'd been quite excited when she'd last stayed in a Premier Inn.

She turned around to face the double doors she'd come through. They were impressively tall and sleek. She closed them and then flung them open and sashayed through – it felt amazing. 'We all need double doors in our lives. These are incredible.' She repeated the routine a few times and added 'Ta-dah!' Curtis coughed. 'What?'

'I thought you were used to living indoors but it's not apparent from your behaviour.'

'But these are fabulous,' she said, coming through the double doors and striking a pose with a pout.

'But you have seen doors before?' His lip twitched.

'Curtis, it's called having fun. You know what they say. Growing old is compulsory but growing up is optional?'

He seemed to consider it. 'I would have thought they were the same thing.'

'Er no. You have fun though, right?'

'I used to as a child.'

'Wow. You've forgotten how to have fun.'

'Not exactly, there's not really any call for it. Or time for it either. I work.'

'But not all the time?' she asked, although she had a feeling she already knew the answer.

'I work every day because I don't have any commitments. I have time to fill and work does that.'

'You can work *and* have fun. I have fun every day at Bloom with a View.'

'At work?'

'Yep. I always swore that if I didn't, I would quit. So, I do a job I love. You're there far too many hours not to.' It was also something her mum had instilled in her. She'd always say, 'Rather be a happy dustman, than an unhappy duke'. Although Ruby had never worked out how you got the job of a duke – she was pretty sure it wasn't something you could apply for on Monster.co.uk.

Curtis scrunched up his features in thought. 'Interesting theory. Even more so because it comes from you.' He joined her in the bedroom and closed the doors to the bathroom. 'I take it we're done with the doors?'

'I just really like them. They make you feel amazing.' He gave her a doubtful look. 'Seriously, you need to try it. Go on,' she added.

Curtis looked uncomfortable. Eventually he gingerly stepped forward and opened one of the doors.

'No, no, no.' Ruby gave him a gentle shove into the bathroom and shut the door with him on the other side. 'Both together. Like this.' She demonstrated the dramatic entrance one last time and a rush of something coursed through her system. She felt like she could do anything, be anyone. It was great. Curtis, on the other hand, had only just managed to get out of the way in time to avoid being smacked in the face. 'Your go,' she said. 'And no half-hearted nonsense. Enjoy it.'

Curtis swallowed hard. Ruby shut the door and waited. A couple of moments passed and she could imagine him psyching himself up on the other side. The doors flung open and Curtis strode through, making Ruby gasp. His jaw was clenched in concentration – moody but determined.

Despite his very neat appearance seeing him materialise like that gave him a film-star quality.

'How was it?' she asked.

'Fine. Can we go to Leeds now?' Despite his words she could sense he'd secretly enjoyed it – just a little bit.

Chapter Sixteen

Ruby was pleased that Curtis had sorted out the train tickets for both of them. Better still, he said he'd cover them as a work expense because they were going to discuss her workload during the journey. They had a seat with a table and Curtis faced the way he wanted to, giving Ruby full view of the carriage. Curtis tapped away on his laptop and she watched a couple who were sitting a few seats down. They were younger than her and there was something about their body language that caught her attention. The way they touched each other, the facial expressions and how they happily invaded each other's space. They were clearly in love and Ruby had to concentrate not to let out a heavy sigh.

Curtis shut the laptop with a slap, making her jolt. 'What is it?' he asked, placing both hands on the closed lid and giving her his full attention.

'It's the couple down there,' she said in a whisper and nodded her head.

Curtis leaned out into the aisle for a good look behind him.

'Don't be that obvious. You're as subtle as a truckload of bricks.' Curtis gave a mock scowl over his shoulder. She instantly realised her mistake. 'Sorry.' Curtis stayed leaning into the aisle for a while. 'Curtis,' she hissed and he righted himself.

'I see two people acting quite childishly. What is it that you see?'

She tilted her head. It was obvious to her. 'Two people in love.'

'Really?' But before she could answer he was having another unsubtle look. 'How on earth do you deduce that? Neither is wearing a ring. I've not seen them kiss. And we can't hear what they're saying.'

'It's the way they look at each other. How comfortable they are in each other's space. The fact that happiness is practically radiating off of them.'

'Hmm. Interesting.'

'It really is interesting. Well, it is to me. I love that they've found their ideal partner,' said Ruby, folding her arms and trying hard not to stare at the couple.

'What are you looking for in an ideal partner?' he asked.

She narrowed her eyes. 'Why do you want to know?'

'For one I'm meant to be introducing you to suitable potential partners and I'm also genuinely interested. Relationships fascinate me. Though they also confuse me.' He grimaced as he spoke.

'I know what you mean. I read a lot and the men in the books are nothing like reality.'

'I suppose that is why it's called fiction,' he said.

'Good point. But it's not only finding someone. It's finding the *right* person and making it last.' A thought struck her. 'Adam and Eve couldn't make their relationship work long-term and they were in paradise – what are my chances in Sheffield?' She chuckled at her own joke.

Curtis didn't. 'I'm not sure location is a big factor in longevity.'

'Maybe not, but if you think about all the permutations of what you and they want from a relationship, the odds of finding a match are stacked against you.'

'Go on then. I won't judge. Your top-three things you're looking for in an ideal partner.' He tilted his head expectantly.

She loved things like this and it was a surprise that it was his suggestion. 'Hmm. Someone I can trust.'

'I agree,' he said. 'Integrity is vital.'

'It's a lot harder to find than you'd think.' He was watching her intently. She had a little think about what she would want in a partner. 'Someone who makes me laugh and has the same interests as me, so we've got something in common. They need to have the same goals too.' A picture of Chris Hemsworth cradling a baby popped into her mind.

'You set goals in your relationships?' Curtis opened his laptop and started typing.

'Are you making notes in a spreadsheet?'

'I might be.' His guilty face peered over the top of the lid. 'I'm intrigued. Especially now you've said goals.'

'When I say goals, I mean that I want a long-term relationship and children.'

'I see, and the men you usually meet want sex and no ongoing commitment. Correct?'

She was about to become defensive but he'd actually hit the nail on the head. 'Yep. That's basically the issue.'

'Fascinating. Thinking about your criteria, my first suggestion would be Bob. And you've already met.'

Bob? Who the hell was Bob? Ruby's mind raced back to the meeting and the dull bald man in his forties. 'Bloody hell, Curtis.' She didn't want to be rude about Bob but she needed to shut this down quickly. 'For starters, I'm guessing Bob lives in London, he's probably shorter than me and when I ran over his toes with the chair there wasn't exactly a spark between us.'

'Spark?' he asked.

'You know. That instant connection. Something that draws you to someone. A little frisson of excitement.'

Curtis was still watching her closely, his fingers poised over the keyboard. 'I'm not sure I know what you mean.'

'Okay. You know when you meet a woman . . .' she was suddenly aware that she had talked a lot about her relationship problems and desires but knew nothing of his '. . . or a man, I don't know what your preference is. But anyway. It's that sense you get when you meet someone you're attracted to. A strong feeling. It's that little something that tells you they feel the same.'

Curtis pressed his lips together. 'I don't tend to have strong feelings for people either way.'

'I think I probably could have guessed that.' They both went quiet while they pondered this.

'Shall we go through the progress you've made on the emails I sent over and what else I need you to do?' he said eventually.

'Sure.' She got out her list. The young couple hooted with laughter, instantly distracting them. Both Ruby and Curtis leaned into the aisle to get a better look.

Ruby liked Leeds – she'd been a few times. It made a change from Sheffield and it wasn't far away. They had all the good shops too. Some fancy big ones and some interesting little independent ones – neither of which she could afford but she liked looking. They had devised a plan on the train. Or more to the point Curtis had said, 'I suggest we take the ring into the jeweller's and ask them if they can contact the purchaser for us.' And Ruby had agreed.

They entered a stunningly beautiful Victorian arcade with a glass-domed roof and intricate tiled floor. The jeweller's was tiny and had an entry bell. Curtis went to push it and Ruby stopped him.

'Hang on.'

'Why?' Curtis stepped back to read the signage. 'This is the right jeweller's.'

'Yeah, but look.' Ruby pointed to a notice in the window, which read 'Robbery 13th April. A number of items were stolen from these premises in an armed raid. Police are looking for any information that will lead to the recovery of the items and prosecution of those involved.'

'Do you think—' began Curtis.

'Well, I do now!' Ruby pulled him away from the door. 'We need to think about this.'

'If it's stolen we need to return it,' said Curtis.

'But if Lewis didn't know it was stolen, he will lose the ring and be out of pocket.'

'But if it *is* stolen, it means we are handling stolen goods and that is an offence.' Curtis's eyes widened.

'Not if you don't know they're stolen.'

Curtis tapped the notice. 'But we do.'

'Not for sure.'

Curtis's expression said otherwise. A face appeared on the other side of the window display, giving them both a start. A smartly dressed woman pretended to rearrange the things on show whilst eyeing them both with a level of suspicion of someone recently robbed.

'Come on,' said Ruby. 'We can't discuss this here.' She started to walk away but Curtis wasn't moving.

'If we knew what was stolen, we would know if the ring

was one of the items or not,' he said, getting out his phone and searching the news. 'No details or photographs on here. It just says jewellery to the value of fifty thousand pounds.'

'Wow,' said Ruby, but then given the price tags she'd seen that was probably only a few handfuls of stuff.

'And I bet this ring is one of them.' Curtis was looking unsettled.

'We can't exactly ask.' A thought pinged into her head. 'But we could pose as a couple looking for an engagement ring. One with yellow diamonds.' Ruby was warming to her plan but Curtis was already shaking his head. She returned to the window and started to peruse the rings and she pointed at a couple.

Curtis moved closer. 'What are you doing?'

'Is the jeweller shop woman still watching us?' she asked.

Curtis checked. 'Yes.'

'Great. Right, here's the new plan.'

Curtis didn't like the new plan and had made that very clear but Ruby was on a mission. They'd been for a walk around the city centre and gone over the plan a couple of times. They were now back in the arcade and approaching the little shop.

'I don't think I can do this,' said Curtis, stopping and backing away.

'Come on, it'll be fun.'

'No, it won't.' He'd gone all rigid and was gripping his laptop bag tightly like a life raft. 'I'm not good at pretending. I was never picked for parts in the school play. I was always the narrator.'

'And I was Dopey – I get that we aren't always suited

to our parts. But all you have to do is follow my lead. Got it?'

'They'll see through the charade and it will end badly. I'm not happy,' said Curtis.

'And now I'm grumpy,' said Ruby.

'Can we please stop calling out dwarves?'

'Look, I know you're uncomfortable about this. But seeing as you're pretending to be getting engaged – and, can I point out, engaged to me – you should be very happy. Ecstatic in fact.' Curtis blinked repeatedly. 'You could do worse, you know,' said Ruby, trying not to be offended by his terrified expression.

'I've not thought about how I would behave if I were betrothed.'

'You're not trying for a BAFTA, Curtis. We just have to look believable as a couple.'

'That's what's worrying me,' said Curtis.

Ruby narrowed her eyes. 'Am I not good enough? Is that it?'

'On the contrary. I'm just not sure we would be a likely pairing.'

Ruby flicked her hair over her shoulder and put her hands on her hips. 'Who do you see yourself with then?'

'Let me think . . .' Curtis took an inordinate amount of time. Eventually he shook his head.

'Exactly,' said Ruby, trying to calm herself down. She pressed the doorbell before Curtis came up with any more excuses. The door buzzed open. Ruby grabbed Curtis's hand and pulled him reluctantly inside.

The woman behind the glass-topped counter slapped on a smile. 'Good afternoon, how can I help you?'

'We're looking at engagements rings,' said Ruby.

'How lovely. Congratulations.'

'Thanks,' said Ruby. She gave Curtis's hand a squeeze.

'Thank you?' he said but somehow made it sound like a question.

'Did you have something in mind?' asked the jeweller.

Ruby rocked from side to side. 'I'm not sure. You see diamonds are traditional, right?' The woman nodded. 'But I kind of like a bit of colour. I mean I'm going to be wearing it for the rest of my life.' She heard Curtis swallow hard. She rested her head on his upper arm because she couldn't reach his shoulder. He stiffened.

'What sort of budget are you looking at?'

Curtis opened his mouth but Ruby spoke. 'Sky's the limit. My Curtis said I can have exactly what I want.' Curtis's eyes bulged in alarm.

The woman appeared delighted. 'I see,' she said, scanning the shop.

'Nothing too large. I've got dainty fingers.' Ruby waggled her left hand in front of the woman for effect.

The jeweller proceeded to bring out rings one at a time for Ruby to look at. She fell in love with a ruby and diamond twist and was admiring how pretty it looked on her finger when Curtis coughed, bringing her back to reality.

'Do you like this one?' she asked him.

'But . . . I . . . er . . . we're not . . .'

Ruby could sense he was going to blurt something out so she did the only thing she could think of and kissed him quickly on the lips. She figured the shock would keep him quiet for a while. Curtis stopped talking but was now blushing from the collar up. 'It's so adorable when you can't find the words – that's why I love you,' she said tilting her head at him admiringly for the jeweller's benefit. 'You know what? I love yellow,' said Ruby. 'And I quite fancied the ring you showed us with the three stones. I don't suppose you do one like that but with yellow stones?'

'We can make one. We did one with a stunning central yellow sapphire.'

'Diamond,' said Ruby a little more sharply than she'd intended. 'You can get diamonds in yellow. Right?'

'Of course. It would be a special order but we could have that made up within four to six weeks to your exact design. It would be in the region of—'

'Do you not have one available to buy today?' Ruby leaned forward a little. Curtis was still busy turning red.

'No, I'm sorry.'

'So you don't have one with yellow diamonds in the shop?' asked Ruby. The woman gave her a puzzled look and Ruby worried that she'd said too much. 'Only I thought I remembered seeing one in your window ages ago. But I might have been mistaken.'

'It's not a piece that I can recall. But then I was working at our York store until a couple of months ago.'

Ruby felt her shoulders sag. 'You've been really helpful. And given us lots to think about.' She turned to Curtis who was now looking like rigor mortis had set in. 'Hasn't she, darling?'

'Yes?' said Curtis.

'Let us mull over everything and hopefully we'll see you again very soon. Thanks,' said Ruby and she gave Curtis a tug to get him moving.

Outside she let out a puff of a breath. Curtis still appeared somewhat stunned. 'You okay?' He blinked. She realised he had a smudge of her lipstick across his top lip. 'You might want to . . .' She pointed and he seemed to snap out of his trance.

'What?'

153

'Lipstick. Sorry.' Although she wasn't that sorry. His lips had been soft and she'd caught a hint of a rather nice aftershave. 'That was a big waste of time.'

He rubbed a thumb over his lips. 'And now we can never take the ring back because they'll know we were lying all along.'

He had a point.

Kim had had a quiet morning in the shop. Mondays always were. But it was a good day to do admin. It was surprising how much admin there was with a florist – it definitely wasn't all petals and bows. She'd not heard from Adrian since Saturday. After Hayley had arrived it had all felt a bit awkward. Hayley had said 'Hello' but after that she'd pretty much monopolised her father. If Kim was being paranoid she would have said Hayley was actively excluding her. Kim had made her apologies and left.

She'd been doing a lot of thinking about Boomerang and as the only other person who had seen him, she would have liked to have chatted things over with Adrian but she reminded herself theirs was simply a casual friendship, as Adrian wasn't ready to move on from Justine, so she decided to leave it.

There was a flurry of activity at lunchtime and then it went quiet again, giving her time to make a phone call.

'Hi, Margaret. It's Kim. I visited your rescue centre on Saturday.'

'Hello. Now have you made a decision? Is it the yorkie? I've got a ten-pence bet on with myself that it's the Yorkshire terrier.'

'She is lovely but no. I wanted to have a bit of a chat. You see I can't get Boomerang out of my mind and I know you're going to say he has issues but I really want to give him a home.'

There was a long pause. 'Kim, I'll be honest with you. A part of me wants to hand him over immediately but I'm desperate for him to have a forever home. And that's the issue. The last two homes couldn't cope and each time he comes back he's a bit more damaged.' Kim's heart actually ached. 'We've been here twice before and I can't do it to him again.'

'Okay. How about you coach me?' Kim was making it up on the spot but she'd never felt like this about an animal before. 'I can come to the kennels every evening and all day on a Sunday, if that helps, and we'll do whatever we have to do to help Boomerang adjust.'

'I don't know,' said Margaret.

'And I'll only bring him home if and when you're happy that it's going to be his forever home. What have you got to lose?' Kim could sense Margaret was wavering.

'I guess we could give it a try. Kim, this isn't going to be easy. He's a very troubled little chap.'

'I know but I'm up for the challenge. Thanks, Margaret, you won't regret this. I'll see you later.' Kim was over the moon.

Chapter Seventeen

It was Tuesday lunch break and Ruby and Kim were catching up on each other's time off as they always did on a Tuesday. Ruby had brought Kim up to speed on yesterday's Leeds trip and had now fully explained about the part-time admin she was doing for Curtis and thankfully Kim was fine about it. Ruby was logging all her hours in one of the many spreadsheets Curtis had shared. He had travelled down to London this morning to set things up for the testing but was continually sending her emails, so she'd switched off her phone.

'Wow, you're getting a dog?' asked Ruby, pausing briefly in between eating her sandwich.

'It's going to be a slow process. I saw him last night and he won't stay still unless he's eating. I fed him. Margaret said it would help the bonding process. But he just hoovered it up, had a poo and went back to being crazy.'

'Sounds like a typical bloke to me,' said Ruby with a chuckle.

'Not all men are like that.'

Ruby hoped any Curtis found for her were an improvement on her past experiences. 'You never know, I might meet someone in my new executive assistant role.'

'Ooh, how about Curtis?' Kim was leaning forward.

'No, not Curtis.' The memory of her kissing him flashed into her mind. 'It opens me up to meeting new people that's all. And I have a backup plan if that doesn't work.' She liked having two plans – it made her feel in control of her life, something she hadn't felt for a while.

'Another dating app?' asked Kim.

'No. It's a sperm donor.' Ruby fixed her smile and watched the one on Kim's face slide away to leave something resembling stunned mullet. Kim opened her mouth a couple of times but closed it again. 'Well, say something,' Ruby prompted.

'Sorry, Ruby. It's just, a sperm donor . . . that feels like something someone does as a last resort.'

'It is. I've mined the dating cesspool and it's full of crap. IVF is too expensive. This way works better.'

'But you're still young. I'm sure if you keep looking you'll find someone.'

'I don't feel young. I'm almost thirty-five and I know you're trying to help but the soul-mate connection thing you and Vince had is one in a million. Most have to settle for someone who is far from ideal and I don't want to settle. I don't want to muddle along with someone who is bearable, because inevitably it'll end and then I'll not only be a single mum, I'll also have an idiot ex I have to see regularly. Most likely someone I now detest and who loathes me but despite that we'll slap on fake smiles every Friday when we hand over the poor kid. I'll spend the weekends thinking about what lies and junk food he's feeding them. We'll argue over who should pay for school uniform and then he'll go over the top with Christmas and birthday presents just to make me feel bad. And then he'll find "the one" and she'll be amazing and my child

157

will end up wanting to be with their new mummy more than me.' Ruby stopped because she could feel panic rising.

'Wow, you really paint a picture don't you?' said Kim, her eyes wide.

'If I can't have the full-on fairy-tale romance then I'll do it my way.'

'With a donor? What will they put on the birth certificate for the father?' Kim was looking pained.

'Same as they would if it was any one of my exes – just another wanker,' said Ruby with a smirk. 'I didn't find me a Vince so . . .'

'Right.' Kim was giving her an odd look. 'The thing about Vince and me is . . .'

But the door chimed and Ruby leaped to her feet. 'I'll go.' She didn't want to give Kim an opportunity to pull apart her backup plan. Despite her protestations she was on very wobbly ground with the sperm donor idea but the more she thought about it the more she felt it was the right answer. Dating was exhausting: the constant being on show and having to feign interest and be charming and funny. And how long into a relationship before you knew it was right enough to start a family? That could take years.

The customer was Dean. 'Ruby, you're back. Hallelujah! I'm at the "I want you to know I think you're special" stage, you know?'

'Kim said you were in on Friday but this sounds like it's moving fast.' Dean usually spent a lot longer in the wooing stage, which proved lucrative for the flower shop.

'But when you know, you know. What can I say? She's special,' said Dean, going all coy.

'Then we need lilies and lots of them. As long as she doesn't have a cat.' Ruby paused.

'No, she's got tropical fish. Why do you ask?'

'Lilies are very poisonous to cats.'

'Ah, Ruby, you think of everything.' Dean got out his wallet and Ruby set to work selecting the prettiest blooms for the bouquet. She wondered what went wrong with Dean's relationships. He always seemed thoughtful and attentive and yet they always ended. 'And something extra special on the card. Okay?'

'Sure,' said Ruby, clicking on her pen. At least she was helping someone get their fairy tale even if she couldn't sort one for Lewis and she wasn't likely to get one herself.

That evening Ruby couldn't decide on anything to watch so was quite pleased when Curtis called. He'd been quiet after she'd kissed him in the jeweller's, which was a bit awkward. She'd been looking at old photographs – always a double-edged sword. The memories made her smile but also brought on what she called happy-sad tears. Making her feel happy and incredibly grateful to have had the loving mother she'd had but they also brought her grief to the surface. A picture of Ruby as a toddler on the beach with a bucket on her head was on the top of the photo pile; it was a photograph she couldn't remember being taken although her mother had told her the story so many times she could picture every detail, almost smell the salt in the air and hear the seagulls. It gave her an idea.

Curtis gave her an update on a number of things she didn't understand but it made her feel like part of the team and it was still better than binge-watching something for the sake of it.

'Both Bob and Cordelia have asked after you,' he said. Now she was interested. 'What did they ask?'

'Only mundane and perfunctory matters but I think

it's a good sign from Bob. I know he's a little shorter than your ideal but would you like me to make enquiries on your behalf about his likelihood to engage romantically with you?'

'No, thank you.' She was already becoming practised in responding in a calmer manner to Curtis's unconventional suggestions. He was only trying to help.

They covered off a few things on the spreadsheet and Curtis seemed satisfied, although it was hard to tell – he was never going to go over the top with praise.

'Are you happy with what I'm doing so far, Curtis?'

'Happy?' She'd clearly used the wrong word.

'Is it okay?' She was pretty sure he would say if things weren't up to scratch.

'Yes. Your work is of an acceptable standard. I would even say good in places. You are definitely saving me time and I am happy with our arrangement. Although, I feel I may be failing on my side as we don't have many prospective males as yet.'

'That's fine, Curtis. It's only day two and it was always a long shot.'

'Bye then.'

'Hang on,' said Ruby. 'I've been thinking about what you said yesterday. About not having fun and working all the time. And I don't think it's good for you.'

'I'm not sure I follow.' She could sense the tension in his tone.

'I think you need to have more fun and I'm adding it to my spreadsheet.'

'And what exactly will it entail?' he asked. She was pleased that it wasn't a straight no.

'I haven't decided yet but it's not healthy to work all the time. The brain can't operate at that level for long

160

periods. I read somewhere that taking a break means you come back better than before, meaning it would be beneficial to you to have a day off. Especially as you've got some long hours coming up with the testing in London,' said Ruby, feeling that she'd put forward a good case. There was silence from Curtis and she could imagine him considering her argument. 'I've pencilled in Sunday as your day off.' She went into his calendar and updated it as she spoke.

'Right. Okay. I'll not do any work on Sunday. Thank you . . . I think.'

'You won't regret it!'

'I strongly suspect that I will.'

Kim wasn't sure why she kept putting off telling Ruby about Vince. She'd had a couple of opportunities but when she'd tried to get the words right in her head they seemed like a jumble. And then the moment had passed. She knew what was really stopping her – she was afraid of what Ruby would think of her. She didn't like what she thought of herself, let alone what Ruby would make of it.

Kim knew lying all this time hadn't been the smart thing to do but the longer it had gone on the harder it was to come clean. Like Adrian, she'd valued being able to talk about Vince in the way she wanted to remember him – the loving and attentive husband. She hadn't wanted to face the fact that at some point she must have stopped making him happy. Or maybe the acupuncturist made him happier – she'd never know. Over time things had felt better and she had moved on. What she needed to do now was work out what she was going to say to Ruby and just do it. But that was easier said than done.

She was now visiting Boomerang every day after work

and, although it was early days, she felt they were making a tiny bit of progress. He'd taken a couple of morsels of food out of Kim's hand and he'd stood still long enough for her to give him a bit of a fuss – she'd felt like she'd won the lottery. It was baby steps but it was progress and she was content to go at a pace that suited Boomerang. There was no rush.

Friday came around and with it a flurry of customers. Some days it was completely straightforward and others it was anything but. Kim was dealing with a miserable-looking man in his forties who was there because, in his words, he needed 'something to get the wife off my back'.

Kim had suggested all manner of floral arrangements and plants and they were now back at the cheapest bunch, which was where they'd started twenty minutes ago.

'Maybe I should get her something else. I mean flowers are going to die anyway right?'

She gave him her best fake smile. 'Yes, and so are we.' *Some of us sooner than we planned if you don't make a decision,* she thought. Her menopausal rage was rising. 'What's it to be, flowers or no flowers?' She gritted her teeth.

'Go on then.' He made it sound like he was doing her a favour. 'But I want ones that'll last, not just what you want to get rid of.'

'Right.' Kim took his money and began putting together a mixed spray – he wouldn't be getting a penny more than what he was paying for.

'You can put some more leaves in,' he said pointing to the myrtle. 'They're free, aren't they?'

'No, it's a filler but it still costs money.'

'But if you get it free out of fields you shouldn't be charging for it,' he said.

162

'Myrtle doesn't grow wild in this country. I buy it from the wholesaler the same as the blooms. Do you want extra myrtle or not?' The snap in her voice made them both flinch.

'No, it's okay.'

Kim finished the spray, wrapped it in cellophane and floral paper and handed it over.

'What, no bow?'

She was ready to shove the flowers somewhere uncomfortable when in walked Adrian and with him came an air of positivity. He waited while she finished serving the awkward customer.

'Sorry, no bow with the basic bunch. Anything else?'

'No.' He turned to leave.

'Have a lovely weekend and I hope your wife enjoys her flowers.'

'Another happy customer?' asked Adrian as the grumpy man left.

'Something like that. What can I do for you?'

'A couple of things. Did you see in the local paper there have been a spate of burglaries?'

'Yeah, it was the talk of the bakery when I went to buy lunch. Not much to nick from a florist though and I cash up every night.'

'Still, be careful,' said Adrian, giving her a look that made her feel that he really cared about her welfare.

She felt a bit self-conscious. 'Anyway. We've got some beautiful pale pink peonies in. Would you like some of those for Justine's bouquet? Maybe with a couple of roses and some gypsophila?'

'Sounds terrific.' He hovered nearby while she made up the bouquet. 'Actually, Kim, I saw an advert for something I thought you might be interested in. They're streaming

163

a couple of Michael Frayn plays live to cinemas and I wondered if it was your sort of thing. It's cheaper than the theatre . . . but that's not why I'm asking. I'd happily pay for the theatre. It's just . . .'

Kim watched his colour rise and felt something flutter in her gut. Then she gave herself a mental shake. They were friends, nothing more, despite her wishing that they could be. 'Sure, when are they?'

Adrian took a breath. 'This Sunday is the next one.'

'I'd love to.'

'Then I'll get tickets.'

'If you're paying for those, then I'll shout us a pizza beforehand.' Kim always liked to pay her way.

'Great.' He beamed a smile and she felt herself mirror him. It was contagious. 'I could pick you up at six?'

'Ah, that kind of clashes with my daily Boomerang visit. But it's Sunday so I could go earlier.'

Adrian smiled. 'How about I pick you up at five, we visit Boomerang and then go for a bite to eat before the show?'

'That sounds great.' Kim tucked a stray piece of hair behind her ear and made a mental note to do more with her hair.

Adrian paid and took his flowers. Kim watched him leave.

'Wa-hey! Someone has a date,' said Ruby, emerging from the back room and flinging the beads wide, attempting to make a grand entrance but failing badly as she got tied up in them.

'It's not a date. He's a friend.'

'A friend you go on dates with,' said Ruby, twisting out of the grasp of one string of beads only to get wrapped in another – this time her hair got caught. 'Argh! Help, I'm stuck.'

'Serves you right,' said Kim, wondering if there was anything suitable in her wardrobe for a non-date.

'If you help me escape, I'll show you the super-cute chicken toy I bought for Boomerang.'

'That's sweet of you.'

'You see I'm a good person who needs to not be tied up in these things.' Ruby rattled the beads like they were chains.

'But it might be a bit early for toys for Boomerang. Could you keep hold of it and you can give it to him when he's a bit calmer?'

'Sure. Can you untangle me . . . please?' asked Ruby.

'I'll think about it.'

'Kim!'

Chapter Eighteen

By the time Sunday came around Ruby was beyond excited. She had done some planning and had got lots of things lined up. She had loaded up her car and double-checked she had everything they needed. It was just after nine when she buzzed the bell on Curtis's hotel room. Ruby rocked on her heels as pent-up excitement threatened to overflow. She was about to ring it again when she heard the lock turn and got the distinct sense she was being peered at through the spyhole. She leaned in and grinned. The door opened a fraction.

'Ruby? Is everything all right?' asked Curtis with a yawn.

She looked him up and down. 'You're not dressed.' She was beyond surprised.

'No, I was late to bed. You see I was busy with something . . .'

'Oh, crap.' Ruby lowered her voice. 'Is she still here?'

'Who?'

'The woman you were getting busy with.'

'What are you talking about?' Curtis scrunched his eyes up and then pinged them wide as if trying to wake himself up. 'You'd better come in.'

'Great.' She followed him in and shut the door. 'Why the lie-in?'

'I didn't get to bed until the early hours because, like we agreed, I am taking today off so there were a few things I wanted to get done.'

'Okay. Great. I'll wait while you get showered and changed.' She waved her hands in the direction of the bedroom to encourage him to hurry up.

Curtis ran his hands over his face. 'I'm sorry but I'm rather confused as to why you're here.' Both his cheeks twitched at the same time.

'For our day out.' She resisted the urge to do a ta-dah.

'Day out?' Curtis puffed his cheeks. 'No, sorry you'll need to explain further.'

'We arranged it. I said you needed a day off to recharge your batteries and I promised you that you'd have fun.'

Curtis took a step back. 'Then I'm afraid there has been a grave misunderstanding. I thought having a day off meant not working not . . . not . . . whatever you have planned.'

'Curtis, relax. It'll be fun. I promise. Now be quick or we'll miss the best bits.'

'Right.' He hesitated before disappearing into the bedroom but was back a nanosecond later. 'What should I wear?'

'Do you have anything here other than a suit?'

'Only my gym kit.'

'Perfect. Now go.' And she shooed him back into the bedroom. 'And bring your swimming shorts too.'

The early June sunshine was warming things up when Curtis appeared at the car, his hair wet from the shower, wearing a plain white T-shirt, black shorts and carrying a rolled-up towel. 'Are we going swimming?' he asked.

'All will be revealed. Hop in.'

167

Curtis did up his seatbelt and stared ahead. He looked apprehensive and on red alert. Ruby had been keen not to give anything away but she didn't like the tense vibe he was emitting and she wanted him to enjoy the day.

'Curtis, please relax. Today is all about you having fun. There's nothing to worry about. Trust me,' she said.

Curtis nodded slowly. 'Okay,' he said, but as soon as she set off, he gripped the seat. She quickly glanced across – his teeth were clenched and he kept flinching.

'There's no rush, is there?' He shot a look at her speedometer and sighed at its reading, then gave a dramatically sharp intake of breath.

'What?' snapped Ruby, scanning the road for a hazard she'd surely missed.

'I didn't put the *please clean my room* sign on the door.'

'Bloody hell, Curtis! I thought I'd hit something.'

To try to divert his attention from her driving, she suggested a game.

'I don't think you should be distracted from driving,' he said.

'It's going to take us about an hour and a half to get to where we're going.' She glanced over and saw the fear in his eyes and knew a game was definitely the right thing. 'Let's play Shag, Marry, Push off a cliff.'

'What now?' His voice rose in alarm.

Ruby snorted out a laugh. He was funny. 'You know. The one where you pick three people and the other person has to say whether they would shag, marry or push them off a cliff.'

Curtis chewed his lip. 'Why would I want to push anyone off a cliff?'

'Curtis. It's not real. It's a game. Lighten up. I'll go first.' She had a brief think before deciding on her three that she felt were fairly straightforward. 'Okay. Anne Hathaway—'

'Shakespeare's wife?'

'No, the actress.' Curtis's jaw tightened, but she continued. 'So, Anne Hathaway, Michelle Obama and Demi Lovato.'

'Who is Demi Lovato?'

It was going to be a long journey.

Ruby parked the car. Curtis let go of the seat and flexed his knuckles until the colour started to return. They'd had a good if somewhat quiet trip with very few hold-ups and they found a parking space not far from the beach.

'Welcome to Cleethorpes!' announced Ruby, splaying her arms and almost whacking Curtis in the face.

'I wasn't expecting that,' he said. She wasn't sure if he meant Cleethorpes or the near smack in the face.

Ruby got out of the car. 'Curtis, you are going to have fun today even if it kills me.'

'I do appreciate what you are trying to achieve. And I promise I will embrace my day at the beach.' He held his towel aloft and smiled at her.

'You can leave your swim stuff. We won't need that until later.' Curtis returned his rolled-up towel to the footwell like a child being asked to leave their toy behind. 'First up, it's the fun fair,' she said, locking the car with a flourish. Curtis's smile slid away.

Fifteen minutes later they were choosing rides. There was actually a point where Ruby thought he was going to vomit and that was just in the queue while they were watching the ride spin above them. His face was the same colour as his T-shirt.

They climbed into their seats and she could hear Curtis

sucking in deep breaths. She started to feel a bit guilty that she was stressing him out. 'You can bail out. I don't want today to be traumatic.'

'No. I read a book called *Feel The Fear and Do It Anyway* and this is a good opportunity to put that theory to the test.' Curtis gripped the safety bar.

'Can I give you some advice?'

'Yes, please do. Unless it is make sure your will is up to date because, thankfully, I've already done that.' Curtis flinched as a kiddies' coaster whizzed by behind him.

'Curtis, you're not going to die. I promise you. That's exactly what you have to remember. That's kind of the whole point of fun fair rides and roller coasters. You think you're going to die, but you're not. You're quite safe. Relax and enjoy being scared.'

Curtis was mouthing the words 'enjoy being scared' when there was a jolt and the ride started to move. They were in a small cage for two people on the end of a long arm. Both the arm and the cage rotated whilst the whole thing was turning like an errant Ferris wheel.

Ruby threw her hands above her head and screamed. Curtis clutched the safety bar and screamed – a very different sort of scream. 'You're safe!' she shouted at him. 'Let go!'

He held on tight. Ruby thumped his fingers and he instantly let go. She started to laugh and after a brief pause Curtis did too. Every time they twirled, he squealed and it made them both laugh more.

When the ride ended Ruby had a stitch from laughing so hard. She had to help Curtis off as his legs had gone to jelly. 'Okay, something less manic now,' she said, leading him to the dodgems.

'You should be good at this,' said Curtis.

He spent the whole time trying to avoid people whilst Ruby happily careered into as many others as she could. But it was good to see him laughing. After the dodgems they had a go at throwing beanbags at cans where Ruby won a garish pink teddy bear and gave it to Curtis. They went back to the car and collected some things from the boot and headed down to the beach.

The sun was shining – it was the perfect sunny June day. Great swathes of golden sand stretched in both directions but Ruby knew where she wanted to set up camp. It was where she and her mum had been going as far back as she could remember. There was a wide stretch of beach near the leisure centre and whilst there were people there, it wasn't heaving. They found a good spot and settled themselves. Ruby had brought two picnic rugs, which she laid out and weighed down with stones. She flopped onto one of them, opened up the cool box and handed Curtis a beer.

'Ham or cheese and pickle?' She waved two foil-wrapped packages at him.

'Cheese and pickle, please.'

They sat and ate whilst they watched the water gently lap the sand. Children ran to the edge, dipped a toe in, screamed and then retreated. Parents smothered their children in sun block until they looked paler than Curtis had on the fun fair ride. Ruby handed him some sun cream, then pulled off her T-shirt to reveal a red bikini underneath. 'Can you do my back please?'

There was a brief pause from Curtis. 'Of course.'

She rolled over and he very gently rubbed the cream across her shoulders.

'Thanks. Shall I do you?' she asked.

'No thank you. I'm keeping my top on.'

'You'll get those weird T-shirt tan lines,' she warned.

'I think I can live with that.' He proceeded to cover any exposed flesh with sun cream.

'Right. Cricket!' Ruby jumped up, produced wickets, and a bat and a ball from her bag and handed the children's sized bat to Curtis who regarded it with interest.

'Cricket?' He was grinning.

'Beach cricket,' she said and she stuck her tongue out. Ruby marked out a pitch in the sand and Curtis disputed its size. 'Right, let's get a few people involved.' Ruby soon rounded up a couple of families and before long they had a full-scale cricket match on their hands. One of the dads was taking it all a bit too seriously and wouldn't let the kids have a go until he was out and that was proving hard to do.

'Throw me the ball,' said Curtis. 'I'll bowl.'

Ruby had her reservations, Curtis didn't strike her as the sporty type, but it wasn't a real cricket ball so he couldn't do too much damage. He eyed up the batsman who swung the bat around a bit in preparation for whacking it into the sea again. Curtis took a few strides up the beach, turned and then ran and bowled with a perfectly straight arm. The wickets almost jumped out of the sand as the ball hit them straight on. The kids all rejoiced and the dad walked off scratching his head.

'You can bowl!' said Ruby, unable to hide her surprise.

'Harry taught me. He came to every cricket match I ever played in.'

Ruby wanted to hug him but instead she settled for a slap on the back. Curtis really got into it and was terrific at helping the kids to beat the adults; only a few times did she have to step in over boundary disputes. Everyone had fun together but especially her and Curtis. He seemed to relax into the familiarity of a game he clearly loved. He even copied her little dance when he hit a six – but only until Ruby put her hands on her hips and gave him a look.

Cricket over, they returned to their rugs and after a lot of persuading Curtis changed into his swim shorts whilst lying under a towel. He tiptoed his way into the sea as far as his ankles. Ruby took a few steps back and then ran into the water, sending spray in every direction. Including all over Curtis.

'Whoa!' he yelled, trying and failing to avoid the icy droplets.

Ruby dived under the surface, re-emerged and waved at Curtis to join her.

'Don't splash,' he said, his voice going all school-teachery.

'Is that a dare?'

'It's a request. Please.'

'You've got three seconds before I splash. Three . . .'

'You wouldn't.'

'Two . . . One!' But before she could start Curtis had dived under the water. He popped up a few feet away and she had to swim to reach him. He powered away from her and she gave chase. After a couple of minutes he stopped swimming, turned onto his back and kicked his feet, frantically splashing Ruby's face.

'It's all right once you're in, isn't it?' said Ruby.

'It's my first time in the sea.'

'No way!'

'I remember paddling once but I wasn't keen. I used to sit and read.'

'But you can swim.'

'Lessons at the swimming pool,' he explained.

'How posh,' said Ruby. 'My mum taught me to swim here.' She looked back to the shore and could almost see her mother waving and clapping with pride at her first doggy paddle.

'Race you to the breakwater,' he said and he was off before she could reply.

They dried out on the beach until Ruby produced the buckets and spades. Curtis eyed them warily. 'I am not four,' he said.

'No, but do you remember being four and how much fun building sandcastles was?'

His lips lifted at the corners briefly. 'Perhaps. But I'm an adult now.'

'Do you know anyone here, apart from me?'

Curtis scanned the beach. 'No.'

'Then what's the problem?' She thrust a bucket at him before he had a chance to object. 'Get digging.'

Curtis proved to be an enthusiastic if somewhat picky sandcastle builder. After a lot of adjustments, they stood back to admire their handiwork. A large central mound of sand with four resplendent turrets was encircled by a moat with a painstakingly built bridge.

'Good job, Curtis. Now you get to jump on it.'

Curtis looked horrified. 'I couldn't.'

'That's the best bit.' She grabbed his hand. 'One, two, three!' And they both jumped.

After a bit more paddling and people-watching, Ruby declared they had a train to catch. They packed up their things and wandered back up the promenade.

'But we came by car,' Curtis pointed out.

'Ahh, you'll see,' said Ruby with a wink. She wasn't sure why she winked. It wasn't usually something she did. It was, however, something her mother had used to do. She remembered seeing her mum wink and feeling a little flurry of excitement that something good was coming. Curtis didn't appear to be reacting the same way she used to do. Although he didn't look quite as terrified as he had earlier in the day, which was progress.

'Quick,' said Ruby, breaking into a jog.

They came to a halt by a small white land train ornately decorated and almost full of people. 'This is the lollipop train,' said Ruby. She paid the driver and hopped on board, making space for Curtis.

The driver came around and handed each of the children a lollipop. 'Ahh,' said Curtis.

'Ta-dah!' said Ruby, pulling two lollipops from her bag.

They sucked their lollipops and watched the Cleethorpes seafront go by as the train pootled along, showing them the sights of Cleethorpes beach including donkey rides and the garden, eventually coming to a stop near the pier and the car park. They dumped their beach stuff and Curtis went to get in the car, his lollipop stick sticking out of the corner of his mouth.

'Where do you think you're going?' asked Ruby.

'Home?'

'Nope. Still loads to do. Come on.' She linked her arm through his and they walked back towards the pier and then a little further on until they reached the crazy golf.

'I had better warn you that I am a reigning champion,' said Ruby, handing him his putter and blue golf ball.

'Then you can show me what to do.' He gave her a warm smile. At last it seemed Curtis was relaxed.

They giggled their way around the course, tackling pirate ships, tunnels and castles until they reached the last hole. Ruby totted up their scores. 'I won by one point!'

'I demand a recount,' he said, making a grab for the scorecard and missing.

After a brief tussle she handed it over. He scanned the numbers. 'It's a draw,' he said, breaking into a grin.

They had a friendly discussion as they walked to the pier. Cleethorpes pier was shorter than most after the council dismantled a great chunk of it during World War Two, fearing the Germans would use it should there be an invasion. It might not have been as impressive as the likes of Cromer or Brighton but it held a special place in Ruby's heart. It was where they had scattered her mum's ashes. But she had lots of happy memories too. She remembered sitting on the pier and eating ice creams and the many times she'd tried and failed to catch a crab with a crab line and a piece of bacon rind.

'Are you okay? asked Curtis, touching her arm.

'I just zoned out. I'm fine.' She'd been dreading coming back to Cleethorpes but with Curtis to focus on she'd surprised herself and enjoyed it.

'What now?' asked Curtis.

'I present to you the country's largest fish and chip shop,' said Ruby, throwing out her arms and gesturing to the enormous restaurant taking up the lion's share of the pier.

'Let me pay for these.'

'Nope. Today is on me,' said Ruby, joining the queue.

They made their choices, paid and collected the orders. Clutching the warm packages, they walked until they found a bench and sat down to eat their food out of the wrappers with a wooden fork – just as you should at the seaside.

'Why do fish and chips always taste better at the seaside?' mused Ruby.

'I don't know,' said Curtis. 'I do know they taste better with you.' It caught her off-guard and she wasn't sure how to respond. Thankfully a large gull swooped down and snatched the chip Curtis had poised on his fork and the comment was forgotten.

Chapter Nineteen

Kim was quite pleased with how her hair had turned out. It had been coloured and now she'd put it up in a messy bun and it looked quite good. Sort of sophisticated but not too fancy. After much teeth grinding she'd settled on a black and white patterned shirt over a vest top and black trousers, which she hoped was smart casual. She reminded herself again that it wasn't a date before adding an extra coat of mascara and redoing her lipstick. She checked herself in the mirror – she looked good. She pledged to make the effort more often – not for anyone else but for herself, because looking good made her feel good too. Recently the menopause had been getting her down and this was just the thing to give her a bit of a boost.

Adrian arrived on time, said lots of nice things about how she looked and had brought some sweets for the performance. He was keen to point out he was happy to pay cinema prices for drinks but drew the line at chocolate that he could get for a third of the price at the supermarket. She agreed – she hated being ripped off.

At the rescue centre, Adrian waited outside the kennel

while Kim took in Boomerang's food. The sky was clouding over but Adrian had a pac-a-mac with him. Kim would have put money on him having been a Boy Scout. For a few minutes they did their usual routine of Boomerang pogoing around like he had a hornet up his bum and Kim talking calmly until eventually he'd take some of the kibble from her hand.

'Look at you two,' said Adrian, his voice low and soft.

'I know,' whispered back Kim, proudly. 'It's not much but each time I see him he improves a little.' With her free hand she gave Boomerang a rub around his ears. Kim put down his food and using a brush Margaret had given her, she went carefully over his brown and white coat. He was definitely getting used to her.

Kim and Adrian chatted nonstop about Boomerang whilst they ate their pizza and were still chatting when they took their seats at the cinema. They settled themselves down and Kim remembered why she hadn't been to the cinema for a while – it was stiflingly warm.

They sat through the usual adverts and then the lights dimmed and someone introduced the live-streamed performance. Kim was quite excited. She was also starting to overheat. A hot flush was surging over her skin. She undid the cuffs of her shirt and rolled back the sleeves – it made no difference. She was thankful for the low lighting; she knew she'd have a sheen of sweat on her face and would be looking quite pink. Her temperature went up another notch. That was it, the shirt had to come off or she'd be reduced to a puddle. She needed to remove it quickly and efficiently and without drawing too much attention to herself. She decided to swiftly pull the shirt over her head. Kim kept her eyes on the screen. She took a deep breath and tugged the shirt off. She rolled it up and shoved it in her bag. Job done. It was a huge relief. She felt instantly cooler. Now she could relax and enjoy the performance.

Kim got lost in the play. It was hilarious and the first half seemed to fly by. The actors left the stage and the cinema screen darkened as the lights went up. Adrian turned to look at her with a broad grin on his face, which suddenly changed to a more startled expression. 'Uh . . . where's your top gone?' he asked.

She was a little narked that he'd drawn attention to her taking off her shirt. There was nothing wrong with her vest top. Although when she looked down she could see there was something wrong – it had disappeared. She was sitting in the cinema wearing just her bra. And not even a fancy one at that. It was a comfy, slightly greying one, of a utilitarian nature.

'Sod it! I must have pulled off my vest top along with my shirt.' She began rummaging in her bag as her temperature shot up again, this time thanks to embarrassment. 'As I get older, I get hotter and not in a good way.'

'Oh, I don't know,' said Adrian. 'Here.' He expertly popped open his travel mac and offered it to her.

She quickly put it on. 'Thanks,' she said, wondering if maybe dissolving into a puddle wouldn't be an entirely better look.

The journey back from Cleethorpes seemed to go way faster than the trip there – why was that always the way? Ruby and Curtis chatted nonstop about the day. It made her realise how much they'd packed into it and whilst she had done it all ostensibly for Curtis, she'd had a brilliant time too. It had made her think of all the fun she'd had as a child and how wonderful her mum was but for the first time thinking about her mother didn't make her want to cry and that felt like a real milestone.

'The size of that seagull? I thought it was going to make off with the whole thing,' said Curtis with a chuckle.

'Your face was a picture. I thought you were going to scream . . . *again*.'

'Hey, that fun fair ride was terrifying. I actually thought my heart was going to stop the first time it went up in the air.'

'Just the first time?' asked Ruby, taking her eyes off the road for a second to give him a look.

'Maybe a couple of times.'

'I can't believe that was the first time you'd swam in the sea.'

'I'm trying not to think about what I might have been swimming in,' said Curtis.

'Yeah, it's probably best you don't.'

Ruby drove into the hotel grounds. It was impressive all lit up by floodlights. She parked near the entrance as it was starting to rain. She stifled a yawn. 'Night, Curtis. Don't forget your towel and pink teddy,' she said.

Curtis undid his seatbelt and twisted in his seat. 'Thank you, Ruby.'

'You're welcome.'

'What made you do it? You must have planned it all.' His eyes seemed to search her face for the answer.

She shrugged even though she knew why. He was still waiting. 'It was what you said about growing up in foster care and not having fun now you're an adult.'

'The two aren't connected. My childhood was fine. I was happy. And lately, I guess I've been caught up in the routine of work. Today made a surprisingly good alternative.'

'I'm glad.' There was something about the intensity of his gaze that made her look away. She yawned. It was a bit of a fake one this time, although she was tired. She always slept well after a day at the seaside. The sea air makes you sleepy – that was what her mother had always said.

He scratched his head. 'Thank you doesn't seem enough. I have to tell you I was somewhat alarmed when you announced our day out this morning but I have genuinely enjoyed it . . . well, apart from on the way there when you inched over the speed limit and the near-death experience at the fun fair. And possibly whatever waste and bacteria I have ingested in the sea water. Apart from those things, I really did have fun. Thank you, Ruby.'

'I had a good time too, Curtis. You need to make sure you make time for fun in the future. Okay?'

'Absolutely. I will put a recurring reminder in my diary.' She could tell he was joking and it was good to see his self-deprecating side.

She rolled her eyes at him. 'Why not go the whole hog and make a spreadsheet?'

He laughed and the sound seemed to fill the small car. 'I might just do that.'

Tuesday rolled around. Kim had been looking forward to her weekly catch-up with Ruby. As soon as Ruby walked in the shop she pointed at Kim.

'You've changed your hair. I like it,' she said.

Kim was pleased. Buoyed by her evening out with Adrian she'd done something similar with her hair again and slapped on a bit of lipstick and she felt better for it. She needed her hair tied back for work. She couldn't be doing with it always flopping in her face and it was better off her neck in case a dreaded flush materialised, but the

182

new messy bun was a huge improvement on her usual 'ponytail in elastic band' effort.

'Ooh, is this the walk of shame?' asked Ruby, scanning Kim's outfit.

'No!' But she was quite pleased that Ruby thought her capable of being out all night and then rocking up to work. Those days were so far behind her they were a mere smudgy dot she'd need glasses to see.

'How was your date?' asked Ruby, putting her bag down in the back room.

'Really nice but it wasn't a date,' said Kim, trying to sound stern and failing.

'Did you get lucky?'

'At my age getting lucky means finding my glasses before I have to buy new ones.'

Ruby gave her a hard stare. 'Did you kiss?'

'Of course we didn't kiss. Friends don't kiss each other.'

'What? Not even a peck on the cheek?' asked Ruby.

Kim glanced up from sorting the flowers in the cooler and Ruby was giving her a disbelieving stare. 'Air kissing isn't *actual* kissing.'

Ruby did an exaggerated pout. 'I think the clue is in the title but okay.' She held up her hands in surrender. 'How was the play?'

Kim gave a brief summary of the performance and then in great detail recounted her bra reveal disaster and Ruby laughed hard, even holding her sides at one point. 'I'm glad you find it hilarious,' said Kim but even she could see the funny side of it now. She'd been sitting in the cinema for a good hour in just her bra. She was thankful there hadn't been more people there to witness it.

'You should have said it was a bikini top.'

'There was no way that industrial hammock was going

to pass as part of a bikini. Not one from this century anyway. Thank goodness Adrian had his pac-a-mac.' Ruby started laughing again. Kim threw a broken stem at her. 'How was your grand day out with Curtis?'

Ruby finally managed to get her giggles under control and started to set up the shop. 'It went well.' She lugged a heavy bucket into place and paused. 'He said he enjoyed it and I really think he did. He thanked me on the day and again yesterday in a formal email.'

'Oh, he *thanked you* on the day, did he? And what format did that thank you take?' asked Kim, managing to squeeze a whole heap of insinuation into her voice.

'We didn't hook up if that's what you're asking.'

Kim was disappointed. 'But might that be on the cards in the future?'

The momentary pause before Ruby spoke said far more than the words that followed. 'No. Definitely not. However, I have had another thought that I wanted to run by you.' Ruby put down a large container of chrysanthemums and bit her lip.

'Go on, then.' Kim was intrigued.

'I'm thinking about asking Curtis to be my sperm donor. And before you give me a million reasons why it's a bad idea, hear me out.' She held out her palm and began counting them off on her fingers. 'One – he's super smart so the child wouldn't struggle at school. Two – he is emotionally disconnected from people, so he'd not want to get involved with parenting. Three – he's local so good Yorkshire stock.'

Kim felt she had to butt in at this point. 'Hey, he's not a prize bull.'

'Don't interrupt but okay noted. Four – he fits my physical criteria because he's tall and doesn't look like he fell out of the ugly tree and hit every branch on the way down. And five – he's loaded so he might do it for free or a reduced price.' She'd run out of fingers. 'And bonus point – he's a business person so would be able to treat this as the simple business transaction that it is.' She folded her arms, her shoulders tense and her gaze fixed on Kim.

Kim was a bit stunned. The argument Ruby had presented was a good one. Kim didn't like being put on the spot but she could see that Ruby had thought this through. It wasn't the way she would have gone about things but she was warming to Ruby's logic and if this was the route she was determined to pursue then someone who could see it as a business arrangement was probably the ideal candidate. Ruby was waiting expectantly for an answer.

'Well, if you're sure this is what you want then . . . I have to admit Curtis seems like the ideal donor.'

Ruby's shoulders relaxed and she smiled. 'Excellent. Then all I need to do now is ask him.'

Chapter Twenty

That evening Ruby curled her feet underneath herself and zoomed in on the spreadsheet she'd created on her phone. It was a pros and cons list for using Curtis as her sperm donor. In fact she had two lists: one was from her perspective and one from his. The latter had been hard to do as she'd had to try to see the situation as he would and getting inside Curtis's head was always going to be difficult. She wanted to be ready with any objections he might raise and needed a strong list of benefits she could persuade him with, although that was proving tricky. All she had on the pros side for Curtis was 'Help out Ruby'. It probably wasn't enough to win him over.

Seymour was curled up next to her. He stretched and opened his wonky eyes. He looked how she felt after studying the spreadsheets on the tiny screen for so long. Surely there were more benefits for Curtis? It would be unkind to say it might be his only opportunity to have children – but given he was one hundred per cent focused on his job and seemed to struggle with people it probably wasn't far from reality. But she couldn't use that, not only because it was mean but also because it implied he would have some sort of involvement in the child rearing and that was exactly what she was trying to avoid by having a donor. She sighed heavily.

She had a lightbulb moment and quickly added: 'Pass on your smarts', then she reworded it so Curtis would understand: 'Pass on your clever genes'. She was uncertain as to whether that would be a strong selling point but it was all she had. She flicked the screen to her own spreadsheet. Her pros list was looking a lot happier. Her only cons were that she didn't want to damage their friendship and she didn't know his medical history but if he had grown up in foster care it was likely he didn't know it either.

She pictured her mum laughing at her making a spreadsheet. Usually when she thought of her, she saw her in the hospital bed towards the end of her life but more recently the images were of her mother laughing. She'd laughed a lot. Despite all the blows life dealt her she was always upbeat. Maybe this approach wasn't what her mum had in mind but Ruby knew if she could have a relationship with her child like the one she and her mother had shared she would be very happy indeed.

Her phone rang. Spookily it was Curtis and she almost dropped it in her fumble to answer.

'Good evening. Ruby Edwards, Curtis Walker's executive assistant,' she trilled.

'You do know it's me?'

'Yes, I'm just showing you how I answer the phone to your customers.'

'Clients.'

'Yeah, those too. Anyway, I'm glad you've called,' she said.

'Why?'

Sod it, she thought. She'd not meant to say that out

loud and now she had to come up with a reason. 'Because . . .' She looked at Seymour and her eyes almost crossed too. 'Because we need to talk about what we're doing about Lewis's engagement ring.' Seymour slunk off for a bite to eat.

'I thought we could post it to the jeweller's,' said Curtis.

'No, not now. I don't want to talk about the ring now.' This was no good – she needed to be face to face to ask him about being the donor.

'Why not?'

She waved her free hand around in the hope of conjuring up another quick and plausible answer. 'Because I think Lewis and his girlfriend deserve better.' What was she talking about? She had no idea. 'I mean we owe it to them to have considered all options . . . perhaps we should draw up a spreadsheet and detail all our attempts to return it. With dates.'

She waited. There was a moment's silence. 'I suppose that would provide a robust audit trail should he ask why it has taken this long to get it back to him.'

'Exactly.'

'I was ringing to ask if you could contact a new client. It's just at the initial enquiry stage but I'm swamped here with the twenty-four-hour testing and I'm struggling to call them back.'

Ruby resisted the pull to apologise. This was another week in London and it was kind of all her fault. 'Of course. Whizz over the details and I'll have a natter to them.'

'Natter? You need to establish what their requirements are and . . .'

'Curtis. I was joking. Chill out. I've got this.'

'Of course. I will email you their details.'

'Great. And shall we catch up when you're back from

London to talk about the ring?' Ruby giggled. 'We sound like Hobbits.' She switched her voice to Gollum. 'My precious.'

Curtis cleared his throat. 'Yes. That's fine.'

'Okay. I'll pick you up from the station on Friday night. Text me what train you're on.'

'Actually that—' But she ended the call. Ruby wanted to see him as soon as he was back. She felt like she'd been waiting to do this for a while already and she didn't want to waste any more time. If he said yes, this time next week she could be pregnant.

Friday in the flower shop was a good one. They'd had a steady flow of customers, all of whom had been happy ones, which added to the general feeling of excitement bubbling away inside Ruby. Today was the day. She'd had multiple trial conversations with Seymour standing in for Curtis where she'd put her well-thought-through plan to him and responded to all of his possible counter-arguments, making her feel ready for the real conversation. Although she feared Seymour would prove to have been slightly easier to convince than Curtis. One whiff of catnip and he was anybody's.

Kim seemed to be having a day of two halves. She'd told Ruby that her shower had packed up and the plumber couldn't come until Monday but on the plus side Adrian was picking her up from work and they were off to see Boomerang together. Ruby had noticed this had become a regular thing as long as Adrian's train got in on time.

An older gentleman came into the shop and Ruby went to serve him.

'Hello, how can I help?'

He checked his list. 'Do you have any chlamydia?'

Ruby blinked and tried to avoid Kim's jiggling shoulders as she failed to control her laughter. 'Well, I hope not.'

'Why, is it not very nice? Because my wife wants some.'

Ruby pressed her lips together to compose herself. 'It depends exactly what you're after. Can I get a look at that list?' she asked. He handed it to Ruby. The writing was appalling and it did look like she'd written trailing chlamydia. 'I'm going to take a guess that she's after trailing clematis. And if it's wrong, keep the receipt and bring it back. Okay?'

'But is it the same thing?' He looked quite concerned.

'No, it's not. Trust me, clematis is a lot nicer. Chlamydia isn't pretty at all.'

He cheered up. 'Okay then, that sounds grand.'

Ruby sorted him out with a purple flowering plant and managed to keep her giggles inside until he was completely outside the shop.

She raced to the back room where Kim was doubled up with laughter. 'You were no help,' she scolded.

'That was a corker. I've had someone ask for pee on knees instead of peonies before but never chlamydia.' Kim pulled herself together. 'Although I did know a Births, Deaths and Marriages registrar who swore blind someone wanted to name their baby Chlamydia.' That set them off again. The door chimed and they both peeped their heads out to see who it was.

Adrian waved back at them. Ruby was relieved it wasn't the elderly man changing his mind and coming back to insist she give him chlamydia.

'I'll just be a minute,' said Kim. She pulled her head back through the beads and straightened her top. She pulled her lipstick from her pocket and added a quick sweep across her lips.

'Only a friend, huh?' whispered Ruby and Kim gave her a playful swipe before she strode nonchalantly into the shop.

'Hi, Adrian, I made up a bouquet for Justine.' She produced the bunch of mixed roses with a flourish.

'They're lovely. I managed to catch the earlier train. I'm a bit early, aren't I?'

'That's fine,' said Ruby, joining them. 'You go; I'll lock up. I'm not picking up Curtis for another hour and a bit. I figured I'd sit here and read my book until I need to get him.'

'You sure?' asked Kim.

'Of course. You two kids go and enjoy yourself,' said Ruby with a friendly smirk.

Kim stuck her tongue out at her as she went to get her bag. 'And you'll cash up and everything?'

'No, I'm planning on leaving the money strewn around the shop and the door wide open with a sign saying, "Help yourselves".'

'That's not funny after all the burglaries.' Kim gave her a long-suffering stare.

'Sorry. Of course, I'll do everything,' said Ruby. 'Go, quick before I change my mind.'

'Thanks, you're a star,' said Kim as she headed for the door.

'Bye,' she said, waving them off.

Ruby checked her watch – ten minutes to closing. She started to pack up the shop. It wasn't likely she'd have any more customers but there was always the odd one who wanted to grab some flowers on the way home. She sorted out the stock, tidied up, hoovered the floor and wiped down the surfaces until the little shop was all spick and span. She put all the old stock to one side and wrapped them up into two makeshift bunches. They weren't good enough to be used tomorrow but they would cheer up Curtis's dad's nursing home and as it was near the hotel, she planned to drop them in on the way. She figured it also wouldn't do any harm to have Curtis on her side before she asked him the big question.

Ruby cashed up. She flicked the lights off in the back room and picked up her bag ready to leave. The bell chimed. *Sod it,* she thought, she'd forgotten to lock the door and turn the sign over.

'Sorry, we're closed,' she said, stepping into the now sparse-looking shop. A man she would have put in his fifties was standing right up against the door. She smiled but he didn't – if anything he looked on edge. Alarm bells started to ring in her head. All the talk of recent burglaries filled her mind. Her exit was blocked. She'd never seen this man before. Her eyes darted to his hands checking for weapons – nothing obvious. She straightened her back. This was one of those moments she really wished she was tall. She raised her chin and her voice. 'I said we're closed.'

He scanned the shop. 'Is the owner here?' He leaned to one side to look past Ruby towards the back room.

'No . . .' As soon as she'd said it she wished she hadn't because now she'd told him she was all on her own. Alone and vulnerable. Her pulse started to thud in her ears. She weighed him up. If it came to fight or flight, he had the weight advantage. She stepped towards the back room. If she had to, she'd grab the scissors off the wall and wield them like a ninja. Or at the very least, a mildly dangerous harpy. 'She'll be back any minute.' Ruby blurted it out in the hope he'd fear being interrupted and leave.

'Right. Then I'll wait.'

Nooooooo! That was not part of the plan. She was trapped in the shop with a burglar. There was no way out. Kim wouldn't be back until tomorrow. Was that when they'd find her body? She was seriously panicking now. 'You can't wait because I have to be somewhere.' Her throat was dry, making her voice sound all wobbly. *Show no fear*, she told herself as she gripped her bag to stop her hands from shaking.

'You all right?' he asked.

'Actually, no, I'm not. I need to leave.' She snaked her hand into her bag. If she could reach her phone without him seeing maybe she could dial 999. Would they be able to work out that she was in a hostage situation?

'How long is she likely to be?' he asked.

'I don't know exactly. She will be back. But you can't wait.' She was making no sense. She bit her lip as she rummaged around her bag with one hand. It was extremely difficult to identify items when you couldn't see them. She had far too much rubbish in her bag. She found something squishy – eurgh, what even was that?

He stepped forward and Ruby thought her heart was going to leap out of her chest. She pulled the first thing she could from her bag and waved it menacingly. They both stared at the rubber chicken. For a moment Ruby was as confused as the burglar. Then she remembered it was the toy she'd bought for Boomerang.

She threw it at his head, shot to the back room and grabbed the scissors. She spun around to find he had followed her.

'That's far enough!' she shouted and she made a stabbing action with the scissors. Although it would have been more menacing had she opened them up.

'Whoa. Calm down. I'm not after any trouble.'

'Then why did you barge in here and corner me?'

'The shop was open and you were acting a bit strange.'

He had a point. 'That's not the point. Who are you and what do you want with me?'

'I've come to see Kim. I'm Vince.'

Chapter Twenty-One

Ruby was a bit dazed. She was sitting in her car just outside the train station, staring out of her windscreen but not really seeing anything. All she could think about was Vince. Vince – the husband Kim said was dead, but it appeared was very much alive and who, once she'd stopped waving the scissors at, had got her a drink of water to help with the shock. The living, breathing man who she thought had come to rob the shop and murder her, but it turned out only wanted to see Kim, his wife. None of it made any sense.

Someone tried the passenger door handle and she screamed. She'd been miles away, trying to understand what Vince had told her.

'You all right?' asked Curtis, sticking his head in the car.

'No. I'm not. I've just had a conversation with a dead man,' said Ruby.

Curtis scanned the back seats. 'Is he still here?'

'What are you on about it?' She didn't need Curtis going all obtuse on her.

'I thought maybe you thought you saw a ghost.'

'Something like that. Get in and I'll tell you on the way to the nursing home. Then we're going to the hotel bar, where we are going to have too much to drink and I'm going to tell you a story that will melt your brain. Then I'll get a taxi home.'

'That crystal ball of yours has been worth the money,' he joked.

She scowled at him. He quickly got in the car and did up his seatbelt.

They had been driving for a few minutes before it registered with Ruby that Curtis hadn't queried her setting out her plans for the evening and inadvertently his. Her head was far too full of Vince for her to contemplate raising the donor issue and that hitched up her annoyance at Kim even further. She'd tried to call her after Vince had left the shop but it had gone straight to voicemail. That was probably for the best. She wanted to see Kim face to face when she challenged her about this.

'It's occurred to me that there may be a reason why you want to get drunk. Is there something wrong?' asked Curtis.

'I didn't mean to take over your evening. I can drop you at the hotel if you like?'

'The plans you have outlined for the evening are fine but that doesn't answer my question. Is there something wrong?'

'You are going to wish you'd not asked,' said Ruby, pulling up outside the nursing home. 'I'll tell you later.'

Inside it was dinner time and the staff were charging about trying to ferry everything from the kitchen while it was hot. Ruby held up the flowers, feeling bad for interrupting.

'I just thought these might cheer up some of the residents,' said Ruby to a stressed-looking young woman carrying a full gravy boat.

'That's such a nice thought. But I'm afraid I don't know when I'll be able to put them in water.'

'If you point me to some vases, I'll do it,' said Ruby.

'Okay. Straight through those doors. Round to the right, you'll find the cleaning cupboard. Top cupboard, top shelf. Help yourself.' And with that she sped off.

'I'll go and have a quick five minutes with Harry if that's okay?' asked Curtis.

'Sure.' Ruby went in search of the vases. She noticed she was grinding her teeth – quite rare for her to do it while she was awake. That's how cross she was with Kim.

She arranged the flowers into three separate vases and by the time she had tweaked the last arrangement she could feel the tension leaving her jaw. Flowers always had a calming effect on her. Ruby took one vase through to the television lounge where a few residents were eating off trays. Nobody looked up. But then to be fair the shepherd's pie did look and smell particularly good. Ruby took the second vaseful into the dining room and was greeted like a returning hero by Dot.

'Look who it is and those flowers! Are they for me?' Dot's face lit up and Ruby instantly felt bad.

'They're for all of you to share.'

'They're beautiful. Here, let's have a sniff.' Ruby wafted the blooms under Dot's nose.

'Gaw-jus,' she said. 'Now sit down and update us on everything.' Dot picked up her fork and carried on with her meal but her eyes never left Ruby.

'Oh, what the hell,' said Ruby. She needed to get it all off her chest. She recalled her encounter with Vince, including wielding the rubber chicken in his face, which she got out for demonstration purposes and had the room in uproar. By the time she'd finished her story and the ladies had gasped and hooted in all the right places Ruby was feeling somewhat unburdened. She caught sight of the clock.

'I need to dash. But I'll be back soon. I promise.' She gave Dot and Kitty a quick hug and jogged off to get the last vase of flowers.

She headed upstairs and found a door with Harry's name on a laminated card slotted into a holder. An odd reminder of how easily replaceable those name tags, and the room occupants, really were. She knocked on the door.

Curtis appeared.

'I brought these for your dad,' she said, offering him the vase.

'You can come in if you like?' As usual he was hard to read but she got a sense that maybe he wanted her to. She went into the room and closed the door behind her.

'Harry, this is Ruby who I was telling you about,' said Curtis. Harry's eyes fluttered open.

'Hi, Harry, I brought you some flowers,' she said, finding a space on the table so he would be able to see them from where he was sitting in bed. He was a slightly built old man with a shock of thick white hair and an oxygen mask covering half his face. 'How are you feeling?' she asked.

Harry gave her a thumbs up. 'The antibiotics seem to be working,' said Curtis, sounding flat.

'That's good then.' Ruby pulled up a chair. 'If you keep on like this, you'll be back training for the London marathon soon enough. Or at the very least you'll be able to join the others in the lounge.' Harry rolled his eyes. 'Oh, now hang on a minute. Am I sensing that you don't get on with someone?' Harry didn't react. 'Or . . . is it the opposite? Is there a someone who you do get on with? Perhaps you'd like to get on with them even better. A certain lady of the female variety. Maybe Dot?' Harry's eyebrows jumped. 'Or Kitty?' Harry started to laugh and it instantly turned into a hacking cough.

Curtis scowled at Ruby as he got to his feet and helped Harry into a more upright position.

'I'm so sorry,' said Ruby, feeling mildly panicked that she'd triggered the coughing fit.

Harry pulled off the mask. 'He said you were feisty. He's not wrong, is he?'

'To be fair I've been called a lot worse,' said Ruby.

Harry's breathing was laboured and he needed to pause before speaking again. 'Thank you for the flowers.'

'I work in a florist's – it's one of the perks. Don't go thinking Dot has a rival for your affections. I don't want to get mixed up in a love triangle.'

Harry beamed back at her before Curtis replaced the oxygen. 'I think we should probably go.'

'Lovely to meet you, Harry. Keep up the good work,' she said. Harry gave her another thumbs up and she could see he was smiling.

They walked back to the car. 'How do you do that?' asked Curtis, shaking his head and glancing back at the nursing home as if he was trying to figure something out.

'Do what? The flowers? It's just practice. The trick is not to try to be symmetrical with blooms. You—'

'Not the flowers. The chat. Despite having known him for over half my life I frequently have no idea what to say. I had been sitting there in silence for at least five minutes. But you . . . You're able to chat to a complete stranger about . . . actually I have no idea exactly what you were talking about but I know that's the most animated I've seen him in weeks. It's the first time he's smiled in a long time.'

'Oh.' For once she didn't know what to say. 'Gift of the gab, my mum used to say.' She tilted her head. 'Verbal diarrhoea my teachers called it.'

'I think it's a gift.'

'Thanks,' said Ruby, liking how good she felt about herself right at that moment.

Kim hadn't been out of the shop all day, but she had seen that it had been chucking it down all afternoon. Thankfully the evening had brought a brief respite although it was still cloudy. Kim and Adrian were waiting for Margaret to let them in.

'I like your top,' said Adrian.

She'd had a good rummage through her wardrobe and discovered a few nice things she'd forgotten all about. She wasn't sure when she stopped thinking about what she was wearing but she was conscious that, of late, she'd been living in jeans and T-shirts and she was enjoying the change. 'Thanks. I'm planning on keeping this one on tonight.'

'That's good to hear.' Adrian scrunched up his shoulders. 'Not that it was a problem last time. And it wouldn't be in the future. You know . . . if you wanted to take your top off.'

Margaret flung open the door and scowled at Adrian, clearly having overheard their conversation. 'Everything all right?' She addressed her question to Kim whilst Adrian ran a finger around his collar.

'All good,' said Kim. 'Keep that pac-a-mac to hand,' she added, smiling at Adrian, and they went inside.

'We had the canine psychologist here for Boomerang today,' said Margaret, her voice gruff.

Kim spun around. 'How did it go?'

'Well . . . that's debatable. I think you'll notice a change in him. Anyway . . .' Margaret marched ahead.

'What does that mean?' asked Adrian.

'I have no idea.'

As they approached, the usual barking started. Margaret shouted and the barking dwindled except now there was one lone ear-splitting solo echoing around the yard. Kim and Adrian looked at each other. 'Boomerang?'

They reached his kennel and received their answer. Boomerang was sitting in the outside run, and for a moment Kim was overjoyed to see him looking calmer but he had his head back and was howling at an ear-bleeding pitch.

'Blimey,' said Adrian, putting his fingers in his ears.

'Boomerang,' said Kim but she got no response. 'Boom – er – ang,' she called in a singsong voice.

The dog stopped howling and looked at her.

'I say, someone has the magic touch,' said Margaret. 'Shall we try taking him for a walk?'

It took a while to get the harness on him. He was over-excited and bounced around like Tigger after a couple of red bulls.

Eventually they were ready to venture out on a walk. Kim held on to the lead tightly whilst Margaret snapped instructions at her. It was beyond stressful. The dog was pulling hard and Kim was surprised by how much power he had. He wasn't a big dog but his power-to-weight ratio was impressive. As was his ability to have his front half off the ground most of the time, like he was trying to take off. Boomerang seemed to think he was in a race and was determined to be first across the finish line.

'Tell him, heel!' insisted Margaret.

'Heel,' said Kim. Boomerang continued to strain against the lead. It was making Kim's arm ache.

'I don't think he's listening,' said Adrian.

'Pull the lead back and tell him,' said Margaret and Kim caught sight of her shaking her head. She was doing her best.

'Heel!' she said firmly and gave Boomerang a tug.

Underfoot it was slippery thanks to the rain and for a moment she skidded. Her heart leaped but she regained her footing. Over the last few days she'd thought about what it would be like to take Boomerang out on lovely long walks – having her arm tugged out of her socket had not featured in those daydreams.

They were doing the same circuit they had done with the Yorkshire terrier and the Labrador – and now they were on the homeward stretch. Kim was looking forward to relaxing the muscles in her arm.

'You okay?' asked Adrian.

'Yes, fine,' said Kim. She figured if he was going to be her dog, she had to get used to walking him. 'I'm sure he'll calm down.'

Margaret snorted a laugh and at the same time Boomerang went into overdrive, catching Kim unawares. She had the lead looped around her wrist as Margaret had instructed, which was good as it meant when the dog lunged, she didn't let go or rather couldn't let go. But this was also bad because the jolt coincided with a particularly slippy bit of track and Kim slid along for a moment like she was water skiing before reaching a grippy bit where her shoes stopped and Boomerang kept going. Propelling her face first into a muddy puddle.

'Boomer!' spluttered Kim. For the first time the dog seemed to respond. He turned around and jumped into the puddle with her, finishing off the job of covering the rest of her in mud.

Adrian was laughing so hard she thought he'd rupture something. And she could imagine the sight she looked, which set her off too.

'Come on, Boomerang,' said Margaret sullenly, taking the lead from Kim and marching off ahead.

Adrian helped Kim to her feet and she dripped muddy water back to the kennels.

'I think that was positive,' said Adrian. They both studied the mud dripping from Kim. 'I meant specifically the part where he came when you called him Boomer.'

'Maybe he doesn't like his name,' mused Kim.

'I like Boomer better.'

'Yes. Me too,' said Kim, flicking some drips off her chin.

By the time they got back, Margaret had already put Boomer back in his kennel and fed him.

'The Yorkshire has been rehomed but the Labrador is still available and we've got a Beagle cross called Sherlock I don't think you've seen,' said Margaret, locking the pen.

'Er, I'm only having the one dog,' said Kim.

'Wonderful.' Margaret looked relieved. 'Which one?'

'That one,' said Kim, pointing at Boomer who was now back to cavorting up and down the length of his enclosure.

'You still want him?' Margaret looked aghast.

'Of course,' said Kim. 'He's a handful but I'm not giving up on him just because of a bit of mud.'

'Terrific. He's come on leaps and bounds thanks to all your efforts. If you're absolutely sure I'll get the papers. And you can take him whenever you like.'

'Great. But not tonight,' said Kim, indicating her muddy coating, which was starting to dry in places, giving her a certain crusty quality.

'Of course. Tomorrow?'

'Yes. Okay.'

'Wunderbar!' said Margaret in a dodgy German accent and she almost skipped off.

'I need to get home and in the shower,' said Kim. 'Oh, crap.'

'Problem?'

'My shower died on me this morning. Plumber can't come out until Monday. Maybe I could get in the washing machine.'

'Come over to mine. You can have a shower and while your clothes are on a quick cycle, we can have a take-away. How about that?'

It sounded perfect. 'I usually only do naked take-away on a Sunday but . . .'

'I'm sure I have something that would fit you. Unless you really wanted to do the naked take-away.'

'I could be persuaded as long as it's nowt too hot . . .' said Kim. 'That's a burn I wouldn't want to have to explain at hospital.'

Chapter Twenty-Two

The hotel bar was sumptuous and swish. Ruby was making her way through a bottle of wine when Curtis joined her, freshly showered and without a tie – his only nod to this being an informal meeting.

'Does your wardrobe consist entirely of suits, shirts and gym kit?'

'Pretty much.' He scanned what he was wearing. 'Drink?'

The barman appeared. The bar was quiet and he looked keen. 'Half a lager shandy please,' said Curtis.

'You might need something stronger once I've told you what I've discovered today.'

Curtis pulled up a bar stool. 'Let's start with the shandy and I'll see.'

Ruby repeated the story she'd told at the nursing home, this time without the rubber chicken and without any interaction from Curtis. When she reached the end, she fixed him with a stare. Curtis remained attentive but gave no response. 'So, what do you think?'

'That Kim has lied to you.'

Ruby rolled her lips together. 'You reckon?'

'Definitely, if the husband she said was dead is in actual fact—'

'I was being sarcastic.'

'Oh, I see.' He sipped his drink.

She needed to give him more pointers on the kind of interaction she was hoping for. 'What I mean is: what do I do?'

'It's not really any of your business.'

Ruby almost toppled off her chair in shock. 'Seriously? Of course it's my business.' She was outraged.

Curtis shook his head slowly. 'No, it's not. She's your employer. This information has no bearing on your job.'

Ruby became animated. 'She's my friend too. And she lied to me.'

'I suppose that may put a slightly different light on things. Although I assume she has a good reason.'

'That's the thing.' Ruby leaned forward conspiratorially. 'Vince says that after he had his heart attack, she wouldn't have anything to do with him. Dumped him when he was in hospital. And since Kim has been lying all this time, I'm inclined to believe him. He said she had some sort of breakdown and even sold their house!' She pulled her head back, expecting Curtis to react to her bombshell but there wasn't a flicker from him. 'You're no fun,' she said, finishing her wine and refilling her glass.

'I am trying though. I made a concerted effort whilst I was in London to incorporate fun activities into my week.' He looked quite pleased with himself. 'I visited the Science Museum, which was most interesting. I crossed both Tower Bridge and the Millennium Footbridge.'

'That's great, Curtis. Well done.' She offered her glass for him to clink and he did but very carefully.

Maybe it was the wine. Or maybe sometimes things

just fell into place. It felt like the right moment to ask him about being a donor. She swallowed hard. 'Curtis, there's something I want to ask you. Let me explain and then I'll take questions at the end.'

'I had something I wanted to share too. But it can wait.'

'Okay.' Ruby paused. Now she was intrigued. 'No go on, you first.' She waved a hand at him. She needed a moment to compose herself anyway because her palms were going all sweaty. She was once again at a pivotal moment in her life.

'It's sort of connected to the fun thing.' He took a deep breath and she sensed he was nervous too. 'You see I've very much enjoyed the time we've been spending together. Especially the trip to Cleethorpes. It was both enjoyable and informative. You've given me a great deal to think about and on some level, I have reassessed my life goals.'

'Go on.' Was this going where she thought it was? Perhaps she'd never need to ask her question. She gave herself a mental slap. Getting free sperm would be a deplorable reason to go out with Curtis. She looked at him afresh as he took a long draw of his shandy. Was that to steady his nerves? Bless him. He was classically good-looking in a Cary Grant black and white movie sort of way. She'd never met anyone like him – although this was probably because there literally was no one like him. He was sweet in a lovely, unspoiled way. He was also quite odd but there was something that drew her to him. Not least that she liked who she was when she was with him. His gaze seemed laden with something. Her pulse quickened as she imagined him leaning forward and kissing her. *What was going on? Where were these feelings coming from?*

207

He cleared his throat. 'The thing I wanted to say was that I'm considering embarking on a relationship . . . with Cordelia.'

Ruby was glad she'd swallowed her mouthful of wine or she may have inadvertently spat it in his face.

'Dressing gowns are underrated,' said Kim, joining Adrian in the kitchen. She was wrapped in a thick white towelling one – it was so chunky she couldn't turn the cuffs back so they covered her hands.

'I never wear one. That was a Christmas present.'

'Well, someone knows their dressing gowns. Washing machine?' she asked, her dirty clothes bundled in her arms.

'Utility room. It's ready to go. Just sling in a pod and shut the door.'

She padded off in the direction Adrian indicated. The utility room was standard and like the rest of the house it was tidy. As she turned around, she spotted a photograph on the wall. Adrian and a woman. It was a selfie where they were both laughing and seeing it made her smile.

'Is this Justine?' she called.

He appeared in the doorway. 'Yes. That's her.' His eyes rested on the picture.

'It's a lovely photograph,' said Kim, now looking at him rather than the picture.

'It's daft really. We were bored waiting for a train and started making silly faces.' His mouth lifted at the corners.

'You look so happy.'

'We were.' She loved how much he still loved Justine even if it did mean there was no chance of them developing a relationship. They exchanged smiles. 'Cup of tea or something stronger?'

'I'd love a gin but I'd better not.'

'Sorry, no gin in the house but let me know what sort you like and I'll get a bottle in for next time.' The doorbell sounded. 'That'll be the take-away – perfect timing,' said Adrian, going to answer it. Kim made herself comfy at the breakfast bar where Adrian had already laid out plates and cutlery.

They'd decided on Mexican and as Kim didn't know much about Mexican food Adrian had ordered while she'd jumped in the shower.

'We have bean enchiladas, chorizo quesadillas, rice, and beef chimichangas. Dive in!'

They helped themselves. 'This is amazing,' said Kim. The flavours were making her taste buds sing.

'I'm glad you like it. We should go to the restaurant sometime. They have some great specials.'

'I'd like that.' Kim went to tuck some hair behind her ear as it was wet and dripping in her face.

'I'm sorry I've not got a hairdryer,' he said.

'Don't be daft. It's better if it dries naturally anyway.' Kim ran her fingers through her sodden mop. She probably looked a fright but it was better than the muddy dreadlocks she'd had earlier.

They chatted and laughed their way through the meal until Kim couldn't fit in any more. She was grateful she was wearing the dressing gown as it was very forgiving in that respect. It was a shame dressing gowns weren't acceptable work wear. Although this one did have a habit of coming loose. She'd had to quickly tighten the belt a couple of times for fear of boob-flashing Adrian over his chimichanga.

She sat back and then remembered that it was a bar stool just in time. Adrian reached out an arm to catch her and they both paused as he held her safely in place. 'So, gin,' said Adrian, righting himself and letting go. 'What's your favourite?'

'Rhubarb, but I'm not fussy really. What's your poison?'

'Wine mainly and tea. I drink lots of tea. Talking of which, I'll pop these in the dishwasher and then make some,' said Adrian, gracefully sliding from his seat.

'Let me help.' Kim grabbed both plates and tried to hop down from the stool. It was easier than it looked. The stool turned slightly catching the open edge of the dressing gown and as her feet met the floor the dressing gown tie gave up and the gown opened. Her naked body was spotlighted perfectly by the kitchen lighting.

Kim gasped, which made Adrian spin in her direction. His eyes went cartoon wide.

At that very moment there was a loud rap on the kitchen window making them both look up. Hayley glared back at them. Kim really wished she'd use the front door like any normal person.

Kim was still holding two dirty plates, which she promptly put down and then quickly gathered the gown around her, while mumbling apologies at Adrian.

'What the hell is going on?' demanded a slightly muffled Hayley from the other side of the window.

'Hayley, love. You remember Kim,' said Adrian. Kim had to admire his easy tone. She was sweating so much she'd need another shower at this rate.

Adrian opened the back door. 'Come in.'

'Hello again,' said Kim, trying to match Adrian's breezy tone but failing. Hayley glared at Kim. 'My clothes got muddy. They're in the washing machine.'

'I bought you that dressing gown for Christmas,' said Hayley, speaking to her father as if Kim wasn't there.

'It's very nice,' said Kim, stroking the material and then stopping herself because it was quite a strange thing to do.

'Anyway . . .' said Hayley. 'I dropped round to remind you about your suit fitting tomorrow.'

'I know. I wouldn't miss it for the world. You sure you don't want to stop for a cuppa?' asked Adrian.

'I wouldn't want to intrude.' She kissed her father and shot an icy glare at Kim before tutting and marching off.

'Sorry,' said Kim, grimacing.

'It's okay. She's getting married in four weeks. She's a bit stressed that's all.' He shut the door and turned to face Kim. 'Umm, you might want to . . .' He waved a finger in a zigzag up and down her body.

Kim glanced down and saw the gown was gaping again and she was showing a few acres of cleavage.

'Oh, for heaven's sake!'

Ruby ordered another wine and tried hard to arrange her thoughts. Curtis was looking quite pleased with himself and had almost reached the end of his shandy.

Their drinks arrived and Ruby took a steadying swig. 'When you say you're considering embarking on a relationship with Cordelia, what does that mean exactly? You're thinking about asking her out or . . .?'

His brow puckered. 'Do I have to do that formally?'

'Not in writing, no.'

He tilted his head. 'We have been out. We had dinner together Wednesday night.'

She found she was pouting. 'How did that come about? Did you ask her? Were other people there?'

'Just the two of us. There were meant to be a couple of others but they came for a drink and then left.'

Ruby realised she was squinting and stopped. 'Why was Cordelia there? Was she staying over in London too?'

'No, she lives there.'

'And how did it go?'

Curtis's eyes widened a fraction. 'We ordered food. We ate food. We went to bed.'

'Bed!' Ruby shrieked the word out far louder than she intended. 'Bloody hell, Curtis, you move fast. Sex on a first date.'

His eyebrows jumped. 'Not in the same bed and certainly not for sex. We went to our respective beds.'

She wasn't sure if she was relieved by that for her or disappointed for him. 'Do you like Cordelia like that?'

Curtis took an inordinate amount of time to think this through. Ruby waited and sipped her wine, now very aware that she'd eaten nothing and drunk a lot. 'I have thought a lot about what you said.'

'What *I* said?' Ruby couldn't think of anything she'd said about Cordelia. And was a little discombobulated that Curtis thought much about anything she'd said.

'Yes. You said what you were looking for in a partner was someone you trust, makes you laugh, has the same interests as you, so that you have something in common and the same goals.'

'I said that? I sound like a fortune cookie.' Drunk Ruby was impressed with fortune cookie Ruby.

'It's actually very astute.' She was slightly wounded that he was surprised by that. 'I considered those points in relation to Cordelia. Do I trust her? Yes. She has given me no reason not to. In fact, she is highly respected both within the company and in her field.'

Ruby snorted. 'In her field. Makes her sound like a farm animal.'

Curtis scowled at her and she went back to her wine. 'Does she make me laugh? Not as much as you, but laughing is something I rarely do anyway. Do we share the same interests? Yes. IT systems. Do our goals align?'

'Whoa! Back up there, buddy. The thing you have in common is IT? Nowt else?'

'You didn't specify how much we had to have in common.'

'True.' Her head was starting to swim. 'However, usually you want to have a few more things in common like . . .' She looked about for inspiration and caught sight of the car park out of the window. 'Does she like cars? Or is she . . . autophobic?' She gestured with her hand as she thought of the word.

'Autophobic?'

'Fear of . . . automobiles.'

'Autophobia is a fear of being alone,' corrected Curtis. She screwed up her face. 'Really?' He nodded. She went to carry on but was still baffled by the autophobia revelation. 'Nothing to do with cars?' He shook his head. 'Being alone. Seriously?'

'Yes.'

He really was a mine of information. 'What I meant was have you got enough to talk about. If she isn't interested in something you love it rarely works. I'm thinking that IT is very worky and you might want to leave that at the office. And then what would you have in common?' She waved an arm expansively and almost threw herself off the stool. She gripped the edge of the bar. It was time to get a cab home. 'I need to leave.'

'Curtis checked his watch. 'Perhaps we could continue this conversation another time.'

'Sure, any time.'

'I would value your opinion, Ruby.'

213

'Blimey. I hope I remember that when I'm sober.' He helped her steady herself and she waved him away. 'Goodnight, Curtis.'

'Actually. Didn't you say you wanted to discuss something? Was it the ring?'

'Umm . . . that's going to have to wait.' She tapped her temple. 'That's just one of many things I want to talk to you about.'

Chapter Twenty-Three

Ruby's head felt like someone had used it for football practice and then a bit of basketball for good measure. She opened her eyes. Everything was a bit fuzzy and the sight of cross-eyed Seymour up close wasn't helping her focus. He yawned and his fishy breath made her gag. She groaned.

'Good morning,' said Curtis from the doorway.

'Cwap!' said Ruby through her mouthguard and it was louder than her aching temples could cope with. She glanced hastily at the other side of the bed. Surely they'd not? She spat out her mouthguard. 'Curtis, what's going on? How did I get home?'

'You got a cab.'

'Alone?' She remembered being in a taxi but she didn't remember Curtis being there.

'Yes.'

'Hallelujah.' That was a relief. But it didn't explain her unexpected houseguest. 'Then why are you here?'

'I said I wanted to continue our conversation and you said, "Sure, any time".'

She let her head flop back on the pillow and pretended this wasn't happening. 'When I said *any* time . . . oh, never mind.'

'I got you a red bull and two paracetamols.' He held them out towards her. 'Although I'm now wondering whether they should be ingested separately.' He went to take them away.

'Give them here,' she said, taking the can and knocking back the tablets. 'How did you get in?'

'When you initially couldn't find your keys at the hotel and pulled out a rubber chicken you told me that your neighbour at flat four B had a spare. When I couldn't rouse you this morning, I feared you may be unwell so I took the liberty of calling on them.'

'At this time? Actually, what time is it?' Seymour re-arranged himself into a tight ball as if conveying that it was time to go back to sleep. Ruby squinted at the clock. 'Seven o'clock. On a Saturday?'

'I don't understand what the problem is.'

'Everyone has a lie-in at the weekend.'

'But you work.'

'Yeah, but unless there's a wedding we don't get in until just before we open up, which is 9.30 a.m. on a Saturday.'

Curtis was nodding along. 'I see.'

Ruby waved her arms around in the hope of getting more of a reaction from the man who had interrupted her sleep. She usually cut it quite fine on a Saturday. When he didn't respond she had to say something.

'My alarm is set for eight thirty.'

'You can cancel it now,' said Curtis with a smile.

'Grrr,' said Ruby and she fell back on the bed causing Seymour to glare at her, or possibly the wardrobe – she never could tell.

'Umm,' said Curtis followed by silence.

'What?!' Ruby raised her voice and instantly wished she hadn't. It was echoing around her hungover brain.

'When are we going to chat?'

She scrunched up her eyes. There was no point even trying to get back to sleep. 'Give me five minutes, then I'll have a shower and get dressed and then we can chat while I eat the toast you've made me.'

'I've not . . . ah, got it. Breakfast on its way.'

Once the tablets and fizzy drink kicked in she started to feel a little more human and less like the incredible hulk with PMT. She'd not drunk that much for a long time. The previous evening flashed through her mind while she showered. She could remember most of it. She certainly remembered his revelation about Cordelia and couldn't think of it without sighing at her foiled plan. She could hardly ask him to be her sperm donor now. She wouldn't want to split up Cordelia and Curtis before they'd even begun. She couldn't help feeling that she'd lost a little more than the donor opportunity. She was struggling to understand what she was feeling. As if by stealth Curtis had grown on her. Although she had to admit that he and Cordelia were a far better match than they were. Not that that had ever been a consideration. Stick to the plan, she told herself. But what was the plan now? She had no idea.

She finished showering, got dressed, dried her hair and joined Curtis at the table where he was drinking a cup of tea. The smell of which wafted in her direction. 'Did you find another one of those fancy-arse teabags?'

'No, I brought my own fancy-arse Lady Grey teabags with me.'

'Lady Grey? Is that Earl Grey's grandma?'

'It's a variation of Earl Grey tea invented by Twinings in the 1990s to appeal to the Nordic market. It's flavoured with bergamot oil, lemon and orange peel. I've another bag if you'd like to try it.'

Ruby wrinkled her nose. 'No thanks. It's still tea. Thanks for this,' she said, sitting down to a plate of toast and a glass of orange juice.

'You're welcome. Can we talk now?'

She took in his expectant expression. 'Yes, Curtis. What did you want to discuss?'

'Cordelia.'

Ruby forced herself not to harrumph. 'Okay. What about Cordelia Two Smoking Barrels?' The woman had unknowingly derailed Ruby's donor plans so she wasn't feeling quite as warm about her as she had been when she was eating her company's free biscuits, but that wasn't Cordelia's fault.

'Would you consider her a good match as a partner?'

Ruby tried to keep a straight face. 'Well, I usually like my partners taller, wearing less make-up than me and a bit more muscle . . .' Ruby bit into her toast.

Curtis's forehead was puckering, something she was used to seeing when he wasn't quite understanding something. The frowning stopped and a smile appeared. 'Very funny. Not as a partner for you, and by the way I am aware that I need to deliver on that side of our agreement. I meant Cordelia as a partner for me. Actually, that is a good point. What if she's a lesbian?'

'I don't think she is.'

'Should I ask her?'

'No! I can check with Jonty,' said Ruby.

'Right. I wish I'd brought my laptop.'

'You don't need a spreadsheet for this.' She smiled at him. He was endearingly naïve. 'The tricky thing about relationships is that you can't work them out with a spreadsheet. You just know if that person is a match or not.'

Curtis tilted his head. 'But you said you've been out

with lots of unsuitable men. So, at what point does the mismatch become apparent?'

'You've spotted the flaw in my method. The trouble is that whilst I know they aren't the best match I continue to hold out some hope that maybe they could be. In my defence they don't usually reveal their true selves and arsehole tendencies until about date four or until after I've slept with them.'

Curtis was blinking. 'It's incredibly confusing.'

They sipped their drinks in silence for a while before Curtis spoke. 'And didn't you want to finalise what we're doing with the engagement ring?'

The word 'finalise' didn't sit well with Ruby. It made her realise that once that ring was returned they would have just formal work things to interact over and then probably only until the end of the project. Non-work Curtis was her friend now and she didn't want that to fizzle out. 'Yeah, we need to think about that,' she said noncommittally.

'Weren't you completing a spreadsheet?'

'Was I?' She racked her brains for the last conversation about the ring. Bugger it. She had suggested a spreadsheet to log their attempts to return it. 'I thought we could do it together because you love spreadsheets. And to make sure I've got the dates right. I've been wondering about Lewis and his girlfriend. There must be more we can do.'

'I agree,' said Curtis. 'But I'm not sure what.' She inched forward and got a whiff of cologne.

'New aftershave?'

'I may have been doing some research of my own into relationships.' He broke eye contact and concentrated on finishing his tea.

She sniffed the air. 'Good start. I like it.'

'I've been thinking about the ring and I believe we have two options. We either courier it to the jeweller's because if it was stolen from them then it is theirs or if it is legitimately Lewis's they will contact him. Or we hand it in to the police and say we found it on a train. The latter we probably should have done right at the start and I would be uncomfortable having the conversation with the police as to why we have not done this sooner. They may think we've been trying to sell it and have failed.'

'I have to be honest – I don't like either of those ideas.'

'I appreciate your honesty. But do you have another suggestion?'

'I do. Social media.' She leaned back and downed the rest of her juice with satisfaction.

Kim was miles away as she unlocked the shop. She let out a yawn. Another virtually sleepless night. The combination of warm weather and night sweats was killing her. She'd been going over the previous evening. At least she and Adrian had been able to laugh about her impromptu flashing episode.

Despite low energy levels, she was excited. Today was the day she was going to become a dog owner. She'd ordered all sorts of dog-related paraphernalia, which a kind neighbour was going to take in for her, and Adrian was picking her up later so they could fetch Boomer together. She pottered through to the back room and put the kettle on. She was considering having one of Ruby's Cokes; she needed a boost and maybe caffeine was the answer.

She heard someone knock on the door. It must be Ruby, she thought, and in a daze she went to let her in. As she flicked the catch she caught sight of who was on the other side a fraction too late to stop them pushing on the door.

The sight of him made her gasp. 'Vince?'

'Hi, Kim, I was hoping we could talk.' He pointed into the shop.

She did a bit of a goldfish impression before she pulled herself together and managed to form a sentence. 'No, Vince. I don't want to hear anything you've got to say.'

'Please, Kim. It's important.'

'Not to me it's not.'

Vince chuckled. It was a familiar sound despite the missing years. 'You don't know what it is yet.'

'But I know you.' She stabbed a finger in his direction, wishing it were a sword and that running someone through for being a cad was still socially acceptable.

Vince shook his head. 'I've changed, Kim. Really I have.'

She stood up straight and looked him in the eye. 'Does your acupuncturist agree?'

'We've parted ways.'

'Ooh, shame.' She sounded bitter even to her own ears. 'So that's why you're here. You're homeless and you think I'll be mug enough to take you back. Jog on, Vince.' She tried to waft him out like a bad smell.

'No. It's amicable. I've got a lovely place in Mablethorpe.'

Kim waved a hand to stop him. 'I'm sorry, I think you've mistaken me for someone who actually gives a crap.'

Vince chortled. 'This is what I've missed. Feisty, straight-talking Kim.' He took a minute to appraise her. 'You've not changed. You look amazing.'

'Thank you, now I know you're talking grade-A bollocks because I feel like shit and look like Mrs Doubtfire.'

'You've always been too hard on yourself. I think—'

'No, Vince.' She shook her head. 'You need to go. Now, please.' He needed to leave before Ruby arrived for work. She held the door open for him.

221

He pressed his lips into a thin line. 'Okay. I'll go but can we meet up later? Maybe go for a meal – my treat.'

'No.' She was starting to lose her remaining shred of patience and Ruby was due in any moment.

He held his palms up in surrender. 'I'm going.' He paused in the doorway and she wanted to kick him through it. 'How about Sunday lunch?'

'Out!'

Vince rested a hand on her shoulder. 'Kim, I didn't want to have to tell you like this but . . . I'm dying.' The words slapped her hard and she knew it must have been written all over her face. 'I'm sorry. I wanted to tell you myself. That's why I sent the letter asking if we could meet. I'm here because I want . . . no, I need to put things right between us. That's all I'm trying to do.'

She could feel unexpected emotion bubbling up. After all these years and everything that had happened, she still cared. 'But you look . . .' She stopped herself saying something crass. Telling him he looked well probably wasn't helpful.

'It's one of those invisible killers. Cancer.' She felt tears prick her eyes.

'Thanks for telling me, Vince, but I think it's better if things between us are left as they are.'

He sighed deeply. 'Right . . . okay . . .' He nodded solemnly. 'I understand. Of course. I hope you didn't mind me coming. It's been good to see you again. Goodbye, Kim. Take good care of yourself.' He stepped outside.

'Bye, Vince.' She closed the door and slid the lock.

Chapter Twenty-Four

Ruby was thinking over her conversation with Curtis as she walked from the car to work. Curtis fascinated her. It was like he'd been living in a cave most of his life and was only now emerging. There was a little bit of her wondering if maybe they could have been more than friends or was that the hangover addling her brain? She'd grown close to him very quickly and she valued their friendship above all else. It was actually quite sweet how he was running his thoughts on Cordelia past her. It made her feel like she was being useful. If there was something she knew a lot about, it was relationships. Maybe what she knew about them was how they failed but perhaps somewhere, in amongst the failures, there was the secret to how to make them work.

She felt a little like Curtis was an experiment. What did that make her? The mad scientist? At least even if she couldn't have her happy ever after maybe she could help Curtis find his. As she neared the shop, she saw someone leave. It wasn't even open yet, so that was odd. The light was on inside and she could see Kim was already setting up.

She watched the familiar man crossing the road. 'Hey!' She waved and ran after him.

Vince turned and waited for Ruby on the corner. 'Hello again. I'm sorry if I startled you last night.'

'It's fine. All forgotten. Have you seen Kim?'

'I have.' He nodded earnestly.

'And?'

Vince seemed pleased. 'We're having lunch tomorrow. I'm picking her up. Blast, I've forgotten what number she said her house was. She'll think I'm getting dementia. Twenty something, no that's wrong . . .' He turned to head back to the florist's.

'Forty-five Marr Ter—'

'Marr Terrace,' said Vince, clicking his fingers. 'What am I like?'

'Is everything sorted between you?' asked Ruby.

'It's early days but . . .' He held up two pairs of crossed fingers. 'I'd better dash. Bye, Ruby.'

'Bye,' she said then crossed back to Bloom with a View and tapped on the door. She watched Kim through the glass; she initially seemed alarmed when she looked up but her expression softened when she saw it was Ruby.

'Good morning,' she said, opening the door and shutting it quickly once Ruby was inside.

'Shall I put the kettle on?' asked Ruby. 'Then we can have a chat.'

'Thank you, it's not long boiled.'

Ruby got the drinks while Kim finished setting up. Ruby handed Kim a mug. 'So . . .' she said, now not quite sure how to broach the resurrected husband issue.

'Did he say yes?' asked Kim, blowing on her tea.

'What?' Ruby was wrong-footed.

'Curtis. About being your sperm donor,' she said.

'No,' replied Ruby and Kim visibly drooped. 'No. Not *no*. I've just not asked him yet. He dropped a Cordelia-shaped bombshell and talking of bomb—'

The door chimed; Kim jumped as a customer came in.

'Tell me later,' said Kim, handing her mug to Ruby and going to greet the customer. That was Ruby's opportunity gone for now. She wouldn't ask her about Vince in front of customers. She'd have to bide her time and wait until there was a lull or, worst case, after they closed.

The customer was Hayley. 'Hi, Hayley,' said Kim. Pictures of her flashing her naked body at Adrian's daughter loomed large in her mind.

'Hi,' said Hayley, her eyes darting around as she checked out the shop. 'What a lovely job, playing with flowers all day.'

Kim saw Ruby flash her a look as this was one of Kim's pet hates – when people made the assumption their job was akin to a toddler playing in the sandpit. Anyone can plonk cut flowers in a vase but what they did took real skill and flair. It annoyed her that it was often dismissed as easy.

Kim kept her cool. She was sure Hayley wasn't trying to wind her up. She pasted on a smile. 'How can I help?'

'Is there somewhere we can talk in private?' Hayley asked, scanning the shop.

'Sure.' Kim led her out the back. 'Is everything okay? Is your dad all right?'

'It's Dad I wanted to talk to you about.' Kim held back the beads and Hayley stepped through. 'Um, no door?'

'No.'

'Right.' Hayley glanced through the beads. They could both see Ruby was watching them but she turned away and began humming, which made Kim smile. The door chimed and Ruby went to serve. 'Here's the thing.' Hayley pulled a face like she was sucking on a lemon wedge but someone had just nicked her tequila. 'I'm worried about Dad.'

'What's wrong?' Her stomach plummeted as she feared the worst.

'Mum's death has been hard for him and he's still coming to terms with it. He spends a lot of time at her graveside. I worry about his mental health.'

Kim was relieved it wasn't anything more. 'It's lovely that you're concerned about him, Hayley. I think he's probably coping better than you think.'

Hayley squared her shoulders at this. 'Maybe I'm not being clear. He still loves my mother. There's no room for anyone else.'

'Oh, I see. You're warning me off,' said Kim, trying not to smile. 'It's okay. We're just friends.'

'That wasn't how it looked to me.' Her lips puckered like a cat's bumhole. 'Every time I go around, you are there wearing increasingly less clothing. You can see that he has money. You've got him ferrying you about like a frigging taxi service. I think your intentions are pretty clear.' Hayley folded her arms and returned her lips to their tight pose.

Kim chuckled. 'You think I'm after his money?'

'You said it.'

Mardy mare, thought Kim.

'Hayley, please let me put your mind at rest. I'm not interested in your dad's money and I assure you we're just friends. Okay?' The door chimed and Kim glanced through the beads to see two customers enter the shop. She needed to get back to work.

Hayley paused. 'No. Kim, it's not okay. I'd like you to stay away from my father.'

'Hayley, I appreciate that you're looking out for him. Really, I do. But you can't intrude on your father's life like this. He's a grown-up. It's down to him to make his own decisions.' Kim was rapidly losing patience.

Tears welled in Hayley's eyes. 'My mother only died recently. He's vulnerable and you're taking advantage!' Her voice was rising.

'Hayley, Justine has been gone for over two years.' Kim regretted her blunt approach as soon as Hayley spluttered a tearful gasp. 'I'm sorry but it's true. And your dad is doing fine. You can't expect him to spend the rest of his life alone. It's up to him who he sees.'

'You would say that. Someone like you.' She pointed her finger at Kim. 'Someone who's desperate to get her claws into my dad's money.'

That was the point where Kim's patience packed its bags, put on an out-of-office notice and buggered off. 'You're barking up the wrong tree. But honestly, he could be shagging all of Sheffield if he wanted to – it's really none of your business.'

'We'll see about that!' snapped Hayley. She turned quickly, swatting the beads out of the way and they immediately responded by whacking her back. In her temper Hayley's arms flailed about, making the end of one string whip up and slap her in the face. 'Ow!'

Everyone in the shop turned to look as Hayley marched out clutching her eye. Kim switched into pleasant florist mode. 'Who's next?' Nobody looked very keen.

It had been a busy Saturday and Ruby was glad to flip the sign to closed. 'Right. Before we get any more interruptions, we need to talk,' she said, realising that she sounded like she was about to dump a partner not question her boss.

'Ooh, sounds ominous,' said Kim, sorting out the stock that would be past their best by Monday. 'Do you want some of these for the nursing home?'

'Er, yeah. Please,' said Ruby. 'Can you stop for a minute?'

'What's wrong?' asked Kim, looking over her shoulder.

'Vince,' said Ruby.

'Um . . . what?' Kim almost stumbled headfirst into a bucket. She righted herself, her cheek twitching.

'Vince. Your husband who is very much alive and well and who turned up here last night and scared me half to death.'

'What did he do?'

'He caught me off-guard and I freaked out a little and then he told me who he was and I freaked out a bit more. Then he got me a glass of water and was quite lovely really. He's told me everything about what happened after his heart attack.' She was still a bit shocked that Kim had dumped him while he'd been ill in hospital but Vince had said Kim was having a breakdown at the time. Kim looked alarmed. 'Which is none of my business, but I'd like to know why you lied to me.' Ruby folded her arms. When she'd gone over this with Curtis the previous evening she'd been quite cross about it. Now that temper had ebbed away.

Kim sighed. 'I'm so sorry, Ruby. I never set out to lie to people. Especially not you.'

'When you said he'd gone to a better place I thought you meant heaven, not sodding Mablethorpe,' said Ruby with a smile.

'And now he's back and—'

'I know. How good is that?' said Ruby.

Kim's expression was somewhere between a grimace and a snarl. 'It's not good at all.'

'But this could be a second chance.' She loved a second chance love story. She read them all the time. 'You've always said how brilliant you were together. Didn't you say he was your soul mate? Your missing puzzle piece? The one person you could be yourself with? Don't you want that again?'

'Well, yes . . . I guess. But, Ruby it's not that simple. You don't forgive someone just like that.'

'Why not?' It seemed to Ruby like Vince had already forgiven Kim for dumping him.

Kim chewed the inside of her mouth. 'Do you forgive the microwave thief or the kettle pisser?'

'No, but this is different. This is you and Vince. He wants to put the past behind him.'

'He does?' Kim steadied herself by holding on to the shelving unit.

'Look, Kim. We all do things we're not proud of but if someone still loves us deep down and can forgive us then why wouldn't you have another crack at your happy ever after?' Ruby was rather proud of her little speech.

'I don't know.' Kim put her head in her hands. 'Some things are impossible to forgive.'

'Do you not think you should at least think about it?'

Kim exhaled loudly. 'It's all too late.' She handed the past-their-best blooms to Ruby.

The door clanged open, making them both turn. Kim slapped on a smile at the sight of Adrian. Ruby suddenly realised why Kim might be having doubts about rekindling things with Vince. She had two men vying for her attention now.

'Hiya, Adrian,' said Ruby. She glanced at Kim. 'Think about what I said. I'll see you Tuesday.'

For once Kim was relieved to see Ruby leave. Her attitude to Vince had taken her by surprise. She'd thought of all people, Ruby, would have been ready to lynch Vince from the nearest lamppost now that she knew what he'd done. Ruby knew what it was like to be cheated on, to have men disrespect her, so it was odd that she thought getting back with Vince was an option for Kim. Ruby must have got the wrong end of the stick. Surely Vince couldn't expect to turn up out of the blue and pick up as if the acupuncturist hadn't happened? Ruby was a romantic at heart so this was the most likely explanation. But it had made her wonder if she should have at least given him a chance to talk to her. Now she knew he was dying it did kind of put a different spin on things.

'You all right?' asked Adrian, flipping the sign to closed. Seeing him cheered her up and she liked that. It was hard not to compare him to Vince. They were very different. Vince was all charm and swagger. 'A bit of a wide boy' her dad had called him. Adrian was steady and dependable. Not that she was looking at him as a suitor – they were just friends. That didn't stop the fluttery sensations she got when she was around him, but he remained devoted to Justine, so she certainly wasn't going to make any moves.

Maybe if she'd met someone like Adrian earlier on it would have been different. But then was there anything she really wanted to change about her life? Only the lack of children. Not being a mother still made her sad heart ache. But she had a lot to be thankful for. She had her house and her little shop and now she was about to get a dog. She'd have her very own fur baby. Actually, things were looking okay.

Kim took a deep breath. Adrian. Lovely Adrian was here. She felt her shoulders relax a fraction. 'Yes. I'm fine.'

'Sure?' He was studying her closely. 'Anything you want to tell me?' His eyes held a look she'd not seen before.

'Oh, Hayley came to see me earlier. I take it she's told

you.' She hoped her comment about him shagging the whole of Sheffield hadn't got back to him.

'She's told me.' He looked like he was clenching his jaw. 'You're not denying it?'

'Look, I might have overstepped the mark a little but—'

'A little? Bloody hell, Kim. You hit her!'

Kim snapped her head back as if she was the one who had been slapped by the beads. 'No, I didn't hit her. She copped a strop and the beads sort of smacked her.' Adrian looked doubtful. Kim took hold of the end of the beads and tried to re-create the incident, which was quite difficult and probably made her look a bit deranged as she whirled them around.

'That's not what she says.'

Kim felt like she was being told off about a playground brawl and the thought made her snort a laugh, which was possibly not appropriate. Adrian didn't look impressed. 'This is silly. She's making it up.'

Adrian shook his head. 'You're saying she's lying? I've seen her eye, Kim.'

'Well, these beads can give you a fair old whack.' Kim swung them about a bit more but they were not giving off the deadly weapon vibe they had earlier.

'Hayley's really upset. And this close to the wedding she doesn't need any additional stress.'

'Adrian, what are you saying?'

'I'm sorry, Kim. I can't be around someone who lashes out like that.' He looked pained as he turned and made for the door.

'She came around here to warn me off,' she said, somewhat belatedly as the door closed with a cheery tinkle.

* * *

231

Half an hour later, she was hanging on to the lead while Boomer tried to launch himself into outer space. She was starting to wonder what she'd done.

'It's like he knows he's going to his forever home,' said Margaret, placing a lot of emphasis on the word forever. 'He's excited.'

'Me too but I'm managing to keep it in.' Kim grimaced.

'Sign here,' said Margaret, waving a form almost within reach of Kim. Kim grabbed the proffered pen, scrawled something illegible and handed it back to Margaret.

'That's it, the donation has gone through. Here are his vaccination records and some leaflets about insurance, worming and um . . . dog training classes.'

They both watched him bound about like he'd sat on a hedgehog. 'I think we might be needing those.'

'I know he's a handful,' said Margaret, her eyes pinging up and down as they tried to follow Boomer's antics. 'But I do believe that you and he have got a bond. If you have any problems, please ring me sooner rather than later. I want this to work out as much as you do.' Margaret looked sincere.

'Okay. I wi-ill,' said Kim as Boomer lurched and dragged her off towards the exit.

Kim could sympathise with the dog a little. He'd been in kennels on and off for over a year. She'd be excited to be out if she'd been shut in for that amount of time. They raced across the car park at top speed and the dog paused briefly to cock his leg on two other cars before they reached Kim's. Kim opened the car door and showed him the blanket on the back seat. Boomer put his nose in to sniff it and grabbed it. There then followed a tug of war. His tail went wild – he was clearly very happy with the game. He readjusted to get a better grip and in the second he let go Kim snatched the blanket from his jaws.

'Let's try without the blanket,' she said.

Kim knew that Boomer was smart. On the first command he jumped onto the back seat of the car. However, a moment later he jumped back out again and so it went on. In the end she instructed him to jump in and then jumped in beside him and quickly shut the door at which point he promptly jumped all over her in his abject delight at being at eye level with her.

'Noooo,' said Kim, but she was laughing through the frantic doggy kisses. 'Boomer. Stop it, you loon.' After a lot of tussling and a few mouthfuls of fur she managed to get him clipped into his travel harness. Kim didn't want him straining to escape again so decided that she'd have to get to the driver's seat without getting out of the car. She attempted to crawl through the gap in the seats. It was a bit of a squeeze and she had to twist to one side. She slid down slightly on the faux leather covering and her hip met the central console and armrest. Her middle was wedged. Kim tried to heave herself through but she was jammed in tight by the seats. Maybe she did need to lose a few pounds. She felt a paw scratch at her backside.

'Thanks for your help, Boomer,' she said.

She tried to reverse but that wasn't an option if she wanted to bring both breasts with her. She was stuck.

Chapter Twenty-Five

Ruby was giggling when she pulled into the rescue centre car park. Kim's car was parked on its own and she stopped alongside it. At first, she couldn't see anyone inside but when she got closer the whole sorry situation was presented to her. Or, more accurately, Kim's backside stuck between the seats was. Ruby walked around the car to eyeball Kim. She held in her laughter for all of a nanosecond and then fell about – it was one of the funniest things she'd seen in a while.

'How the heck did you get in this mess?' she asked.

'Don't ask,' said Kim.

Ruby looked in the back and a happy spaniel face complete with lolling-out tongue appeared at the window. 'Hello, you must be Boomerang. Aren't you gorgeous? Yes, you are. You're gorgeous. Yes—'

'I think we've established who's gorgeous and who is a woolly mammoth. I'm definitely going on a diet.'

'You're the only person who thinks you're big. I think you look fabulous,' said Ruby.

'Thanks but can we concentrate on shifting my huge bum?'

Ruby opened the door and immediately Boomer was interested and tried to jump onto Kim but was thankfully held back by his seatbelt and harness.

Ruby kneeled on the passenger seat and leaned over Kim to fuss the dog. 'He's lovely.'

'He is but this is all his fault, you know.'

'Who's a clever boy,' said Ruby.

'Do you think we could focus on the main issue here?' Kim waved her free arm.

'Sorry,' said Ruby, crouching down towards Kim's head. 'What shall I do?'

'Get me out of here.'

'Yeah, but how exactly?' Ruby could feel a fit of giggles returning and clenched her jaw to stop them.

'Try moving the passenger seat forwards or backwards.'

'Okay.' Ruby sat down, felt under the seat for the lever and gave it a tug while she pushed with her feet. It sent her backwards at speed.

'Ow! Boobs!' squeaked Kim. 'It's like you've run them over.' She gave her chest a rub.

'Whoops. Can you move now?'

'I'm not sure.' Kim was in an awkward position but a lot less stuck than she had been. After an inelegant couple of minutes she managed to clamber fully into the driver's seat. 'Blimey. I don't know how that happened. I've climbed between the seats before with no problem.'

'Maybe you've put on a few pounds?' suggested Ruby.

'Tell me something I don't know.'

'Salad tastes nice,' said Ruby with a grin.

'Bloody cheek!' said Kim but she was laughing. 'And no, it blooming well doesn't. Unless you're a rabbit. Being big runs in my family. To be honest it's the only thing that runs in my family.' Kim smiled. Although she had a feeling Boomer was going to change that.

* * *

235

That evening Ruby gave Jonty a quick ring.

'I'm really sorry to bother you on a Saturday night,' she said.

'Hang on, my boyfriend is watching the football.' That statement confirmed one thing for her.

'You're not a footy fan?'

'I am but he's not. It's more of a tutorial because he's trying to fit in at a new job. It's a nightmare. I said get them all to watch *Queer Eye* and be done with it.'

'Sound advice. Anyway, Curtis is in London again next week and he wants to reciprocate the meal that Cordelia paid for. I was after the inside track of what sort of thing she likes.' She hoped that was subtle enough.

'Ooh, do we have some grade-A gossip here? Is Curtis trying to hook up with Cordelia?'

Whoops. Rumbled. 'Noooo. Don't be daft, this is Curtis we're talking about. He has the emotional range of an IKEA chair.' Jonty snorted down the phone. 'I just thought it would be best if they went somewhere she liked and also if you have any top tips on what she's into that I could brief Curtis on, in case conversation dries up.'

There was a cheer from the background. 'Either someone has scored or there was a Diet Coke advert. I'd better go. I'll email you a few suggestions. Okay?'

'Perfect.'

After her call, she had a brief text exchange with Curtis. Brief from his end not hers. She didn't subscribe to the short response. She texted like she spoke – often at length and without vetting. Not always wise but she was pretty safe with Curtis. As they were both free on Sunday and Curtis still had relationship questions (which he had now organised into a spreadsheet) they agreed to meet up. To kill two birds, Ruby was picking up Curtis and they were dropping the flowers into the nursing home along with a stack of books Ruby thought Dot and Kitty might enjoy. After that they were going somewhere for lunch.

The next day, Curtis was waiting on the steps of the hotel, holding his laptop bag. He smiled as she pulled up.

'Good morning,' said Curtis, opening the car door.

'Is it?' said Ruby, deciding on the spur of the moment to give Curtis a bit of a test when it came to conversation with women.

Curtis froze, still holding open the passenger door. 'Er . . . It's not raining and you're on time,' he said with a little hesitation.

'Aren't I usually on time?' she snapped.

He started rapidly blinking, something she'd noticed he did when he was flustered. 'Yes, yes you are. Can I get in?' Ruby nodded and Curtis slunk into the car. He put the laptop bag at his feet and fastened his seatbelt but the whole time he kept his eyes on Ruby like a wary mouse watching a prowling cat.

'Are you not going to tell me I look nice?' Ruby was struggling not to laugh. She clenched her teeth tight together and stared at Curtis who was now hastily scanning her from head to foot.

'You look nice.'

'That's it. I look nice. *Nice?* What's that in Amazon stars, two?'

The blinking increased. 'Er . . . well.' He swallowed. 'You look like . . . you,' he said with an uncertain smile.

She couldn't keep it up any longer and burst out laughing, making Curtis recoil. 'I'm messing with you! You can relax.'

'Do you gain pleasure from that?' He ran a finger around his buttoned-up shirt collar.

'A little bit but that wasn't why I did it. You need to think about each of your interactions with a woman. You need to sense her mood.'

'I do?'

'Yes. And I'm going to coach you.' She grinned at Curtis. 'I've decided that if you want to impress Cordelia you need someone to prepare you so you know what to expect.' She was very proud of her selfless idea. Curtis appeared mildly terrified.

As they walked into the nursing home Ruby handed the two large bunches of flowers to Curtis. 'Here, you can take those in.'

'Is this another test?'

'You could say that. I'm guessing it's been a while since a man brought Dot or Kitty flowers. You'll make their day.'

Curtis looked down at the blooms and back at Ruby. 'Should I buy Cordelia a bouquet?'

'Not yet. You need to be in some sort of relationship first, otherwise it's a bit creepy.'

'Fully established relationship first. Then flowers?'

'Nooooo,' said Ruby, with a laugh. 'Don't wait that long – she'll think you've cheated on her. Come on,' she added and she strolled inside, leaving Curtis blinking back his confusion on the threshold.

'Hello, ladies,' said Ruby, walking into the TV room and placing down her bag of books which was met with interest. 'And look what else I've got for you,' she said with a wink.

Curtis cautiously entered the room and Dot, Kitty and a few others all swooned at the sight of him and the large bunches of flowers. Dot clapped her hands together. 'Are they for me?'

Curtis's eyes swivelled around warily. 'Yes, they are,' said Curtis, giving them one each. They giggled like schoolgirls as they sniffed the blooms, pointing out all the flowers and colours before swapping to admire the other bunch.

'They're beautiful. Thank you. What a lovely man you are,' said Kitty, wiping away a stray tear.

'Come here,' said Dot, opening her arms for a hug. Curtis stepped back.

'I'll pop them in some water, while you have a chat to Curtis,' said Ruby, taking back the bunches.

Curtis grabbed her arm. 'Don't leave me.' His eyes were wide.

'This is a *real* test. They are pussy cats compared to Cordelia. Ask them about themselves and then listen and smile,' she whispered.

'That's it?' He gave her a disbelieving look.

'Yep. Beginner level only.'

He nodded and pulled up a chair. He offered his hand for them to shake. 'Hello, I'm Curtis,' he said.

Ruby watched from the doorway.

'Are you Harry's boy?' asked Dot.

'Yes, I am.'

'You look like him,' said Kitty.

'No, I—' started Curtis but Ruby coughed and he looked round.

'Listen,' she mouthed. He nodded and turned back.

'You do look like him,' said Dot. 'You've got his eyes.'

'And his chin,' said Kitty. 'I like a man with a strong jawline. It hints at a strong character. I like a tight little bum too. I mean, who doesn't?'

'I'd like a man with a strong heart,' said Dot.

'Do you mean romantically?' asked Curtis.

'No, just one without heart disease. I've buried two

239

husbands because of it.' And she started to laugh. Curtis gave a chuckle and glanced over his shoulder at Ruby who gave him a thumbs up. She decided he was probably going to be okay for a few minutes, so she left him to it.

When she came back, with two vases, she was surprised to see that Curtis now had a circle of women around him and most of them were hooting with laughter. Ruby put the flowers down. 'What's going on?' she asked.

Curtis leaned in. 'I have no idea.' But at least he didn't look alarmed.

'I was telling Curtis about the time I met the lord mayor and my trousers fell down,' said Dot and everyone laughed.

'I'm afraid I need to go,' said Curtis. 'But it's been lovely.'

'Bye,' they chorused.

'Well done,' whispered Ruby at the door.

'Thank you,' said Curtis. 'You really know your stuff.'

Ruby smiled. 'That's just the tip of the iceberg.'

Thankfully, by the time Kim had got him home on Saturday night, Boomer had calmed down a fraction. He'd looked up at her with his big dark eyes and she'd felt the same sensation she'd experienced on the day she'd met him. He'd stolen her heart and this was why she'd persevered. Everyone deserved a second, or in Boomer's case a fourth, chance. This was a new start for them both. She'd wondered if maybe she'd been too hasty to dismiss Vince.

Kim had walked Boomer around the house on the lead and he'd jumped on everything and sniffed everywhere. She'd taken him into the garden and praised him when he weed, which he did a lot. After that it was all a blur. A literal blur because as soon as she let him off his lead, he'd spent the rest of the evening racing from room to room and out into the garden and then repeated it, dashing past her in a fuzzy swirl of white and brown.

She'd tried ignoring him. She'd tried intercepting him. She'd tried distracting him. Nothing had worked. She'd shut him in the kitchen and he scratched at the door and howled until she let him out. She'd eventually gone to bed in the hope he would tire himself out.

However, she did get a lovely greeting when she came down for breakfast on Sunday morning which was a million times nicer than an empty house. After a few laps of the garden, she managed to put on his harness and take him for a proper walk. More accurately, he dragged her round the park at full speed. She was sure her right arm was getting longer. His saving grace was that he was the friendliest thing. He loved meeting other dogs and she felt bad but she daren't let him off his lead; given that he didn't obey any commands, she feared he'd simply run off and never be seen again – apart from possibly on the news.

Boomer was the perfect distraction needed from the Hayley and Adrian mess. She'd gone over and over the discussion in her mind. All the things she should have said to him instead of trying to get the beads to re-enact what had happened with Hayley. Without her noticing, Adrian had crept in and taken up a vacant spot in her life and she was already missing him. The silly text messages and harmless flirting but most importantly his friendship. She completely understood why he'd taken Hayley's side. What else was a father going to do? But the thought that she wouldn't be spending time with him saddened her far more than she had expected.

She was sitting in the garden watching Boomer destroy his third tennis ball of the day when the doorbell sounded.

241

Boomer pricked up his ears. 'Stay', she told him and she left him in the garden while she went to answer the door.

She had a smile on her face to greet her visitor until she saw who it was.

Vince beamed back at her. 'Hi, Kim, please can I come in?'

She wanted to tell him where to go. To ask how on earth he had got hold of her home address and what the hell he thought he was doing turning up unannounced like a crazy stalker but she didn't. Truth be told, it hadn't been just Boomer who had kept her awake. She'd gone over and over what Vince had said and whatever way she looked at it she felt bad about sending away a dying man and not granting him his last wish to make amends.

'Look, Vince. I'm sorry if I was a bit off yesterday. It was a shock seeing you again.'

'Not as much of a shock as it was for Ruby. She thought I was already dead.' He tilted his head questioningly.

'Well anyway, I'm sorry, but you can't come in. I've got a dog and I'm not sure how he'll react.'

'I love dogs.'

'Do you?' She couldn't recall him ever being that keen.

'Sure thing. I wish I'd had one but it's too late now.' Vince looked at her the same way that Boomer did.

She felt her resolve eroding. Perhaps if she let Vince talk, they could then both move on. 'We could take him for a walk and chat, if that's what you've come for.'

'Or Sunday lunch somewhere? For old time's sake. Split the bill.'

She'd been hoping he didn't have that much he wanted to say, not enough to occupy a whole lunch. Surely 'sorry' wouldn't take that long. 'I'm not sure, what with the dog and everything.'

'The Rising Sun allows dogs.' He pointed back to the Fulwood Road.

Kim was running out of excuses. Boomer howled his protest from the garden. 'Okay. Give me five minutes.'

Thanks to Boomer they got there in double-quick time. The sign said it was dog-friendly, but she wasn't sure whether it would be Boomer-friendly. On the way she and Vince mainly talked about what had and hadn't changed in Sheffield over the last seven years. It turned out Vince was staying at a friend's place for the weekend before going back to Mablethorpe.

They found a table and Vince got them drinks and menus. Boomer tried to eat the menu but Kim managed to persuade him otherwise. She could see people looking as he wrapped himself and his lead around the table legs. He didn't like lying by their feet but once he'd jumped up next to Kim he did, at last, settle down.

They sipped their drinks and Kim felt oddly awkward. In the early days, after Vince had left her, she'd fantasised about him turning up and them talking everything through. After seven years, here they were but everything had changed. She glanced at him; she didn't want to stare. He looked well. She didn't want to ask how long he had left but she would have liked to have known. This Vince was a stranger she couldn't ask personal questions of.

'Has there been anyone since we broke up?' asked Vince.

The question caught her unawares. 'Nowt serious. No acupuncturists if that's what you're asking.'

'Touché. Do you remember—'

'Look, Vince,' she cut in. 'I'm sure this is a terrible time for you but I don't want to go down memory lane. What was it you wanted to say?'

'Right. Sorry. I thought it might be nice to catch up.'

'I thought you wanted to put things right between us?' She was confused.

'I do.' He nodded and ran his lip through his teeth. 'I am truly sorry for what happened. I honestly never stopped loving you, Kim. What I did was stupid. I was flattered by the attention of another woman.' He chuckled. 'I'm such a cliché. And I know I must have hurt you and I'm sorry. Can you forgive me?'

It wasn't easy and she would have loved to have vented all her frustrations and the hurt she'd been holding on to for seven years but this was her moment to be magnanimous. Her opportunity to let go of the past and to do the right thing for a dying man. She took a deep breath. 'Of course I do, Vince. Consider yourself forgiven.' His face was the picture of relief and she felt a warm happy glow.

'That's a weight lifted. Thanks, Kim. You're a good person. There was one other thing.' He looked serious. 'I've not got much time left and it makes you question what you want to do with it . . .' He held her gaze. 'I've missed you, Kim. And I want to spend what time I have left with you.'

Kim snorted out a mouthful of cider and Boomer leaped up, knocking the glass out of her hand. As cider seeped through her clothes she stared at Vince. 'You what?' She couldn't have heard him right. Boomer frantically licked up the cider; at least that might make him sleep.

Vince looked sincere and reached across for Kim's hand. 'I want us to give it another go.'

Chapter Twenty-Six

Ruby decided to treat Curtis to one of her mum's 'free days out'. They'd driven into the Peak District, parked up and taken a country walk she'd done many times before. Soft undulating hills criss-crossed with ancient drystone walls and a sprinkling of sheep. She loved a picnic and they'd dined on sausage rolls, Pringles and Dairylea triangles with Curly Wurly bars for dessert. They were sitting on her mum's checked picnic blanket at the top of a hill. Ruby looked out towards Stanage Edge, while Curtis scrolled through a spreadsheet he'd made earlier.

'Question seven,' he said. 'At what point would a relationship be confirmed?' He looked up. 'Basically, I want to know when I've achieved my goal.'

'Interesting. I think an offer of sex from her would be a clear indicator.'

Curtis speed typed the answer into his spreadsheet. 'Question eight and the last one for now.' Ruby openly sighed with relief. 'An internet search suggested we should have pet names for each other.' Ruby snorted but Curtis continued. 'It recommended a shortening of their first name. Do you think I should go with Cord or Delia?'

'Does that make you Curt by name and by nature?'

Ruby grinned but Curtis was serious, so she tried to chase the grin away with a frown. 'Well, Curt, let's see . . . Cord makes me think of old men's trousers and Delia is a celebrity chef who shouts at football matches.'

'I might have to rethink that one.' He tapped away on his keyboard.

'I don't think this is working,' said Ruby, trying to get a signal by waving her mobile about.

'The spreadsheet or the phone?'

'Both.'

'You won't get any reception up here,' said Curtis.

She put down her phone and sipped her Coke. 'I was going to check if Lewis had been in touch.'

Curtis turned his body towards her. 'Explain.'

'Don't get your hopes up. I tweeted about Lewis and the engagement ring and asked people to retweet it. I'm hoping we can find him through social media.' She jiggled her bottom across the rug towards Curtis and showed him her phone screen. 'If it was working, it would show me how many people have shared the tweet and liked it. That all helps more people to see it.'

'Can you target an area or people by age group?' he asked.

'No, it's not that sophisticated. It's just people who follow me or look up the hashtag.' Now she thought about it the chances of finding him were pretty slim. 'I wish I'd taken a photo of Lewis. That would have been easier; I have a much bigger reach on Insta.' Curtis chuckled. 'What?' she asked.

'That wouldn't have been odd at all. Taking a photograph of a stranger you'd just met on the train.'

'True.' He had a point.

'I've never subscribed to social media. It looks like a thorough waste of time.'

246

'I thought you were the techy king,' she said with a smirk.

'Only serious technology.'

Ruby gave a mock gasp and held her palm to her chest like she'd been shot. 'I'm wounded. Are you saying selfies and photographs of your dinner aren't serious?'

'Precisely.'

'Is Cordelia online?'

'I don't know.'

'When we get back to civilisation, I'll stalk her.' Curtis looked momentarily anxious. 'Not in the weird "go through your bins" way. In the "look you up on Facebook", completely acceptable way.'

Curtis didn't appear convinced. 'Do you think social media is something we could have in common?'

'Not if you're not genuinely interested in it. When I said you needed more in common I meant you needed to talk to her to find out what those things are, not ask what she likes and then pretend that you like them too.'

'That may prove quite difficult. You see, Ruby, I'm not a very interesting person.' His eyes seemed sad and she wanted to hug him but she refrained.

'Curtis, you are anything but that. In fact, I will put my neck out here and say you are without doubt the most interesting person I have ever met. With the possible exception of my Great Uncle Norris who was a hoarder. Going up his stairs was like crossing a land mine site. You had to be super careful where you put your feet, or you'd tread on a bag of muesli. I fell once and bags exploded around me like oat confetti. Boosh!' She acted out the mini explosions and he laughed.

'Thank you . . . I think. Perhaps I shouldn't pursue a relationship with Cordelia. Like you say, it's probably doomed to failure.'

'I never said you and Cordelia are doomed. Me and any male on the planet – yes. But not you two. Don't give up.'

'Do you get lonely?' he asked.

For a moment she was going to laugh it off but this was Curtis and something compelled her to be real with him. 'Yeah, sometimes I do. I miss my mum. I know that sounds lame at my age, but I do. I miss being able to tell her stuff. I miss her laugh. Grief keeps catching me unawares. I go a few days without crying and I think I'm doing okay then wham.' She clapped her hands together. 'It comes out of nowhere like that ninja guy from Inspector Clouseau.'

'Cato Fong.'

'That's him . . .' She paused. 'How do you know his surname? I didn't even know he had a surname.'

Curtis shrugged. 'I remember stuff.'

'I've noticed. Do *you* get lonely?'

Curtis lay back and stared at the clouds. 'I'm not sure I do. I fill my time. I suppose that's all we're doing here on earth. Filling time however we see best.'

Ruby sighed and lay back too. 'Makes life seem a bit pointless really.'

'Ultimately it is.'

'Aren't you a ray of sunshine?' She looked across at him and saw him smile.

'Apart from procreation. That makes it worthwhile. Continuing the species,' he said.

'Is that what's driving the whole sperm donor endeavour? The need to reproduce?'

For a moment she wondered if he'd want to continue the species with her but a giant image of Cordelia popped into her head and stopped her. 'I think it's a bit deeper than the timer on my ovaries going off.'

'Or maybe it's the desire to solve your loneliness issue?'

She thought about what he was suggesting. Both were possibilities. Her head started to fill up with questions. Why was she so focused on having a baby? She sat up quickly. 'Shit, Curtis! I thought I just wanted to be a mum. Now you're making me think all sorts of things.' And some of them she didn't like the idea of at all.

Kim wiped the cider off her chin. She wanted to think Vince was joking but she could see from his face that he wasn't.

'You're actually serious?'

'Deadly. No pun intended.' He gave a cheeky grin.

She laughed even though it wasn't funny. 'After what you did?'

'You just forgave me!' He looked indignant.

She snatched up some serviettes and started mopping up the spillage. 'Vince, I know this is a tough time for you and I sympathise, I really do, but you can't just click your fingers and expect me to forget what happened.' She'd only forgiven him to be nice and a little because she felt cornered, but she could hardly tell him that. 'Forgiving is one thing. Forgetting, now that's a whole other issue.'

'I know. And I'm not saying make a decision now. I'm saying think about it.' She went to protest and he held up his palms. 'Please, Kim. Think about it. Not for too long though eh?'

She suddenly felt the weight of what he was asking land on her. She had been expecting him to apologise and then leave her in peace – not this. She stood up. 'This was a bad idea.'

'Come on.' He waved his hands for her to sit back down. 'I'm sorry. I shouldn't have put you on the spot.

Please don't leave. Forget I said anything. We'll have a nice meal and then . . . well . . . that's up to you what happens afterwards.'

'Nothing, Vince. Nowt is going to happen.'

'Okay.' He nodded. 'I get it.' He waved his hands for her to sit down and against her better judgement she did.

Ruby lay back, watching a butterfly's wonky flight and pushed the thoughts of what was driving her need for a child to the back of her mind to concentrate on things that were far easier to deal with.

'If you're set on Cordelia we need to do some serious shopping and more coaching.'

Curtis puffed out a breath. 'I was afraid of that.' He sat up. 'I think we need a plan.'

She held in a smile. 'And a spreadsheet?'

'Definitely,' he said, his face deadpan. 'I'm not joking.'

'Oh, I know you're not.' She gave him a gentle nudge with her elbow and after a brief pause he reciprocated. 'Here you go,' said Ruby, pulling something from her pocket and handing him a crumpled piece of paper with something scribbled out on one side. 'I've been doing some preparation of my own.'

'And this is?' asked Curtis, scanning both sides, choosing the one where everything was crossed out.

'Rough calculations of my menstrual cycle, which you don't need to know about.' She'd been working out the best dates for her to conceive a baby before the whole London trip fiasco. She turned the page over in his hand. 'This, however, is a list of areas I think we need to cover.' She gave it a tap. She was quite proud of what she'd come up with. She was definitely more organised since she'd been working for Curtis. She had to be. Juggling the two jobs was tricky sometimes but it made the week go quicker and she had a bit more cash – it was all good.

Curtis read the page. 'Clothing – purchase of casual outfits. Capsule mix-and-match wardrobe. Communication – conversation, discussion topics, no-go areas and texting.' He glanced at her over the top of the page. 'You've put a lot of thought into this.'

'I have. Next weekend we could go shopping. Carry on – Jonty gave me the lowdown on Cordelia's interests.' She waved at him.

'New hobby – investigate one of the following: singing in a swing choir, Zumba, upcycling furniture or baking. But you said I wasn't to pick something she liked and say I liked it too.'

'No, but this is a way of you trying out what we know she already likes and seeing if you like it too. That's different. And to be fair, you need a hobby.'

'Accepted.' He read on. 'Body language.' He stared at the page for a moment and then at Ruby. 'That's all it says.'

'Did you know that the words we use only account for seven per cent of how we communicate?'

'Yes. That's Albert Mehrabian's theory.'

Of course he knew. 'Right. But do you apply that theory?'

'No. In my experience I've found if you are clear with the words you can interact effectively.'

'That's not going to work with Cordelia. Research by psychologists at Harvard University has shown that women are far more alert to body language than men.'

'Harvard?' For a moment there was a smile on his lips.

'Yeah. The more I think about this one the more I think it's important. Women have a sixth sense. We can tell when men are lying.'

251

Curtis pouted. 'Can I refer my learned friend to the sperm donor in West Ham?'

Ruby thought for a moment. 'If my initial conversation with Neil had been face to face and not by email I probably wouldn't have gone ahead because I would have known he wasn't telling the whole truth from his—'

'Cardigan?' suggested Curtis.

Ruby folded her arms abruptly. 'No.'

Curtis narrowed his eyes in thought. 'Height?'

'No, his body language.' She watched him roll up his shirt sleeves. 'I think we've got a lot of work to do.'

Chapter Twenty-Seven

Curtis had unwittingly given Ruby a lot to think about. Why was she set on having a baby on her own? She'd thought she'd known the answer but now the waters were as muddy as if a herd of elephants had trampled through them. She'd been sure her motivation had been triggered by her mother's last words and that she would achieve her dream of being a mother without the hassle of a useless man, but now Curtis had sown some different seeds.

Ruby had to admit it was uncomfortable to think that perhaps on some level she was lonely but she was pretty certain that wasn't what was driving her need to be a mother. She checked the various dating apps she had previously subscribed to. One of them was offering a limited-time reduced membership and it was tempting. She chewed her lip while she thought about it. She was still vetting her options for a sperm donor. There was no reason why she couldn't have a last little foray into the world of dating whilst also thinning down her donor options. She clicked on the app and began scrolling.

At the end of the day she was a romantic at heart. All the books she read told her that the man for her was out there somewhere and despite skip-loads of evidence to the contrary, she harboured the dream of finding someone who truly loved her. Maybe one last try in case her Prince Charming was lurking amongst the weirdos.

Ruby was due in early that Tuesday to finish the wreaths for a big funeral that morning. She knocked on the door and was met with frantic barking as Kim was dragged to the door by Boomer.

'Come in quick,' shouted Kim, flicking the latch and hanging on to the dog's lead.

Ruby did as she was told and dropped to her knees inside the shop, which was an open invitation for Boomer to jump all over her. 'How are you, gorgeous?' The dog left a little trail of wee around her in response.

'Someone's excited to see you,' said Kim, fetching the mop.

'I have that effect on a lot of people.' He jumped around Ruby like he'd been fitted with springs. 'He's still quite excitable.'

'We've got our first training class tonight. It's for diffi-cult-to-train dogs.'

'He'll be fixed by tomorrow then,' said Ruby.

'You're funny.' Kim led Boomer into the back and gave him instructions to lie in his bed, which he ignored while she tied his lead to the bench leg. After some barking and whining, he eventually lay down and stared at them as they set to work.

They updated each other on what had been happening in their lives and the time soon ticked away while the wreaths stacked up.

'Let me get this straight,' said Kim, waving a yellow chrysanthemum in Ruby's direction. 'You are coaching Curtis in how to pull another woman?'

'I'm helping him, yeah. What of it?'

Kim pouted. 'You are willingly going to send gorgeous, tall, eligible Curtis and his grade-A quality sperm into the arms of another woman? More than that, you are actively orchestrating it?'

'You missed out sensible and smart.'

'Exactly. Curtis is a catch and you're lobbing him at someone else without even considering him.'

'I'm not *not* considering him.' Ruby busied herself with finishing the ribbon on the large heart cushion arrangement she'd been working on.

'So, you are considering him?' Kim was leaning forward, trying to make eye contact.

Ruby titivated the bow while she thought. She didn't like to admit that the more time she spent with him the more she liked him because that wasn't helpful at all. 'We have nothing in common. He's way too clever for me. He's not shown any interest in me like that and . . .' She tailed off.

'You once told me you were holding out for the full fairy tale. Is that still the case?'

'I guess but it sounds ridiculous when you say it. I'm going to have one more shot at dating and then I'm going to do the sperm donor thing but properly this time.'

'Curtis is lovely. Why isn't he the fairy tale?'

'Because he drives me crackers. He knows everything about everything but then he knows nothing about life or people. He is obsessed with spreadsheets and order. He dresses in the same suit, shirt and tie – he's got, like, loads of identical outfits. He is consumed by his work – that's literally all he does. He has no hobbies or outside interests. Curtis is so far from the fairy tale he's a horror movie.'

'Hmm,' said Kim.

'What do you mean "hmm"?'

Boomer started to whine and Kim inserted the last of the chrysanthemums with a flourish and went to give him a fuss. 'Bloody hell, Boomer,' said Kim.

'What is it?' asked Ruby but she could already see the problem. While they'd been talking Boomer had been happily munching on the strands of beads until they were a chewed, straggly mess.

Kim picked up the scissors and started giving the curtain a haircut. 'Do you fancy going out for a drink sometime? My local has some . . . entertainment coming up.'

'Yeah. Okay.'

'Great,' said Kim, looking pleased with herself.

Kim was delighted with how Boomer's first couple of days at the shop had gone. Apart from an initial attempt at destroying the beaded curtain and some barking he'd been pretty good and the customers loved him. She was glad she'd got Boomer because he was keeping her occupied and that meant less time to think about Vince and Adrian. Although in reality Vince and Adrian were all she'd thought about. Vince kept messaging her to say he wasn't pressuring her, which he obviously was by the multitude of messages and she hadn't seen Adrian since he'd accused her of hitting Hayley and walked out. She couldn't see a way to fix things with Adrian without calling his daughter a liar.

Her phone rang as she pulled into the car park near where the dog training was taking place. She didn't need to look at the screen to know it was Vince. She switched it off. A rap on the window made Kim scream and Boomer barked furiously, triggering the woman to leap away.

Kim buzzed down her window and shouted over the din of Boomer's barking. 'Sorry!'

'It's okay. I was asking if this was where the dog training was but I think you've answered my question.'

The woman was well dressed, wearing full make-up and was chewing gum. Her French bulldog, Nelson, had the opposite problem to Boomer. Nelson was apparently scared of everything and everyone – apart from, it seemed, Boomer. They went inside and Kim started filling in the form she was given until she dropped the pen and Boomerang demolished it almost before it had hit the floor. She was pleased she'd already paid online, or he might have eaten her credit card too.

Kim found it reassuring. As more and more dogs arrived, the volume increased and rather than all the perfectly behaved dogs that she had met on her walks, these were a bunch of misfits and tearaways. They did introductions and most were rescue animals. The woman she'd met in the car park was called Elaina.

There were a mixture of breeds including a couple of greyhounds, two other spaniels, a sausage dog, three that were something crossed with a poodle and a German shepherd with bladder issues and a very apologetic owner. There was also a couple who had inherited a spoilt yapping Shih Tzu when their grandad had died.

Elaina whispered in Kim's ear. 'That one fits his breed name, he's a right little shi—'

'Evening, everyone,' said the good-looking organiser, bouncing a tennis ball and gaining the attention of anything with more than two legs. Sadly, one of the rescue greyhounds only had three. 'Thanks for the introductions. I will try to learn your dogs' names by the end of the course but rest assured I won't remember yours.' Everyone laughed.

'Shame,' said Elaina, 'I was hoping he'd be screaming mine by the end of the course.' She laughed at her own joke while her French bulldog relieved himself on the Shih Tzu.

He started off by telling them there were no untrainable dogs, only untrainable humans. At which point Boomer slipped his lead and raced over to meet the German shepherd who promptly wet herself. 'Sorry,' said Kim as she and Boomer did the walk of shame back to their spot.

The group exercises were pretty hard with everyone trying to gain their dog's attention. However, the parts where some past graduates stepped in to help were more effective as they were looking at the issues specific to each dog.

The trainers showed Kim that because Boomer was easily excited a silent approach with no eye contact was the quickest way to calm him down. It took a while but eventually he stopped jumping up and as soon as he sat down, they rewarded him with a morsel of food and praise.

The leader started bouncing the ball while Kim was distracted by the three-legged greyhound trying to mount the incontinent German shepherd, and Boomer was gone. He raced over with his lead trailing behind him, snatched the ball and destroyed it in record time.

'New balls please!' shouted Elaina and followed it with a screech of a laugh that was enough to stop even Boomer in his tracks.

'Sorry,' said Kim, finally wrestling what remained of the leader's tennis ball from her dog's jaws.

'Not a problem.' He turned his attention back to the group. 'This is a great example of your dog attention-seeking. This is when you must ignore his behaviour until he presents you with behaviour you want to reward.'

If she did that at home Boomer would destroy the place in ten minutes flat. She figured she'd have to pick and choose the bits of the course that worked for her. The time flew by just like Boomer after a ball and generally she felt it had been very helpful. Granted, Boomer spent most of the session trying to make friends and destroy tennis balls but overall Kim felt it had been a positive session.

Elaina grabbed her arm as they left. 'Don't you get expelled for chewing someone's balls?'

The man with the three-legged greyhound made a lewd comment, which they both ignored. 'Apparently it's okay so we'll be back next week. Will you?' asked Kim.

'Maybe. Definite lack of fit blokes at this one though.'

Kim's brain started to whirr. 'You've been before?' She glanced at Elaina's French bulldog, sitting obediently next to her.

'It's our eighth course. Shhh.' She put her finger to her lips, which did nothing to suppress the cackle of a laugh that escaped. 'Take care.' She waved as she walked back to her car.

Kim was desperate to share what had happened with someone else who'd find the evening funny. She bundled Boomer into the car and dialled Ruby's number. It went straight to voicemail. She stared at her phone for a moment. Who else could she call? She dialled his number and waited.

Chapter Twenty-Eight

'Welcome to Meadowhell!' declared Ruby that Sunday.

'It looks that way.' Curtis swallowed hard as busy shoppers barged past him.

'How can you not have been here before?' Ruby asked Curtis. He was blinking rapidly at the sight of Meadowhall shopping centre.

'I have clothes I like. I reorder more of the same online.'

It was hard to argue with his logic. 'That is a little restrictive. Don't freak out about the size of this place because we are targeting a few key stores. I wouldn't be so cruel as to take you on a full-on browsing session. That's the sort of thing you need to build up to.'

'Or not.'

'Or not,' she agreed, registering his already obvious distress. 'I'm thinking Hollister, Jack & Jones, Jack Wills and Levi's to start.'

'To start?' His eyes pinged wide.

'Trust me. I'm going to make this as painless as possible.' She gave him her best smile to which he shook his head.

Ruby had thought through what Curtis's casual style might be. She'd actually done extensive online research, which mainly consisted of googling Ryan Reynolds,

Nicholas Hoult and Robert Pattinson. But it had helped her to carve out a style she thought would suit him. He was most definitely not a sweatpants and baseball cap kind of guy but short-sleeved shirts with tailored trousers or shorts might possibly work.

Their first stop was Levi's. 'If we can nail the jeans, the rest will flow.'

'But, jeans.' Curtis scanned the shop. 'They're all the same. Blue denim created for goldminers.'

Ruby gasped. 'The same? Oh boy do you have a lot to learn.' Having already obtained his sizes she went along the shelves and rails, pulling out styles she thought might suit him and adding them to the ever-growing pile in his arms. When at last she was happy they had at least one pair of each of the key cuts she shooed him into the changing rooms. 'Try them on, but can you come out to show me?'

Curtis raised an eyebrow. 'This is like school uniform all over again.'

'I promise you won't have to grow into these though. Go on.' She waved him into the changing rooms and he reluctantly retreated.

The first few pairs were a bit too fitted, which was apparent by the level of squirming Curtis was doing. It was no good if he was going to be uncomfortable. The next were too baggy. He had a nice bum – it would be a shame not to frame it in well-fitting denim. On the fifth pair he trudged out looking like a broken man.

'Stand up straight.'

'It really is like school.'

'Stop moaning. I think these could be the ones.' She circled him like a lioness eyeing a tasty gazelle. They looked good – slim on the leg, grazing the top of his shoes and nicely cut over his backside but not tight.

'Does that mean we can stop?' he asked, straightening his body and showing off the jeans.

'Yeah.'

'Wonderful,' said Curtis.

'We can stop looking for jeans, but we need lots of other things.' Curtis began to droop again. 'Uh-huh,' she said, waving her arms and he reluctantly straightened up. 'Sold,' she said, clapping her hands together. 'We'll have a coffee break because I'm kind like that – and then the real fun begins.'

'I'm not even going to ask,' muttered Curtis and he traipsed back into the changing rooms.

After a quick coffee and Coke break, they set off again. They didn't last long in Hollister – the noise and smell were too much for Curtis – but she did manage to get him to try on a couple of nicely fitted plain T-shirts before she admitted defeat. He was a lot more at home in Jack Wills, the slightly formal side of casual was right up his street. Ruby found a few things she wanted him to try and he offered up a couple more. She felt a small drop of pride as he presented her with a striped shirt.

'That would look amazing with these.' She pulled some navy chinos off a rail, ushered him over to a mirror and held the clothes against him.

Curtis stared at his reflection. 'I like them,' he said at last and Ruby wanted to hug him.

'Try them on. That's my top tip. Always try clothes on and remember the sizing is just a guide. Don't get hung up on it. If you need a size bigger then go bigger.' She heard her mum's voice in her own.

Curtis didn't look like he fully understood but he said okay and took the bundle they'd acquired off to the changing rooms. This time when he came out, he looked different and not merely because of the clothes. The way he held himself, the comments and critique he made about the fit showed his interest. On his third change he came out in a logo'd T-shirt and tailored shorts.

'I'm thinking yes to the shorts but no to the T-shirt,' he said, leaning forward as if seeking her approval.

'Totally agree. Try the pink T-shirt, with those shorts.'

'Pink.' He didn't look sure. 'Okay,' he said, nodding his head vigorously as if he needed to psych himself up.

When he emerged, Ruby felt a little emotional. 'Look at my little boy all grown up,' she joked.

'Is it all right?' He turned to check himself in the large mirror.

'You look great.' He looked more than great. He looked amazing. Gone were the formal suits and shirts and with it the crusty hard edges of Curtis. The man before her was like the male equivalent of the caterpillar to butterfly transformation. He definitely looked fanciable now and she was proud of the part she'd played in his metamorphosis.

'And you think Cordelia will approve?'

Hearing her name brought Ruby back to reality. They were doing all this for another woman. 'Of course, she'll love you. I mean it. She'll love *it*.' How could she not?

It was a busy Friday in the shop and Ruby was finding it hard to concentrate. Unhelpful images of Curtis in a variety of new outfits kept popping up in her mind, especially the one of him trying on a pair of swimming shorts. They'd been in the sale, so she'd added them to the pile and he'd come out of the changing rooms to show her, like for all the other outfits, only on this occasion he had been topless.

'Hey. You okay?' asked the customer, waving a hand in front of Ruby's face. She'd zoned out *again*.

'Me? Yeah. Sorry. You want to pay for the Curtis . . . I mean cactus.' She could feel Kim's eyes dart in her direction but she ignored her. She finished the transaction and then went into the back room to give Boomer a fuss. He jumped about a bit, so she ignored him as Kim had instructed her to do and eventually, he sat down and she gave him a head rub.

What was happening? She didn't fancy Curtis. Being attracted to Curtis would be like being turned on by a robot. It made no sense. Her phone sprang into life, making the dog bark and Ruby jump. It was Curtis.

'Hey, you,' she said and cringed at the false way it sounded.

'Hello, Ruby. I know this isn't within your job description but I've been told that I can move back into my house and I was wondering if . . .' Ruby's brain filled in the slight pause with a multitude of options, some of them including Curtis in his swim shorts '. . . you'd be interested in helping me purchase new soft furnishings?'

Okay that wasn't one of the things she'd imagined. 'You want me to shop with you?'

'It's something you appear to be well qualified for. The builders have finished and I'm moving back in tonight but the place is a bit sparse as a lot had to be disposed of. I'm not good with interior design but I have a feeling you are.'

She didn't want to seem overly keen. 'I guess I could come over and give you a few suggestions. Let me check my diary . . .' She left a pause.

'I was thinking you could come over this evening to see what I have that's staying because anything new would need to match. And then perhaps we could shop online?'

'I can probably move a few things around,' she said, trying to sound nonchalant.

'I'm sorry. If you're busy that's fine. I can google someone local to—'

'No, no, no. I've checked and I'm free,' she said in a hurried voice.

'Great.' He sounded pleased. 'Do you like cottage pie?'

'Yeah. Who doesn't? It's as English as Saint George,' she said, marvelling at her own geekiness.

'He was Greek.'

'Right. Thanks for that nugget – it's good to know. I still like cottage pie.'

'Then I'll cook. I'll pay you, too, for your time.'

'Just the cottage pie will be lovely,' she said.

'Excellent. Seven o'clock?'

'See you then.'

She ended the call and held the phone to her chest. He was going to cook for her and then she was going to spend his money on soft furnishings – it was pretty much her ideal date.

Kim's head popped through what was left of the beaded curtain and she coughed, making Ruby hastily stop hugging her phone and shove it back in her pocket.

'Customers,' said Kim and she disappeared.

Ruby served an elderly gentleman while Kim was taking details of an order. The door chimed and in walked Adrian. He glanced at Kim but waited behind the elderly gent as if waiting for Ruby. She gave the man his change and he left.

'Hi, Adrian. Usual?' asked Ruby.

'Please.' He gave a trite smile and watched her closely while she made up the bunch of flowers for him. Usually he would have been talking to Kim but, even if Ruby hadn't been serving him, she got the distinct impression the two of them wouldn't have been chatting. It was such a shame. Everything had become complicated thanks to Hayley.

Kim finished with her customer and scuttled out the back where she had a word with Boomer. Ruby saw Adrian lean to one side to get a look at the dog – or was it Kim? 'You can go and say "Hi" if you'd like,' said Ruby. 'To Boomer.'

'What? Oh, it's okay. Thanks,' said Adrian, handing her his card.

Another customer came in and Kim reappeared shortly after the door sounded. 'How can I help?' Kim asked the young man who was wearing a fluorescent jacket and carrying a couple of small bunches of sad-looking chrysanthemums.

'I'm a bit short of cash but I want to give my girlfriend a really nice bouquet. Could you rewrap these with a big bow? What would that cost?'

Ruby braced herself for Kim's response. This had been happening more frequently after they'd done it a couple of times and now folk were taking advantage they'd had to put a firm stop to it. With Kim's current mood this bloke was likely to get a very blunt response indeed.

'Apart from my credibility and sanity?' Kim's eyes were doing that fixed stare you saw villains do in films right before they glowed red.

'Sorry?' The man looked confused.

'Let me put it this way: would you buy a steak from Aldi and take it to The Ritz and ask them to cook it for you?'

'No, but wouldn't that be a lovely thing to do?' He flashed Kim a cheeky grin but it only seemed to make her scowl harder.

'Sod off!' She waved her arm at him. The ferocity made him bolt for the door.

He checked over his shoulder as he left. 'You've lost my business.'

'Good!' Kim slammed the door behind him.

Adrian cleared his throat. Ruby was still holding his bouquet, transfixed by the exchange.

'Here you go,' she said, handing it over. Adrian took it and with a glance at Kim gave an imperceptible shake of his head.

'Have you got something to say?' asked Kim, her hands shooting to her hips as if in challenge.

'Your temper is losing you customers now.' He reached for the door and Ruby prepared for Armageddon.

'What, him?' Kim laughed. 'He's not a customer. He wanted something for nowt. I'm worth more than that. And anyway, I'm completely calm.' She relaxed her stance, put her hands in her pockets and slumped against the counter at an odd angle, making her look like she may have had a stroke.

'Boomer seems well,' said Adrian, looking uncomfortable.

'Why wouldn't he?'

'Okay, Kim. You know what? It's none of my business any more.' He held up his hands, and the flowers, in surrender and went to move towards the door.

Kim beat him there and opened the door for him. 'You're right, it's not.'

Adrian paused for a moment and Ruby was willing him to say something that would make things better between them. She so wanted those two to get together.

'Hello,' called out a cheery voice. Vince stepped through the open door.

Kim swallowed hard. 'Well, hello, Vince.' She said his

name clearly and Adrian's head snapped up. Their eyes met and Kim's eyebrows jumped up, daring him to comment.

'Bye, Kim,' said Adrian. He put his head down and left. Kim watched him leave until Vince's arm snaked around her shoulders and seemed to bring her attention back to him. She shrugged off his arm.

'You okay?' he asked.

'Yes, I'm fine,' she said, shutting the door and pasting on a smile.

Chapter Twenty-Nine

Curtis's house looked quite different from the last time Ruby had seen it. The lorry had gone, the fencing had been replaced and there was no sign at all, apart from the freshly painted frontage, that there had ever been an accident. She noted the returfed section of lawn as she knocked on the door.

'It's open,' came his muffled call from inside.

She walked in and the smell of home-cooked food assaulted her nostrils. Her stomach rumbled in response. She shut the door and lingered a moment in the hallway to look at the single photograph on the plain white wall. A couple and an awkward-looking teenage boy smiled back at her. She could tell the man in the photograph was Harry and behind the braces, she could see Curtis.

'Good, you did hear me,' said Curtis, poking his head into the hall. He saw what she was looking at.

'Your mum was beautiful.'

'Yes, she was. Her name was Ayida,' said Curtis and then he disappeared. Ruby followed him towards the increasingly strong scent of dinner. He was wearing one of the Jack Wills polo shirts in navy and had successfully teamed it with the cream chinos. She wasn't sure about the flip-flops but the rest of the outfit looked good. He caught her scanning him over.

'Does it not go together? Because you said stick with opposite colours. Light and dark so I thought . . .'

She waved his words away. 'It looks great. You've got it spot on.'

'Only thanks to you.' He took some cutlery from a drawer and handed them to Ruby. He nodded at the table at the far end of the kitchen. 'Five minutes to dinner. Could you lay the table?'

'Sure.' Ruby looked around the kitchen. Gloss white units, white-washed walls and a plain slate grey floor. The room was in monochrome just like Curtis. Or how he had used to be. She snuck another look at him in his new outfit but he was bending over, so she quickly looked away.

Curtis served up the food and they sat down to eat. Ruby tried a corner of her cottage pie. The flavours were a riot on her tongue. There was the mix of the creamy mash and the rich mince gravy she was expecting but there was a hint of spiciness too. 'This is really good.'

'You sound surprised.'

'If I'm honest, I am. I suppose we all make assumptions about people but I figured you were all numbers, spreadsheets and logic and that is my bad. You're a great cook.'

'Thank you but cooking is very logical. And I always find it odd that people praise the cook when all they have done is read a recipe. The skill is in the balancing of flavours, the alchemy of mixing ingredients in the correct quantities, not the reading and following of instructions.'

'I'd not looked at it like that,' she said in between fork-fuls. 'Who have I got to thank for this recipe? I'm guessing it's not a Delia Smith.'

'It was Ayida's recipe. I've a few like this. Her parents were Jamaican. She told me as a child they ate mainly Caribbean food at home but she loved to go to friends' houses for tea because the food was different. When she cooked for herself, she sort of took the best of both.'

'Great idea and this is delicious.' Ruby noted that she was almost finished and she slowed down.

'My favourite is her jerk roast chicken followed by banana, pineapple and chocolate trifle for dessert.'

'I love pineapple. Stop, I'll be moving in.'

Curtis appeared momentarily startled at the prospect. 'I can share the recipes with you. Ayida wrote out my favourites when I went to university. They are very straightforward. Like I said, it's just reading.'

They ate in silence for a while. She took time to pour herself a glass of water from a jug already on the table.

'I might have found you a man,' said Curtis.

Ruby wasn't sure how she felt about that as it had been a while since she'd even thought about their arrangement. 'Let's have some details then.'

'His name is Martin and he is single. He's one of the new testers and has an interesting background in analytics and—'

'Stop.' Ruby held up her fork. 'I'm not looking to employ him. What's he like as a potential boyfriend?'

'I have a photograph.' He got out his phone and showed the screen to Ruby. A slightly bewildered looking fortyish male was looking into the camera; assuming he had been propositioned by Curtis, the confused expression was understandable. Curtis continued. 'He's clean and tidy and calm in a crisis. I understand he enjoys snooker, both playing and watching it, so was very interested that you live near the Crucible. He is indifferent to Cleethorpes and the seaside but has made pension provisions and has no allergies to cats.'

'Wow. You've done your research.'

'Of course.' He seemed mildly affronted at the inference that he wouldn't have. 'Shall I pass on your details?'

Martin didn't sound like he was going to set her world on fire but Curtis looked pleased with his work. She really didn't have anything to lose. 'Er, yeah. Why not?'

Curtis took a photo of her with her mouth open. 'Hey!'

'He asked for a photograph.'

'Then we'll take a flattering one with filters after dinner,' she said, taking his phone off him and putting it out of reach.

'All right.'

She had another look around the pristine kitchen. 'They've done a good job in here. But it needs some colour to liven it up. Maybe some coloured small appliances; kettle, toaster that sort of thing. Plus a bright blind for the window and some pictures on this wall.' She pointed to the expanse of white behind him and he spun around. He turned back to look at her with his usual slightly puzzled expression.

'This room wasn't affected. I didn't think anything needed to be done in here.'

'Whoops. Sorry.' She focused on finishing her cottage pie.

'It's okay, Ruby. I value your opinion.' He glanced around the room as if seeing it in a new light. 'I suspect you're right. I'll add those things to the list. Could you choose an appropriate colour?'

'With pleasure.'

* * *

They stacked the dishwasher together. To be more accurate, Ruby started to stack it until Curtis took out the couple of things she'd put in, as he had an optimum way of filling the dishwasher. After that, she handed him the dirty stuff and let him do it his way. They retired to the living room with drinks.

Ruby took it all in from the doorway. It had the same white walls – she was sensing a theme. The room was spacious and uncluttered but somewhat sterile.

'No sofas or chairs?' she asked.

'They were wrecked in the accident. I'll get something for us to sit on.' He disappeared and she studied the room: a wood burner and the sturdy wooden beam above it were the central focus, not a television like in most homes. A small TV was in the corner – from its angle she got the feeling it was little used. A large white bookshelf was crammed with books but at a glance she could see none of them were novels – they were all academic and if she wasn't very much mistaken, they were in alphabetical order by author. There were no pictures, no photographs or ornaments.

Curtis appeared with two garden chairs and offered one to Ruby.

'Thoughts?' Curtis opened his laptop and was poised, studying her closely for a reaction.

'It's a lovely room. There's lots of light.'

'That would be the windows,' he said with a half-smile.

She stuck her tongue out at him. 'I'd say start afresh and go with a whole new colour scheme. What colour were you thinking?'

'White.'

'That's not a colour scheme. It's the blank canvas you start with. Like the kitchen, it needs some colour.'

'But what colour?' he asked.

'Hmm, good question. What colours do you like?'

Curtis scratched his head. He took a while to answer. 'There aren't any I don't like.'

'But what's your favourite?'

He narrowed his eyes. 'Why would I have a favourite colour? I'm not seven.' To anyone else he might have sounded rude but knowing him, as she now did, she just laughed.

'Because normal people have preferences for this sort of stuff. It's how the rest of the folk on this planet express themselves, by the choices they make and the impression they show to the world.'

He blinked. 'I see. That's insightful.'

'That's me.' She gave him a cheesy grin. 'I like lots of colour.' She ran a hand from her shoulder to her toes over today's vintage outfit and Curtis's eyes followed it.

'I had noticed that.'

'Rude!'

'Not at all. It's a hard thing not to notice.'

'Again, rude. But I get your point. I guess that's my thing. I want people to notice me but not because I have red hair. When I was a kid I stood out because of my hair.' She self-consciously ran her fingers through it. 'I was teased because of it, called names – and that was just my family.' Curtis gasped. 'Joke, Curtis. You should be able to spot those by now.'

'Yes. Sorry. Continue.'

'Kids at school were mean but that's what kids do. They find what's different about you and they isolate you because of it. I thought I'd left it behind when I went to university but no. Our dorm all had nicknames and mine was Red. However much I tried to introduce alternatives they never stuck. Although I was Miss Whippy for a couple of terms.' Curtis's eyebrows jumped and stayed there. 'Long story, it's to do with ice cream. Anyway, the point is I wanted people to see something other than the hair, so I started dressing in bright colours and patterns and it kind of became my USP.'

'Interesting.'

'Anyway, what's your favourite colour?' she asked.

'I have absolutely no idea.'

Kim found herself making spaghetti Bolognese for two while Vince tried to wrestle a tennis ball off the dog before he devoured it. She wasn't entirely sure how it had happened. There had been the phone call after the dog training class plus a few other messages. And today he'd offered to help her close up and they'd got talking. He told her he was back in Sheffield for a couple of days and before she'd really paid much attention, they were heading back to hers.

There was a comfortable familiarity with Vince. That sense of ease with another human being was still there. The hurt was too, but it was long since dealt with and filed away.

Kim watched Vince through the kitchen window as he raced after Boomer. He looked really well. A little over-weight, but then she could hardly talk. You'd never know he was counting down his last days. She didn't know much about the cancer that was killing him. He understandably didn't want to talk about it. She tapped on the glass and two heads snapped in her direction.

'Dinner,' she called out and they both raced inside.

Over their meal they chatted. There was nothing contentious this time and the conversation was easier. She'd missed many things about being married but this was an unexpectedly big one. The mundane chatter that she had taken for granted. The silly things they'd talked about. The in-jokes that only they had laughed at. These things had walked out of her life along with Vince. Loneliness had crept up on her like a changing tide. Slowly engulfing her and dragging her down.

They took glasses of wine through to her small front room and sat side by side on the old sofa they had spent many evenings curled up together on.

'I like your new place,' he said, giving a cursory look around.

It had been all she could afford after the divorce. He had wanted half of what little equity had been in their old house and she hadn't been able to borrow much thanks to a fledgling business. But he didn't need to know that. She was starting to realise she had to stop beating him with the same stick. 'Yes. I like it too. It suits me, and now Boomer as well.' At the sound of his name he trotted in from the hallway, where he had been suspiciously quiet. He put his head on Kim's lap and she stroked his ears, thankful that he wasn't doing his usual frenetic laps around the living room.

'I've been thinking, Kim. I want to make amends.'

'There's no need—'

'No, hear me out. I messed up and I'm sorry. I've managed to save a bit. Got a nice little place in Mablethorpe. Bigger place than this.' Was that a dig? She shook the thought away. It was just fact, she was being oversensitive. 'Anyway, I'd like you to have it all when I go.'

'What?' she spluttered the word out with a half laugh. Was he serious?

'I don't have anyone else.'

'You've a niece and nephew.' Who she sent a tenner to every Christmas.

'Oh, sure. Of course, and I'll leave them something but . . .' He took her hand. Boomer became interested and started to lick their intertwined fingers. 'I want you to have the rest.'

Kim didn't know what to say.

An hour flew by, culminating in Curtis reading through a varied list of items in his online basket. 'Shall I press buy?' His finger hovered over the button.

'Yep, it's all good. When you're next back from London we can go to that art gallery in Shef and you can pick a couple of interesting pictures. They'll make a talking point. Something to discuss when you're courting the lay-days.' Why she said it in a singsong tone, she had no idea.

'Yes. Good idea.' He pressed the button.

'Now, we need to talk about your new Cordelia-friendly hobby. Which one have you decided to go with?'

Curtis moved his garden chair closer to Ruby, his thigh rubbing against hers. He shared his laptop screen with her. 'I did a risk-benefit analysis for each of the options. And as you can see, baking is conclusively the best option.' He tapped his screen showing the longer list of positives.

'Conclusively,' said Ruby, quickly skimming the list. 'I'm quite disappointed the Zumba didn't come out on top.'

There was a brief frown before he spoke. 'Yes, me too.'

'Wow, is that sarcasm Mr Walker?'

'That's what I was aiming for.'

'Very good.' Her protégé was heading for graduation. 'How are you planning to get your Paul Hollywood vibe on?' Why was she talking like a dodgy DJ? She suspected it was something to do with the heat from his thigh that was radiating up her body and pretty much all she could focus on.

'Do you mean how am I going to increase my knowledge of baking?'

Apparently not ready to graduate yet. She rolled her lips together. 'Yep.'

'I thought I might knead some help.' He motioned with his hands. 'Failing that, I'll read some books on the subject and maybe even set up a rival to Greggs.'

'More sarcasm. My word, you're a regular Chandler Bing.'

'I have no idea who that is.'

'From a TV programme called *Friends*. My mum and I used to watch it. Anyway, the hobby seems to be under control. Let's go through the plan of action for next week in London.'

'There's a plan? I'm impressed.'

'I knew you would be.' She tucked a stray piece of hair behind her ear and pulled out her phone. 'Monday, you'll probably be working late because the project is going live – you could take her to the Thai restaurant in Leicester Square – she's a regular customer so ordering will be quick. Tuesday, I suggest you play it cool unless she asks you out, in which case check where it is and what to wear and go with it. Wednesday is the project party, so anything goes. But great opportunity to chat to her and bring up the subject of the new hobby you're starting.'

'But you'll be at the party too?' He was watching her closely.

'Er, no. I thought I'd give it a miss.' What she'd actually thought was that she only knew a couple of people and she didn't want to spend the evening playing gooseberry to Curtis and Cordelia.

'That's disappointing. It would be a good opportunity to meet Martin and you know there'll be free food and drink?'

'Yeah, I know but it's not really my thing.' She scrunched up her features as if she'd tasted something sour.

'I would have thought parties were very much your thing. Especially ones with single men and free alcohol.' He was like Boomer with a tennis ball – he wouldn't give it up.

'Anyway. Back to the plan. Thursday is your last night and I've booked dinner for the two of you at her favourite restaurant. Wear the dark chinos and the white casual shirt from Jack Wills and remember to mirror her body language where you can without looking like a Covent Garden mime artist.' She wanted to add: 'And if you haven't wowed her by the end of that, you're never going to.' She closed her list on her phone and saw the time. 'I need to make a move.' She stood up.

'Hang on, we need to discuss the ring.' She sat down, this time making sure there was a gap between his thigh and hers.

'I had no luck with social media.' She only had a few hundred followers and very few of them seemed keen to retweet her plea to find Lewis.

'Shall I hand it in to the police?' he asked.

'I think that's best.' They had exhausted all their options to return it. Maybe it was time to let it go.

'And what's our story if I'm questioned?'

She chuckled. 'You won't be questioned, Curtis. It's not *Line of Duty*.' He opened his mouth. 'It's a TV show,' she said before he asked.

'I think I might at least be asked why we've held on to it for this long.'

It was a good point. She had a dip into her imagination. 'How about you say we tried to get it to him at the London Eye but when that failed you thought it would be safest at home while you tried to track Lewis down. And that your girlfriend loved it so much, you've had a replica made. And that's all taken time.' She was pleased with her novel-worthy explanation.

Curtis didn't look convinced. 'Or I could say I was caught up with sorting out my house because of the accident and it slipped my mind.'

'Your version sounds more believable. Let's go with that.'

Chapter Thirty

Vince had put the television on and they'd spent an hour sitting together. There was some series on that he said she had to watch. It wasn't her sort of thing but it was something she knew she would have sat through with him in the past. She hadn't really been watching it. Her mind was fully occupied with his declaration that he was leaving her everything in his will. She was flabbergasted. More than that she was sad. Sad about the lost years, the fact that underneath it all, Vince was in fact a decent man. A decent man who had made a mistake. Here he was trying to fix things before his time was up.

He was leaving and she followed him out into the hallway. 'My solicitor might want to speak to you. I want to make sure everything is sorted out before I kick the bucket. I don't want any loose ends.'

'Right. Okay.' She was still a bit overwhelmed by it all. 'Vince . . .'

'Yeah?'

'Thank you. This is very kind of you.'

'That's me.' He beamed at her and she felt a little nostalgic for the years they had spent together. His expression changed. Almost as if he knew. He leaned forward and his lips brushed hers.

Boomer barked and came skidding into the hallway. The interruption pulled Kim back to her senses. 'Right, bye then,' she said, trying to reach the door handle and awkwardly darting an arm either side of him, like she was trying to spear something.

'Oh. Okay. Thanks for dinner.'

'My pleasure.' She held on to the dog by his collar while Vince went to leave.

'Whoops,' he said. 'Almost forgot my shoes. What an idiot.' He jogged through to the kitchen.

'Bloody hell!' he shouted. 'That sodding . . .'

'What's wrong?' she said, still holding on to both Boomer and the door.

Vince came back into the hallway. He was smiling but Kim knew him well enough to know it was forced and he was cross about something. 'The dog has only gone and eaten my shoe.' He held up the evidence and Boomer leaped to try to retrieve his chew toy. The shoe was trashed – there was a large hole at the toe and the tongue was hanging by a thread.

Kim stifled a laugh. 'Sorry,' she said.

Vince pulled a disgusted face as he put his shoe on. Boomer strained for the chance to finish off the job and Vince lurched away. Kim pulled the dog back. He whined and leaned against her leg, gazing up at her hopefully.

'Anyway, thanks again,' said Vince, standing up straight and stepping closer to Kim. He ran a finger across her cheek. She wasn't sure if he was trying to re-create their earlier moment but it had definitely passed.

'You're welcome.' She stood back with the door open.

'Right. My solicitor will probably give you a call.'

For a second she thought he meant because of his shoe

and then she remembered the will. 'You don't have to do this, you know.'

'But I want to. Night, Kim.' He gave her a brief kiss on the lips and left.

Boomer let out a whimper at the sight of his chew toy disappearing. Kim was quite pleased to close the door.

Ruby was watching her phone for more updates from Curtis on what she was calling Project Cordelia. He was becoming quite the regular messager. Tuesday in the shop had been quiet, except for Boomer who had had a bit of a noisy day. He was definitely calming down but because of that he seemed to overreact when he heard something and excitedly barked every time, so Kim had to settle him. He genuinely seemed thrilled to see everyone and the customers liked that.

A teenager was browsing the plants as they had quickly established he couldn't afford to buy his mum flowers for her birthday. He kept asking the price of each of the plants although the sign clearly explained the pricing and she was starting to ponder the similarity of the nearest plant to his haircut.

He picked up another pot and waved it at her. 'How much is this one?'

Ruby marched over. 'This, this and this are all the same price and they are the cheapest thing in the shop.'

'Still they're not exactly cheap, are they?'

'They will last, require minimum care and they're beautiful when they flower,' she explained.

'Is that it?'

What exactly did he expect a pot plant to do? 'If you feed it, it will grow.'

'Nowt else?'

'It plays "God Save the Queen" on the bagpipes. But only on Thursdays.'

He huffed, plonked one on the counter and a five-pound note next to it. 'Can you gift-wrap it?'

She gave him a tight smile, wrapped the tiny plant in reams of cellophane and finished it with a giant pink bow.

'Cheers, that's wicked.' He left appearing genuinely thrilled, she hoped his mother was equally pleased.

'How's Project Cordelia going?' asked Kim through the sparse beads.

Ruby groaned.

'That good eh?'

'Yes, and that's the problem. He's in London this week and he keeps updating me on how well it's going. They seem to be hitting it off. They're having lunch and tea together each day. I got him to buy a stapler for her as a comedy gift to remember him by.'

'A stapler?'

'I suggested he put a tag on it saying, "To hold things together after I've gone".'

'Cheesy, but good,' said Kim.

'Apparently she thought it was hilarious and showed everyone in the office. She's told him she'll have to get him something special too.'

'Ooh what?'

'No idea, it hasn't materialised yet. Grrr!' said Ruby and she laid her forehead on the counter.

'I'm sensing a problem,' said Kim.

Ruby kept her head on the counter but turned her face to Kim. 'You think?' She sighed and straightened up. 'I don't know what's wrong with me. This was the plan and it's working. I can't find myself a match but it's okay

284

because I'm helping Curtis get together with his. So why do I feel utterly shitty?'

Kim opened her mouth and paused. Ruby waited. Kim shut her mouth and waved her finger about like a Hogwarts first year with a dodgy wand. 'You're going to have to work that one out for yourself.'

She was about to challenge Kim but the door sounded and Boomer barked a welcome, which distracted her.

That evening Ruby was settling down on the sofa in her pyjamas with the latest Jill Mansell novel, Seymour and a hot chocolate when her phone lit up – it was a FaceTime from Curtis. She was instantly intrigued as they'd not FaceTimed before. She answered it before she remembered her PJs and then had to hold it at a very odd angle so only her head was in shot, which made her head fill the screen.

When the video connected, she saw Curtis baulk at the sight of her giant face and then disappear through a door. 'What's going on?' She peered closer to the screen. Where was he?

Two doors suddenly opened and Curtis appeared in a flourish. 'Ta-dah!' he chorused.

'Double doors,' she said with a gasp.

'You'd love these. There's even low-level lighting that comes on at night for you to find your way.'

'That's brilliant.' Her grin was making her face ache.

Curtis picked the phone back up. 'Are you wearing your pyjamas?' he asked.

'I might be. Anyway, was there anything else?'

'No, just the doors. I know you're busy but I had to show you.'

'Thanks. You've made my day. And good luck with Project Cordelia.' She showed him her crossed fingers.

He nodded, waved and ended the call. The joy of seeing Curtis and his double doors vanished with him. She stared at the blank screen and felt the loneliest she had in a long time.

After reading only a few chapters of her book, Ruby's phone rang and she answered it, expecting it to be Curtis again – she was already smiling at the prospect.

'Hi, I'm calling from Park View Residential Care Home. I'm trying to get hold of Curtis Walker but his phone goes to voicemail and it gave your number.'

'I'm his assistant. What can I do?'

'His father is asking for him.'

'I'm afraid he's away for work. Is it urgent?' She feared this was one of *those* phone calls.

'No, his health is the same as it was. He was just keen to see Curtis as soon as possible.'

'He's in London until the end of the week,' explained Ruby.

'Okay, I'll let him know. Thanks for your help.'

'No, hang on. I'll come over. Give me thirty minutes.'

True to her word, in less than half an hour she was knocking on Harry's door. He opened his eyes when she entered and she was sure she saw him smile. He was a man who was fading. It was like his batteries were slowly losing power.

'Hi, Harry, they called me in because you're driving Dot and Kitty wild again.'

His smile broadened and he struggled to lift his oxygen mask to speak. 'They wish,' he said with a gasp. His breathing had deteriorated. 'Where's Curtis?'

'He's living it up in London.' Harry raised a doubtful

eyebrow. 'Honestly. He's even going to a party tomorrow night.' *And probably pulling the woman of his dreams*, she thought sadly. 'So, you've got me instead.'

'Thank you. I don't get many visitors. Curtis is one of the few who keep in touch.'

'That's a shame. Did you foster many children?' she asked.

'One hundred and eighty-seven over twenty-two years.'

'Wow. That's a whole lot of kids.'

'I take it as a compliment that they don't keep in touch.'

'How do you work that out?' Ruby sat down on the bed.

'It means they went on to be even happier. We were always only meant to be a stopgap.' He took a moment to breathe deeply on the oxygen. 'Apart from Curtis. They found him adoptive parents three times but each time he came back to us.'

Ruby's heart ached for the lost little boy Curtis once was. 'Why was that?'

Harry sighed deeply. 'I think everyone has a picture of what their child will be like and Curtis never really matched anyone's expectations. Children aren't performing seals; they are fully formed individuals from a young age.' He took a shaky breath. 'That's hard for some prospective parents to understand. It's like any relationship – you have to accept people as they are. No good comes from trying to change them into something they're not.'

His words hit home. 'You're right. None of us are perfect.'

'True,' said Harry with a cough. 'We loved Curtis with all our hearts. I fear I've not told him often enough.'

'I'm sure he knows.'

He reached out and with a cold bony hand he clutched

287

hers. 'I've not got long.' Harry's expression was grave and it broke her heart a little.

'Nor me, there's a film on I want to watch,' she said with a wink.

He chuckled and it turned into a cough. 'You know what I mean. And there's things I need to tell Curtis.'

'Okay. Are we talking "I've got a map detailing ancient buried treasure" or is it some pearls of wisdom?'

'Both,' he said, returning the wink.

'Now I'm interested. You could tell me and I'll write it down?'

'Please.' He squeezed her hand again. 'You're perfect for our Curtis.'

She laughed out of embarrassment. 'Thanks, but I don't think he thinks of me like that.' She leaned closer. 'Don't say I said anything but he's interested in a woman at work.'

'Oh.' Harry looked crestfallen.

Ruby pulled her hand free from his and took out her phone. 'Right, you talk and I'll type.'

It was Wednesday and Ruby was very aware that tonight's party was likely to be the clincher between Curtis and Cordelia. Kim had done her best to keep Ruby busy all day and to her credit the day had flown by in a flurry of online orders and deliveries. Kim had promised her a night out and now she was quite looking forward to it, if only to take her mind off Project Cordelia. The taxi dropped Ruby off and she knocked for Kim. She hadn't been *out* out for a while, so she'd made an effort and done her hair and make-up.

'You look nice,' said Kim, exiting the house.

'Thanks. So do you.'

'Ta. I think I've lost a couple of pounds already thanks

to Boomer taking me for a walk every day. I've not worn this dress in ages.'

'It suits you,' said Ruby as they began to walk towards the pub.

'Right. Confession time,' said Kim.

'Oh dear. What have you done?'

'It's more what I'm about to do.' Kim scrunched up her shoulders. 'It's speed dating night.'

'Oh, Kim. No. I wanted to have a good girly natter. Not spend the evening being judged by some chancers looking for a quick hook-up.'

'Trust me. It's not the usual cheap and tacky set-up,' said Kim.

'They're all cheap and tacky.' Ruby shook her head, she couldn't hide her disappointment.

'This one is twenty quid and it's VIP dating.'

'Does that stand for Vomit-Inducing Plonker?'

'Hey. I've paid your twenty quid. Don't go slagging it off until we've at least checked it out. Tony behind the bar said it was bringing people in from all over. He's expecting a bumper night. And I thought it would be a giggle. Goodness knows we could both do with one.'

Ruby huffed out a breath. 'I don't know.'

'Aw, go on. We'll have a laugh and if it's rubbish then I promise we'll leave. Please,' begged Kim.

'You've given up on Vince and Adrian then?' asked Ruby.

'Vince comes with more complicated add-ons than satellite TV and I've not heard anything from Adrian. I saw the speed dating poster and thought it would be fun. Fun is what we both need right now.'

'Fun? There speaks the voice of a woman who hasn't had all her optimism trampled on by cocky middle-aged men in Marks and Spencer's brogues.'

'Come on,' said Kim, linking arms with Ruby and picking up the pace. 'Let's find you a man.'

They were about to go into the pub when Ruby's phone lit up.

'Just a sec, it's Curtis,' she told Kim as she accepted the FaceTime call.

Noise instantly blared out and Curtis's moving face blurred across the screen. 'Hellooooo from Londinium!'

Was he drunk? 'And hello to you,' she said, finding herself chuckling at the sight of Curtis letting his neat hair down.

Cordelia appeared at his shoulder and waved. 'Where are you, Ruby?' she asked, her voice sounding slightly slurred too.

'I'm in Sheffield. Are you all having a good time?' She could see that they were and she suddenly wished she'd gone. That feeling dissolved when Cordelia rested her head on Curtis's shoulder and he didn't flinch. She screenshotted it in her mind. It was hard to hear them over the general noise of the party.

'Yes, I'm having a time with lovely Curtis. . . I mean a lovely time with Curtis.' She hiccupped, which seemed to surprise her and she disappeared from view.

'This is Martin.' Curtis angled his phone at a snogging couple. 'I think you may have missed your opportunity there.'

'Never mind.' She shrugged.

'What?' he asked, clearly having trouble hearing her.

'I said. NEVER. MIND.'

'Shhh,' said Curtis, putting his finger to his lips and giggling like a child. 'I've found more double doors.'

She couldn't help but laugh along. 'Curtis, you're becoming obsessed.'

'I know. But you're right. You feel amazing when you walk through them. I'll show you.'

She caught a glimpse of people chatting, a waiter, and then they were somewhere slightly quieter. She stood up straighter, glued to the screen. Two double doors with port holes appeared.

'I'll turn you around for the full experience,' said Curtis. He pushed on the doors. 'Ta-dah!' There was a loud crash and Ruby caught a brief glimpse of a waiter lying on the floor covered in what looked like mini quiches. 'I am sooo sorry. Ruby, I've got to go.' He ended the call.

Inside the pub was actually quite nice. It had had a make-over since the last time Ruby had visited and although she wasn't going to let on to Kim, the few men already at the bar looked quite hopeful. Maybe this was what she needed. The discounted rate on her dating app had only brought in a new bargain basement of disappointment. What did she have to lose? Apart from a couple of hours and another drop of pride?

'Ooh, cocktails are half price,' said Kim, picking up a menu. 'Well, a few of them are.' She passed it to Ruby.

Ruby read them out. 'A Slow Comfortable Screw, Sex On The Beach, Screaming Orgasm and Slippery Nipple. Just the suggestively titled ones then.' Maybe this wasn't quite the classy VIP dating evening Kim had been sold.

'I like a Slippery Nipple,' Kim declared.

'Ladies, are you here for our VIP evening?' asked the barman.

'Yes,' said Kim, getting out her tickets.

'Excellent. Here's your score sheet. There's three rounds and a break after each one. I'll get you some drinks and

291

then you can make your way through to the back room. What can I get you?'

Ruby sighed. The nice-looking guys at the bar probably weren't there for the dating. 'I'll have a white wine, thanks,' said Ruby. She turned to Kim. 'If it's rubbish we leave after round one.'

Kim pondered. 'That's like three pounds a bloke.' Ruby raised her eyebrows. 'Okay, fine. If there's nobody you score more than half marks, we'll decamp into here for a natter instead. Deal?'

'Okay.' Ruby scanned the score sheet. Marks were to be awarded out of ten for Appearance & Hygiene, Personality, Conversation, and Sense of Humour. 'This is harsh.'

They took their drinks and wandered through to the other room. Ruby was still studying the score card and wondering how she would fare. She was freshly showered and doused in deodorant but she wasn't feeling particularly witty. She wished she was at the party with Curtis.

The woman on the door took their tickets, wrote their names on stickers and directed them to tables explaining that to start with they needed to sit facing the wall and then turn around when the bell sounded. A few other women were already sitting down facing the wall like they were in detention.

'Where are the men?' asked Ruby, suddenly thinking Kim might have signed them up for lesbian night.

'They have to wait at the bar.'

Ruby's enthusiasm lifted a little. After a few minutes the woman announced that the men were joining them and then the bell would sound and the first round of dating would start. She got that little squiggle of something in her gut. Was it excitement, anticipation or merely fear? She wasn't sure but right then and there she decided this was the last time she was going to put herself through something like this. All the judgement, the scrutiny and the whiff of desperation needed to end and tonight was that night. She immediately felt better about it all.

'Just enjoy it,' said Kim, reaching across and giving her arm a friendly squeeze.

Ruby heard footsteps enter the room and her pulse started to quicken. This was crazy but she had to admit it was quite exciting. The bell sounded. Ruby took a deep breath. She saw Kim turn slightly ahead of her.

Ruby turned around fully to face her first date. The man was putting his phone away. It was his jacket she noticed first and then the hair. He looked up. She couldn't quite believe it.

'Lewis?' It couldn't be, could it?

Chapter Thirty-One

Ruby found she was doing the rapid blinking thing she'd often seen Curtis do, but it wasn't changing the image in front of her. Lewis was sitting at her table large as life.

'I can't believe it's you.'

Lewis was giving her an odd look. 'Do I know you?'

'I'm Ruby from the train a few weeks ago. I've been looking for you.' She was beyond excited to have found him and was doing that slightly crazy arm-waving thing she sometimes did. 'I've got your ring. Not me exactly. A friend, who I also met that day on the train. He's got it. It's in his safe. So, it's . . . um, safe.' She was rambling. She gave a short smile.

Lewis's expression changed and his shoulders seemed to relax. 'Ruby! Oh my God, it's really you. And you found the ring – that's terrific. I thought I'd never see that again.'

'Sorry. We tried to get the ring back to you. We went to the London Eye but we must have missed you.'

'Wow, that was super kind of you. I can't believe you recognised me.'

'I've got a good memory for faces and it was such a big day for you. And I've been thinking about you a lot.' She felt her cheeks flush. She was wording this all wrong. 'I mean, wondering about what happened with your proposal after you'd lost the ring. Did your girlfriend say yes?'

There was a brief pause and she was aware of the intense chatter from the other tables around her. 'Er . . . No.' His lips made a flat line. 'Turns out I didn't need the ring after all. She stood me up.'

'What? She missed her own proposal?'

'She'd been seeing someone else so turns out it was a lucky escape. And that's why I'm here tonight.'

'Oh right. Yeah.' She'd almost forgotten she was at a speed dating event.

'My mate dragged me along actually. It's a bit soon after the split for me.' His face crumpled but he swallowed hard to compose himself.

'You must have been devastated.'

'I was. I thought she was the one.'

'I'm sorry. But at least you didn't give her the ring. We should swap details – then you can have your ring back and I can have my phone.'

'Crap. Your phone.' His hands shot up in the air. 'I am really sorry about that. I felt like such an idiot. There were so many people getting on and off I just hopped off the train for a second. Next thing I knew the train was leaving.'

'But you've still got my phone?'

His jaw tensed. 'No, I handed it in to lost property . . . at Kings Cross station.'

'St Pancras?' It was basically the same station but Curtis always called it St Pancras.

'Yeah. That one.'

'I didn't think to ask there. But I can give them a ring. Ha, ring . . . because you had a ring.' Why was she talking like a fool? It was best if she shut up.

'It's good to see you again, Ruby,' said Lewis, his eyes appraising her.

'It's good to see you too.' He reached for her hand and gave it a brief squeeze. Her heart gave a little flutter. The bell sounded and all the men stood up.

'I'll catch you in the break, yeah?'

She nodded and he beamed back at her as he moved on to Kim who was looking at Ruby and Lewis with interest. She mouthed at her that it was Lewis but Kim was rubbish at lip-reading.

A man a little older than Ruby with a buzz cut sat down opposite her but it was hard to drag her eyes away from Lewis. He was her ideal man apart from having a girlfriend but now he didn't. Maybe she could slot in her place and claim the fairy-tale ending for her own. She gave herself a mental slap and tried to concentrate.

'Hi, I'm Ruby.'

'Hey, Ruby, I'm Jackson. I love your hair.'

'Thanks. I like . . .' She was going to say she liked his and then realised he hardly had any.

'It's okay. I know I look like I've had nits. I shaved it off for charity.' He ran a palm self-consciously over his shorn head. They chatted and he seemed nice. He asked about her and he listened. But each time she glanced at Lewis he was looking right back at her. This was fate. She was absolutely sure of it.

When the break came, she was in dire need of another drink. Seeing Lewis had been the nicest shock ever but it was still a shock. Kim was chatting to the last man at her table and from what she could overhear, Ruby ascertained it was about spaniels.

She tapped Kim's arm. 'The queue at the bar will be huge.'

'Whoops, sorry. Got to go,' she said to the man. 'But lovely to meet you. Might see you dog walking,' said Kim and he nodded enthusiastically.

They went through to the bar and Ruby scanned the room for Lewis. It was busy and she couldn't see him.

'Any get over half marks? Are we staying for round two?'

Ruby glanced at her score sheet. She hadn't even bothered to mark Lewis. 'We can do. But something amazing has happened.'

'Ooh, which number was he?' asked Kim.

'The first one for me, and your second one. He was Lewis.'

Kim had the look of a toddler trying to answer questions on University Challenge. She scanned her own score sheet and read through her notes. 'Campervan T-shirt?'

'What?' asked Ruby.

'He was wearing a T-shirt with a campervan on it. Travels a lot for business. Really funny. I had to make notes or I'd forget who was who.'

'He's the guy I met on the train to London. The one whose engagement ring I found.'

'Wow. That Lewis?'

'Exactly.'

'And he's engaged and he's come to this?' She was frowning her disapproval.

'No, that's the best bit. He split up with his girlfriend. She dumped him!' She tried very hard not to sound too thrilled at this news but it was difficult not to. He was the kind of man she'd been searching for all along. Someone kind, funny and unafraid of commitment. But she needed not to get too excited. Just because he ticked all her boxes didn't mean she did the same for him.

Kim's head was on a swivel as she scanned the bar area. 'Where is he now?'

'No idea. We've arranged to swap numbers so I can give him the ring back.'

'Wasn't he about to propose like a month ago? Isn't it a bit quick for him to be doing this?'

'It was more than a month. Maybe four and a half weeks. And his mate dragged him along. Just like mine did.' She tipped her head at Kim. A space came free at the bar and Ruby linked arms with Kim and pulled her forward. 'My turn to get the drinks in. What are you having?'

Kim perused the cocktail menu again while Ruby had another surreptitious look for Lewis. The bar was packed and quite warm. The speed dating night had definitely been a success. She took her time to scan all around the room, checking every face for Lewis. There was no sign of him. Had he left already?

Kim's phone rang and a quick glance told her it wasn't a number she recognised. She almost rejected it. 'I'll have another Slippery Nipple,' Kim said to Ruby, before pointing at her phone and taking the call. She squeezed through the crowded bar with the phone to her ear but it was difficult to hear what the person was saying. 'Hang on,' she told the caller as she made her way outside.

The cool evening breeze was a relief. 'Right. Sorry about that.'

'Hello, is that Kim Baxter?' said the clipped female voice.

'Yes, it is.'

'I'm Sally Burrows, the solicitor acting for Mr Vincent Baxter. I understand you're expecting my call?'

Not at this time of night she wasn't. Her head wasn't

really in the right place for a serious conversation. 'Yes, but I'm out at the moment. Any chance you could call back tomorrow?'

'Sorry, I've been in court all day. This is the first chance I've had to speak to you but of course I can call back at a more convenient time.'

Kim felt bad. She walked a bit further up the road. 'It's okay. You can talk to me now if it's not going to take too long.'

'Thank you. I appreciate that. My client has made a new will and named you as sole beneficiary. This means his house, its contents and any money in his bank account will become yours upon his demise.' Even though Kim knew this, hearing it from someone official made it all seem too real. This was actually happening. Vince was dying. She took a steadying breath and listened. 'It would be helpful to me if you could provide details of your bank account so that in the event of his death his assets and the property proceeds would be easily transferred to you.'

'Right. Okay.'

'You can call me back with the details. You should also consider obtaining a power of attorney. That's a legal document that needs to be registered with the Office of the Public Guardian. I can do this for you but I'd need some identification from you.'

Kim's head was starting to spin. 'Look I'm sorry. This is more to think about than I realised. It's a lot to take in and like I said I'm not at home right now. Can I call you back tomorrow?'

'I'm afraid I'm in court all day again. I'll call you. Thanks for your time. Goodbye.' The phone went dead.

* * *

Ruby definitely needed a drink and the house white wasn't going to cut it. She fixed her eyes on the barman who was now making two Slippery Nipples. That way she wasn't tempted to keep scanning the bar. She was starting to look desperate and a balding plumber from the Manor Estate winked at her every time she turned round. She didn't know what Lewis did for a living although Kim had said he travelled a lot for his job so she must have asked him some questions when they'd had their one-to-one. Perhaps he'd been called away. Ruby was feeling that she'd quite like to have a proper one-to-one with Lewis and have a chance to find out a bit more about him.

She saw Kim come back inside and start fanning herself. She made her way through the bar and slumped an elbow on the counter. 'That was Vince's solicitor.' Kim rolled her eyes.

'At this time?' Ruby looked around for a clock and had another crafty look for Lewis – still no sign. The plumber gave her a wave and a wink and she hastily turned back to face Kim.

'She's been in court all day,' explained Kim. 'It's definitely happening. She's confirmed that he's leaving everything to me: his money, his house and its contents.'

Ruby twisted her lips. 'Blimey. Does that mean you have to sort through all his stuff after he . . .'

'Dies?' She finished the sentence for her. 'I guess so. That would be strange. The solicitor wants my bank details and asked me to consider getting a power of attorney so I can pay for things when he gets sick.'

Ruby thought about this. 'I think that makes sense.'

'I'm not sure.' Kim chewed at her thumbnail.

'Two Slippery Nipples, ladies,' said the barman, presenting them with two shot glasses both filled to the brim.

A hand clutching a twenty-pound note came between Ruby and Kim. 'I'll get these,' said Lewis, giving them both a broad smile. The barman took the note.

Ruby was so pleased to see him she could have hugged him but instead she picked up her glass and eyed him seductively over the top. 'Thank you for my Slippery Nipple,' she said.

'You're welcome. I called St Pancras lost property.' Lewis pulled a face. 'I'm really sorry but they only keep things for a few weeks and after that they go to charity. They've not got your phone any more. But I have a mate who can get second-hand phones at a good price. I'll get you a replacement. Is that okay or do you hate me right now?'

He looked at her with persuasive eyes. How could she hate him? 'It's not a problem. I've got a new phone already through my job.' She pulled it out of her bag. 'And I don't hate you, but you do owe me.'

'Something more than a shot?' He gave her a cheeky smile. He was very sexy.

'Definitely. I think dinner at least.' She sipped her drink and the alcohol buoyed her confidence. 'But first I need your phone number so I don't lose you again.'

'Of course.' He took her phone and punched in the number.

The bell rang. 'VIP daters, it's time for round two!' bellowed the barman.

'I think I'll give it a miss,' said Kim, looking a bit glum and red-faced as she fanned herself with the cocktail menu. 'I've got too much to think about.'

'Yeah. Me too,' said Ruby as Lewis handed back her phone.

Chapter Thirty-Two

Ruby rang Curtis's phone for ages before he answered it and then all she heard was a groan. 'Curtis? Are you all right?' she asked.

'My head – it feels awful. And it's like someone has sandpapered my tongue.'

'Do you think that might be a hangover?' suggested Ruby.

'I suppose it must be.'

'Tell me this isn't your first one.'

'I don't usually have more than one alcoholic drink.'

'You must have got wasted at university?'

'Ow, it hurts when I shake my head. No, I was there to study. Others drank a lot and then they vomited. I couldn't see the appeal.'

'When you put it like that . . . Anyway, take two paracetamol and drink lots of water. Then have a shower and call me back.'

'Yes, right. Why?'

'Because I've found the elusive Lewis.' She gave a little screech and then realised her mistake.

'Ow . . .' There was silence. 'Well done. I look forward to hearing all about it. Bye.'

Ruby paced the flat and Seymour appeared to be watching her from the comfort of the sofa. The minutes ticked by. Exactly how long did it take someone to shower? Weren't men supposed to pride themselves on being super quick? She'd got up early and waited until eight before calling Curtis and she still got the impression she'd woken him up. But it was an emergency. She needed to know how soon she could get the ring from his safe so she could arrange her dinner date with the lovely Lewis and return it to him.

The thought of him made her emit a soppy sigh. He was exactly as she'd remembered from the train: kind, interesting and drop-dead gorgeous. Unfortunately, they hadn't been able to talk for long. Lewis's mate wanted to get his money's worth at the VIP dating and Kim was quite down after her conversation with Vince's solicitor, so they'd said their goodbyes. Ruby had promised to message him once she'd been able to arrange the collection of the ring.

Her phone sprang into life and Ruby leaped on it.

'How are you feeling now?' she asked.

'Like my brain is trying to tunnel its way out of my head and I fear I may vomit at any moment.'

'Excellent. Let me tell you all about Lewis.' She gave him a potted update of her evening and awaited a response. 'Say something, Curtis.'

'I'm not sure you can claim to have *found* Lewis. It's purely coincidence.'

'You're splitting hairs. I made contact with him. It's the same thing. Anyway, what train are you getting back tomorrow? I thought maybe I could meet you and get the ring?' She bit her lip in anticipation.

'Hopefully before five o'clock. I can text you when it leaves.'

'Great. Thank you.' She punched the air in celebration and Seymour seemed to think she'd thrown something and spent the next couple of minutes trying to find it.

She belatedly remembered to ask about his evening. 'I'm sorry, Curtis. How did Project Cordelia go?'

There was a long pause. 'My memory appears to have been impacted by the alcohol.'

She chuckled at his turn of phrase. 'It's a bugger when that happens. Any clues? Like, is she asleep in your bed with her underwear hanging from the lampshade?'

'I didn't have sex with her if that's what you're trying to ask. In fact, I can't remember much after Jonty bought a round of tequila shots.'

'They're the worst. Look, don't worry. I'll call Jonty and get the lowdown – he won't have missed a thing – and then I'll update you. Don't do anything until I call back.'

As she had suspected, Jonty was full of all the gossip, much of which was about people she either didn't know or had met the one time but it was nevertheless quite entertaining. 'I mean seriously, who snogs four different people at a works party? That's outrageously slutty.'

'Don't beat yourself up. It's tough when you break up with a long-term partner.'

'Thanks, Ruby. You're lying but it's kind and I appreciate it. I'm not sure how I'm going to face Frank in the office. He's retiring soon and I get the distinct impression I was the first person he'd kissed in a very long time.'

'Then you probably made his day. And that's a good thing. Like care in the community.'

'Okay, now not as kind. But sadly, very true. Anyway, you missed a good night. Next time you're down we should go out.'

'And invite Frank along,' she suggested with a giggle.

'You're funny.'

'Thank you. No gossip on Cordelia then?'

'There's a loaded question. Oh my God, have our bosses hooked up? Spill the dirt – I want it in truckloads after what I've confessed to you.'

'No, no, no. I was just fishing,' she said, worrying that she'd dropped Curtis in it.

'Oh, that's disappointing. I had high hopes that those two might get it on. Cordelia is like a cat on heat at the moment. This job seems to have been the kiss of death for her love life.'

'So, what happened?'

'Cordelia passed out after the tequila shots, I put her in a cab and by the time I got back to the party Curtis was in a similar state, so I did the same for him. Pair of lightweights – they're made for each other.'

'Thanks, Jonty. You're a star.'

'Twinkle, twinkle. Don't be a stranger.'

Ruby ended the call and immediately rang Curtis to update him. She suggested that he check Cordelia was still on for dinner that evening and she wished him every success and this time she really meant it.

The work day started well as Ruby breathed in the scent of the sweet peas. They were glorious and filled her with joy, although she was already feeling pretty maxed out on that spectrum. Curtis was a few nudges away from dating Cordelia, and Lewis had sent her a couple of flirty texts and they'd arranged dinner at the fancy Italian in town. She had temporarily put her motherhood plans to one side in case Lewis was the answer to all her dreams. Everything felt like it was lining up.

Boomer was lying on his back on the shop floor with his tongue hanging out and his legs lolling around while Kim rubbed his middle.

'He looks happy,' said Ruby.

'You'd look like that if you'd tried to mount the postman and then had a packet of bacon and a tennis ball for breakfast.'

'I'm not sure I would. But he's definitely calming down,' said Ruby, making up a giant bouquet for Dean who had called in his order earlier.

'I wonder why dogs love this?' asked Kim.

'I'll rub your stomach and you can tell me.' Kim stuck her tongue out. 'Are you okay?' asked Ruby. 'I get the feeling something is bothering you.'

'Well, I slept in a vest top and both my boobs escaped in the night. I woke up to Boomer chasing one around the bedroom.'

'That's not true,' said Ruby.

'Sadly, it is, apart from the bit about him chasing one. He was actually lying on top of my left boob. I had to pull it out from underneath him. No wonder I'm over-heating at night. He insists on sleeping right up against me.' Kim rubbed the dog's tummy harder.

'He loves you.'

'At least someone does.' Kim sounded glum.

'Oh Kim. What's wrong?' Ruby wanted everyone in her life to get a happy ending and Kim more than most.

'I've given Vince's solicitor my bank details. I'm not sure if it was the right thing to do.'

'It's no more than the info on a cheque,' said Ruby, pausing what she was doing. 'You're definitely going to accept then?'

'What else can I do? If he wants to make amends and

leave it all to me that's his choice. But I'm not doing the power of attorney thing because that feels like too much responsibility.'

'And what about you two hooking up again?'

'That's the thing. I don't want to and now he's offered me the money it feels even weirder. Like he's paying me.'

'That's sleazy.'

'Exactly. But that makes me feel a bit bad because he's dying and then I go around the same stuff again and again and it's driving me crackers!' Her voice spiralled into a shout and Boomer leaped to his feet. He did a quick lap of the shop, barking at every corner in case there was danger lurking behind a bucket. Kim coaxed him to her with the rubber chicken and he took it to the back room for a good chew.

Kim slumped onto the stool behind the counter. 'I'm exhausted with it all.'

'You know you've got to do what's right for you.' Kim opened her mouth and Ruby waved any protests away. 'Nobody else. Just you. Don't feel guilty or pressured or blackmailed into anything.'

'I thought you were all for us getting back together?'

'Not if it's not what you want. I've said it before. You're too kind, Kim. Sometimes you need to do what you want and to hell with everyone else.'

'You are very wise.' Kim slumped her head onto the counter.

'Any takers from the VIP speed dating?'

Kim twisted her head in her direction. 'Nah, I wasn't really hunting.'

'Anything from Adrian?'

Kim let out a long sigh. 'Nope. I think that's properly over. And it's not what might have been that gets me, it's the loss of what we had. The friendship. It was worth much more to me than anything else. And Hayley has gone and spoilt it all.'

'With a little help from our beads,' added Ruby, tying the bow on the giant bouquet with a flourish. As if on cue, Dean strolled in and Ruby proudly held the flowers aloft. Even if she did say so herself, they looked stunning. The pastel colours all blended together beautifully.

'Ruby, they're amazing. Have you written the card?'

Ruby was particularly pleased with today's wording. She handed it over and waited. 'Wow, girl, that's awesome.' He paid for the bouquet and slipped Ruby a five-pound tip. Life was definitely looking up.

Kim needed to clear her head after a busy day so decided a very long walk around Rother Valley Country Park was just the ticket. Boomer still took a few goes to get in a car but he loved sticking his head out of the window once it was on the move and he had been securely strapped in.

Kim had thought a lot about what Ruby had said and she was right. It was up to Vince who he left his money to, but that shouldn't be a deciding factor in whether or not she wanted to rekindle their relationship. She no longer harboured any romantic feelings for Vince. They might have shared a happy marriage but his adultery and the passage of time had killed the love she'd once had for him. If she went back with him it would be purely for his benefit and only because he was dying – all the wrong reasons. The issue now was that she needed to tell him. And that was easier said than done.

She needed some head space to think through what she was going to say and work out her responses to any counter arguments Vince presented. She'd need to stand her ground and not be manipulated round to his way of thinking. If he changed his will she didn't care – she'd never expected a penny anyway and she was doing fine on her own.

She parked the car and they set off at their usual jolly speed. She'd found it was easier to go at Boomer's pace than try to hold him back. At least the extra exercise was doing her good.

They headed towards the lake. The sun sparkled on the surface like a thousand sunken stars. The ducks were sleeping by the edge of the water and quacked their protest as Boomer barked an excited hello. It was half five and still rather warm. She'd call Vince when she got home and arrange to meet as soon as possible.

A little further on Boomer found a nice spot to bob down. Kim was now used to the routine – well, as used to picking up another creature's excrement as you could be. She was hovering over it with her hand in a bag ready to scoop it up when she heard footsteps approaching.

'Hello!' someone called. Kim lunged for the poo but Boomer ran towards the voice, almost pulling her over. She stood up fast and clung onto his lead. 'I thought it was you,' said a happy-looking man with a golden cocker spaniel lolloping along beside him. For a moment Kim was puzzled and then she remembered. She'd met him at the speed dating.

'Oh hi,' she said, not sure what else to say. She was keeping one eye on Boomer and the other on his deposit – the last thing she needed was to step in it.

'I'm Ray and this is Florence. Well, I call her lots of things. She's often Flo, Furry Flo Flo, Floodle Poodle, Flumpy Floo or Furry Baby. Do you do that?' He looked hopeful and not nearly as embarrassed as he should have done.

'Er, no, not really. This is Boomerang. Boomer for short.' Both dogs were frantically checking out each other's bums while their tails wagged faster than a teacher's finger during playground duty.

'There you go. That *is* the same.'

It clearly wasn't. 'Okay. If you like. Anyway, nice to see you. I need to um . . .' She held up her poo-bag-covered hand. She lugged Boomer away from his new best friend and nearer to his earlier deposit.

Ray didn't seem to take the hint and followed her at close proximity. 'I didn't know you lived around here.' He hovered at her shoulder while she attempted to grab Boomer's poo. It was more than a bit off-putting being watched.

'I don't, we just fancied a change of route.' On her second lunge she successfully scooped it into the bag and swiftly tied a knot whilst hanging on to the lead – no mean feat. With the challenge completed she carried on her way. Ray trotted to keep up and came in step alongside her.

'It's nice to see you again. Especially with you being a fellow spaniel lover.'

Kim thought about what Ruby had said. 'Look, Ray. It is nice to see you again too.' He appeared thrilled and she felt even worse for what she was about to say but she steeled herself. 'But I've got a lot going on right now. I need some alone time to think.'

'Dog walking is great for that,' he said, continuing to walk beside her.

Kim stopped walking. She needed to be firmer. She could do this. 'Bye, Ray, and perhaps I'll see you again on another walk.'

'Right you are. Another time. Nice to see you, Kim and Big Boy Boomy, Boomer, Boomerang.' He chuckled to himself as, at last, he walked on.

She looked around for the nearest bin and made off towards it. Boomer was reluctant to walk in a different direction to his new friend, but once he picked up the smell of something else they were off. Kim's thoughts went back to her planned conversation with Vince, which she feared was going a lot smoother in her head than it would in reality.

Her phone pinged in her pocket and she went to retrieve it. At the same time Boomer did a lap of her legs and literally tied her in knots as he scrabbled to get somewhere or see something. She shuffled towards the bin.

Ray suddenly popped up beside her, which explained Boomer's excitement as he and Florence got to know each other all over again, but this time his lead was cutting off the circulation to Kim's lower limbs. 'I was going to say, Florence and I go to fly-ball. It's great for spaniels. Here's a leaflet.' He waved it in her face, and her annoyance levels hitched up a notch.

'My hands are full.' She held up her hands. Showing him the lead, phone and poo bag.

Boomer went in reverse and spun her around the other way and as she passed the bin, she saw her opportunity. She launched the bag at the bin. Or at least she thought she did. The moment her phone left her hand she realised her mistake and watched in slow motion as her mobile sailed through the mouth of the bin and landed with a cushioned thump on heavens only knew what. Although she had a sinking feeling she was about to find out.

'Anyway. Here you go,' said Ray, pushing the leaflet into Kim's now free hand. *What a shitty day,* she thought.

Chapter Thirty-Three

Ruby had it all planned out. Curtis was on an early train; she was collecting him from the station and they were going back to his to get the ring. Then she was off home to spend the best part of two hours getting ready for her date with Lewis. She'd picked out what she was going to wear – smart and sexy but not too much. She wanted to keep something in reserve for when she really wanted to wow him. She was looking forward to the dinner and getting to know Lewis better.

Kim had given her some flowers for the nursing home, which was lovely but this time Curtis would have to drop them off as she was on a tight schedule, especially if she was going to do her hair in tousled curls. Ruby felt a pang of guilt that she hadn't visited her new friends at the home for a while. She'd been caught up with things. She made a mental note to visit over the weekend and the guilt dissipated.

She was waiting in her car by the station when a text popped up.

Train at a standstill just outside Chesterfield. Will update when we move.

This was bloody typical. He was only about fifteen

minutes away. She took a deep breath. She had left plenty of time – it was fine. She texted back.

No worries. Waiting in usual spot. Keep me posted.

She checked her email. Nothing much. Things had gone quiet since the project had completed. There was something planned called a post-implementation review but apart from that, it was done. She feared it also signalled the end of her job with Curtis. He hadn't said as much but the hours on her timesheet were dwindling and he wasn't sending a lot her way any more. With the ring going back to Lewis she feared she wouldn't be seeing much of Curtis going forward. A sigh escaped her. She didn't want to lose him from her life.

She played a game on her phone to while away a few minutes and to stop her from checking the time every couple of seconds. It was only a temporary solution. Fifteen minutes and no update from Curtis. The delay was eating into her getting-ready time. Maybe she didn't need to curl her hair. It was probably a bit too fancy for a first date anyway. She didn't want to look like she'd tried too hard.

By the time she'd emptied out her glove compartment, eaten three of the four mints she'd found in there and reordered everything in it, she was getting to the grumpy stage. She put the other mint in the rubbish pile because it was covered in fluff. But it was a job well done as she generally opened the glove compartment, slung stuff in and then shut it quickly until the next time. It had been full of car park tickets, Greggs paper bags and sweet wrappers.

It was coming up to forty minutes and her phone pinged. 'At last,' she said, pouncing on it.

Moving slowly. Expect I'll be another thirty minutes. You don't have to wait. I can take a taxi and you can get the ring another time.

'Grrr!' She composed a reply.

Need the ring tonight as meeting Lewis for dinner.

The three little dots came up and swirled there for ages. She watched and waited. They disappeared. Why did that happen? Had Curtis started replying and then changed his mind? It was so frustrating. The dots reappeared. Ruby waited. And waited. Ping.

OK.

Ruby dropped the phone onto the passenger seat. This was driving her nuts.

She got out of the car and had a walk around to stretch her legs and calm herself down. She got back in, picked the fluff off the other mint and ate it.

Eventually she saw people spilling out of the station and started the engine like a getaway driver pre-empting the escape. She wildly skimmed the crowd searching for Curtis. At last she spotted him striding towards her. She leaned over and opened the passenger door – she wasn't sure how many nanoseconds that would save her but it felt like it all counted.

'Hello. That was annoying,' he said.

'Get in, get in. We need to go,' she said, revving the engine.

He did as he was told but not at the speed she would have preferred. He carefully did up his seatbelt while she stared at him.

'Is everything okay?' he asked.

'Not in the slightest. I've got a date in about an hour's time.' She indicated and pulled into the traffic.

'Where?'

'Shef.'

'Then there's no rush,' he said happily. 'You've plenty of time.'

'I need to get showered and changed and make myself look fabulous.'

'I see.' Did she sense a hint of disapproval in his voice? 'Where is Lewis taking you?'

'That fancy Italian place.'

'Not Greggs?'

'Oh, you're funny,' she said, crunching the gears and they both winced. 'How was your date last night with Cordelia?'

'Was it a date? I'm not sure. We ate a meal together. I walked her back to her apartment.'

She found herself glancing in his direction. 'And what happened then?'

'I'm not sure I follow.'

'Did you linger outside? Did she invite you up for coffee? What happened *exactly*?'

Curtis paused and she could almost see him replaying the video in his head. 'She said, "This is me." I said, "I know it's you." Apparently, she meant we had reached her building. I said goodnight. She said, "There's a lovely view from my balcony." I said, "Which way does it face?" and she replied east. I commented that I prefer north-facing as I don't like to overheat in bed.'

Ruby found she was nodding furiously in an attempt to get to the juicy bits.

'Are you all right?' he asked.

'Yeah. Keep going. But maybe speed it up.'

'Right.' He carried on but was speaking faster, like the people who give out terms and conditions at the end of adverts. 'She asked if I wanted to see the view. I said as it was dark and it appeared her side of the building was predominantly facing another block of flats, I'd rather not.' Ruby snorted out a laugh at the picture of Cordelia's best

315

chat-up line being given the Curtis brush-off. 'She then invited me in for coffee, which I explained was a very bad idea at that time of night if she was expecting to get any sleep at all. To which she said there were more pleasurable things than sleep.'

Curtis took a deep breath, then got his phone out and started flicking through it. Ruby was on tenterhooks like the end of an episode of a soap opera – and she wasn't happy to wait a week for the next instalment. 'What did you say to that?'

'I said that sleep was necessary rather than pleasurable. And she kissed me.'

Ruby went rigid, like she'd been smacked in the face with a frying pan. Her knuckles were white as she gripped the steering wheel. Cordelia was definitely a woman on a mission. And despite this being ultimately what she'd planned she wasn't feeling as happy about it as she was probably meant to.

'Was it a peck on the cheek? Or a Nanna smacker? Or . . . ?' Ruby didn't like how much she needed to know and she liked the images it was conjuring up in her mind even less.

'A gentleman never tells.'

'Curtis!' she snapped and he almost dropped his phone.

He put his phone away carefully. 'If you insist. It was a light kiss on the lips. It caught me unawares so really just the edge of my lips. I have to say I panicked slightly.'

Ruby wondered what form that took and had hopeful thoughts of him shoving Cordelia into the Thames. 'That's understandable if you weren't expecting it. Did you have . . . coffee?'

'At that time of night? No, it would have been madness. I said goodnight and went back to my hotel.'

Ruby was relieved. 'That's excellent, Curtis. I'm really pleased for you. And for Cordelia.' She relaxed her grip on the steering wheel; she needed to accept this because it was the right thing for Curtis. And anyway, she had Lewis, so everything was fine.

'She invited you up for coffee. You'll be ticking off your goal very soon,' she said.

'I don't follow.'

'Coffee is code for sex, Curtis. She invited you up to her apartment to have sex with her.' Sometimes you had to spell it out for him.

Curtis jolted so hard that it reminded Ruby of the time she'd forgotten she'd left the flower shop scissors in her back pocket and sat on them.

'You're winding me up.' He let out a tinkly laugh.

'Nope. Coffee is the universal code for sex. Surely everyone knows that.'

A quick glance at Curtis's expression told her otherwise.

He sat back in his seat, looking thoroughly confused. 'Actually, now that you mention it, I have noticed on the rare occasion I've watched television programmes – often because they are on before the news – that when someone suggests coffee at the end of an evening it's usually followed by kissing.'

Ruby did her crazy arm wave. 'There you go. Coffee equals sex.'

'Fascinating. Are there any more code words I should be aware of?'

Ruby had a think while she negotiated a roundabout. '*It's not you* means it absolutely is you. *It's fine* is code for nothing is fine. *I'll think about it* means definitely not. And *We need to talk* translates to you need to listen.' Ruby stopped because Curtis was looking like she'd flicked his nose with every statement. 'You okay?'

'And does everyone know this?'

She pondered. 'Women do. Men not so much. Apart from the coffee thing.'

'Then, I guess I'm dating Cordelia Stuart-Bruce.'

She turned briefly to see that he was smiling.

'I guess you are.' And now all she had to do was to find it in her heart to be happy for him. Which she was sure she could do, if only she could ignore the little niggle burrowing into her brain.

Once they got to Curtis's house, he insisted on showing Ruby the things they had ordered.

'Why are they still in the boxes and wrappers?'

'Because I need you to supervise where they go.'

'You need me to supervise *you*? Blimey how times have changed,' said Ruby with a snort. 'I'll come over on Sunday. Right now I need to grab the ring and go.' She remembered the flowers in the back of the car. 'And I almost forgot, Kim gave me some more flowers for the nursing home. You'll need to get them over there either tonight or tomorrow or they'll wilt. Maybe pop them in water tonight. Back in a mo.'

When she returned Curtis was on the phone. She knew instantly that something was wrong.

'I'll come over straight away. Right. Thank you,' he said and ended the call.

'Harry?' she asked.

'Yes. I know I've had The Call before but I fear this really is it. His blood pressure is low and he's unresponsive.'

Ruby watched him fiddle with his phone and she made the easiest decision of her life. She thrust the flowers at him. 'Get in the car. I'll take you now.'

'I can drive myself.'

Ruby did a double take. 'You've got a car?'

'Yes. In the garage.'

Ruby shook her head. She'd ponder that later. 'You're shaking. It's better I drive.'

'But you've got a date with Lewis.'

'If it's meant to be, he'll wait.' At this rate, if she had time to brush her hair it would be a miracle.

Chapter Thirty-Four

Kim poured herself a glass of wine and switched on the television. Boomer was busy eating his bed. She'd rung Vince's mobile and it had gone to voicemail – she'd have to tackle that issue tomorrow. She put her feet up, relaxed into the sofa and sipped the cold wine. She was going to have one glass and then have a long soak in a hot bath until she was the colour of a cooked prawn. The doorbell interrupted her reverie. With a deep sigh she got up to answer it. She shut Boomer in the living room and went to the front door.

Vince was standing on the doorstep and the second she opened the door he attempted to walk inside. She stood in his way. He pulled his head back and shot her a questioning look.

'Hey, gorgeous, how about a cosy night in with a takeaway and your favourite film?' He held up a *When Harry Met Sally* DVD.

'Vince, I'm really tired and I've got a bit of a headache. So, before it turns into a full-on head-banger, I'm going to bed.'

'Oh.' He looked deflated. 'I've driven all the way from

Mablethorpe. I was kind of hoping you'd made a decision about us.'

She took a deep breath. This was her cue to launch into her prepared speech and tell him it wasn't what she wanted but looking at him standing there, with his expectant expression, how could she? 'I think maybe there's some middle ground.'

'Full sex, no foreplay?' he joked. She scowled at him. 'Sorry. Poor taste. Okay go on.'

'The opposite. I'm thinking we can spend time together but nowt else. I don't feel like that about you any more, Vince. I'm sorry. I'd be lying to both of us if I said otherwise.'

He looked a little crestfallen. 'Okay. You haven't called my solicitor back. She needs a copy of some ID.'

Kim rubbed her forehead. 'I'll do it tomorrow.' He gave her a look. 'I promise. Night, Vince.'

She tried to shut the door but he put the DVD in the way. Billy Crystal was looking at her hopefully from the cover. 'You sure you don't want to take a couple of paracetamols and snuggle up?'

'No, but I might be able to manage a bit of this. Thanks.' She took the DVD and shut the door.

Ruby and Curtis ran to the car and set off at speed. 'Thirty limit,' said Curtis and he nervously scratched his ear.

Ruby slowed down. The last thing she needed was a speeding ticket or, worse still, an accident. Ruby mentally plotted out the fastest route for that time of the evening.

When they finally pulled up at the nursing home, she moored the car and they both charged up the steps and went inside, Curtis clutching the flowers. At the top of the stairs, only a few feet from Harry's door, Curtis stopped abruptly and Ruby almost cannoned into the back of him.

'What is it?' she asked.

'I don't know. It all feels very final. When Harry's gone, I will be all alone.' His Adam's apple bobbed.

Emotions swelled inside her. At that moment she knew exactly how he was feeling. She'd been there. She *was* there. She squeezed his shoulder. 'You're not alone. I'm here. And I'm not going anywhere.'

Curtis glanced at her, his face serious. He nodded, handed her the flowers and went into Harry's room. Ruby waited in the doorway. She watched the carer get up from the chair next to Harry's bed and whisper something to Curtis. Harry looked so frail. The nurse joined Ruby at the door.

'How is he?' she asked.

'I'm afraid it's a waiting game now. He'll go when he's ready. Can I get you a coffee?'

'No, thanks.'

Ruby joined Curtis in the room and they sat in silence for a while watching Harry's chest rise and fall unsteadily. An air freshener nearby made the room smell strongly of vanilla.

'I had better get these flowers into water before they . . .' She didn't want to say the word. She gave them a little shake and went to leave. Curtis caught her arm, the unexpected contact sending a shiver through her.

'Thanks for bringing me. I do appreciate what you do for me, Ruby.'

'What are friends for?'

'I've never fully worked that out. But anyway, you need to get to your date.'

She checked her watch. Poor Lewis, he was probably on his way to the restaurant. 'I think I'll have to cancel.'

'Why? Not on my account. I'd feel awful. This could be your happy ever after.'

She smiled at him. 'You don't believe in those.'

'No. But you do.'

'I can't go looking like this. I've not even showered.' She pulled at her hair and her top in turn.

Curtis studied her closely. She felt oddly scrutinised and a little self-conscious under his gaze. 'You look very pretty.' He leaned slightly forward, his nose almost touching her right boob. 'And you don't smell at all.'

She laughed. 'Thanks, Curtis. That's reassuring.'

'I'm serious. If you go straight there, you'll be marginally late. I'd forgive you that.'

'And what will you do here?'

He looked about as if searching for inspiration. He held up his phone. 'I'll learn all about social media.' He glanced at Harry. 'And I'll wait.'

There wasn't much she could do. Perhaps she'd be more useful to him after the inevitable happened. And she did really want to see Lewis. 'Okay, but promise you'll call me if there's any change.'

'I promise. Now please go,' he said, taking the flowers from her.

Ruby screamed into Eldon Street car park and was relieved to find a space. She hastily paid for a ticket, slung it on the dashboard and hurtled off in the direction of the restaurant. She came to a halt a few metres away and took in a few lungfuls of air, trying to calm her pulse. She ran her fingers through her hair and hastily applied a smudge of lipstick. She checked how she looked in her phone. A little pink from the running but otherwise okay.

Curtis's words invaded her mind. He'd said she was pretty.

323

She watched her reflection smile. She shook her head; she needed to focus. Tonight was about her and Lewis and the ring. 'Bugger it!' She said it a little more loudly than she'd intended, making a woman nearby almost fall off the kerb. 'Sorry.' In the whole Harry emergency dash, she'd forgotten the ring. Her shoulders slumped. It was all a waste of time. *Oh well,* she thought, *I'll just have to explain to Lewis what's happened.* What else could she do?

She took a deep breath and strolled into the restaurant. It was lovely inside. In her flustered state she was grateful for air conditioning and if the smells were anything to go by the food was going to be good. A waitress approached her and at the same time she spotted Lewis sitting forlornly at a table near the back. As she approached him, he looked up and beamed a welcoming smile at her.

'I thought you'd stood me up.' He greeted her with a brief kiss on the cheek.

'I'm sorry. It's a very long story but a friend of mine, the one from the train who's got your ring, got a phone call that his dad was seriously poorly, so we dashed over there and . . .' She took a breath, aware she was gabbling. 'I forgot the ring. Sorry.'

Lewis shrugged. 'No worries. We'll have to go out again.' And just like that she felt herself relax. Thankfully most of the other people were dressed casually so she didn't look out of place in her patterned top and leggings. She thought of Curtis and how he would have likely worn a suit and not even noticed he was the only one.

They shared small talk while they perused the menu. A waitress took their order and the conversation continued.

'You actually went to the London Eye that day?' Lewis shook his head. 'I can't believe you did that.' He rested his forearms on the table and listened attentively.

'We did. Curtis had this important presentation at a big company and I . . . had an appointment. And we couldn't agree over who should look after the ring. So, we had to go to both things together.' The thought of that day made her laugh. She replayed it in her mind: her knocking over the flipchart, him rescuing her from Neil the sperm donor. 'Then there was all this maintenance on the Tube and we had to get a bus . . .' She saw Lewis check his phone. She was rambling again. 'Anyway, we got there and waited but you didn't show up.' She wanted to tell him about going to Covent Garden with Curtis, sitting outside and watching the world go by. It had been such an unexpectedly good day.

Lewis nodded. 'I got the call that I was dumped so I pretty much got on the next train home.'

'And where is home?'

Lewis talked quite a bit about being from Barnsley but moving to Sheffield as a teenager. He shared a flat with a friend and there was a funny story about them trying to get into a neighbour's flat when drunk but Ruby's mind was drifting. She was thinking about Curtis. While she was happy to be out on a date with Lewis, there was also part of her that wished she'd not left Curtis. She was worried about him and what he was facing alone. She smiled and nodded in what she hoped were the right places as Lewis moved on to amusing anecdotes about his Sunday league football team.

Their food arrived and the waitress ground black pepper onto their meals.

'This is amazing,' said Lewis, cutting her a piece of his lasagne. 'You have to try this.' He offered her his fork. A picture of Curtis and his chips on Cleethorpes seafront shot into her mind. She pushed it aside as Lewis was waiting.

It appeared he was going to feed it to her. She wondered what Curtis would say about that. She took the fork from him and swapped it with her, as yet unused, one.

'Oh, okay,' he said.

She ate the lasagne. 'Mmm that's really good. My friend . . .'

'Curtis?' he interjected.

'Yeah, Curtis.' Had she mentioned him too often? 'He makes this amazing cottage pie with a Caribbean twist.'

'Uh-huh. You and this Curtis. Is he like a jealous ex who's likely to want to thump me?'

'No.' She tilted her head. 'He's the guy from the train who I told you about.' Despite his attentive look had he not listened to her at all?

'Right. That guy.'

'What did you say you did for a living?' She tucked into her meatballs and she had to admit they were mighty fine. She was regretting the spaghetti a little when she felt sauce stick to her chin but hopefully he'd not noticed.

'I travel quite a bit and it pays the bills. How about you?'

'Travelling is interesting. Different places or the same ones repeated?' she asked keen to find out more.

'All over really. What was it that you do?'

'I'm a florist, and I'm an executive assistant for Curtis but you were saying about your job. What is it that you do exactly?' She still wasn't sure that he'd actually told her.

'It's just dull stuff with computers.'

'Ooh Curtis is a consultant in computer technology – maybe your paths have crossed.'

'I can't say I remember him. Anyway, a florist – that must be a lovely job, playing about with flowers all day.'

Ruby was glad Kim wasn't there. 'There's a bit more to it than that. But, it's a good job. I like not knowing what I'll be doing from one day to the next.'

'Making something with flowers I'm guessing.' He laughed as he forked up a huge piece of lasagne.

'Yeah, but some days it's bouquets, another it's funeral wreaths, or church sprays and table centres for weddings. Quite varied really and very different to the admin work I do for Curtis. I'm lucky because I enjoy both my jobs.'

'That's good. There's not many people who like one job, let alone two.'

'I suppose.' She pondered this for a minute. She was very lucky with both her jobs and especially with the people she worked with. They chatted some more and moved on to dessert. Ruby wasn't entirely sure she had room but she couldn't say no to tiramisu.

'Have you got your own place?' asked Lewis.

'I have. It's a little flat but it's big enough for me.'

'I'd like my own place but . . .' Lewis's attention was drawn to the front of the restaurant where Ruby was vaguely aware of slightly raised voices. She followed Lewis's gaze and was surprised to see Curtis.

Chapter Thirty-Five

The waitress's arms flopped down in an 'I give up' gesture as Curtis strode past her and over to Ruby's table.

Ruby feared the worst and sadness clutched at her heart. 'What's happened?'

'I've been on social media,' said Curtis.

Not the answer she was expecting. 'And your dad?'

'He's the same.'

Lewis's eyes were darting between the two of them. 'Hello, mate,' he said, standing up.

Curtis spun in his direction. 'I'm not your mate by any definition of the word. I'd like you to accompany me to the police station,' said Curtis, holding his head high.

Lewis leaned over the table towards Ruby. 'Is he dangerous?'

'No,' she replied, feeling very defensive of her friend. Ruby felt at a disadvantage as the only one sitting down so she stood up too. 'Curtis, what's going on?' she asked, aware that other diners were starting to pay attention to the drama unfolding at their table.

'I decided to look at hashtags, as Cordelia had suggested. I started with swing choir because it's something she's interested in and I know little about. However, searching the hashtag swingers was obviously a mistake.' He gave a little shudder. 'I moved on to railway-related things. And I discovered there has been a spate of mobile phone thefts on the Sheffield to St Pancras line. By this man here.'

Lewis looked about him uneasily. 'You've got the wrong guy.'

'Five people have described someone borrowing their mobile and then exiting the train at the next station.'

'But I handed Ruby's phone in,' said Lewis.

'No, you didn't. I called St Pancras lost property. They record everything and retain it for twelve weeks. No mobile phones were handed in from our train and also none at all that day that matched her make and model.'

Ruby's head was spinning and her throat had gone dry. 'Lewis?' Her voice was a croak. Had Curtis been right all along? Was it all one big charade to steal her mobile? 'Is this true?'

Lewis put his hands together as if in prayer. 'No, I swear. I don't know what he's going on about.' She desperately wanted to believe him.

'Curtis, you can't go barging in and accusing people of things. You need proof.'

'But what he did is the same as the stories on the internet,' said Curtis, suddenly sounding like doubt was creeping in.

'Don't go believing everything on the internet, mate,' said Lewis. He scratched his head. 'It's a coincidence. I'll call you, Ruby. Okay?'

'Oh, don't go,' said Ruby, hating how desperate she sounded. Lewis went to leave but Curtis blocked him.

'My apologies,' said Curtis inclining his head. 'It must have been a mistake. Please don't go on my account.'

'Stay. Please finish your meal,' said Ruby, sitting down

329

in the hope that Lewis would do the same. How was she ever going to recover this?

The waitress bobbed about behind Curtis. 'The manager would like you all to leave. Please.' She pointed to a woman who appeared to be hiding behind the till while taking a telephone call.

'It's all right. No harm done.' Lewis ran a finger around his collar. There was a moment where Curtis and Lewis glared at each other. Ruby placed a hand on Curtis's arm. He moved to the side and Lewis went to pass him.

'You'd best have your ring back,' said Curtis, handing him the ring box.

Lewis automatically went to take it. 'Thanks.'

Curtis moved the ring out of Lewis's grasp. 'I shared a photograph of the ring with one of the women who had reported the phone thief. She said it was exactly the same as the one the man on the train had shown her when he'd told her all about the elaborate proposal he had planned. Is that a coincidence too?' asked Curtis.

Ruby's stomach plummeted and the look Lewis gave her said it all. She'd been a fool. Curtis had been right all along. Lewis was nothing but a con man.

Curtis grabbed him by the arm. 'Shall we go to the police station now?'

'Get off me!' shouted Lewis, trying to wrench his arm free as he bumped into a nearby table, knocking over their bottle of wine.

'Hey!' yelled a man at the table.

'Ruby. Tell your nutjob friend to let me go or I'm going to knock him out,' barked Lewis.

'Curtis, he's not worth it. Let him go.'

'No. He's committed a crime and he's upset you,' said Curtis.

Ruby raised her voice. 'Let him go!'

Curtis nodded and released his grip on the struggling Lewis who straightened his shirt. He snatched the ring box from Curtis, flipped it open and smirked to see the ring was inside. 'Thanks, *mate*,' he said, closing and pocketing the box. He turned on his heel and strode confidently towards the exit. Ruby and Curtis watched his retreating back. She felt a part of her was leaving with him and taking her last hope of a fairy-tale ending along too. Romance really didn't exist. She'd put a lot of faith in Lewis, spent so much effort trying to return the ring to him and the whole time he was nothing more than a common thief.

As Lewis reached the glass door, two policemen appeared on the other side and Lewis froze. He checked over his shoulder where Curtis and Ruby were watching him. The waitress approached him and brandished the extra large peppermill. He had nowhere to run.

Whilst the restaurant staff had called the police because of the disturbance, the officers were quite interested in the evidence Curtis happily shared with them. A couple of police radio exchanges ensued and a few minutes later Lewis was arrested. Ruby watched from her seat at the table where her tiramisu sat untouched and she hugged a hot chocolate despite it being a warm evening.

Curtis ended a phone call before sitting down opposite her.

'There goes another happily ever after. I can't believe how much time I wasted on Lewis.' Ruby slid down a little in her seat.

'Look on the bright side,' said Curtis.

'Which is what exactly?' Ruby shook her head. All was lost.

Curtis thought for a moment. 'You returned Lewis's ring to him.'

Ruby huffed – it wasn't much of a bright side. 'And that must have been a big old fake just like Lewis. I wonder if any of it was true,' mused Ruby.

'I doubt it. The girlfriend certainly wasn't.' He got something up on his phone. 'Was one of these his "girlfriend"?' he asked, showing her a series of pictures of women next to palm trees.

'That one,' she said despondently as the picture of the pretty girl on the Caribbean beach popped up. 'Grrr.' This time Curtis didn't recoil. 'I'm such an idiot.'

'No, you're not. An idiot is someone of low intelligence and you've proved to be anything but while you've been working for me.'

She was starting to get grumpy. 'But you know what I mean when I say that. I'm an idiot because I'm the one Lewis chose to play out his charade with. He must pick out certain people as his victims.'

'I suspect he thought you'd have an expensive phone.'

'Thanks for that. He didn't choose me because I'm a nice person. Just because I might have a decent phone.'

'And possibly be gullible.' He had the decency to look away as he said it.

'Bloody hell, Curtis. You're infuriating.' He looked up again. 'You're so nit-picky. You know what I'm trying to say but you have to make me feel an even bigger idiot by correcting me. You're a . . . quibbling perfectionist.'

There was a long silence. Ruby's heart was beating slightly faster than usual thanks to her getting riled. Curtis's jaw was tense. Eventually he spoke. 'The word you are searching for is pedant.'

'Bloody hell.' She threw up her arms. 'I'm going home. This is the perfectly crappy end to an absolutely crapulous day.'

'You're right. It has been a crap day,' said Curtis.

She stood up and picked up her bag but Curtis stayed where he was. 'You should be getting back to the nursing home.'

'No need.'

'Why?'

'They called just now. Harry died a few minutes ago.'

It was early Saturday morning in the shop and Kim felt like she had done the right thing by agreeing to spend some time with Vince. But whilst it might have been a good thing to do for him, she was feeling wretched. It went against everything her instincts were telling her but she'd been backed into a corner and couldn't see a way out without appearing totally heartless.

Boomer was on form and happily rolling around the floor groaning in ecstasy – oh to be that easily pleased.

Ruby came in and Boomer went berserk and, for the first time he didn't wet himself when he saw her. 'Good boy,' said Ruby.

'How was your big date?' asked Kim, keen to immerse herself in someone else's hopefully more successful love life.

'A total and utter disaster,' said Ruby, dropping her bag in the back room and slumping onto a stool.

'Did you and Lewis not hit it off?'

'You could say that.' Ruby proceeded to update Kim on the previous evening's events.

Kim listened intently. When Ruby got to the end of the

story she reached out and squeezed her shoulder. 'Oh, Ruby, you do pick them.'

Ruby rolled her eyes. 'If it wasn't so tragic it could be an actual gift. I could maybe get them tattooed as a warning to all other females. This is a Ruby Edwards confirmed arsehole.'

'And poor Curtis, losing his dad. How is he?'

Ruby shrugged. 'He said there was nothing he could do. He got a taxi home and I drove back to mine.'

Kim knew she was giving her a schoolteacher look. 'Was any of what happened with Lewis, Curtis's fault?'

'Noooo,' said Ruby, sounding remorseful. 'Now I feel awful. It was just that it was Curtis who revealed what Lewis was really like. And a little part of me – the stupid part – didn't want to know. I wanted Lewis to be the lovely guy I met on the train, the one who was besotted with his girlfriend and had planned this amazing proposal.'

'But he never was that person.'

Ruby pursed her lips. 'I know that now. I did text Curtis this morning and he said he was fine.'

'Is that likely after what's happened?'

'No. I'll call him.'

'Excellent idea,' said Kim, leaving Ruby and going to flip over the shop sign.

The first customer through the door was Dean and he hovered around, waiting for Ruby to get off the phone. 'I left a message for Curtis,' she said to Kim before putting her phone away and giving the customer her full attention. 'Dean. Just the person I need to see today.'

'Yeah?' Dean gave a little swagger. 'What can I do for you?'

'Tell me all about your latest girlfriend. I need to know that romance is alive and well.'

'Sure thing. I want to do something for our anniversary. Can you do me five single red roses, individually wrapped. One for each week we've been together and add one of your messages to each one.'

Ruby sighed. 'You see, this is what I need,' she said, choosing the best of the blooms. 'I need a man like you, Dean. Someone who values women and treats them well.'

'That's me.' Dean preened himself. 'You know, Ruby, you're a fine-looking woman. I might have room for you.' His eyebrow puckered suggestively.

Ruby turned around slowly with the roses in her hand. 'How do you mean, Dean?'

Kim sensed this could end badly. 'I'm sure you're joking, Dean. You already have your hands full. Am I right?' said Kim.

'Oh, yeah.' Dean laughed. 'I'm messing with you, Ruby. I have enough on my plate if you know what I mean.'

Ruby seemed to relax and began putting the roses into individual wraps. She counted out five cards. 'Tell me five things you love about her?' She had her pen poised.

'I love her eyes. I can tell her mood by the look she gives me.' Ruby wrote out the first card. 'And she's fun to be around. You know what I'm saying?'

'Got it,' said Ruby, jotting something on a second.

'She's positive. She sees the good in everything and it makes me look at things differently. I love that about her.' Ruby finished the next card. 'She's beautiful. I could look at her all day like a painting.'

Ruby completed another card. 'Okay. Last one.'

Dean seemed to have to think about it. 'I trust her. Like I trust her completely.' Ruby was nodding. 'I mean I have to, right. If she told my wife that would mess up everything.'

Kim noticed an almost imperceptible shudder go through Ruby before she scooped up all five roses and began beating Dean about the head with them.

'You cheating, no-good, scumbag arsehole,' she said as she battered him with the now limp-looking flowers.

'Hey! I thought you knew!' shouted Dean, trying to dodge the onslaught.

Kim dashed over and intercepted the roses. 'You all right?' Kim asked them both. Dean shrugged. Ruby nodded. 'Coke break?' Kim suggested to Ruby, tipping her head towards the back room. She could see she was fighting back tears.

'Okay,' said Ruby, and with a death stare at Dean she left them.

'Man, that was some over-reaction,' said Dean. 'But the cards look cool. If you get me some new flowers, I'll be outta here.'

'No,' said Kim.

'I'm not reading you?'

'No. Ruby is right. Men like you are total scum. You are no longer welcome in my shop. Please leave and don't come back or I'll tell your wife.'

He held up his hands in surrender. 'Hey. Isn't there some code of practice that says you can't do that?'

'We're not doctors, you moron. Now clear off.' She shooed him out of the shop with the limp roses.

In the back room, Ruby was sobbing and a sorrow-ful-looking Boomer had his head on her knees. 'Come on,' said Kim. 'He is definitely not worth tears.' Kim wrapped her in a hug.

'It's not just him, or Lewis or Curtis.' She sniffed as she got the tears under control. 'It's all of them. There's no such thing as romance. It's all a lie peddled by Netflix and

336

publishers. I really believed it, Kim. I thought if I searched, I'd find it. But the world is full of Deans and Lewises.'

'There are also Curtises and Adrians too. And there will be someone for you. I'm sure of it.'

Ruby shook her head. 'I'm done. I quit love. It's a big con and this time I'm done with being the fool.'

Chapter Thirty-Six

Ruby's Saturday improved a little. She was cross at herself for losing her temper with Dean but it had been the proverbial last straw. All the times she'd written messages for him and each one had been for a mistress. It made her shiver. She felt that somehow she'd colluded in his deceit. Being battered with roses was too good for him, although she did feel bad about the poor flowers.

They had a break for lunch. 'Thanks for backing me up with Dean. I know he's a good customer.'

'We'll survive. Women have to stick together.' Kim gave her a hug. 'Have you tried Curtis again?'

'I'll do it now.' She pulled out her phone and dialled his number while she unwrapped last night's tiramisu – it would have been a shame to waste it.

'Hello Ruby,' said a distinctly female voice.

Had she misdialled? A quick look at the screen told her she hadn't. Ruby swallowed her spoonful of pudding quickly. 'I was after Curtis.'

'He's busy right now.'

'Uh. Okay. Sorry, who is this?'

'It's Cordelia.'

Ruby froze with her spoon at her lips. 'Cordelia, hi. Is

Curtis all right? I've been worried about him, what with Harry passing away.'

'That's kind of you, Ruby. I got the last train up from London to be with him. You really don't need to worry. I have everything in hand.'

'Right. Um . . .' Ruby wasn't sure what else to say.

'Was there anything else?'

'Can you tell him I called and . . . I'm sorry about . . . Actually, just tell him I called.'

'Of course. Bye.'

The call ended before she could say the same.

'Problem?' Kim was watching her closely.

'No. I think everything is as it should be. Cordelia is with Curtis and that's good. Right?'

Kim nodded.

'I don't need to worry about him any more.' Ruby nodded so much she felt her neck twinge. Who was she trying to kid? Curtis was, without doubt, the most unusual person she'd ever met but he was also the most genuine. He never pretended to be something he wasn't. Yes, he was blunt, reserved, and lived his life in black and white but at least she knew where she was with that. He was also driven, loyal and funny – although often unintentionally. She'd been so focused on finding the fairy-tale man she hadn't noticed the reference book one right under her nose. She scooped up a spoonful of tiramisu and promptly dropped it in her lap. Yeah, everything was just great.

Kim turned the sign to closed and let Boomer have a trot around the shop while they finished up. The afternoon had been steady and they had all been lovely customers but Ruby's mood hadn't improved. She was sure Boomer could sense it as he followed Ruby around with his rubber chicken in a vain attempt to cheer her up.

'Look, I'll finish up here. Why don't you get off?' suggested Kim.

'And do what?' Ruby shrugged. 'Sorry, I've only got another long evening on my own stretched out in front of me. The highlight of which will be if Seymour pays me a visit and even those have become less common. I'm sorry, I'm on a bit of a downer.'

'Can I do anything?'

Ruby shook her head. 'No. I need to sort my life out. But that's easier said than done.'

'Why don't you take these to the nursing home?' Kim handed her some mixed roses.

'They're perfectly fresh,' said Ruby, eyeing the tight blooms.

'I figure sometimes we should all experience the best life has to offer, instead of settling for cast offs.'

'Thanks, that's really kind. I will.' She got her bag and took the flowers. 'Night, Kim.'

Kim held on to Boomer's collar while Ruby exited the shop. She'd barely shut it again when there was a tap on the glass. She turned to see Adrian peering inside. Her stomach flipped at the sight of him.

'Hi,' she said. 'Come in.'

Boomer seemed to recognise him as he leaped about wildly. 'Hey, boy. You're looking well.' He gave the dog a fuss.

Kim watched them for a moment. 'Sorry, Adrian, but I was shutting up. Was there something?'

Adrian stood up quickly. 'Yep, sorry. Look please say no if this is bang out of line. I don't want you to think I'm taking advantage. But you popped into my head and

I couldn't think of anyone else.' Kim's heart started to race. He took a step closer and her skin prickled with anticipation – or possibly a flush, but she wanted to believe it was the former. 'I need you—'

'Yes,' said Kim without thinking.

Adrian's head shot up. '. . . to do me a huge favour.'

Kim licked her lips. She was no longer sure where this was going. Her imagination had swept her away on a torrent of happy feelings and now she'd hit a dam. 'Sorry?'

'Actually, it's Hayley really. Her florist has gone bankrupt and the wedding is on Friday. Can you help?'

'Er . . .' was all Kim could manage.

'I know it's difficult after everything. But she's distraught and I didn't know what else to do. But if you're too busy or it's too weird, just say.'

Kim gave herself a mental shake and went into professional mode. She was the bigger person here and she liked the idea of coming to Adrian's rescue even if it meant helping his scheming daughter too. 'What's she after exactly?'

Adrian pulled out a handwritten list. 'Essential,' he read out. 'Bride's bouquet. Three bridesmaid's bouquets. One flower girl posy. Wedding party buttonholes and corsages for eighteen. Top table centrepiece.' He looked up and gave her a fleeting smile before carrying on. 'Desired but not essential – twenty-two table centres, baskets of petals to throw instead of confetti, bouquet to toss, church flowers . . . There's quite a long list after that including arrangements for the altar and pews et cetera.'

'Let me check the diary.' She was glad of the distraction of being able to scroll through their orders. Her pulse began to settle – what a fool for thinking he was there to patch up their friendship. 'I've got a wedding on Saturday but Friday is clear. We do most of the work the day before anyway. That's assuming she's happy we stick to the essentials list and I'd suggest she reuses the altar spray for the top table and throws the flower girl's posy – less likely to take an eye out. What colours and flowers does she want?'

'Um.' Adrian scanned his list. 'Doesn't say. I think at this point anything you can conjure up would be wonderful.'

'I can call my wholesaler now and see what he's got coming in. We usually order at least a week in advance.'

Adrian threw his arms around her and squeezed her tight. She froze. 'Kim, you're a life-saver. Hayley will be over the moon.' He released her and she let out a breath she didn't know she was holding in. Adrian seemed to realise how intimate his gesture had been and returned to making a fuss of Boomer.

'Will she?' queried Kim, remembering the last time they'd met and thinking about the blatant lie she told her father about being hit in the eye.

'Of course. She needs wedding flowers.'

'Did you tell her you were going to ask *me*?' Kim fixed him with a stare.

'No, she actually asked me *not* to ask you but there is literally nobody else.'

'Thanks, Adrian – way to make me feel special,' she said with a chuckle.

'Sorry. I'm sure she'll be able to see past your disagreement.'

'Hmm I'm not sure she will. But I'll leave it to you, Adrian. The offer is there if she wants to take it up. But I'll need to know tonight so I can order the extra fresh stock from the wholesaler in time. We need them in store two days before to recover. We're running out of time. Why not give her a call now?'

Adrian ran his bottom lip through his teeth and looked a little awkward. 'Okay.' He pulled out his mobile and made the call. Kim continued to pack things away while keeping a discreet ear tuned into Adrian's conversation. 'Hayley, I've found a florist who can do the essential flowers for the wedding.' He pulled the phone away from his ear as she excitedly screamed her reply. 'And you can have a chat to her now about what she can do. And it's Kim,' said Adrian, his voice speeding up at the end. He quickly passed his phone over.

Kim took the phone to hear Hayley was still talking. 'Dad, seriously? Is this a joke? There must be someone else.'

'I doubt it,' said Kim. 'I can do what you want though I can't promise specific flowers and colours, but if you tell me what you had planned, I'll do my damnedest to get it as close as possible.' There was silence. Kim and Adrian waited. 'Hayley, I need to know now because I have to order the stock otherwise it's whatever I can cobble together from shop leftovers.' She gave a shrug for Adrian's benefit.

She heard Hayley sigh. 'The bridesmaid's dresses are pale sage, so all the arrangements and bouquets had a lot of foliage, white roses and lots of very pale blush pink flowers but I don't know what type they were. Mine was going to be a beautiful . . .' Hayley paused and Kim heard her sniff.

'I know how important wedding flowers are, Hayley. How about I find out what I can get my hands on and I'll bring my catalogue over to your dad's tonight and we can work out what we can do?'

She heard Hayley take a deep breath. 'Thanks, Kim.'

'No problem.' She handed the phone back to Adrian

who was blowing her kisses and making her heart melt. Maybe this was a step to them being friends again. She very much hoped so.

Kim rang Vince and explained why she couldn't see him that night. He was quite annoyed at being fobbed off – apparently, he had something his solicitor needed her to sign. He said he felt she was blowing hot and cold and not taking his situation seriously but before she could protest, he ended the call. Oh well, she'd deal with him tomorrow. For now, she was focused on coming to Hayley's rescue, although it was clear who she was really doing it for.

Kim showered and changed into a plain summer dress she'd found in her wardrobe, something from her 'one day I'll be slimmer' collection and she was thrilled that it fitted her again. She did her hair and make-up. She told herself it was because she wanted to look professional for Hayley but that was a big fat lie. After being away from him for what felt like ages Kim realised she had feelings for Adrian. Big obvious heart-a-flutter feelings for him that wouldn't go away.

She left Boomer with a carrot. She'd only be gone an hour and he was getting better at being alone. Hopefully he'd sleep. She checked there was nothing obvious he could eat, chew or destroy before she explained where she was going and how long she'd be. He concentrated on his carrot.

It was a short drive to Adrian's and she had to keep reminding herself seeing him wasn't the main purpose of her visit. Adrian let her in. 'Hayley's a bit delayed but she'll be here soon.' He seemed on edge. He showed her through to the living room where they settled uneasily on separate chairs and looked at each other. Kim put her albums of photographs and catalogues on the floor. Adrian checked his watch. 'I'm not sure what we do to keep ourselves amused while we wait.'

'I could take my clothes off,' said Kim, trying to lighten the mood. Adrian appeared to tense up in alarm. 'Because the last time I was here . . . Well, I had the dressing gown on but . . .'

Adrian clicked his fingers and seemed to relax. 'I remember, yes.'

They both emitted something like canned laughter and returned to looking awkwardly at each other. 'Tea!' said Adrian, making Kim jump. 'Would you like a cup?'

'Yes, please.' The relief was palpable from them both. Kim sank back into the chair. What had happened to the easy friendship they'd had? She could hardly believe she was here to help out the very person who had destroyed it. Ruby was right: she was too kind for her own good. She got to her feet and had a little snoop around. Nothing intrusive, she was simply interested in the many photographs dotted about. She had a good look at all the happy family pictures and wondered if in a parallel universe that could have been her and Vince. If a child would have stopped him from straying.

A key in the front door had her dashing back to her chair. She caught her toe in the rug and stumbled in an ungainly fashion towards the chair, getting there just before Adrian entered the room.

She hastily sat down and took the tea that Adrian was clutching. 'Thank you,' she said in a small voice. That was close.

As Hayley appeared behind her father, Kim was relieved that she wasn't meeting her in a state of undress this time. 'Hello, Hayley, how are you?'

Hayley was looking from her father to Kim and back again. She too seemed surprised to find Kim fully clothed.

'Hello, love. Tea?' asked Adrian.

'Okay,' said Hayley, taking a seat on the sofa, her eyes still flicking around the room.

Once Adrian had left, Kim felt she needed to set out her stall. 'I'm here in a professional capacity so—'

'This doesn't change anything, you doing the flowers. I stand by what I said – it's too soon for Dad,' said Hayley in a low voice.

'Hayley, I don't want to get into that again. And I think you're well aware that your little stunt has had the desired effect. Our friendship is over because your dad thinks I'm some sort of violent harpy.'

'You need to move on,' said Hayley.

'I was hoping you were going to come clean about lying but clearly not.' The small spark of hope was snuffed out.

'I didn't lie. I was very upset and my eye had puffed up. He just assumed you'd hit me.'

'You did nowt to change that assumption though.'

Adrian cleared his throat and they both swivelled in his direction to see him standing in the doorway. Kim wasn't sure how long he'd been there but from his expression she could guess.

'Hayley, is that true. Kim didn't hit you?'

Kim was trying hard not to look smug but it was simply too difficult. She sipped her tea and watched the floorshow.

'Dad, I can explain.' Hayley looked to Kim as if pleading with her to help. Kim shrugged. Hayley continued, 'I was upset. She said some things.' Hayley pointed at Kim.

'Hayley, for goodness' sake you accused someone of actual bodily harm,' said Adrian, rubbing his hand across his chin.

'I wouldn't go that far,' interjected Kim. 'It was actual *beadily* harm to be honest.' She chuckled. Neither Adrian nor Hayley were smiling. 'Because it was the beads . . . on the curtain . . . never mind.' Kim indicated they should continue their confrontation.

'I'm so sorry,' said Adrian, turning to Kim. 'And after all this you still agreed to help with the flowers.'

'Yes, flowers,' said Hayley seeing her opportunity to change the subject. 'Are those your books? Shall we have a look at them?'

Chapter Thirty-Seven

It felt odd to walk into the nursing home knowing Harry was no longer there. Ruby had shed a few tears over Harry and she'd only met him a handful of times. Perhaps her tears had also been for Curtis.

Ruby got a warm welcome from Dot and Kitty and a few of the other residents she was getting to know. 'More flowers,' said Dot, delightedly sniffing them. 'They're beautiful.'

'They are,' said Ruby, admiring the best blooms.

'You look unhappy,' said Kitty, rummaging in her bag. 'Here, have a sweetie.' She offered Ruby the packet.

'Thanks, I'm okay.'

'Is the wedding getting you down?' asked Dot, sniffing the flowers.

'There's no wedding,' said Ruby. There was a sharp intake of breath from someone nearby – although it could have been asthma – followed by the scraping of chairs as people moved closer.

'The toerag!' said Kitty.

'No, no, no,' said Ruby. 'There never was a wedding. We're just friends,' she added assuming they meant Curtis, although it was difficult to keep track who they meant half the time.

'But there was a ring,' said Dot, frowning as if in deep thought.

'Ah, yes. I see where you got confused. There was an engagement ring but . . .' The faces around her were already looking bewildered. This was too complicated. 'It turns out the ring was a fake and Lewis has been arrested.' There was a huge collective gasp. She figured she might as well give them the juicy bits even if they might not fully follow the story. She recounted the restaurant confrontation and she found that in the retelling, Curtis came out the hero. Kitty started a mini round of applause.

'Your life is better than Emmerdale Farm,' said Dot.

'It's not called that any more. Not since Annie Doo-Dah left,' said Kitty.

'Sugden,' said a familiar voice behind her. Ruby turned to see Curtis filling the doorway.

'Annie Sugden,' said Kitty clapping her hands and the conversation drifted off.

'Hi' said Ruby. 'I didn't expect to see you here any more.' She suddenly didn't know what to do with her hands, so she folded her arms.

'I needed to collect Harry's things. The clothes are going to charity but there were a few other items.'

'I see.' Ruby nodded. Awkward was an understatement. 'How's Cordelia?'

'She's well. She's gone back to London but she'll be back for the funeral.'

'That's good. I'm pleased you two are getting on.'

'Actually, if you have a few minutes I did have some questions.'

'Sure.' Ruby said her goodbyes and followed Curtis out. They strolled down to a bar on the Chesterfield road as the sun started to fade. They didn't do much in the way of small talk on the way. They ordered drinks and found some stools in a cosy corner.

'I'm sorry you weren't there when Harry died. I kind of feel responsible,' said Ruby.

Curtis shook his head. 'Not at all. Statistically it was very unlikely I would have been there when he actually died. I think it's far more important I was there while he was still conscious.'

Logical as ever. 'You know he loved you very much,' said Ruby. She thought about the night she'd chatted to Harry when Curtis had been in London.

'Yes, it was one of the last things he said.'

Ruby had to swallow hard not to get emotional. Grief was a regular visitor who she had to slam the door on. She took a deep breath and tried to sound bright. 'I'm glad we've seen each other . . .' He looked intrigued. 'I wanted to say I was sorry if I was a bit off last night.'

'I ruined your date. I understand.'

'No,' said Ruby. 'You saved me from another waster. So, thank you.'

'You're welcome,' he said with a nod.

Curtis reached forward and his hand brushed her cheek. The intimate gesture caught her off-guard. What was he doing? 'Curtis?' her voice was barely a whisper.

'Spider,' he said, retrieving it from her hair and letting it drop to the floor.

The question she wanted to ask him popped into her head. 'Curtis . . . can I ask you something?'

'Yes.' He was studying her face.

She wondered what he'd say if she asked him what was bubbling in her mind. But now wasn't the right time. 'What was it you wanted to talk about?' she asked instead, reaching for her glass.

'Cordelia.'

Her name alone conjured images of the two of them together. 'Anything specific?'

'Indeed. She stayed at my house . . .' Ruby immediately wanted to know what had gone on and also *didn't* want to know at the same time. 'And I noticed she'd forgotten her toothbrush, underwear, some make-up remover, and some other make-up products. I offered to post them to her and she said she didn't need them. Now should I dispose of the items or post them to her anyway?'

Ruby scratched her eyebrow. 'Neither, Curtis. You need to keep them at yours.'

'Indefinitely?'

'She's planning on becoming a regular visitor.' Something lurched inside Ruby's gut.

'I see. That explains why she said I should use non-biological washing liquid in the future.'

'Things are progressing well then?'

He pursed his lips. 'I'm not sure.'

Ruby leaned forward. 'What makes you say that?'

'Because I'm not sure I know what progress looks like in this context.'

'Usually, once you've established there's a mutual interest, you kiss and if that goes well, you move on to . . .' he was watching her intently '. . . physical things. Then it sort of fizzles out and you realise that that was all it was – just a physical thing. Or, if you're luckier than me, your relationship develops. And you talk. Learn about each other. Discuss what you want for the future: family, career. You settle into something that's both exciting and reassuringly familiar.' Her mind unhelpfully played her a film reel of their trips out, Curtis making her breakfast and him holding her in the restaurant when Lewis was arrested and how right it had felt to be in his arms. It was all too much.

'I can't do this.' She stood up. 'I'm sorry, Curtis, I really want it to work out for you and Cordelia, I honestly do, but I can't hold your hand any more. I've got to go. Bye.' She hastily took money from her purse and placed a ten-pound note on the table.

'Ruby?' She turned back. What could he say that would make her stay?

'There will be change.' He pointed at the note. Same old Curtis, always practical.

'Leave it as a tip,' she told him and left.

By the time Thursday rolled around Kim could tell as soon as Ruby walked in that things hadn't improved. They set up and Kim went through the blooms she'd managed to get from the wholesaler for Hayley's rush-job wedding flowers. 'And I figure if I pop into the reception at the end, I can whip the table centre vases back for the Saturday wedding.' Ruby was staring out of the window. 'Here,' she said, giving her a tenner. 'I think bacon butties are needed.'

Ruby didn't crack a smile but left to get the food. Kim was laying out the flowers for Hayley's bouquet and was pleased with the mix of white hydrangeas, blush peonies, freesias and silver dollar eucalyptus. Boomer barked as a customer entered the shop. Kim went to serve.

'Curtis, how lovely to see you. You've just missed Ruby; she'll be back in a minute.'

'Is it all right if I wait?'

'Of course. You don't mind if I carry on, do you? We've got a rush job for a wedding tomorrow.' Curtis followed her to the back room. Boomer strained at his lead to get a good sniff at the new person. Kim rewarded his not

352

jumping up with a treat and felt quite proud. 'How's things with you and Cordelia?'

He puckered his eyebrows. 'I'm still working that out. Kim, can I ask, have I upset Ruby?'

'She's not said anything to me. You'd have to ask her.'

'I fear she wouldn't tell me if I had. She was going to ask me something on Saturday night and then she just left. I've messaged her a few times and called but she's not responding.'

'You saw her Saturday night?'

'Not intentionally. We were both at the nursing home. We went for a drink and she was explaining about the stages of a relationship.'

'Was she now?' The thought of it made Kim smile.

'Yes, she was. But she said she had something to ask me and I've been puzzling over what it was and why she didn't ask.'

Kim bit her lip. It was clear Ruby had bottled out. If she was fixed on going down the sperm donor route then Curtis was by far her best, safest and most straightforward option. 'Look, she's been thinking about this for a while. Please don't let on I've said anything. The thing is, she wants you to be her sperm donor.'

Curtis's eyebrows jumped and stuck in a very high position. They relaxed a fraction and he started to blink rapidly. 'I see. I certainly wasn't expecting that.'

'Please don't say I blabbed but at least now you have a chance to consider it and be prepared for when she does ask you,' reasoned Kim, hoping she hadn't done the wrong thing by telling him. 'And don't mention it to Cordelia.'

'No. Um.' He checked his watch twice in quick succession. 'Thanks, Kim. I think I'll catch Ruby another time.'

'You sure?'

'Yes. Bye, Kim.' He left the shop like someone fleeing a burning building. *Damn*, thought Kim, *what have I done?*

Kim served a customer and Ruby returned with the bacon butties. 'Curtis called in.'

Ruby started tucking into her sandwich. 'What did he want?'

'Um. He thought you were holding back on asking him something. So—' Kim's mobile rang. 'Hang on,' she said to Ruby before accepting the call.

'Yes . . . Oh, hi . . .' She mouthed to Ruby that it was the bank and she gave an eyeroll. 'Er . . . No . . . Absolutely not . . . Okay . . . Should I come down? . . . Right . . . Thanks.' Kim was stunned; she couldn't believe what she'd just been told.

'Problem?' asked Ruby, licking ketchup off her fingers.

'Yes, a bloody great Vince-shaped one.' She grabbed her bag and raced for the door. 'Hold the fort. I'm going to lynch him.'

'That's not a good idea,' called Ruby but Kim was already at the door. Boomer whimpered at the sight of her leaving.

The bank manager had told Kim there was no need for her to come down but she disagreed. She was fuelled by pure adrenaline, loathing and a lot of temper, plus she'd missed out on her bacon butty – another reason to hate Vince. She marched into the banking hall, past the queue for the till and desks of smiling staff. She knew where the manager's office was and through the glass she could see the manager, Vince and a woman with her back to the door. The sight of Vince made her clench her jaw. How could he have fooled her a second time?

Kim flung open the door and strode inside, shutting it firmly behind her. She was pleased to see Vince almost topple off his chair in surprise. His head spun rapidly from her to the manager and back again. The woman next to him looked up and smiled but the smile quickly faded as she registered Vince's reaction.

The bank manager looked startled. 'Madam, this is a private—'

'Hi, Vince,' said Kim, trying to sound blasé. 'I didn't know you banked here too.'

'Uh, well, er. You see the thing is—' He appeared to be looking for another exit as his head swivelled around the small glass-walled room.

The face of the woman was etched in Kim's mind. She'd only ever seen her once before and it was at Vince's bedside – she was the acupuncturist. 'Hi, I'm Kim Baxter. And you are?' Kim asked, offering a hand for her to shake. She stared at it like it was a loaded gun.

'Ah,' said the manager, getting to his feet. 'I suggest you wait in the other office while we sort this out, Mrs Baxter.' He looked from Kim to the seated woman and then pointed at Kim as if to clarify which one he meant. 'This Mrs Baxter.'

'There is only one. She's the imposter,' said Kim, jabbing a finger at the seated woman.

'That's where you're wrong. I am the *current* Mrs Baxter.' Not the ex-partner Vince had led her to believe. And her voice sounded uncannily like that of Sally Burrows, Vince's solicitor. Kim was rapidly realising that pretty much everything Vince had told her was a lie.

'You might be, but you're not the Mrs Baxter with the account at this bank. You pair of crooks are trying to steal my money!' snapped Kim, holding on tightly to her temper, which was on a fraying thread. The repeated request from the 'solicitor' for some ID was now making sense; they obviously needed it to defraud the bank.

355

Vince stood up and nudged the woman to do the same as he hastily made for the door. Kim blocked his exit. 'Going somewhere?'

'Kim, don't get yourself all flustered. You can't blame me for trying. I walked away with nothing.'

'You had half the bloody house!' She was furious.

'But none of the business and you've got to admit I helped build that up. Half of it is rightly mine.'

'Is it hell. It had only been up and running five months and I used my mother's money to set it up. It's all in my name. I don't owe you a penny, Vince Baxter.'

'Really, Mrs Baxter, we do have this in hand,' said the manager. He turned to Vince. 'We have CCTV footage. There's not a lot of point in running.'

'I disagree,' said Vince, shoving Kim into the manager and wrenching open the door. He darted out, promptly tripped over someone's shoe and hit the floor like a dropped plank.

'Whoops, sorry,' said Ruby, stepping on his hand. Kim was delighted to see her.

'Ow!' He pulled his hand from under Ruby's heel and scrambled to his feet.

'Vince!' shouted the other Mrs Baxter, from the office where Kim was blocking the doorway. 'Don't leave me!' She didn't look happy.

'He does that,' said Kim.

'Move out of the way, Kim,' said Vince. A crowd was now watching them. A sheen of sweat formed on Vince's top lip.

'One question,' she said. 'Are you dying?'

He snorted a sickening laugh and shook his head. 'Come on,' said Vince, leaning past Kim, grabbing his partner's arm. Ruby and Kim blocked their exit.

The bank manager stepped forward. 'Really ladies, I must insist you—' he started.

'Ge'ore!' chorused Ruby and Kim together.

'Bloody hell, it's Floral and Hardy,' said Vince, with a chuckle. He tried to push past Ruby, knocking her to the floor in the process. Kim took a swing at him as two police officers rushed inside and intercepted her.

'Hey, not me. I called you to arrest him!' she shouted.

The manager nodded his agreement and the police officers let Kim go, placed a hand firmly on Vince's shoulder and marched him back into the manager's office.

Chapter Thirty-Eight

An hour later Adrian was forcing a cup of hot sweet tea onto Kim. 'Here, get this down you. It's good for shock,' he said, giving her shoulder a friendly squeeze.

'Thanks for minding the shop,' said Kim.

'You've already thanked me,' he said.

'Sorry, I dumped that on you,' said Ruby. 'But I knew there was trouble brewing and I couldn't just lock up with Boomer here.'

'My pleasure,' said Adrian. 'I quite enjoyed it. I sold a pot plant to someone who really wanted a bouquet and have booked in baby flowers and a blue balloon for delivery as soon as you can.' He tapped a note on the counter.

'I'll crack on with Hayley's flowers,' said Ruby, putting down her Coke can.

'Oh goodness, the wedding,' said Kim.

'It's fine. I've got it covered,' said Ruby. 'You relax and mentally stick pins in Vince's testicles.'

Kim's hands were shaking as she cupped her hot tea. Her head was spinning like an Olympic ice dancer. 'I can't believe it was all lies,' she said to nobody in particular.

'He took me in too,' said Ruby. 'I can't believe he wasn't really dying.'

'Only dying to get his hands on my money. Not that there's much. But there is a sizeable overdraft that I don't use. The police think they were going to empty the account, with her posing as me, max out the overdraft and flee the country.' Kim was still shaking.

Adrian crouched down in front of her. Boomer instantly joined him and demanded a fuss. 'Can I get you anything, Kim?' he asked.

'No, thanks. What was it you came in for?'

'Crumbs – I completely forgot.' He picked up a bag from behind the counter and handed her a bottle of rhubarb gin. 'It's just a little something to say thank you for doing Hayley's flowers at such short notice and after everything that happened.'

Kim could have cried at the thoughtfulness. 'My favourite.' As tears welled in her eyes, she sniffed them back, making quite an unattractive sound and she wished she hadn't done it.

'You sure you're okay?' he asked, his face full of concern.

'I'm fine. I bet there's a million and one things you need to do before the wedding tomorrow. You should go.'

'If it's okay with you then I will. I've written and rewritten my speech a dozen times and I'm still not happy with it.' He ran a hand through his hair.

'It'll be perfect. A wedding reception is the ideal audience – everyone is happy and they all want you to do well. Don't worry about it. Go,' she said, shooing him with her free hand.

'But we'll catch up soon. Yes?'

'Very soon. I'll be dropping off the flowers in the morning.'

'Of course.' He jokingly slapped himself on the forehead. 'Okay great. I'll see you then.' Adrian paused to wave twice as he headed for the door. 'Bye.'

Ruby appeared through the beads with some flowers in her hands. 'He's lovely. And as far as we know, not a criminal. I think you two should get it on.'

'Thank you for your sage advice but it's a bit complicated. What with Hayley not being keen and me getting caught up with Vince, I'm taking a leaf out of your book and swearing off men for a while.' Boomer dropped his head in her lap, almost knocking her tea. 'Apart from you, boy.'

'I don't blame you.' Ruby began wrapping stems together to make one of the bridesmaid's bouquets. 'I've got a new plan. It's early days but I've made a few enquiries.'

Kim was pleased to be distracted from thoughts of Vince. 'Go on, what's the new plan?'

'I'm investigating fostering. It would be instead of the sperm donor idea. And who knows, fostering might lead to adoption.' Ruby did a gleeful jiggle and looked elated at the prospect.

Kim recalled her conversation with Curtis. 'Ah. You're definitely not doing the sperm donor thing?'

Ruby fixed her with a worried look. 'What? Do you think fostering is a bad idea?'

'No. I think you'd be amazing at it.'

'You get all sorts of training and support and you get paid too. I might need to speak to you about reducing my hours but I don't want to get ahead of myself.' Ruby tied a perfect bow – *if only everything could be tied up as neatly,* thought Kim.

'Ruby . . .' Kim bit her lip. 'I've got a confession to make.'

Ruby was very fond of Kim but she had overstepped a line. She'd kept it together in the shop while Kim had confessed to telling Curtis that Ruby wanted him to be her donor. There was little point ranting and raving –

Kim was her boss and on top of that Kim had had a totally rubbish morning thanks to Vince. They'd worked on the wedding flowers until late. But it meant Ruby had bottled her frustration and now she was pacing around her tiny flat trying to work out what to do for the best. Seymour was lying on the back of the sofa and he took a playful swipe at her each time she went past and every time he missed.

She wanted to speak to Curtis about fostering – that had been what she'd wanted to ask him about but it had felt personal and the moment hadn't been quite right. Now things were decidedly awkward. If she explained to him that Kim had got it wrong, he'd know Kim wouldn't have made it up so it would look like she was lying. If she said she had a new idea would it make her look fickle? She didn't want him thinking the fostering thing was a whim. She'd been mulling it over for weeks. In fact, pretty much ever since she'd known he was a foster child.

The more she'd thought about it the more certain she had become that it was the right path for her to take. There were thousands of children who came in and out of the care of social services and if she could do a little bit to make their lives better then she'd feel she was doing something worthwhile. It was an opportunity to share the love she had and become a parent to someone who truly needed one.

She was also coming to terms with the fact that Curtis was probably right about her having autophobia. She didn't like the idea of being alone and this was a good way to solve that and at the same time give a happy temporary home and lots of love to a child who needed it. She realised her mother's legacy was love. She missed her terribly and that would take time to heal but what she had shown her was that loving another human being was what made you happy – regardless of how they came into your life. And at least she was being honest with herself about her motivation for doing it. She paused her pacing. Seymour took three swipes at her and caught her on his third attempt.

'Hey, you,' she said. Seymour went to give her an affectionate head bump, missed and almost fell off the sofa. 'I'll feed you before I go, I promise.'

She needed to speak to Curtis tonight but it had to be a face-to-face conversation. She fed the cat, grabbed a bottle of wine as she didn't like the idea of turning up empty-handed and set off for Curtis's house. She went over what she was going to say on the way there. She'd be honest and explain that she had been considering him as a sperm donor but she felt fostering was a far better option all round. Whilst, on paper, he was the ideal candidate she wanted them to stay friends and something like that would definitely complicate things.

She pulled up outside and could see there were lights on. He was in. She rang the bell and waited. As the door opened she held up the wine as a peace offering and came face to face with Cordelia. Ruby was gobsmacked. She lowered the wine and the smile slid from her face. Somehow with everything else that had been going on she'd forgotten about Cordelia. It wasn't that she didn't like her – she did. She was obviously a better fit for Curtis than she was. And whilst she wanted Cordelia and Curtis's relationship to go well she hoped there was an opportunity for her and Curtis to continue their friendship because she had come to really value it.

'Erm, hi,' said Ruby. 'Is Curtis in?'

Cordelia was staring at the wine bottle. She stepped outside and pulled the door to. 'Ruby, can I have a quiet word?'

'Sure.' She had a bad feeling about what was coming next. She hoped Curtis hadn't said anything to her about the sperm donor idea.

'I get that you and Curtis are . . . close.' She had a way of saying it that made it sound like incest. 'But as employer and employee I think it's better for everyone if there are clear boundaries. Don't you agree?' As she'd feared, Cordelia was one of those women who were uncomfortable with their partner having female friends.

'No,' said Ruby, and she revelled in the stunned look on Cordelia's face. 'I've worked for Kim for over three years and in that time we've grown really *close*,' she said, mirroring Cordelia's odd inflection of the word. 'And everything is better because of it. We know each other inside and out, which makes us more productive, more creative and happier people.' She gave a broad grin; she was definitely happy in her work and that was largely down to her relationship with Kim.

'Perhaps flower arranging is unique in that regard but with—'

'Ruby, hello,' said Curtis, opening the door fully. 'I thought I heard your voice. You'd best come in.' She retained her grin as she jauntily walked past Cordelia, leaving her to shut the door behind them.

They gathered in the kitchen. Ruby noticed he had a new roller blind. 'I like the Orla Kiely blind. The colours work really well.'

'I chose it,' said Cordelia, snaking an arm protectively around Curtis. He seemed to stiffen slightly. 'And I bought him matching oven gloves as a gift.'

'Because you're too hot to handle?' quipped Ruby, thinking about the note on the stapler Curtis had given Cordelia.

Cordelia's brows puckered. 'No. They're so he doesn't burn himself.' *These two are made for each other*, thought Ruby.

'No double doors yet, though,' said Ruby, looking around.

Curtis chuckled. 'No, I'm still working on those.'

'That's good to hear,' said Ruby, revelling in their exchange.

Cordelia appeared confused. 'Is that some sort of in-joke?'

'Very much so,' said Ruby. 'It's all part of our *close* relationship.'

'Was there a purpose to your visit, Ruby?' asked Cordelia, her tone unamused.

Ruby put the wine on the counter. This was a bit awkward. Her planned speech didn't work quite as well with his girlfriend present. She'd just have to make some amendments on the hoof.

'This.' She pointed at the wine. 'Is to say sorry for the confusion over what Kim said to you today. I admit I had considered . . . it, but I've decided against it partly because of . . .' she glanced at Cordelia '. . . certain changes in your relationship status. But mainly because I have a better idea.' Curtis was nodding; at least it appeared one person knew what she was talking about. 'What I actually wanted to talk to you about . . . and now might not be the time, was your experience of fostering and your thoughts on me doing it.' She was aware she was doing her arm-waving thing, so she stopped talking and suddenly was over-whelmed with self-consciousness. She realised how important Curtis's opinion was to her. She wasn't entirely sure why she needed his endorsement for this big life decision – but she did.

'Then you'd be leaving Curtis's employ?' asked Cordelia, looking pleased.

'Not necessarily.' She probably would have to but right now she didn't want to please Cordelia. Her little speech about employee-employer boundaries had pissed her right off.

'I see,' said Curtis. His expression unreadable. Ruby waited.

Cordelia appeared impatient. 'Curtis?'

'To summarise,' began Curtis. 'You've decided against pursuing a sperm donor, which also means you have discounted my sperm as an option.' Cordelia gasped. Ruby couldn't look at her. At least she knew he'd not already discussed Kim's revelation with Cordelia, which felt like a bonus. Curtis continued unperturbed. 'You are planning to continue with two jobs and foster as a single parent.'

'Yeah,' she said, her voice a little overwhelmed, which was exactly how she felt now he'd played it back to her.

Cordelia hooted with laughter. 'This is a joke. Some sort of comic wind-up you two have cooked up?' She jabbed a finger at both of them.

'No,' said Ruby. She swallowed hard. Did it sound like a joke? She hoped it didn't because for the first time in a long while she actually had a half-decent life plan mapped out.

Cordelia's laughter faded and her face turned stony. 'You come over here with your in-jokes, cheap wine . . .' it was Ruby's turn to gasp '. . . and ideas about my boyfriend's sperm!' Cordelia's nostrils flared and Ruby wouldn't have been surprised if they'd snorted out fire – she certainly looked angry enough.

'No,' said Curtis, perfectly calmly. 'She said she *doesn't* want my sperm.'

'Do you think this is appropriate?' Cordelia was staring wide-eyed and incredulous at Curtis.

He gave Ruby a sideways look and she shrugged. Cordelia possibly had a point. 'Ruby is my friend. Friends share intimacies with each other,' said Curtis. This didn't help.

Cordelia's face was turning quite red. 'Is there something I should know? Have I been a fool? Have you been carrying on this whole time?'

'That's quite a few different questions,' said Curtis. 'Shall we take them one at a time?'

'Are you friends with benefits?' asked Cordelia.

'Yes, a great many,' said Curtis cheerfully.

Ruby waved for him to shut up. 'No, Cordelia. There's nothing going on between us. There have been no *intimacies* and no benefits. I promise you.' She shook her head at Curtis, who looked perplexed beyond his standard confused form. 'I don't want to cause any issues between the two of you. I should go.'

'I agree,' said Cordelia, straightening her spine. 'I think that's best.'

'Maybe I'll catch you another time, Curtis,' said Ruby. She knew Cordelia was going to lay down some rules once she'd left.

'Yes,' said Curtis.

'No, I don't think so,' said Cordelia. 'I mean, if you worked in my company, Human Resources would be crawling all over this wholly inappropriate relationship. If you had any decency you'd resign.' Cordelia stared Ruby down.

The fight had gone out of Ruby. 'If that's what you want, fine. Consider me resigned.' Ruby paused to look at Curtis, willing him to react, to fight for their friendship. To fight for her – even if it was only as an employee. Did their friendship not mean the same to him as it did to her?

'That really should be in writing,' said Curtis at last.

'Fine,' snapped Ruby. 'I'll send you a bloody spreadsheet!' She snatched up her wine, because they didn't deserve it, and marched out with as much dignity as she could muster, tears welling in her eyes and her heart in tatters.

Chapter Thirty-Nine

On Friday morning Ruby and Kim were both quiet as they loaded Hayley's wedding flowers into the van. As Ruby turned to go back inside the shop, she noticed Kim add an extra bouquet she didn't recognise.

'Dropping it off on the way,' Kim explained. She shut the doors and paused by the van. 'Ruby, I'm really sorry,' she said, for the umpteenth time.

Ruby faced her. 'It's okay.' She didn't want Kim to take the blame for something that was inevitable. 'It's not what you said to Curtis. Having friends of the opposite sex rarely works out well.'

'Was it just a friendship though? I thought you and Curtis had the potential for more than that,' said Kim.

Ruby played with a strand of hair. She didn't want to dwell on what might have been – that wasn't going to help. 'I liked him as a friend but basically it would never work as a romantic relationship. He has as much of an idea about romance as ABBA do about heavy metal.'

'Really? This is the man who took you to Covent Garden at the mere mention it was somewhere you'd always wanted to go. He bought you a new phone having met you only hours before, invented a job for you and cooked you cottage pie. That sounds pretty good to me.'

Ruby was confused by her feelings. 'But he's part robot.'

'Is he? I mean, what are you really looking for in a partner?'

Ruby thought back to the list she'd shared with Curtis. 'Someone I can trust, who makes me laugh and has the same interests and life goals as me.'

'And does Curtis tick any of those boxes?'

'It's more complicated than that. He's Curtis. He doesn't fit the standard tick list. He's completely straightforward and yet utterly complex at the same time.'

'It sounds to me like you're trying to convince yourself he's not right for you, rather than looking at what does work between you.' When Ruby started to protest, Kim held up her hands. 'I'm just saying. Anyway, I've got to go.' She hopped in the van and drove off. Ruby stayed standing on the pavement and watched the van disappear. Kim had given her some food for thought. The sad thing was it was all a bit too late.

Kim dropped off the separate bouquet that wasn't for Hayley's wedding and then arranged the church flowers. There was something calm about being inside a church alone. The altar spray and pew decorations, didn't take long to place but gave the desired effect. She set off for the hotel and felt a little squiggle of anticipation at the thought she might bump into Adrian; he'd said he'd be there early helping to get things ready. She parked the car and went inside to check which room the reception was being held in.

She was shown through and her heart sank a little. There was no one there. Countless tables were ready with name cards and favours, chairs covered and tied with blush sashes and balloons carpeting the dance floor. She stopped by the reception desk on her way back to the van. 'Is anyone from the wedding party here?' she asked nonchalantly.

'No, they were here last night to get things ready. Did you need to speak to someone?'

'No, it's fine. Thanks,' said Kim, trying to stifle a sigh. She'd missed him but she'd catch him at the house when she dropped off the bridal party bouquets and buttonholes.

She spent a while putting out the centrepieces. Each table had a small globe vase and Kim took her time arranging the flowers in every one, snipping fractions off stems so they sat precisely. She made a space on the top table where the altar flowers would sit when they were brought from the church and left a sticky note to be on the safe side.

She had one last look from the door. The room looked perfect. She hoped Hayley and Adrian thought the same.

As soon as she pulled up at Adrian's house, Hayley came running down the path in her dressing gown. Her hair was up and looked beautiful.

'Morning, bride-to-be.'

'Did you have enough for all the tables?'

'Yep, all done. Take a breath. The reception room looks beautiful.'

'Altar flowers?'

'That was my first stop. They look lovely. You just need someone to remember to take them to the reception.'

'Best man, chief bridesmaid and Dad.'

'Three people for one spray? It's not that big.'

'I figured if I asked three of them at least one would remember.' Hayley seemed to be calming down a little.

'Good plan. Now go back inside and I'll bring in everything.' Surprisingly Hayley did as she was asked. Ever since an excited bride had snatched her bouquet and promptly tripped over and destroyed it, Kim had a thing about taking the flowers to where they needed to be. After that it was someone else's responsibility.

Kim carried in the buttonholes, corsages and flower girl's posy. The house was a frenzy of activity with hairdressers and a variety of women and young girls she assumed were bridesmaids and other assorted relatives – but there was no sign of Adrian.

Hayley and the bridesmaids made the appropriate oohs and aahs at the sight of the flowers. 'I've just got the bride and bridesmaids' bouquets to bring in. Is your dad about? You know, to see your reaction.'

'Oh,' said Hayley, her shoulders sagging a little. 'He's gone to pick up Great-Aunt Beryl.'

'Right,' said Kim, chewing her lip and trying not to be selfish. 'Will he be long?'

'Depends on how easily he can get her walking frame in the car,' said Hayley.

'I'll video you,' said one of the other women. 'Then he won't have missed your reaction.'

'Right. I'll bring them in,' said Kim, no longer able to stall things.

She returned from the van with the large box and Hayley burst into tears as soon as she caught sight of the flowers. This was always a special moment for Kim. She didn't like to make people cry but happy bride tears were always the best feedback.

'It's okay then?' she asked, prompting a lot of sniffing from Hayley.

Hayley threw her arms around Kim and hugged her tight. 'They're utterly beautiful. Exactly what I dreamed of.'

'That's good then. Phew,' she said, trying to lighten things.

'Good job I've got waterproof mascara on,' said Hayley, gently smearing black smudges under her eyes.

'Have an amazing day, Hayley. I wish you every happiness for the future.'

Hayley swallowed hard. 'Thanks, Kim.'

'My pleasure,' she said and it really was. 'Oh, and your mascara might be waterproof but I fear your eyeliner isn't.'

Hayley drew a sharp intake of breath and ran off squealing.

Ruby checked the local news on her phone and almost dropped it when Lewis's face popped up. The police were charging him with thirty-one counts of theft and there were details of how to get in touch if you'd been duped by him. She let out a sigh; he even looked good in his mugshot. Her sorry heart still longed for the person he'd pretended to be.

Boomer barked as the shop door opened and Curtis walked in. Ruby straightened herself out. She'd gone over what Kim had said as she left but it was all a bit too late to do anything about it now. But seeing him, looking all neat and insecure, she couldn't help but feel something stronger than friendship for him.

'Hey,' she said, putting away her phone. 'Look about last night. I'm sorry if I upset Cordelia.'

'That's fine.' He rolled his lips together but said nothing.

She looked him up and down. He was wearing a diamond pattern jumper and beige chinos. She did a double take. It wasn't what they'd bought together and, in her mind, it didn't really suit him.

'Could you give a wistful look out of that window and maybe point?' asked Ruby, failing to hide her grin.

Curtis gave the window a cautious glance. 'Why?'

'Because you look like you've stepped out of the Littlewoods catalogue.'

Curtis frowned and shook his head. 'You know I have no idea what you're talking about?'

'Yeah, I know.' She was going to miss this. 'What can I do for you?'

'It's about your resignation.'

'Bugger. I meant to email you but I forgot.' The door pinged as a smartly dressed young man walked in. She was miffed at being interrupted but went into professional mode. 'Hello, can I help?' she asked.

'Do you sell bouquets of flowers?' he asked.

One day she was going to say no, we do them in buckets, bins and bumholes. 'Yes, we do.'

Curtis shook his head. 'The educational system in this country is dire.'

'Shhh,' said Ruby, manoeuvring Curtis out of the way.

'To take away now or for delivery?' she asked the customer.

'Can you waive the delivery charge as it's not that far?'

'No, because it's not just the petrol. The charge is also for my time,' she explained.

'How about you take them at the same time as someone else's – is that cheaper?'

Ruby squeezed her eyes shut. Was this guy for real? 'Sure thing. You leave me the address and the next time we are delivering to the house next door I'll give you a call.'

'Sweet,' he said. There was a brief pause. 'You're shitting me, ain't ya?'

'Do you want to leave the address or take them now?'

'Okay. I'll take them with me.'

'Good decision,' said Ruby. She talked him through some options and made up the bouquet for him. He left a happy customer.

'You're really good with people,' said Curtis.

'What because I'm snarky with them? I think Human Resources would beg to differ.'

'Apart from that. You're good with people. You're good with me.'

Ruby was taken aback. 'Well, apart from the wild partying and double door obsession, you've turned out okay I guess.' She gave him a nudge with her elbow.

'Indeed. I want to help you . . . with the fostering, not the artificial insemination.'

For a moment she was thrilled and then realisation dawned. 'But I don't think you can do either without upsetting Cordelia.' His face was blank. 'She's your partner and you need to run things like this by her now. And if it's anything to do with me, I guarantee she's going to say no.'

'I see,' said Curtis. 'You mean I effectively need to choose between you and her?'

That was it exactly but spelling it out wasn't going to make the situation feel any better. 'Don't think about it like that,' she said. 'They're two different things: a friend and a partner. You said yourself that you and Cordelia are a match. You have things in common. You like each other like that. You have to give that your best shot.'

He nodded. 'Indeed. But you've been guiding me. I'm not sure I'm ready to go it alone with Cordelia.'

'At some point you have to. It's kind of the law. Otherwise you have to change religion and become a Mormon or something.'

'I'll investigate that option,' he said with a smile. 'In the meantime . . .'

'It's been fun. And thanks for the job,' cut in Ruby hastily, feeling sadness come over her in a wave.

'Send me your last timesheet and if you need a reference in the future just ask.' He held out his hand.

They shook hands and the contact sent a shiver through her. 'I'm not sure I'm going to make a long-term career out of being an executive assistant.'

'I meant a reference for the fostering. You'll make a superb mother.'

Ruby was wrong-footed. She swallowed down a lump of emotion. 'That would be great. Thank you.'

'And Cordelia thought you should have this.' He handed her a bag.

She took it cautiously and peered inside. It was the pink teddy bear she had won for him in Cleethorpes. 'Thanks.'

There was an awkward silence broken by someone entering the shop. 'I had better go,' said Curtis.

'Right. Of course. Bye then.' She didn't want him to leave.

Ruby went to step forward to give him a kiss on the cheek goodbye, but the woman who had entered waved a plant in between the two of them. 'This is beautiful. Is it a lily? Because I have a cat and they're poisonous to cats, aren't they? Shouldn't it have some sort of warning on it?'

'It's not a lily, it's a royal white orchid,' explained Ruby as she watched Curtis disappear out of her life, taking a piece of her heart with him.

Chapter Forty

It had been an odd Friday in the flower shop for Kim. Ruby was still out of sorts, Boomer had eaten and thrown up a succulent and she'd spent the whole day thinking about Adrian. She was glad when she was eventually able to pack everything up and head home. She watched something dull on TV but the whole time she was watching the clock, trying to work out when she could feasibly sneak into the wedding reception and collect the centrepiece vases she needed for the next day's wedding. Hopefully she would catch a glimpse of Adrian. He was worth a million Vinces.

She showered, changed and did her hair and make-up – which felt like an odd thing to do at nine o'clock in the evening – and set off for the hotel, leaving Boomer with a chew stick and strict instructions not to eat the furniture.

The hotel was floodlit and looked majestic against the darkening sky. As soon as she got out of the van, she could hear voices and music. She slipped inside the room where the reception was being held and surveyed the scene. Lots of very happy people dancing, chatting and generally having a good time. The tables she'd dressed earlier were now pushed to the edges of the room to make more space for dancing, making it fairly easy for her to collect the vases without disrupting anyone. She scanned the room. She was taking it all in but she was really only looking for one person. Her eyes rested briefly on Hayley. She was dancing with someone who she guessed was the groom, because he was looking at her the way Boomer looked at Kim when she was eating sausage. Hayley was beautiful in a traditional full-length wedding gown. And most importantly she looked happy.

There were a lot of people dancing to the loud music. Kim studied the men in morning suits but Adrian wasn't one of them.

'You looking for someone?' asked Adrian, appearing at her side.

'Ge'ore, you silly sod! You made me jump,' said Kim, shouting to be heard over the sound system and giving him a playful slap. She took a step back. He looked gorgeous in his morning suit. 'Wow.' She said it before she'd had time to engage her brain. 'I mean, you scrub up well, now don't you? You look like a film star.'

'Thanks.' He coloured a little – or that could have been the disco lights. 'And you do too.'

'Ah, but which film? *King Kong*?'

'You shouldn't put yourself down.' His eyes lingered on her for a moment. 'What do you want to drink?' he asked.

She waved his offer away. 'No, I'm working and I've got the van. I'll grab the vases and I'll be out of your hair.'

'We can do that at the end. Come outside.'

Before she could protest, Adrian had taken her by the hand and something akin to a lightning bolt had shot up her arm. They weaved their way through people onto a veranda where some of the party had already spilled out.

'At least it's cooler out here,' she said.

'And quieter,' said Adrian. He was still holding her hand and she wasn't sure if she should point that fact out or just enjoy it.

'Did everything go okay? Your speech?'

'Kim, it's been an amazing day. But do you know the two things that made me cry?'

'Happy tears, I hope.' She smiled.

'Yep, both times. The first was when Hayley walked downstairs. It took my breath away that my little girl could grow up into such a beautiful woman.'

'That's lovely. And the second?'

'After the service, Hayley and I walked around to Justine's grave so she could lay her bouquet there.'

'Ah,' said Kim, knowing what was coming next.

'And someone had laid the most beautiful bouquet of yellow roses.' He raised his eyebrows. 'And I burst into tears.'

'That might have been me,' said Kim. 'I didn't know Hayley was going to do that with her bouquet and I didn't want Justine to miss out on her flowers this week. Sorry they made you cry.'

'Do you know why?' She shook her head. Adrian took her other hand and held them both in front of him. 'Because I knew right at that moment how much you mean to me. You are a beautiful human being, Kim, and I want you in my life.' Kim felt a surge of happiness.

But there was one issue. 'What about Hayley?' she asked.

'She's going to have to get used to it.'

There was an inaudible announcement from the DJ and everyone seemed to tumble outside. Hayley made a beeline for her father. Kim tried to pull away before Hayley reached them but Adrian squeezed her hands reassuringly.

378

'Kim!' Hayley seemed a little tipsy. She gave Kim a one-armed hug as she was holding on to the groom with her other hand. 'You are amazing. Thank you sooooooo much for everything.' Kim glanced at Adrian. This was a turn-up for the books. Hayley whispered in Kim's ear. 'I'm sorry I was such a mardy cow.' She was then propelled away by her new husband. 'Come on, Dad,' she called over her shoulder. 'Fireworks!'

Kim and Adrian walked hand in hand down some old stone steps and onto a perfectly manicured lawn. The July evening was warm and fragrant. The floodlights went out and the fireworks began. Kim only saw the first few because while everyone was watching them Adrian kissed her and everything else melted away.

Ruby was thoroughly fed up. She'd done the right thing. She'd let Curtis go but it hurt like hell. As it turned out she had inadvertently developed quite strong feelings for him. It was an unexpected and inconvenient crush. Ruby told herself it was simply because he was no longer available, like when they cross something off the specials board in the pub and then that's all you want to eat. But even more than that, the friendship they'd grown was more special to her than she'd realised and she was missing him terribly.

Ruby was curled up on her sofa cuddling the garish pink teddy when her phone pinged with a text. Seymour glared at it and so did Ruby. She tapped the screen and a message from Curtis popped up.

One last task. Please can you join me in London on Monday for Post Implementation Review Meeting? Need someone I trust to take notes. Have ordered your train tickets. Curtis.

Technically she was still employed by him as she'd not got around to sending in the last spreadsheet. Monday was her day off from the florist and she had nothing else planned. Cordelia could hardly object. *Oh, what the hell,* she thought.

Sure. Ruby x
She looked at her reply, removed the kiss and sent it.

On Monday morning Ruby looked for Curtis at Sheffield station but there was no sign of him. She checked the time on her prebooked ticket. She'd sent him a text but got no reply. As the train pulled in, she hesitated; if he didn't get on the train with her, she could end up in London on her own. Then she had a thought that perhaps he was already there. Maybe he'd gone down on Sunday and stayed overnight with Cordelia. She banished thoughts of Cordelia and got on the train. She went through to the quiet carriage and sat in her allocated seat. She looked around at the grey faces. Nobody spoke. She sighed. She'd read for a bit and then worry about how she was going to find her way from St Pancras station to the offices when they got a bit closer to London.

Ruby opened her book. It was a new one and immediately she envied the heroine her inevitable happy ending. She was aware of people moving around the carriage but she stayed focused on her novel.

'I think you're in my seat.' She recognised the voice but couldn't quite believe it. She looked up to see Curtis standing next to her. The sight of him made her heart skip. She'd missed him.

'Curtis. I thought you'd missed the train.' She looked him up and down. He was wearing the shirt and jeans they'd bought together and carrying a takeaway cup and his laptop bag.

She put down her book. 'You're not dressed for the office.'

'No. Perhaps I could sit there?' He pointed to the empty seat next to her. 'And I'll explain.'

She moved next to the window so he could have the aisle seat.

'What's going on, Curtis?'

'I got you these,' he said, handing her the cup before producing something from his bag.

'Hot chocolate and a Greggs sausage roll.' She pounced on the paper bag. 'You read my mind; I only had a cereal bar for breakfast. I'm starved,' she said in between mouthfuls. 'Mmm this is delicious. Haven't you got one?'

'Not really my thing.'

She finished her sausage roll and licked her fingers. 'You could have told me it was dress-down Monday.' She indicated his outfit.

'Yes, my apologies. I didn't think of that. But you do look lovely. You always do.' He was giving her outfit the once-over. She was pleased with her charity shop Fifties swing dress.

'Thanks.' She felt some warmth in her cheeks. 'Have you issued an agenda because I haven't seen anything and—'

He held up a palm to halt her. 'Ruby, I do have an agenda.' Curtis pulled a typed sheet from his bag and laid it out on the table in front of both of them.

Ruby scanned it and her heart gave a flutter. At the top of the sheet it said 'Ruby's Fun Day Out'.

'What's this?' she asked, her mouth going dry.

'I wanted you to have a fun day out like the ones you took me on.'

Ruby reread the page. Everything on the list sounded amazing but there was an obvious issue. 'Does Cordelia know about this?'

'We have agreed to keep things on a purely professional level.' Curtis pressed his lips together. 'She bought me a new laptop bag.'

'And that's a chuckable offence because . . .'

'I like *my* laptop bag. I've had it years. It's the last present from Harry and Ayida before Ayida died. Cordelia expected me to stop using it and use the new one. And I realised it wouldn't stop at the bag; she'd want me to change all the old things in my life . . . including you.'

'Hey! I'm not that old.'

'That wasn't what I meant. But she wanted me to change and it didn't feel right.'

'I'm sorry, Curtis. Do you not think maybe you're reading too much into this and that perhaps you need to persevere?' It wasn't that she wanted to convince him to get back with Cordelia but she didn't want him to regret anything.

'I'm afraid there's no point.'

She couldn't deny she felt a certain sense of relief. 'Why ever not?' she asked.

'I have analysed my relationship with Cordelia.'

'Why does that not surprise me?' she said with a chuckle.

'Because I like to analyse things . . . Oh I see, that was sarcasm.'

'Correct. And what did you deduce from your analysis?' asked Ruby.

'That the reason I was interested in pursuing a long-term relationship was because of you.'

'What?' It took her by surprise.

'All the things we enjoyed: shared experiences, laughter, in-jokes and intimacy.'

'Intimacy? Did I miss something?'

'Not sex, Ruby. I mean our friendship. Familiarity that encourages a feeling of being relaxed and at ease with someone.'

'I see. And you didn't have that with Cordelia?'

'Not at all. I knew I was happier in your company, although it is difficult to pin down exactly why.' A frown crossed his forehead.

'Gee thanks.'

'And there was a note with Harry's things,' he said. 'Which I believe is in your handwriting.'

'Ah. I typed it but it felt too formal like that so I copied it out.'

'But when?'

'The nursing home called when you were in London. Harry asked me to do it and it's entirely his words. I had very little to do with it,' said Ruby. The note had been from the heart and full of love and a bit of fatherly advice.

'It was especially kind of you. Thank you.'

'You're welcome.' She wasn't sure where this left things. 'Does that mean it's back to the dating drawing board for you then?'

'No, Ruby. My analysis has shown that you are the key. It's you who I want to be with.'

'Wow,' said Ruby, completely taken aback. 'But you don't believe in happily ever after.'

'Maybe not but I believe in you.'

Ruby gulped down unexpected emotion at his words. It felt like a flutter of butterflies had been unleashed in her stomach. 'I don't know what to say.'

'I know you are seeking someone spontaneous and romantic. And I am aware of my shortcomings in that area. I struggle with spontaneity; however, I can plan. The question is, despite my deficiencies would you be interested in pursuing a relationship with me? But before you answer, today is all about influencing that decision.' He smiled and tapped the printed sheet.

She'd never heard of anything so romantic in her life. 'Mr Walker, this is blatant manipulation.'

'I'm afraid it is.' He inched closer and she felt the warmth of his leg against hers and her breathing faltered. 'Do you think it will work?' he asked.

Ruby twisted in her seat. His face was very close to hers. His blue eyes watched her hopefully. 'We have a friendship and one that I really value and don't want to mess up. Dating crosses a line.'

He leaned back and she missed his closeness. 'I see. Then I have a suggestion.' She nodded for him to continue. 'We spend the day together as if we are on a date as a couple. And at the end of the day we review it. A sort of post-implementation review.'

'And if we don't want to pursue a romantic relationship we stay as friends and forget today ever happened?'

'Exactly. Do we have an agreement?' He held his hand out for her to shake.

'Has the date started?' she asked.

'Yes.'

'Then let's check something first.' She gently pushed his outstretched hand out of the way and leaned forward until their lips met. The kiss was hesitant at first – tender and unsure. But it quickly intensified. Her body zinged as passion ripped through her. They pulled apart. 'Bloody hell, Curtis! You've done that before.'

'Of course I have.' He rolled his eyes. 'I might be staid but I'm not dead.' He pulled her back in for another kiss and she wished the train journey was a lot longer.

At St Pancras, their kissing was interrupted when they were shooed off the train by a cleaner. As they headed for the Tube, Ruby bubbled with excitement about the day ahead.

'Perhaps you could refrain from pole dancing this time,' said Curtis as they stepped onto a train.

'Seriously it's fun. You should try it,' she said, twirling around the central pole. As the train took off Ruby spun out of control, but this time Curtis was there to catch her.

'Thanks,' she said, feeling safe in his arms as he steered her into an empty seat.

'My pleasure,' he said with a smile.

Their first stop was the London Eye. Ruby could hardly contain her excitement as they waited in the queue. They had their photograph taken and got ready to embark. As the pod slowly moved along the walkway towards them, Curtis took her hand and they stepped on together.

They found a spot and Curtis pointed out all the key buildings on the London skyline as they inched their way to the top. Curtis gripped the rail tightly and looked up river.

'What are you thinking?' she asked and instantly wanted to kick herself. They weren't even officially going out yet and she'd committed the cardinal sin of dating of asking a man what's on his mind.

'Good question,' said Curtis. Thankfully he was apparently unaware of the unwritten dating code. 'I was thinking that I might actually be a little acrophobic. Fear of heights.' He nodded at the glass.

Ruby limboed awkwardly under his arm and popped up in front of him. 'No problem. You can look at me instead.'

He chuckled. 'That works for me.' His eyes scanned her face. 'You remind me of autumn.'

'Is it the hair? It's the hair, isn't it?' She twirled a tendril around her index finger.

'No. You can't miss autumn. It makes its presence known and frequently takes your breath away. You are truly beautiful, Ruby.'

It meant so much more coming from Curtis who was never spinning a line. She knew right there that she had fallen big-style for Curtis Walker. 'Thank you. You're not half bad yourself.' She ruffled his hair, making him look a bit more boy band and a lot less tax inspector. Then she remembered Harry's words and smoothed it back into place. 'So, fear of heights is acrophobia. Not vertigo then?'

'No, that's a sensation, like dizziness, which can go with being acrophobic.' She nodded. She had a sort of dizzy feeling right at that moment but it had nothing to do with how high up they were.

He glanced past her and closed his eyes. She leaned forward and kissed him. That would help take his mind off the acrophobia.

When they were safely back on the ground they collected their photograph. Ruby was pulling a face and Curtis looked like he was posing for a passport picture. It reflected their personalities and Ruby knew it was something she was going to treasure.

They hopped back on the Tube and popped up at Leicester Square. She'd seen it many times on the TV when there had been film premieres but had never been. From there they dashed across busy roads and walked through ancient lanes and Ruby recognised where they were heading. Curtis stopped outside a shop.

'I thought you might find something you like in here,' he said, nodding at a display window. 'My treat. As a bonus for all the work you did.'

Ruby scanned the shop front and her heart leaped – they were outside Kurt Geiger's. 'You're paying me in shoes?'

'If that's okay with you?' He looked unsure.

'Yeah, that's very okay with me.'

After trying on an obscene amount of footwear, she chose a pair of raspberry red Mary Janes and swung her bag happily as they strolled through Covent Garden. They made their way towards the restaurant they had been to the first time they came.

Curtis had reserved the same table. 'This is definitely romantic,' said Ruby, her heart filling up with happiness.

'I have to confess. This part wasn't my idea.' Curtis scrunched his face up and Ruby held her breath. 'It was Kitty's.'

Ruby laughed. 'You sought advice from Kitty?'

'And Dot. Although she did suggest I buy you a new car and a property in the Algarve, which I thought a little extravagant.'

Ruby laughed. She loved those two ladies even more now.

After a lazy lunch they walked hand in hand through the tiny streets until they reached a corner where Curtis stopped. Ruby looked around. They were outside a theatre.

As Ruby craned her neck to read the signage, Curtis produced two tickets. 'We have a box for the matinee,' he said.

'*Mamma Mia*?' He nodded. 'Oh my gosh! I want to have your babies!' she squealed and jumped into his arms.

'Now that was something else I wanted to talk to you about,' said Curtis but he was cut short by Ruby's kiss.

Ruby almost skipped into Bloom with a View the following morning. Boomer scampered over and danced around her legs like she'd just returned from an expedition rather than her day off. He left her a little tiddle. She quite liked that she could reduce him to incontinence.

Kim sighed. 'I'll fetch the mop.'

'No, no, I'll do it,' said Ruby merrily.

'Hang on – someone is off-the-scale happy. What happened?'

'I'll put the kettle on – it's a long story,' said Ruby, failing to stop the smile spreading across her face.

Kim almost tripped over a bucket in her haste to join Ruby in the back room. She switched the kettle off and its excited burbles died. 'I've waited a long time to see you looking this happy. Come on, spill.'

After the floor had been mopped they sat down and Boomer joined them. He sat with his chin on Ruby's lap and stared at her adoringly while she recounted her day out with Curtis. Kim gasped, clapped and shed a small tear in all the right places.

'And then we got the train home. First class.'

'Are you seeing him again?' asked Kim.

'I'll see him at Harry's funeral on Friday, if that's what you mean.'

'You know it's not. Come on out with it. What did you decide?' asked Kim, leaning so far forward she was in danger of sliding off the stool.

'Well.' Ruby went a little coy. 'I invited him in for coffee.'

Kim wrinkled her nose. 'But you don't drink coffee.'

'I know.' Ruby did something like jazz hands.

The door chimed. 'Hello,' called out Curtis.

Ruby smoothed down her hair, straightened her top and almost skipped into the shop.

'I bought you both a sausage roll,' said Curtis, holding up two Greggs paper bags. Boomer raced to greet him and danced under the sausage rolls as if trying to work out which one was his.

Curtis wrapped Ruby in a hug and kissed her tenderly.

Ruby stepped back and took her sausage roll. 'You're a keeper,' she said.

Kim joined them. 'Your mum would be so pleased you got your happy ending, Ruby.'

'We all did,' said Ruby, giving Curtis another quick kiss.

'Apart from Cordelia, Lewis, Vince, Neil the sperm donor . . .' said Curtis.

'Okay,' said Ruby, raising her palm to halt his list. 'The people who really matter all got their happy endings.'

'Yes,' he agreed. 'And hopefully there'll be another one for someone when one day in the future we foster a child.'

Kim waved a hand at them, her eyes welling up with tears. 'Stop! I can't take any more.'

The door chimed and in walked Adrian. 'I hope this isn't a bad time,' he started but he tailed off as he spotted that Ruby and Curtis were holding hands. 'What did I miss?' he asked. Boomer leaped about yelping his happiness at seeing Adrian and raced to get his rubber chicken, which he proudly presented to him. As soon as Adrian went to take it, Boomer raced off and began hurling it around the shop.

'He loves tossing his chicken,' said Kim proudly.

Ruby spluttered.

'They hold an annual rubber chicken tossing contest in Iowa,' said Curtis.

And right then she realised fairy tales came in all shapes and sizes and this was hers. 'That's good to know, Curtis,' said Ruby giving him a squeeze. 'That's good to know.'

THE END

Acknowledgements

Hugest of Thank Yous to my fabulous editors Rachel Faulkner-Willcocks and Beth Wickington – I have so enjoyed working with you on this book. This extends to all the brilliant team at Avon who have managed to get yet another book published during the pandemic – no mean feat. And ongoing credit to my agent, Kate Nash, for being there throughout and continuing to reassure me.

Thanks to my fabulous dog owner friends Charlotte, Emma, Heather and Jane for a fun evening discussing the many antics their canine charges have got up to. A special thank you to Anne Marie Robinson-Gall of Anne Marie's Florist in Dunchurch for her expertise and helpful insight into running a florist business. Any mistakes are entirely my own.

Big thank you to Alison May for suggesting a writing retreat to Retreats For You in Devon (highly recommended – by the way!) which kicked off the writing of this story and to Penny Gibbons for going to Comic Con with my daughter so I didn't have to and instead could get on with the first draft!

Thank you to my fabulous and slightly bonkers writing friends – you know who you are! Thanks for the texts, chats, Zooms, RTs and shout outs – I appreciate every single one.

Biggest thank you goes to my family – I am so lucky to have spent the lockdowns with people I actually like as well as love to bits. You are the best.

Big shout out to everyone in the book blogging community for their continued support.

Deep gratitude to you my readers who have bought or borrowed my book and taken the time to read it. I really do appreciate it. I so hope you've enjoyed this as much as I loved writing it and if you have a moment to leave a review that would mean so much – thank you.

A big family. A whole lot of secrets. A Christmas to remember . . .

One Family Christmas

What's Christmas
without a little chaos?

BELLA OSBORNE

Available in all good bookshops now.

Regan is holding a winning lottery ticket.
Goodbye to the boyfriend who never had her back,
and so long to the job she can't stand!
Except it's all a bit too good to be true . . .

'Sweet, charming and brimming with kindness and hope.
An absolute tonic.' Milly Johnson

BELLA OSBORNE

Available in all good bookshops now.

Life's not always a walk
in the park . . .

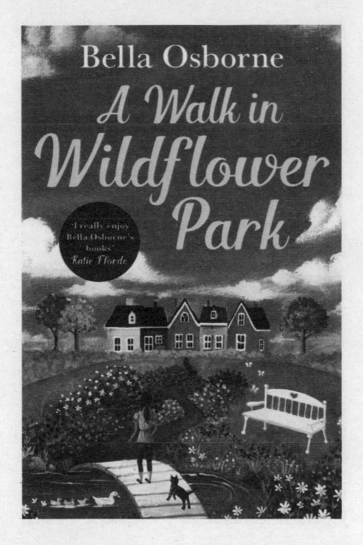

BELLA OSBORNE

A Walk in
Wildflower
Park

'I really enjoy
Bella Osborne's
books'
Katie Fforde

Available in all good bookshops now.

Join Daisy Wickens as she returns
to Ottercombe Bay . . .

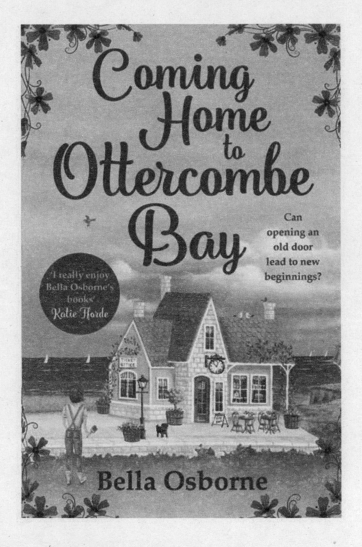

Available in all good bookshops now.

Escape to the Cotswolds with Beth and Leo . . .

Escape to Willow Cottage

'I really enjoy Bella Osborne's books' Katie Fforde

Bella Osborne

Available in all good bookshops now.

Tempted to read another heart-warming romance by Bella Osborne?

Available in all good bookshops now.

As the sun begins to set on Sunset Cottage, an unlikely friendship begins to blossom . . .

Available in all good bookshops now.